I0831502

Grosvenor Square

a novel

Grosvenor Square

a novel

Katherine Ann Meyer

Epigraph Books
Rhinebeck, New York

This book is a work of fiction. Names, characters, places, and incidents either are the product of the author's imagination or are used fictitiously. Any resemblance to actual events, locales, or persons, living or dead, is coincidental.

Epigraph Books
22 East Market Street, Suite 304
Rhinebeck, New York 12572
(845) 876-4861
epigraphpublishing.com

First U.S. edition 2011

Library of Congress Control Number: 2010913545

ISBN 978-0-9829932-0-0

To my mother and father,
who showed me the world
and let my stories take flight

“Beauty is truth, truth beauty —
That is all ye know on earth,
And all ye need to know.”

—John Keats
Ode on a Grecian Urn (1819)

Prologue

The Hathaways did not always live in Grosvenor Square. To fully understand it all, one must really look back to the day Lorna fell into the Serpentine. It was nothing tragic, to be sure, but the events that followed would provide inestimable insight into the family's future circumstances.

At the time of Lorna's little mishap, they lived in a comfortable residence near Hanover Square — not as fashionable or as exclusive as their future abode, but pleasant enough for a family whose fortune and prospects were increasing with agreeable rapidity.

In those days, when the family still employed a governess for the children and bell-shaped crinolines were all the rage, Mrs. Hathaway began to acquire a reputation for her marvelous cook. The praise was well-deserved, and rarely would a guest partake of a dinner at the Hathaway table without extolling Mrs. Hathaway for her judicious prudence in securing such a priceless culinary gem. Naturally, Mrs. Hathaway would turn pink with pleasure at such praise, for it could never be said that she did not relish her budding renown.

Mr. Hathaway would then raise a glass to his wife's merits, pointing out that she was as meticulous at hiring her domestic staff as she was at raising her children, of which accomplishment she had no equal. The guests would invariably follow suit, raising their glasses to the virtues of the lady of the house and concurring that the Hathaway children were unquestionably well-mannered and well-bred.

That is not to say that the youngest members of the household did not enjoy their share of frolicsome play, for they were children, after all, and given to those natural inclinations of which all energetic and carefree young souls are imbued. When they were very small, they could often be seen tumbling about the stable-yard, but as they matured, their governess would take them on outings, for Hanover Square Gardens did not always provide adequate space for the more elaborate play of older children.

It was on one such occasion that they set off upon an excursion to Hyde Park, for the Serpentine could provide much diversion for youthful pleasures, and an early summer day's walk seemed quite in order. The three young charges and their governess (who was not so young) had only just left the house, and had not even turned in the direction of the park, when a gentleman emerged from the residence next door, with the apparent intent of climbing into a waiting carriage. When he saw the children, however, he paused and hailed them.

"Good day, my young friends!" he called out with an affable smile.

"Good afternoon, Mr. Whitney!" returned the children, smiling back, for they were well-acquainted with their neighbor, who was a great favorite with them. He walked over to where they stood with their governess.

"My, my, let me see here," he said as they grinned up at him. He looked them over with mock severity, as if he were a General inspecting his troops. From the eldest daughter — lively, vibrant Lorna, who was nearly past the age of requiring a governess; to black-haired Rosamond, who, although not quite twelve years old, was already beautiful; to Tom in the middle, a good-natured lad who took very seriously his role as the only brother caught between two sisters — each of the children was subjected to the intent and playful scrutiny of their neighbor.

After his "inspection" was complete, Mr. Whitney nodded sagely. "I see that you've all grown taller since Tuesday", he said approvingly, "and must be duly rewarded for your efforts, I suppose."

The children beamed, and they watched with eager anticipation as he felt about the pockets of his coat, which was his usual charade, for the "rewards" were always produced from the same inner-pocket, which was, of course, the last one to be probed. Indeed — "Ah yes, here we are!" he exclaimed, as if relieved to have discovered at last the object of his quest, and he withdrew from that cache a handful of peppermints, which he distributed to the delighted children.

So it was with happy hearts and sweetened tongues that the little party took leave of their kindly neighbor. As much as they adored Mr. Whitney, he was, in truth, the object of some mystification amongst the children, for they never could determine his age, although they had spent many lively hours speculating upon it. He did not appear to be young, though he was a bachelor, and yet his twinkling eyes bespoke of youthful energy, so that one day they were certain he must be only twenty-nine and were just as positive the next day that he was forty-five. But as long as his pockets were well-stocked with sweets and his greetings filled with benign warmth, the children were content to be the recipients of his benevolence.

They did not go directly to the park, but first stopped by a house in the Square proper where resided the Shadwell family, whose children, Hugh and Edith, were such constant companions of the young Hathaways that the governess was equally at ease keeping them in line as she was her own charges. That same governess had found her duties somewhat lightened in recent years, however, as the children no longer required such close supervision as they had when they were small, and this was in evidence once the park was achieved, for the governess settled herself upon a bench in view of the children and promptly dozed off.

A merry hour of play followed, whereby Hugh Shadwell set his new boat to "sea" upon the Serpentine's still waters and even was so generous as to let Lorna have a turn at maneuvering the rope, for she was a very adventurous young lady, while Tom Hathaway climbed every tree in the vicinity, which was his latest favorite pursuit. Rosamond and Edith were content to sit quietly beneath the shade of one such tree and weave daisy-chains to adorn their hair, for they preferred gentler pastimes, and made rather an interesting contrast sitting there together — Rosamond with her black curls, and Edith with her flaxen braid.

The recreation was ended rather abruptly, however, when Lorna, unable to withstand the little boat's pull, toppled into the lake and had to be fished out by Hugh. This greatly upset the governess (who had wakened upon the cries of the two younger girls), and she promptly marched them all home, scolding Lorna for her carelessness.

The governess left her own charges off at their residence, so that Lorna could change out of her dress, and then took the Shadwells to their home. When the three Hathaway children were climbing the steps to their front door, they noticed that a carriage had just pulled up before the house next door, and Mr. Whitney was helping a lady out. They did not see the children and proceeded directly into Mr. Whitney's house, but the children took definite notice of the lady, for she was indeed striking to behold. She was tall and beautiful and very elaborately outfitted in a great deal of silk and jewels, and the cut of her gown's neckline was decidedly ostentatious for such an early hour, but she carried herself with the dignity of a queen. The children could only stare and wonder who Mr. Whitney's companion could be. There was much conjecture amongst them that evening, and Lorna took great delight in imitating the lady's sweeping gait, while Rosamond sighed in admiration over her sparkling necklace.

Although they never learned the lady's name, it was not the last time they saw her, and it turned out that she was inadvertently to play a rather significant role in the Hathaways' situation.

Over the course of the next few weeks, the elegant lady was observed to visit the house next door with increasing frequency, so that even Mrs. Hathaway took notice. Whenever the children pressed her for information regarding the lady's identity or relationship with Mr. Whitney, their mother only shook her head and declared that she could not know. However, this head-shaking was nearly always accompanied by a disapproving pursing of the lips, which only further piqued the children's curiosity in the matter. It was a puzzling situation, to be sure, and little escaped the children's keen observation, partially because they were very interested in the welfare of their kindly neighbor, but more so because the lady herself, in all her proud finery, was so intriguing.

Even young Tom, who initially had little interest in such a lady, began to notice oddities, and one morning he brought one puzzlement before his mother.

"Mama," he said, cocking his head to one side, clearly perplexed, "Last night, I saw from my bedroom window Mr. Whitney's lady visitor arrive at his home. And this morning, when I looked out the same window upon waking, I saw her emerge through his front door and get into a carriage. Does that mean that she left during the night, then returned so early only to leave again? She carried no valise."

Tom was even more bewildered at his mother's reaction, for first her eyes widened, then narrowed, then with a frown, she shooed him away with a stern injunction to pay better heed to his lessons and less to the happenings outside his bedroom window. She promptly paid a visit to the kitchen, whose staff was always well-apprised of the neighborhood gossip, and then spent a great deal of the evening shut in the library with her husband, which only occurred when there were urgent matters to discuss.

There was no immediate change, for during the next few days the children continued to see the mysterious lady come and go (sometimes at the oddest hours!), but it was not long afterward that Mr. Hathaway announced to his children that their family's increase in fortune had accorded them the desirable necessity of removing to more prestigious environs.

Chapter I

So the Hathaway family took up residence in fashionable Grosvenor Square, and in the decade that followed, the children flourished and bloomed in their stately, well-appointed home. The governess was soon cast off. The domestic staff was increased to meet the requirements of the new residence and to provide assistance to the young ladies of the house, whose daily regimen took on new dimensions as they blossomed into young-womanhood. Tom was sent to the University, and his sisters made their highly-successful debut in society, whereupon they were whisked off to the Continent for a "tour" before settling back into life in Mayfair.

London itself was never more splendid than in 1870, as the Royal Albert Hall neared completion, and the soft bustle was fast becoming the height of women's fashion.

The front steps of the Hathaway residence were meticulously scrubbed each morning, at Mrs. Hathaway's insistence, and it was up these immaculate steps that Hugh Shadwell ventured on a fine and breezy September afternoon.

The parlour-maid opened the door and bobbed her curtsey upon recognizing the young vicar.

"Good afternoon, Agnes," he greeted her cheerfully. "Is Mr. Tom at home? He's expecting me."

"He's out at present, Mr. Shadwell. Would you care to wait in the parlour?"

"Yes, thank you."

Hugh was led into the tastefully decorated front parlour and left to his own devices. As the room was very familiar to him, he instantly noticed a new addition — a portrait of the elder Hathaway daughter, newly delivered and still leaning against the fireplace wall, waiting to be hung. He took a few steps toward it, studying it with an interested scrutiny. He contemplated the likeness of his childhood friend, silently formulating his own appraisal and reflecting on the complex nature of the portrait's subject.

Hugh could not think much of the artist, for though the flattering portrait was unmistakably Lorna Hathaway, it did nothing to capture her spirit or her zest for life. The word that immediately came to Hugh's mind whenever he thought of Miss Hathaway was "vivacious", yet this painting reflected none of it, revealing only an attractive, composed young woman sitting on a sofa with an open fan on the cushion beside her. (A posture of exceedingly solemn restraint which Hugh could not recollect Lorna ever to affect in natural life). Still, the painting was done in the latest style, and Mrs. Hathaway probably adored it.

Hugh's reverie was interrupted by the sudden and soft tinkle of piano music — rather faint and distant, for the piano was elsewhere in the house — but piano music it unmistakably was. Hugh knew immediately the identity of the musician, for there was only one member of the household who showed a preference for the instrument. He strode back into the hall and crossed to the drawing room, where he peered through the open door, confirming his speculation as he beheld Rosamond Hathaway seated at the piano, her fingers moving somewhat tentatively over the ivory keys. She did not see him, and for a moment Hugh made no attempt to enter further into the room — rather observing the younger daughter at her practice upon the majestic instrument.

Rosamond was ever the beauty of the family, and the years since her childhood had only increased her loveliness. Even those who knew her well would often find their gaze arrested . . . her black curls and fair complexion striking an exotic contrast with eyes as blue as the Irish Sea at its darkest, deepest fathom.

Not only in appearance, but also in personality and character did Rosamond strike a contrast with her vivacious sister. For Rosamond was demure and graceful, having a fondness for dainty frills, silken ribbons, and delicate lace. She adored equally the ballroom and the theatre, and most of all, she treasured enduring beauty, having cultivated an appreciation for fine art, music, and literature. In company, she tended to be quiet and discreet . . . a paragon of feminine virtue. But those who found themselves on intimate terms and in private conversation with Rosamond knew her to be fond of thoughtful discourse on engaging topics.

At the moment, however, her playing was anything but engaging. The piece seemed pleasant enough, but she hesitated so in producing the notes that Hugh wondered if her mind was entirely on the endeavor. So prolonged was the pause between notes at one point that she actually heard his footfall, soft as it was, as he entered the room. Startled by such an observer, Rosamond immediately ceased her playing, her face coloring prettily as she rose.

"Oh no, no . . .," protested Hugh. "You must not stop. I did not mean to interrupt you. Go on, please."

But Rosamond shook her head.

"'Twas not much to interrupt," she said. "It was a new piece and only my first attempt at it." She smiled at her friend. "I'd prefer to wait until I've had adequate practice on it before performing before an audience." She held up the sheet of music for Hugh's inspection as he approached the piano. "Mr. Cameron brought it yesterday when he called."

Hugh looked up, eyebrows arched inquisitively. "Mr. Cameron? I don't recollect the gentleman. One of your many admirers, I presume?"

"I'd only met him once . . . the night before, at the ballet. He asked if he might call, and what was I to say? I couldn't very well refuse, as it was all very proper."

"Now, now, Rosamond," admonished Hugh, "When are you going

to put all of these ardent suitors out of their torment and actually marry one of them?"

"Why, Hugh, don't you know?" They both turned in surprise at the sound of a new voice. Lorna sailed into the room with an air of jocularity. "She's holding out for *your* proposal. You mustn't string her along so!" She laughed gaily, and Hugh joined her.

"Ah, but I think I'd already proposed ten times before I was thirteen years old, only to be rejected each time. A man has to retain his sense of pride, you know."

Lorna continued with the charade. "Well, I don't know . . .," she said. "If it's been at least a decade since your last proposal, it wouldn't be unseemly to try again. Rosamond would certainly be a decorative addition to the vicarage."

Lorna's good humor was but one of the characteristics she retained from her childhood. Physically, she was pretty enough, though she possessed not the exquisite beauty of her sister. Her wavy hair had darkened a bit since her girlhood, but her eyes were ever the same brown as her mother's, with flecks of amber, creating an overall lighter appearance than may be expected. Her skin-tone might truthfully be said to be a shade deeper than was fashionable at the time, no doubt the result of riding without a sunshade in open carriages, but such conventional trivialities would never concern her or dampen her high spirits.

She crossed to her sister and affectionately patted Rosamond's hand.

"Our dear Rosamond shall marry for love, I'm sure, like a princess in a fairy-tale." She could not resist one more bit of playfulness, though. "I only pray she does not choose Mr. Eggerton, who's been calling rather frequently," she mused. "I don't know which would be worse . . . to have a family member with the word 'egg' in their surname, or to have a sister whose Christian and surnames rhyme."

"Hmm . . .," Hugh contemplated aloud, "*Rosamond Eggerton*. Not a perfect rhyme, but it does have rather a cadence, doesn't it?"

Rosamond herself could not resist joining in the laughter that followed. There was a comfortable familiarity amongst such intimate friends that was a welcome respite from the formalities of society.

"I can definitely put your mind at ease on that point," Rosamond smiled at her sister. "No one should be more relieved than I if Mr. Eggerton would direct his attentions elsewhere." And as that seemed to be the end of the topic, she turned to Mr. Shadwell. "But, dearest Hugh, you've not even received a proper greeting from us," she apologized. "You're looking well. I trust all is well with your parish?"

"It keeps me ever busy!" Hugh declared. "But I cannot complain, for I am well-suited to the work, and I'd much rather be the sole vicar of an outlying parish than be part of a coalition at a large London church."

"Yes, but it seems we rarely see you anymore," admonished Lorna. "For only selfish reasons, we wish you had procured a position in the city."

Hugh smiled at her warm hearted sentiment. "Well, I've ventured into the city today to see your brother, but it appears he must have forgotten our appointment."

"I doubt that," Lorna asserted. "I'm sure Tom will be here at any moment. He often stops at his club after leaving the office."

"Yes, and more often so in recent months," agreed Rosamond. "But he'll surely not linger today, for I know he is always eager to see you."

At that moment, the prattle of chattering voices was heard in the hall, and Mrs. Hathaway and her sister, Mrs. Sarah Blakely, looked into the drawing room.

"Goodness!" exclaimed Aunt Sarah. "The young people are gathered in the drawing room at this hour! Is the parlour occupied? Good afternoon, Mr. Shadwell."

The two women entered the room, still in their bonnets and gloves, their arms laden with packages. Aunt Sarah was as officious as ever, her greying curls arranged in a manner which she perceived to give her a more youthful appearance, but which, in fact, only emphasized her eccentricities. Her features were strikingly austere for a woman of her age, and every part of her seemed to converge at severe angles.

Mrs. Hathaway, on the other hand, was the picture of mature fashion and stylish propriety. With never a hair out of place or a crease in her hat-brim, her matronly figure was always enveloped in a smartly refined ensemble, trimmed with tasteful accents. She was as fastidious about her appearance and manner as she was about her pristine home and polished silver. It was in her nature to be constantly in a flurry, and while this perpetual dither was apt to cause some bemusement upon first acquaintance, it would soon become clear how well-intentioned and kindhearted she was. Above all, she was a dutiful wife and doting mother, for she was proud and tremendously fond of her children. Always concerned for the comfort of others, it was she who spoke up after her sister's remark.

"I'm sure they were amusing themselves at the piano, which is pleasant at any hour of the day, isn't that right, my dears? And Hugh, it's so wonderful to see you. You know, your sister Edith was here visiting Rosamond only last week, and I was struck — really *struck* — with how she resembles your mother when she was the same age. Not that I was acquainted with your mother at that time, of course, but I remember saying to myself, 'I do believe Edith is the very image of how Mrs. Shadwell must have looked when she was a young girl!' Edith is such a sweet child — though I can hardly call her that anymore, can I? She's as much a young lady as my own two girls! But I suppose to a mother, those she raises must always be fondly thought of as her 'children', however they mature!"

Lorna managed to interject. "Hugh had an engagement with Tom, but our brother appears to be somewhat late."

"He's at his club, I daresay," said Aunt Sarah, rather critically. "It seems he's spending more and more time there these days."

Mrs. Hathaway missed the critical tone. "Yes, he enjoys his club as much as his father does. But I'm sure he'll be here soon if you had an engagement. Are you going out?"

"Yes," said Hugh. "We were going to Bloomsbury to look at some horses that are being put up for auction."

"Not for Tom, I hope?" said Aunt Sarah, reproachfully. "Heaven knows this family has no need for another horse."

"No, no," assured Hugh. "I am in need of a new mount for myself. Something gentle and steady would suit my position, I think."

"Well, I hope you'll come back here afterward and dine with us," invited Mrs. Hathaway. "Sir Henry Trainer is coming, and as Sister Sarah is staying on for dinner, that will make an odd number. It's so awkward to set an odd number of places, I always think. Won't you come, Hugh?"

"Oh yes, that would be perfect!" asserted Lorna. "I've always thought you should meet Sir Henry. He reminds us at least twice an evening that he had an early vocation to be a clergyman, but that 'fate intervened'. We've all heard the tale a dozen times, but he'd probably love to have a real clergyman to regale!"

"Lorna!" reproved Aunt Sarah. "That is hardly an appropriate manner in which to speak of such a friend of your father's."

"Oh, Sir Henry and I get on famously, I assure you," certified Lorna. "He would love to meet Hugh. You will come, won't you?" she appealed to Mr. Shadwell.

"I'm sure I would love the company," Hugh said, "but I'm afraid I must decline. I must be back home in time for Evensong."

"Oh, that's a pity," said Mrs. Hathaway. "Perhaps another time, though. You know you are always welcome here." Hugh bowed in acknowledgement. "And now," continued Mrs. Hathaway, "if you'll excuse us, we must put up these packages. We've been in Bond Street doing a bit of shopping — and quite successfully, too, I'm pleased to say. But it was lovely to see you, Hugh. And I wish you the best of luck with your . . . horse endeavors."

Aunt Sarah nodded to the young people, and the two ladies exited the room, still clutching their packages. Mrs. Hathaway called back from the hall, "Oh, here's Tom now!" Then, presumably to that young man—"Tom! Hugh Shadwell is waiting for you in the drawing room." And as the ladies proceeded upstairs, Tom himself entered the drawing room.

Dear Tom! Ever of a genial nature, no one could conceive of a gentler or more agreeable soul than that of the middle Hathaway sibling. His quiet ways and warm-hearted smile made him a favorite amongst colleagues and friends. Affable and considerate, Tom's natural inclination toward kindness put at ease all whom he encountered. Not that any young man should be without flaws — indeed, he possessed not Lorna's assertive wit nor Rosamond's graceful gentility, but his guileless and good-natured disposition transcended any apparent shortcomings. Perhaps as the result of being chronologically between two such self-confident siblings, Tom had a tendency toward hesitation on matters of decision, but this callow unpretentiousness made him all the more endearing. Physically, too, he seemed to fall between his sisters, for his hair was the same brown as Lorna's, but his eyes were as deep a blue as Rosamond's.

Since completing his studies at the University, Tom had been given a position in his father's office, and though he did not possess his father's natural aptitude for business, Tom put forth tremendous effort into every endeavor, so that he might succeed through hard work where he lacked inherent ability.

Naturally, Tom's sisters adored him, and they greeted him now most affectionately as he entered the drawing room.

"I'm sorry to be so late," he apologized to Hugh. "I stopped off at the club, intending to stay but briefly, and was inevitably diverted. Mr. Oakley has just returned from South America and brought back with him some rather impressive artifacts. He was showing them to a group of us, and I'm afraid I rather lost track of the time."

"It's no trouble," assured Hugh. "I've only been here a few minutes and have been admirably entertained by your sisters. I've even secured an invitation to dinner, which I had to most regretfully decline."

"Now Tom," put in Rosamond, "you can't think of taking Hugh away when we've hardly had a chance to visit with him. Surely you need to freshen up a bit before you go out again?"

Tom grinned and nodded. "I suppose I ought to put a comb through my hair." He started back toward the door. "I'll only be a few minutes, though. Oh—" He paused as he reached the doorway. "By the way, Father said to tell everyone to be sure to be at breakfast before he leaves for the office in the morning. He has something to impart to us, I gather."

This offhand remark, delivered most casually, naturally aroused a great deal of interest amongst the young ladies as Tom left the room.

"I wonder what our father means to tell us?" mused Lorna, for it was not often they were summoned to breakfast at such an early hour.

"Nothing unpleasant, I hope," added Rosamond.

After a pause, Lorna concluded, "Well, it must not be overly serious in nature, or he'd likely tell us immediately. We'll have no chance to make inquiries tonight, with Sir Henry here. We'll just have to suspend our curiosity until the morning."

Mr. Hathaway was a man of business. For all intents and purposes, he had made his fortune through a series of extremely shrewd investments, and one of those investments had proved so successful that it virtually secured his future and that of his offspring. In fact, although Mr. Hathaway was but a junior shareholder in the Star of India Tea Company, the senior shareholders — a distinctive group counting amongst its number several titled peers — had been so impressed with his talent for commerce that they had appointed him Senior Director for the entire corporation. And they had not been disappointed, for under Mr. Hathaway's enterprising management, the company had profited and expanded, to the delight of that elite body of investors. Unfortunately, his position necessitated his being away from the country for extended periods, as he must occasionally journey to India, but his family accustomed themselves to these absences, and another manservant had been added to the domestic staff, bringing the number to two, for the comfort and security of the family.

Mr. Hathaway was efficient and organized as a businessman, and he expected his household to be operative in the same manner. One can even postulate that this expectation may have contributed to his tremendous satisfaction in his marriage to Margaret Blakely Hathaway. Her scrupulous attention to detail suited him perfectly, and the household was, in general, a paradigm of orderliness. He was a man who believed absolutely in the merit of upstanding morality and honorable integrity, and those virtues he upheld with dignity and sincerity. That is not to say that his household was in any way colorless, austere, or grim, for Mr. Hathaway was very much a family man at heart, who loved being "lord of his castle" and who always encouraged his children to wholeheartedly pursue their interests, be they artistic, cultural, or intellectual. He was also a man of fashion, conscious of his social position and justly proud of his handsome family, to whom he was devoted. He left the management of the household and servants completely to his wife, for that was the proper realm of the woman, and Mrs. Hathaway took pride in arranging everything to her husband's comfort and for the elegant hospitality of society in general.

As loving and devoted as Mr. Hathaway was, he was eminently a man of punctuality, and when he requested his family members to appear at the breakfast table at an appointed hour, they were heedfully prompt. Even Lorna, who was not accustomed to rising at that early hour, appeared in her wrapper and seemed none the worse for her premature awakening. Mrs. Hathaway, always in a flutter, appeared to be exceptionally agitated as she gave direction to Agnes and Betsy, who were waiting on the gathered family members, replenishing toast and butter, refilling coffee cups, etc. Tom was ever calm and quiet, and Rosamond was serenely elegant in her effortless poise.

Mr. Hathaway was not one to waste time or keep people in a state of uncertainty. It was precisely this natural efficiency which had contributed greatly to his success in business, and in accord, he cut straight to his purpose as soon as everyone had taken their seats and been served. (Lorna was the exception, as she took nothing. She could rise cheerfully enough if her father bade, but she could not bring herself to eat at such an hour.)

Mr. Hathaway began by clearing his throat, then proceeded: "My dears, there is a matter that has come to my attention which requires an immediate response on my part and which I felt the necessity of relating to you as soon as possible. Your mother is already aware of the situation, as I disclosed it to her last night." Here a nod to his wife, who duly responded with a twitter of acknowledgement, clearly relishing the exclusivity of the information of which she alone had been apprised. Mr. Hathaway went on: "You may remember me speaking of my cousin, Robert Munroe. His wife died long ago, before any of you children were born, and he himself passed away five or six years ago. They always lived abroad, and it had been many years since I myself had seen him. Robert had but one child — a son, Jasper — who was left alone after his father's death. I confess, I rather lost track of the boy, though I occasionally heard vague reports, generally to the effect that he was traveling about the Continent a great deal. At any rate, I recently received a letter from Jasper Munroe." And he patted an envelope lying beside his plate, presumably the said missive.

"To get straight to the heart of the matter, the lad has fallen on some hard times. It seems he's been in Africa, trying his hand at diamond mines, and in one way or another, things haven't worked out as he'd intended. It appears as if — to put it bluntly — his resources have completely dried up." And here Mr. Hathaway paused, no doubt to let the gravity of the situation sink in. "I'm sure it took a great deal of courage and humility on his part to write to me of his unfortunate circumstances, and I respect those characteristics. I shall do what I can to help the young man. Jasper Munroe will be arriving in London in a matter of weeks. I have agreed to give him lodging in our home until he is established in a reliable profession, which I also intend to assist him in securing. He is a relation, and you know that I shall never turn my back upon a family member in need."

A discernible stirring had occurred amongst the listeners upon the revelation that Jasper Munroe would be lodging in their house. Each of the young people seemed immensely interested in the prospect of such a guest, and each had questions or thoughts upon the subject.

Lorna spoke first. "You refer to him as a 'lad', yet he must be older than us if his mother died before I was born."

"Yes, I believe he is three or four years your senior. His poor mother gave her own life bringing Jasper into the world, but it was only shortly before you were born." Mr. Hathaway smiled at his eldest daughter. "So, I believe he is yet under the age of thirty, and I am justified in referring to him in such terms of youthfulness."

"Poor devil, to have nothing at all in the world," murmured Tom.

"Did his father leave him nothing?" inquired Rosamond.

Mr. Hathaway's brow wrinkled in thought as he considered the question. "They were not wealthy, though I'm sure they weren't without some means. Whatever inheritance he may have come by seems to have been lost, although in his letter he did not elaborate on the course of his misfortune. Probably received some poor advice on his investments." By the tone of his voice, Mr. Hathaway clearly was of the opinion that young Jasper Munroe should have consulted himself on matters of investing. "Be that as it may," he continued, "it is not our place to question his tribulations, but only to give whatever assistance we may in re-establishing his independence and good fortune. I know you will make him welcome in our home and introduce him into your social circles so that he might have desirable connections here in London. We cannot know what hardships he may have endured, and these surroundings shall be unfamiliar to him."

Everyone had more questions, but Mr. Hathaway could do little to satisfy their curiosity, for Mr. Munroe's letter seemed to have been succinct and without many details. Presently, Mr. Hathaway finished his coffee and left for his office, with Tom close behind him. The two gentlemen had hardly been out the door before Aunt Sarah breezed in, with her curl-papers still peeking out from beneath her breakfast cap. It was not her custom to call in Grosvenor Square at such an early hour, but somehow her very perceptive ears had caught wind that there was to be something of importance announced at the Hathaway breakfast table, and though she was not privy to the information at the time it was related, she made certain that she would be the first to hear it subsequently.

"Good gracious, Sister!" cried Mrs. Hathaway, aghast. "You didn't cross town in an open carriage in such a state, I hope?"

Aunt Sarah brushed aside this triviality and demanded enlightenment. Once apprised of the circumstances, she allowed herself to be served some toast and tea, and expressed her thorough approval of the plan to assist young Jasper Munroe. Although she was, herself, no relation to him, she considered herself merely an extension of her sister's family and thus entitled to some sort of indirect claim on the young man's interests. Long after Lorna and Rosamond had left the table, Aunt Sarah and Mrs. Hathaway remained, discussing all manner of plans and prospects for that fortunate cousin. Their designs for him were purely of a social nature, for in their minds, his social prospects were of far greater importance than that of his imminent career. By the time Agnes had cleared away the dishes, the two women practically had Jasper married off, established in Mayfair, and dining with the Queen herself.

Chapter II

The day of Jasper Munroe's arrival several weeks later was fine and warm. The sunlight shimmered mirthfully across the cloudless sky, and there was only the gentlest of breezes blowing through the treetops. It proved to be a popular day for arrivals at the railway station, for the platform was fairly crowded with anxious Londoners, eager to greet their well-traveled relations and friends.

It had been decided that Tom would meet his cousin at the station (and Jasper was always thought of as "cousin", however distant that relationship may be), and Lorna accompanied him, for their carriage would allow ample room for three passengers and luggage. Brother and sister stood on the platform, caught up in the festive atmosphere of anticipation, eagerly watching and listening for that thrilling moment when the great steam engine would *whoosh!* into the station and come to a screeching halt at the platform. When the train, in all of its black, steam-driven majesty, finally came rumbling in, those gathered pressed closer, and as the passengers began to descend down the steps to the platform, there were many clamoring shouts of recognition, hands waving in attempts to direct attention, and general noisy hollering, so that it was a wonder any loved ones were reunited at all. But everyone seemed to eventually fix upon their own party, and practically before the two Hathaways knew it, Jasper Munroe was in their midst.

It is fair to say that every member of the Hathaway family had held a certain preconceived notion in their minds-eye as to their cousin's appearance: weary, worn, perhaps a bit wistful due to his humble awareness of his unfortunate situation. Probably rather subserviently hesitant and retiring. Modest. Melancholy.

Whatever their preconceptions were, the Jasper Munroe who stood before them put all such illusions to rapid flight. The dapper young man who now greeted them could not have been more of a contrast to the deferential figure they'd vaguely imagined. There was nothing timorous or dull about Jasper Munroe. He was dressed in a very well-fitting, flawlessly-trimmed coat, cut in the latest style, which perfectly suited his excellent build. His light brown hair was a bit longer than was fashionable, but there was nothing scruffy or coarse in its appearance. Indeed, he was very well-groomed in all aspects of his presentation. His hat was cocked slightly to one side in a manner which, to use a colloquialism, could only be described as "rakish". His dark eyes gleamed with arch amusement, and his mouth was drawn apart in a captivating, radiant smile as he bent over Lorna's hand and bowed smoothly to Tom. Everything about Jasper's manner was easy and carelessly elegant.

If the siblings showed any indication of their surprise, Jasper did not appear to notice as he adroitly climbed into the carriage with them, and they proceeded toward the house in Grosvenor Square, conversing with ease and pointing out to their new acquaintance many of the fine aspects of the city. Upon their arrival, Jasper was duly introduced to his host/patron, to whom he expressed laconic, but elegant, gratitude. To Mrs. Hathaway — "Aunt Margaret"— he voiced admiration for her lovely and refined home, and as he bent over Rosamond's hand, there was a definite gleam in his eye, as one who appreciates such rare beauty.

Over the tea table and at dinner, Mr. Munroe proved himself to be an excellent and skilled conversationalist, indulging Mr. Hathaway with recollections of his father and bringing fond memories back to the Hathaway daughters as he reminisced of the beauty of various cities and landscapes on the Continent, which they, too, could recall from their travels. Even Tom, usually so quiet and content to listen, was drawn out by the charismatic Mr. Munroe, with whom he shared an interest in horse racing. Aunt Sarah, naturally eager to be introduced, was also included at dinner and proved no match, despite her officious nature, for the beguiling Mr. Munroe, who won her over with his magnetic smile and aloof urbanity. Despite his position as houseguest and apparent lack of resources, he was in no way ingratiating or deferential, comfortably holding his own with untroubled self-assurance.

Although he spoke with familiarity of the capitals of Europe and the natives of Africa, he gave no reference to his profession or to the circumstances that had prompted his removal to London and to his uncle's hospitality. Lorna, with her ready assertiveness, several times discreetly alluded to these facts, attempting to subtly initiate some elaboration on Jasper's part, but each time, although he appeared to give ready and even highly-detailed responses, Miss Hathaway was somehow still left knowing as little about Jasper's background as before his anecdote had commenced.

Jasper gave Mrs. Hathaway substantial praise as to the taste and presentation of the meal, which compliments filled that lady with delighted pleasure. With a somewhat deliberate modesty, she deferred such merit to the illustrious cook, and at the conclusion of the evening, Jasper himself entered the kitchen to deliver his praise personally to the worthy cook, thereby winning the regard of the entire domestic staff, who were accordingly dazzled to have such a magnanimous gentleman in their midst.

The next day, Hugh Shadwell's sister Edith came to visit Rosamond, as the two young ladies had previously settled upon that afternoon for some pleasant recreation and croquet-playing, for that game was currently in vogue amongst the fashionable set. So it was that Jasper Munroe encountered them, along with the servant James bearing the equipment, leaving the house, headed toward Grosvenor Garden. Upon inquiring of their pursuit, Jasper immediately accepted their invitation to join them and gallantly relieved James of the equipment, taking it up himself and sending the amicable servant off to other duties.

When they crossed onto the green, Jasper situated the ladies on a bench near some shade trees, where they waited and observed as he set up the course. When it was prepared, he allowed them to select their colors first, and it was unanimously agreed that Edith should have the first play, as she was a guest. During the course of the game, Jasper showed himself to be an adept player but was singularly unpatronizing in the assistance he offered, never making either lady feel her ability was in any way inferior.

"Now, now, Miss Shadwell, do not be hasty in your determination to make that wicket," he said evenly, crouching down at a vantage-point to her ball, observing at eye level. "I believe, with your proven aptitude for the game, that if you hit it at *this* angle," (here demonstrating with his hands), "it would hit my ball first, thus giving you the continuation stroke, and still make the wicket."

Edith paused, considering this advice, then proceeded accordingly, smiling her thanks to Mr. Munroe.

At another point in the game, he called out to Rosamond: "Excellent play, Cousin! I confess, I could not devise a tactic from that position, but you have proven yourself my superior in both strategy and form!"

Rosamond smiled prettily in acknowledgement of this praise, but her smile lacked the warmth of Edith's. The truth of the matter was that Rosamond had instantly disliked her cousin upon first introduction the previous day. His attitude was far too cavalier, and his smooth and carelessly elegant mannerisms failed to impress a young lady who'd had extensive acquaintance with a host of silver-tongued suitors. She especially disliked the attention he bestowed upon her fair-haired friend. Edith Shadwell was a slight, attractive girl of a gentle and mild nature. She amiably accepted Mr. Munroe's courtesies as the benevolent consideration of one who has the noblest of intentions. But Rosamond was ever her confidante, and Rosamond knew that Edith had in her heart a special fondness for Tom, so that when that young man entered the garden and greeted the croquet-players, Edith blushed slightly in modest affection. Jasper, too, seemed pleased at Tom's arrival.

"But this is ideal!" he asserted. "We were just determining whether to play another round, and now we could have two paired teams. It's much better playing in pairs."

Tom agreed to join them and suggested that Edith choose her partner, but that modest young lady would not presume to show preference for any.

"You should take Edith for your partner, Tom," suggested Rosamond. "You and Jasper should be quite evenly matched in skill, as are Edith and I, so the pairs would be comparably competitive."

All seemed to feel this was an agreeable suggestion, so they proceeded with another round of play. Despite the fact that he was not partnered with Edith, Jasper continued his encouragement and casual assistance to her, although not to the disadvantage of his own game, for in the end, he and Rosamond won. At the completion of the round, both ladies professed fatigue, and Tom and Jasper assiduously collected the croquet equipment and escorted the ladies back to the house, where Edith took her leave, promising to take the well-wishes of the Hathaways back to her parents in Hanover Square.

That evening, Mr. Hathaway and Tom took Jasper to their club, where he was admitted on a "temporary/guest of a member" basis. Jasper took to club life immediately, establishing himself with Tom at the gaming tables while Mr. Hathaway took his pipe and newspaper in the salon. It did not take long for Jasper to establish a solid reputation for himself amongst the club members, for his card-playing was shrewd, and his talk of exotic travels impressed the gentlemen seated around the card tables. Before leaving the premises, Jasper had submitted his name to the list of candidates for consideration into the club's membership rolls. Mr. Hathaway went to bed that night with the contented satisfaction that the prospects for his young relative appeared most promising.

Whereas Rosamond had developed a somewhat negative impression of Jasper Munroe, Lorna had formed an entirely different opinion, for she found in her cousin a ready comrade with a zealous nature that ably matched her own high spirits. The two of them soon became close companions and could often be seen at the University's bowling green (a favorite place of Lorna's since Tom's school days), walking briskly along the new Thames Embankment, or practicing upon the archery grounds in Regent's Park. That is not to say that there was anything unrefined or unseemly in their activity, for Lorna was well-aware of her status and position and always behaved with befitting decorum. However, she had the impression, as she was further acquainted with Jasper, that should she not always conduct herself with propriety, he might not exercise such restraint in his own mien. Despite his laconic suavity and polished manners, Lorna felt as if Jasper was constantly on the verge of breaking forth into some sort of impulsive recklessness, which he admirably curbed in her presence. But this suggestion of audacity merely intrigued her, furthering her interest in this new-found cousin.

Lorna and Jasper found much to discuss during these excursions, for both were natural conversationalists, and Lorna especially enjoyed having such an intimate companion to whom she could express her opinions on arguable topics (for she had opinions on many contestable subjects, which must usually be repressed in polite society). Jasper rarely gave opinions of his own, but he seemed ready enough to hear hers without threat of judgment. She never was able to draw him out on any topics regarding his recent history, but she did notice that he was a keen observer of his present and immediate realm. Thus did Jasper spend many pleasant afternoons partaking of his cousin's lively company and acclimating himself to the city.

In the evenings, however, Tom was his regular host and companion.

Unassuming as Tom was, he shared with Jasper a fondness for gaming and fine spirits, of which Tom's knowledge had been cultivated in the atmosphere of his club. In the beginning, Jasper's card-playing was funded by Mr. Hathaway, who knew the importance of making social connections at the club gaming-tables. Jasper was a natural gambler, although, due to his circumstances, his wagers were modest compared with the gentlemen who had large sums at their disposal. Consequently, his winnings were modest as well, but this was not seen as unpropitious to anyone at his table, as they wagered only for sport and not out of any necessity for income. Jasper, however, did seem to grow frustrated by his lack of significant winnings, despite the fact that he was provided everything he required and could have no useful purpose in obtaining any sum.

One evening, as Jasper and Tom were ambling along toward Pall Mall, Jasper seemed unusually preoccupied. It was not habitual for the two young men to have abundant conversation, for that is not the way of men, but on this particular evening Jasper was absorbed to the point of distraction. Tom gave up conversing, for he was receiving but terse response, and the two continued on their way in silence for a while. At last, Jasper spoke.

"I say," he remarked coolly, "where do other fellows play cards?"

Tom was puzzled by the unexpected question. "What other fellows?"

"The other fellows in town who aren't members of clubs."

Tom's confounded expression clearly indicated that he was still perplexed. Jasper's patience was deliberate as he elaborated. "Surely there are Londoners who have not the financial means to belong to such elite clubs. I rather fancy most of the people we pass on the street would fall into some sort of social class lower than yourself." His tone was cynical, and Tom was rather taken aback by such bluntness. Jasper continued: "My limited knowledge of the working classes leads me to believe that they enjoy a good wager and a good drink as much as anybody. I am merely inquiring as to where they play and drink."

If Tom had been looking at Jasper straight-on instead of walking beside him, he would have seen a derisive gleam in his cousin's eye. As it was, Tom was of such good-natured demeanor that he could scarcely think the worse once he had recovered from his bewilderment at Jasper's unexpected and indelicate reference to class differences.

Tom hesitated in his reply. "I don't know . . . taverns, pubs . . . such gambling-houses as are common in the East End. Of course, we also play at cards during dinner-parties and gatherings at home." He felt the need to add this last bit, thinking that Jasper was perhaps expressing boredom with a single venue for his entertainment, and hoping to reassure him that there would be other opportunities amongst his own circle.

Jasper made no reply, falling back into a reverie. Tom thought no more of the issue, and soon they entered the club, where Jasper had a rather bad time at the gaming-tables and ended up withdrawing to the dining room to soothe his pride with a delectable meal and some spirits. Although Tom enjoyed cards, he was not such a gambler as was Jasper, and he spent a good portion of the evening in the open salon, as his father did, where he could listen to the other gentlemen discuss politics, travel, commerce, or any other topic at hand; or just indulge in a quiet newspaper or some private conversation in one of the peaceful alcoves.

Tom was not the only one who had a puzzling experience with Jasper. A few days later, Lorna approached her mother in the morning room.

"Mother, have you seen Jasper?"

She seemed slightly perturbed. Mrs. Hathaway looked up from her correspondence and smiled, never noticing her daughter's disquietude.

"Lorna! I was just writing of you to Mrs. Safford — you know she's been in Edinburgh since autumn? I was describing that lovely new silk brocade gown you had fitted on Tuesday. I think the seamstress will be ready for the re-fitting by tomorrow or early next week, don't you? I hope you can have it in time for the Connolly's supper party. I call it that, but it's really an evening affair in celebration of their youngest daughter's birthday. At any rate, the brocade will be perfect for it, and I've already thought that Rosamond might wear her blue silk — I'm referring to her new one, the deep blue with the lace — so that the two of you will complement one another and make a lovely picture."

Being the daughter of Margaret Hathaway required a great deal of patience, which was not Lorna's forte. She certainly had no present interest in her attire for the Connolly's upcoming supper party (an event of which she had no knowledge, or if she had, had entirely forgotten).

"Yes, but where is Jasper?" she asked again, her impatience resonating.

"Jasper? I'm sure I don't know. I can hardly keep up with my own schedule, much less attend to anyone else's." Here Mrs. Hathaway smiled again, in that beaming, girlish way that made Lorna think her mother hadn't a care weightier than a feather. Certainly, Mrs. Hathaway's schedule was full of social and domestic affairs, but none, in Lorna's opinion, of sufficient substance to preclude her from knowing the whereabouts of members of the household.

"He promised to go riding with me today, and I can't find him anywhere."

"Why don't you ask Rosamond to go with you? She enjoys riding, doesn't she?"

Lorna was not to be pacified. "Rosamond is going to a concert this afternoon with Hugh and Edith and doesn't want to get mussed up before she goes."

Mrs. Hathaway cocked her head to one side — always an indication that she was ruminating. "Well, then, ask the servants. Perhaps one of them saw Jasper go out, or James may have even fetched him a cab!" This was stated with such bright certainty, as if it was the most satisfactory suggestion ever concocted, and with such finality that there seemed no alternative but to follow her advice. However, upon inquiry of the servants, the only enlightenment Lorna received was from Agnes, the parlour-maid, who could only assert that she had seen "Mr. Jasper" go out the front way about an hour ago.

As it turned out, Lorna ended up going to the recital with Rosamond and the Shadwells and was in rather poor humor throughout, for she had counted on riding in the park and did not take kindly to disappointment. However, she was bound to be further frustrated, for the next few days Jasper was just as elusive. He left after breakfast without leaving word and returned for tea with scant detail as to the nature of his excursions.

It was Tom who discovered the nature of Jasper's mysterious outings, though inadvertently, for he did not know that Jasper had been frequently absent. The two young men still went several evenings each week to the club or to one of the coffeehouses in the vicinity, often meeting up with other acquaintances of Tom, who always took a ready liking to the debonair Jasper Munroe.

On this particular evening, they were strolling through St. James's when Jasper casually remarked, "You know, old chap, I think I'm going to forego the haut monde crowd tonight. There's a place a fellow told me about that rather interests me. I'd like to go have a look at it. You're welcome to come along, if you wish."

Somehow, Jasper had become the host and Tom the guest. This dichotomy was not really sudden, although it had been happening so gradually and so naturally that Tom had been unaware of its progression. He was not an inherent leader, and Jasper's stronger personality had steadily eclipsed that of his quiet cousin. Tom was, in truth, a bit alarmed at Jasper's suggestion, for Tom was a young man of habit, who liked the regular familiarity of his neighborhood, his friends and colleagues, the activity of the hour at which he sallied forth, and the predictable half-moon pattern made in the waning sunlight by the dust on the latch of St. James's gate.

However, he was also earnestly conscientious of his (perceived) role as host, and he was not about to appear inhospitable, so he replied, "Why, certainly. We can go wherever you wish."

Jasper smiled slightly, in an almost condescending manner. "Good then," he said. "We'll need to take a cab."

Without difficulty he hailed a black hansom cab, and the two young gentlemen climbed in. Jasper gave the driver an address that Tom did not recognize. The cab turned around and began its journey away from the park. They passed through familiar neighborhoods at first, along the Strand and toward Temple Bar. They continued into The City, still following the river, then Fenchurch. That was about the time Tom realized he was no longer in such familiar surroundings. He had rarely ventured beyond the financial institutions and the Royal Exchange, though he had frequented those with his father, and when they passed into the East End, Tom was immersed in a part of London to which he had been only infrequently exposed. Here, the streets were narrow and dingy, lined with dark and low buildings. There were few public squares or open spaces, and there was a general feeling of suffocation, as if the close, somber edifices were crowding out, or threatening to topple upon, any forms of life. There was, however, plenty of vitality to be seen. Despite the grim structures and compressed streets, life seemed to be thriving here, for the walkways and streets were teeming with people. Their attire was generally as dull and colorless as their environment, but their energy was vibrant, for the air reverberated with shouts, calls, bellows, bawls, and snippets of lively conversation. Tom was certain, though, that once the sun set, these streets would be as deserted and bleak as a caliginous wasteland.

Streets and alleys that were even narrower than the present thoroughfare angled off in every direction, and the cab eventually turned down one of those obscure passages. Tom sensed they were headed south toward the river. This side-street was not as lively as the main road, and only a few residents scurried along beside them as dusk began to fall.

At last the cab stopped in front of a building whose façade looked like every other — grim, low, featureless, save for some darkened windows and a wooden door. As Tom paid the driver and stepped out onto the uneven cobblestones, he had no way of knowing what sort of establishment this was, for there was no sign that he could discern. However, the cloudy windows were illuminated from within, and the shadows of moving figures could be distinguished behind the hazy windowpanes.

Jasper led the way in through the feeble wooden door. Inside was one room, long and narrow like the streets and just as crowded. The air hung with smoke, reeking with a heady repugnance and whose haze could be seen in the dim yellow light of the very few wall sconces. Small, crude, wooden tables were scattered throughout, though they could not be easily discerned for the number of men clustered about them, sitting on shabby stools and slat-backed chairs. Despite the density of the crowd, the noise level was surprisingly muffled. The low din seemed to be contained to each individual table, juxtaposing into a dull murmuring hum and only occasionally punctuated by a sudden sharp laugh or distressed lamentation. There were a few women in the room, drably attired and mostly plump, whose task seemed to be delivering drinks to the men at the tables.

Jasper steadily made his way to one of the tables and took the only available seat, leaving Tom to stand behind him, feeling rather awkward, but peering curiously at the dealings before him. Jasper seemed to feel no awkwardness whatsoever, for he conducted himself easily and with what would appear to be even some familiarity.

"Now this, Tom," he said over his shoulder, "is where there is some sporting fun to be had. Your card-playing is a gentleman's game, but *here* is where my fortunes shall turn." And his hand swept over the table before him, where the gathered men were throwing dice. Indeed, every table in this gamblers' den was engaged in dice-playing, the sport of the common classes. It was a rowdy way of sporting, and the men were clearly a disorderly lot, fueled not only by the heated excitement of the betting, but also by the ale and cheap liquor which seemed to flow freely, a quantity of which Tom found himself in possession of without being sensible of its origin.

Jasper was in his element, for here his wagers — modest by Pall Mall standards — were princely sums, and the men gathered at the table were duly impressed by his substantial assets. And although it seemed he won and lost with equal measure, as the evening wore on it was plain to Tom that Jasper's winnings were accumulating, as were the number of tankards downed by the assembled company. Tom had no taste for such cheap spirits, and he accepted the distilled concoctions only to occupy himself, for he took no part in the dice-playing, although he watched the proceedings with some interest. The whole scene around him was foreign to one accustomed to the cultivated West End life, yet this bizarre and raucous setting held a sort of grotesque fascination for him, no doubt enhanced by the cumulative effect of the crude liquor downed across the hours. It grew only louder and more boisterous as the night darkened, but however unruly or inebriated the other men were, Jasper maintained his cool, collected composure, smiling genially as if oblivious to the coarseness about him as he threw the dice and passively paid out or collected, however fortune led him.

Eventually, Tom grew very lightheaded and dazed as the liquor and the lateness took their toll on his senses. The yellow-lit room was nothing but a dim and throbbing blur. When he finally followed Jasper back out into the uneven, cobblestoned street, the fresh air was as a tonic, reinvigorating his senses. Jasper seemed to take everything in stride and was completely undaunted by the fact that he had come out only slightly ahead in his winnings.

"There are a hundred other places we could go in this neighborhood," he said laconically. "But I think we'll visit those another night. My purse won't hold out much longer, and you're looking a bit glassy-eyed, which won't do when you go to the office tomorrow, so we'd best find our way home."

That was easier said than done, and they had to trek a while along the river before they were able to find a cab to take them back to familiar territory. By the time he collapsed onto the cab's bench, Tom's head was spinning and an intense drowsiness had overcome him. Jasper must have gotten him safely back to Grosvenor Square, for the next morning Tom awoke in his own bed, in his attractive and comfortable room, with only a headache as concrete proof that his curious experience of the previous night had been real.

The following evening found Tom and Jasper back at the club and in familiar surroundings, in the elegant card-room and the well-appointed salons. Yet, despite Tom's relief to be thus comfortably re-established, he could not prevent his mind from wandering back to the East End gambling house, for it held a peculiar fascination for him and caused him some distraction for several days afterward.

While Tom had gained some valuable insight into Jasper's character, the rest of the Hathaway family remained unenlightened, though Jasper's frequent, unexplained absences had put something of a damper on his comradery with Lorna. Rosamond seldom put herself into situations of any intimacy with Jasper, for her opinion of him had been unfavorable from the start, and Mrs. Hathaway, who seldom paused for reflection of any kind, saw nothing deviant or unusual in Jasper's demeanor. While Mr. Hathaway generally liked his young relation — for Jasper had been fairly well-accepted by the members of his club — he determined that, after a month or so, Jasper had had adequate time to acquaint himself both socially and environmentally, and was ready to begin his journey toward self-sufficiency by way of gainful employment. So Jasper's carefree days of excursions ended, and he was given a very respectable position at a bank, courtesy of Mr. Hathaway's excellent connections.

The morning he was to start, he ambled into the breakfast room about nine o'clock, just as the women of the household were sitting down to breakfast. They looked up in surprise, and all conversation ceased as Jasper took his seat, wishing them all a nonchalant "Good morning".

Mrs. Hathaway was the first to find her tongue. "Why, Jasper!" she cried. "I thought you were to start your post at the bank today!"

Jasper looked completely unconcerned. "Yes, that's right. Betsy,—

do you have any more of that jam?"

Mrs. Hathaway persisted. "What time were you planning on leaving? I thought you'd already gone!"

Jasper buttered some toast. "After breakfast, I suppose."

Lorna leaned forward. "But didn't Mr. Custis at the bank tell you any certain time to arrive the first day?"

Jasper did not look up from his buttering. "Hm? Oh, no, I don't think so. At least, if he did, I don't recollect. Thank you, Betsy," as the servant placed a pot of jam beside his plate.

All three women were amazed at his indifference.

"I'm afraid Mr. Custis will have words with you if you're not punctual," intimated Mrs. Hathaway with some concern.

"I don't suppose it really matters what time I arrive, so long as I get the work done. I'm not in the teller's cage, after all," he added. "I'm to have a desk of my own." And he continued his breakfast in a most leisurely manner, though the ladies were rather at a loss for conversation for the duration of the meal.

It is fair to suppose that Jasper may, indeed, have had some words from Mr. Custis, for the next morning found him awake and out the door before Lorna had even arisen, and without any breakfast at all. But that would not be his pattern for long.

Chapter III

A few weeks after Jasper began his employment with the bank, Mr. Hathaway left to go to India on business, where he expected to remain for his usual duration of several months. Naturally, his family missed him during these occasions, but they had grown accustomed to his absences, and since the children were now grown, their social lives continued on in much the same manner as when their father was at home. Aunt Sarah became a somewhat standard fixture in Grosvenor Square during these periods, for she felt it her sisterly duty to attend to Mrs. Hathaway while her husband was abroad.

So it was that shortly after Mr. Hathaway's departure, Hugh Shadwell and his sister Edith were invited to dine at the Hathaway residence. After dinner, when the gentlemen had rejoined the ladies in the drawing room, Rosamond was enticed to play for them upon the piano. Being an accomplished young lady, Rosamond's tastes were classical, and her fingers ran gracefully over the keys, charming her listeners with the melody of a fanciful bagatelle. She acquiesced when pressed for a second piece, but modestly declined a third, for she did not wish to monopolize the attention of her guests and demurely retired from the piano bench.

"Well, Miss Shadwell," said Jasper, turning to Edith, "since Cousin Rosamond will not play for us more, then you must be persuaded to delight us with your musical abilities."

Edith immediately blushed and shook her head. "Oh no," she murmured, "I don't play half as well as Rosamond."

"Why, Edith!" objected Mrs. Hathaway. "You play very nicely. I'm sure Jasper would love to hear you."

"There now, you see?" And Jasper gave his hand to Edith, who had no choice but to take it, and escorted her across the room to the piano. She threw a beseeching glance to Tom as she passed him, but that young man thought very highly of his gentle guest and only smiled at her encouragingly.

Edith was, indeed, musically inclined, and while she did not at all mind playing before family or friends, she felt ill at ease performing for any outside of that circle, for she was inherently shy. And Jasper certainly would make her nervous when he sat beside her on the piano bench, declaring that he must be her page-turner. Here it was Rosamond who glanced at Tom beside her on the sofa, for it was his usual commission to assist Edith when she played, but Tom could not very well interfere when Jasper had already positioned himself, and so the playing commenced, Edith blushing furiously as her fingers sought the keys. Rosamond's heart ached for her friend, for she knew Edith was nervous with Jasper fawning over her, and when the piece had finally ended, and Jasper entreated her to play another, Rosamond gave Tom's arm a gentle squeeze. He understood its meaning and rose from the sofa.

"We don't want Miss Shadwell to grow fatigued at such an early hour. I, myself, can listen to music at any hour, and perhaps we shall have more playing later on. I am certain Miss Shadwell prefers a rest now." He crossed to the piano and offered his arm to that young lady, who took it with a look of deep gratitude and tender admiration.

"Yes, Edith does look a bit flushed," put in Lorna. "Why don't you take her out on the terrace, Tom? Some fresh air will do her good, and it looks to be a lovely evening." And Lorna cast a smile at her sister, for she had given voice to the thought that Rosamond was not bold enough to suggest.

Edith conceded that she was a bit warm, and Tom escorted her out of the room and toward the terrace door at the rear of the house. Both Hathaway sisters could not resist stealing a glance at Jasper to see his reaction to these proceedings, but that dapper young man was calmly pouring himself a drink at the sideboard and seemed completely unmoved, despite his defeated attempt to keep Miss Shadwell at the piano and at his side.

Hugh picked up the conversation. "I say, the most extraordinary thing happened this morning as I was walking in the park. I was going along the North Walk, opposite the lake, when a fox crossed the path in front of me and settled under a rose hedge, as comfortable as if it were his den."

"A fox in Hyde Park?" exclaimed Aunt Sarah.

"No, no, —St. James's," clarified Hugh.

"Good heavens," murmured Lorna. "It's a wonder every gentleman in the vicinity didn't run home for his rifle and hounds."

Hugh smiled at her. "Actually, the first to spot him, other than myself, was a lady — a nurse, I presume, with her charge, a little girl of four or five. The child pulled on the nurse's hand and said, 'Look! An orange dog!', and she started to run toward it, but the nurse pulled her back, so the child began to cry, which naturally attracted the attention of some older ladies strolling by. They looked to see what the child was pointing at, and when they saw the fox, they were all in a twitter. The whole group edged closer . . . near enough to have a look without startling the creature. Pretty soon a fair crowd had gathered, and when I left, the fox was still sitting there calmly under the hedge, as composed and proud as if it were *his* garden!"

The ladies in the drawing room had a good laugh at the image.

"I suppose this is what becomes of Londoners who never get into the country," said Lorna. "Seeing such a creature that runs so commonly in the countryside is a novelty and a spectacle to our citified bourgeoisie."

"But whatever would a fox be doing in St. James's Park?" queried Mrs. Hathaway.

"Whatever were *you* doing in St. James's in the middle of the day?" inquired Lorna of Hugh, with a friendly arch of her brow. "Don't tell me you're now a man of leisure with nary a duty at the vicarage?"

Hugh chuckled at her suggestion. "Not at all. In truth, there is more to be done there than I care to admit when I tell you that I had been at the National Gallery."

"Oh, did you see the new exhibition?" Rosamond had perked up at the mention of one of her favorite venues.

"The Early Masters?" Hugh shook his head. "That was my objective in going there, but the exhibition hasn't opened yet, it seems. I thought it was to open last Sunday, but it is actually this next Sunday."

"I would like to see it, too," said Rosamond. "Will you take me with you when you go, Hugh?"

"Why, Rosamond," objected Aunt Sarah, "I heard you tell Mr. Braxton that you'd already made plans to view the exhibition with your sister."

Lorna's eyes widened as she looked inquisitively at her sister. Rosamond blushed.

"Yes, I did say that," she admitted. "I didn't want to offend Mr. Braxton, but I really didn't care to go out into a public venue with him, unescorted. Besides, Lorna did say she wouldn't mind going with me." She turned back, appealing to Hugh. "But she really doesn't appreciate art to any extent and always rushes through the galleries, so that I'm left practically alone anyway."

Lorna could not deny it. Hugh smiled at Rosamond's winsome appeal.

"Of course I'd be honored to take you when I next attempt to view the exhibition," he assured her. "And I'll even let Lorna come, if she wishes." He turned to the elder sister and added with mock severity— "Although she must understand that if she chooses to fly thought the galleries, she may have a long wait at the other end, for I shall not leave *this* fair lady's side," and he bowed to Rosamond who rewarded him with a delightful smile. With such friends as Hugh, one could be at ease and jocular and nearly forget that Jasper was in the room.

That young man had been singularly quiet since Tom and Edith had withdrawn, but upon their re-entry, Mr. Munroe immediately rose and crossed to Edith, inquiring if she felt better, and then, leading her over to an alcove, monopolized her for much of the remainder of the evening. However, when Hugh and Edith had bid their hosts goodnight, it was Tom who escorted Edith out the front door, and it was his hand that helped her into the waiting carriage.

Late that evening, when Mrs. Hathaway and her daughters had retired to their rooms upstairs, Tom sat alone in the library. His father often sat there of an evening, enjoying his pipe before the dying fire, and Tom liked to be there in his father's absence, for it seemed familiar when his father was far away. His reverie was interrupted, though, when Jasper strolled into the room.

"I've put out the lights in the drawing room," he informed Tom. "I'm never certain if that's my job or the servants at this late hour, but at any rate, it's done."

Tom nodded absently, still in his brown study. Jasper's next words brought him out of it.

"By the way, I'd say your lady friend is much taken with you." Tom turned to look at Jasper. Jasper nodded easily. "Oh yes, it's obvious. And have no fear; I'll divulge to her none of your faults or even your guilty secrets. Such an ingenuous nature as hers ought not to be tarnished by minor flaws."

Tom stared while Jasper made as if to exit the room.

"Whatever are you talking about?" demanded Tom, though it was not in his usual nature to demand.

"Just what I said." Jasper coolly ambled over to where Tom was sitting. "I know your little guilty secret." And before Tom could protest,

Jasper reached into Tom's coat pocket and procured a small bottle that had been concealed there. Jasper went on: "But as a gentleman of my word and a fellow member of the ever-threatened 'dominant sex', your secret is safe with me." And, handing the bottle to Tom, Jasper sauntered out of the room leaving Tom alone with his bottle, feeling none too consoled by Jasper's saccharine words.

Lorna wished to read the letter from her father, but she also wished to be out-of-doors, for it was a marvelously clear and unusually warm day, and she couldn't bear the thought of sitting in the parlour when the soft breezes and bright sunshine beckoned so enticingly. She decided to reconcile her two desires and take the letter with her to the University campus, where she could find a pleasant, isolated bench beneath an oak tree and enjoy her letter in solitude. She had been absent the previous evening when the letter had been shared with the other family members, and as these patriarchal missives were infrequent — but always extensive and full of interesting news and fond wishes — Lorna wished to have an uninterrupted length of time in which to savor her father's precious words.

So she made her way to the University's park. It had been a frequent haunt of hers during Tom's tenure at the University, for she and Rosamond would often meet him there and bring a hamper full of delectable offerings from Cook, and the three of them, usually joined by Tom's friends, would spread a picnic out on the lawn and partake in delightful diversions from rigorous studies. Lorna loved the University Park, with its fine, ancient trees, its pretty landscaping, and the bustling students always hurrying to and fro, discussing all manners of academic discourse and nonacademic social interests.

As she sat on her bench, she caught fragments of these scholarly and lively conversations and was also vaguely aware of birds chirping in the high branches above her, squirrels scampering across the path in front of her, and the glorious sunshine bathing the lawn in golden warmth, which nicely countered the light chill in the air. But she was mainly absorbed in her letter, transported by its words to a distant, exotic land where natives offered luxurious and mysterious fruits on golden trays, and the evenings were scented with an enchanting lotus perfume. The descriptions intrigued her imagination, and the words of affection were endearingly sincere from one so far across the sea.

The only obstacle hindering perfect enjoyment of the situation was the gusty wind blowing across the park. What had looked to be a gentle breeze in Mayfair blew with irregular and unpredictable outbursts across the open lawn. Lorna had to hold tight to the pages of the letter, and she actually had to sit on a corner of the envelope to prevent its being taken up by a gust of wind. Unfortunately, as she became absorbed in her reading, she forgot about the envelope, and as she rose from the bench, it fluttered away. She bent to pick it up from where it had landed opposite the path, and just as she did so, another gust of wind took the papers from her hand, sending them sailing in several directions across the lawn.

"Oh dear," she sighed, and went after the pages, trying to maintain a respectable gait but hurrying nonetheless before another breeze should blow them farther from her reach. She managed to retrieve one page and was hurrying toward the next, feeling quite foolish for all of her chasing and bending, when she heard a voice from behind her.

"Don't worry, Miss! I've got it!"

Lorna, who had been crouching to pick up a page, looked up to see a young man rushing past her toward the next page, which was simultaneously blowing farther from his grasp. Lorna looked on in amazement, and some consternation, as the young man apprehended that page, then took off toward the next. By the time Lorna had regained her stance, the man had gathered all the remaining pages and was hurrying back toward her.

In her flustered attempts to right everything, Lorna dropped the envelope once more, just as the young man approached her, quite out of breath, and in his haste to extend to her the missing pages, he set foot squarely in a puddle as she bent down to pick up the envelope, splashing mud on her dress and across her neckline.

Lorna would have expected an awkward silence at this point, but the young man seemed not inclined to silence and instead launched into a stream of heartfelt apologies while attempting to procure his handkerchief, presumably to assist in the cleansing of her neck and garments. She stood, aghast, as he finally produced the none-too-delicate square of linen, but she refused to take it from him.

"No, no, that's quite all right," she assured him hastily. "Thank you for your assistance," she continued, taking the wrinkled pages from his grasp and desiring nothing more than to put some distance between the earnest helper and herself. He would not hear of it.

"Oh, but you are dreadfully muddied!" he protested. "I cannot allow you to leave without attempting to make amends for my clumsiness. You must allow me. Now let me think for a moment . . . ." And as he cogitated, Lorna peered a bit more closely at his features.

He must certainly be a student, though a senior one by his appearance. He was neither robust nor in any way handsome. He looked sallowly ancestral, with his ginger-colored hair and pale eyes, but there was something in his countenance that was undeniably likeable and gave him an air of friendliness. His colorless eyes were brightened by an ardent eagerness, and his smile was warm and unassuming. He seemed oblivious to any barriers of class and addressed her with a convivial warmth that bespoke familiarity.

He snapped his fingers. "I've just thought of an idea! I know of a place where we can at least get you cleaned off somewhat until you can get home and bathe."

Lorna was too shocked at this indelicate reference to know what to say. He seemed undaunted by any sense of propriety, but she allowed him to lead her away across the lawn toward the University buildings. She could not imagine why she allowed herself to be thus persuaded. Surely her mother or sister or any other young lady of gentility would have refused and been duly indignant at being wronged so publicly. But Lorna was a girl of some adventure and great curiosity, and she could think of no valid reason to resist one so intent upon helping her. She followed him across the main Green, where the imposing buildings formed a perfect square, and around the side of the farthest building. It backed up to a densely-wooded slope, which was fenced off as it angled down to a shallow ravine. As the young man headed toward a dilapidated gate in the fence, Lorna's suspicion arose and she slowed.

"That's all right," she said, turning back toward the main campus. "I'll just go home and wash up there."

"Don't be afraid." The young man seemed to read her thoughts and smiled reassuringly. "I know this looks odd, but there is something down here that I think you'd like to see."

Lorna was not naïve, but the eager smile of the young man was so genuine, she could not help but smile back.

"Here!" He pulled open the gate with some difficulty, for there was all manner of longstanding overgrowth blocking its path. "There's a set of stairs here, going down. If you want, I'll walk ten paces ahead of you, and if you ever feel frightened or uncomfortable, you can turn and dash back up the stairs with no harm done."

This suggestion seemed a bit melodramatic to Lorna's cultivated mind, but she could see how earnest he was and how eager to set her mind at ease. She edged closer and peered down the stairs. They were wooden and looked as if nobody had tread upon them for twenty years.

"Is it safe?"

The young man nodded. "I know they don't look like much, but my friends and I have been up and down them a hundred times with our weight. They're sturdy enough."

Rather than have him walk ten paces ahead, Lorna allowed him to assist her down the steps. Her curiosity was now fully piqued, and she wondered what was to be found at the foot of the stairs. It was truly not a long flight, probably fifteen steps or so, and at the bottom was a mossy landing surrounded by the massive trees. It was dark and cool and peaceful, and seemed a world away from the bustling life of the University campus above them. At one end of the clearing was something low and angular and covered with more moss. This seemed to be the young man's objective as he crossed to it. He turned and smiled encouragingly at her.

"Here it is!" He beckoned. "This is just what we need."

Lorna crossed over to him, studying the moss-covered structure.

"But what is it?" she asked.

"It's an old well!" He moved aside some of the branches and leaves which had cluttered the well's covering, and Lorna could, indeed, begin to identify the remnants of an ancient well. It was apparently still serviceable, for the young man was already bringing up the bucket on its frayed rope.

"But this is charming!" cried Lorna suddenly. She found herself enchanted by the mossy well, hidden in this peaceful, cool lair. "However did you discover this?"

The young man laughed as he dipped his handkerchief into the remarkably clear water and handed it to her.

"This was the old well back in the days of the original school . . . long before it was the University. My friends and I discovered it several years ago, when I first began my studies here."

"Yet, surely we're not supposed to be here, or they wouldn't have it fenced off?" inquired Lorna cautiously as she dabbed the mud off her neck.

"Probably not," answered the young man tranquilly. "I always liked this spot, though . . . it has kind of an archaic charm, don't you think? And benevolently useful for our circumstance," he added, re-soaking the handkerchief before handing it back to her.

"Yes." Lorna was not usually at a loss for words, but the oddity of the situation impressed upon her a sort of awkward hesitance. She tried to blot the mud off her dress with little success, leaving blotches that she was sure were more dreadful than the initial mud stain. The young man seemed not to notice her self-consciousness. He leaned comfortably against the well as she dabbed at her dress.

"I don't think I've seen you here before," he said. "Are you visiting someone at the University?"

Lorna shook her head. "No, though I used to be a frequent visitor when my brother was studying here. He completed his studies, but I sometimes still like to come and enjoy the campus. It's so lovely, even when the weather is a bit chilly."

"I wonder if I'm acquainted with him?" mused the student. "I've been here quite a while myself. I completed my initial curriculum then decided to take on a different degree, so I've become rather a permanent fixture here these several years. I'm hoping to finish after next term. I teach some of the lower divisions as well."

Lorna was certain that if she'd ever seen him during Tom's tenure she would have remembered him, with that crop of reddish hair. But she politely said, "His name is Tom Hathaway."

He shook his head. "No, the name does not sound familiar. Probably he was in the lower school when I graduated the first time, then I was just starting over again when he took his degree. The lower and upper divisions don't mix much."

Lorna agreed that this was probable. He looked to be about Tom's age, or a bit older.

"So, you are Miss Hathaway?" he inquired with a friendly smile. "It is a pleasure to make your acquaintance, though I wish I could have made a more fortuitous impression upon you. I am Miles Anderson." He gave her a slight bow, and she inclined her head. His was a puzzling character, to be sure. Very different from any in her social circle. "I hope there is no damage done to your . . . papers." He was holding them for her and attempting to smooth the wrinkles.

She shook her head. "Oh, it's a letter from my father. It will be all right. Although I may have some explaining to do when I give it back to my mother." She looked down at her dress, still splotched with mud. "Probably I'll have further explanation for this. I'm afraid mud on green does rather stand out."

Miles Anderson looked troubled. "I am terribly sorry." He was thinking again, she could tell. "My rooms are over on Becker Street. If you would send it over after you get home, I could have my washwoman work on it. She's marvelous in her abilities to render my shirts clean."

Clearly this young man had no idea of her social status. She wondered what he would say if he knew she resided in Grosvenor Square. But she was too polite to mention it. She merely said, "That's quite all right. We have an excellent — washwoman — ourselves." She wondered how Annie, the servant who did the laundry, would feel about being referred to as a "washwoman". Lorna smiled to herself.

"I'm afraid you are being detained from your studies," she suggested.

"No, not today," he assured her. "On Wednesdays I have only half a day, and I've just finished. I usually head to Cooley's for a bite to eat after class, which is where I was headed when I spotted you on the lawn."

Lorna had no idea what "Cooley's" was, but she presumed it was some sort of pub or tavern.

"I'd be pleased if you'd accompany me there, and I could buy you a bite to eat as penance for the trouble I've caused you," he offered.

"Oh no, that's quite all right," said Lorna hastily. "I daren't go anywhere looking like this!"

"I'll see you home then."

"No, really, it's better if I go myself, and I don't want to keep you from your meal. I was going to walk to my brother's office — my father's office it is, too — and go home with him, but under the circumstances—," They both grimaced, looking at her dress, "I think I'll just take a cab from here."

Mr. Anderson helped her back up the wooden steps, which were, indeed, sturdier than they appeared, and they emerged from the shady coolness of the wood back into the bright and bustling world of the University. Lorna looked a bit wistfully down into the ravine as Miles Anderson worked at closing the dilapidated old gate.

"Such a nice little haven down there," she sighed.

Mr. Anderson grinned a delightfully boyish grin. "It will be there when you want it."

Lorna decided it was best not to mention anything of her little adventure to anyone. Her mother and Rosamond (and definitely Aunt Sarah) would be shocked at her boldness and impropriety. As she looked back on the afternoon, Lorna herself was rather astonished at her own audacity. For a lady to descend into an isolated ravine with a complete stranger certainly seemed to contradict every rule of correct and proper comportment. It would be met with resounding disapproval on every front. So she said not a word, but slipped directly up to her room upon entering the house and later had a private conversation with Annie the laundress — with whom she had excellent rapport, for Annie was young like herself and trustworthy in these delicate affairs — and the stains were thus removed from the dress without ado. As for the letter, Lorna asked her mother if she might keep it, to which her mother agreed, pleased that her eldest daughter should harbor such devoted affection for the words of her father, and it was subsequently stowed away in a bureau drawer without her mother's ever seeing it.

She was tempted to tell Tom and Jasper about the well, for Tom would be interested in anything having to do with his alma mater, and Jasper was always game for exploration, but the two of them kept much away from home these days, and she somehow felt that divulging her secret would rob the mossy ravine of its idyllic enchantment.

Although she said not a word about it, during the course of the week Lorna found herself thinking often of the old well and of the new acquaintance who had led her there. It was delightful to have a secret place, unknown to any but herself, to which her imagination could escape and which would no doubt be idealized beyond its realistic limitations as time went on.

After a week had passed, Lorna determined to return to the campus. She may have had some vague notion of returning to the well, although she knew she would never attempt to descend into the ravine alone. (She was singularly adventurous for a female, but she was not foolish). So it was that a mild and cloudy day found her back at the University, crossing the lawn with a small hamper and every so often gazing wistfully toward the region behind the old buildings, where the trees sloped down behind an unseen fence. She did have a purpose to her outing, thus the explanation for the hamper, but she did not hurry, enjoying her leisurely pace that allowed her to take in the sights around her.

"Miss Hathaway!"

She gave an involuntary start upon hearing her name. Turning toward the far end of the park, she recognized the figure sitting beneath the large tree. That ginger hair was such a distinguishing feature, and she smiled in recognition at Miles Anderson. She approached him and observed that he was sitting on a stool with a sketchbook and a box of pencils on the ground beside him. He rose from his perch.

"I see you remembered that Wednesday is my afternoon of leisure," he greeted her.

Lorna was always polite, but she could not let him flatter himself that he was the reason for her presence.

"I'm afraid it did not occur to me," she replied. "I was merely crossing the campus on my way to deliver this," indicating her hamper, "to my brother." This was not entirely true, for the University Park was really not located en route from Grosvenor Square to the offices of the Star of India Tea Company. But she *was* on her way to deliver the hamper to Tom, however out of the way she had meandered on her circuitous journey.

"But what are you about here?" she inquired, peering at his sketchbook. "Don't tell me that you're an artist, in addition to your scholastic abilities and your wilderness ramblings!" Once again, she was taken aback at how freely and familiarly she conversed with this virtual stranger.

He grinned rather sheepishly, once more impressing upon Lorna the friendly geniality of his smile.

"I do not profess to be a Raphael, but it is a favorite pastime of mine." And he was not hesitant to show her his work.

"Why, that's very good!" she exclaimed, without intending to sound surprised. "You've sketched a perfect rendering of that grove over there, and the young man leaning with his back against the tree. I believe you've captured every leaf on every branch, or at least given such impression. This must have taken you quite a long time to complete."

Miles shook his head. "I've been at work upon it for only three-quarters of an hour. But it's not quite finished yet . . . and besides, there aren't so many leaves left on those trees at this time of year." He looked at her thoughtfully. "What a shame I've not brought my paint-box today. I'd like to do one of you in color. Your eyes are really an extraordinary shade of amber in the sunlight. I thought they looked only brown in the ravine."

Lorna blushed. She certainly had no intention of letting this young man render any such image of her upon only a trifling acquaintance. And she was astounded at his impudence in making such personal remarks about her. It was not at all seemly or proper. She did not comment upon it, but merely said, "I have had my portrait professionally done only this past summer. I hardly think it necessary to follow up with another so soon."

"Who was the artist?" inquired Miles.

"Mr. Thomason of Chelsea."

"Hm." Mr. Anderson was unimpressed. "I've seen some of his work. Were you satisfied with it?"

Lorna tossed her head indignantly. "My mother hung it in our front parlour, so she at least was satisfied. He's very much in demand."

Miles shrugged. "That doesn't necessarily mean that he's talented. Many of the world's greatest artists were never recognized during their own lifetime."

Before Lorna could offer a retort to this insinuation, Miles jumped to a new topic. "You must sit down, Miss Hathaway." He indicated the stool he had vacated. "I'm afraid it's not really a proper seat for a lady, but we could probably find a bench somewhere." He scanned the park and lawn.

"This will be fine," said Lorna, seating herself upon the stool. "I can only stay for a moment, after all."

Miles seated himself comfortably on the grass and eyed the hamper, which had been placed beside the stool.

"Is this to be your brother's mid-day meal?" he asked. "And is this your usual task, delivering it to him?"

"Oh no," replied Lorna. "He doesn't usually get a hamper at all, but Cook was putting up his favorite lemon curd and thought to give him a pleasant diversion in the afternoon. She is always thoughtful of Tom, for he was rather a pet of hers when he was a boy; always sneaking into the kitchen for a sweet — and she'd give it to him, too — but he was never very good at concealing it from our governess, for he would be covered with crumbs all down the front of his shirt, and she would scold him and make him take a plain biscuit at tea time." She laughed fondly at the memory. "Of course, I think that only impelled him to go back into the kitchen where Cook would indulge him once more. She has always been fond of us since we were children. I don't know what we should ever do if she would leave us. We'd be quite at a loss. She's presided over our kitchen for so long, I'm sure it could never properly function under another. I've heard my mother say many times that she would be completely distraught if she ever had to hire another cook. But there are biscuits aplenty in the hamper if you'd like one," she offered, reaching down and opening it. Miles took the biscuit she proffered.

"Thank you. I'll have to try one, after hearing such high praise for the one who made them." He bit into the biscuit, settling back once more.

"You must tell me about your family," he prompted. "I know your father is away somewhere and sends you lengthy letters. And you have a brother named Tom who works at your father's place of business. And a mother who would be most displeased to discover a mud stain on your dress and who admires the artistic talents of Mr. Thomason of Chelsea."

Lorna laughed, in spite of the feeling that this young man's impertinence should appall her. His demeanor was so simple and harmlessly good-natured, she could not help but take a liking to him.

"It sounds as if you already have a ready knowledge of my family."

"Have you any other siblings?" he inquired.

"Yes, a younger sister. I am the eldest, and Tom is next, then Rosamond, though we are each separated by only one year."

"Then I suppose your sister is a great deal like yourself?"

Lorna shook her head. "Not at all. You would not recognize her to be my sister, either in appearance or demeanor."

"Then I may not care much for her," said Miles, impudent as ever.

Lorna only laughed. "If you saw Rosamond you'd probably fall in love with her, as all other men seem to do."

"Ah, she is very beautiful?"

Lorna nodded, smiling affectionately as she thought of her sister. "She's beautiful and accomplished and virtuous and amiable. Everything that pleases a gentleman."

"She cannot be without fault," objected Miles.

Lorna raised her eyebrow indignantly. She would not tolerate his impudence longer. "Nobody is without fault. But I'm certainly not about to enumerate her faults, or anyone else's, for you. That would be excessively discourteous, and I hope I may never stoop to such boorishness."

"There are many gentlemen indeed who fall in love with beautiful and accomplished young ladies," conceded Miles. "But there are some men who would discern more profound attributes in a woman."

"Men such as yourself, I suppose?" Lorna was still rather put out at his forthrightness.

He nodded placidly. "Exactly."

"And to what, pray, does a woman need aspire in order to gain your approval?"

Miles leaned forward. "I tell you, I'm interested in a woman's ideals and her philosophies about life and her obligations therein. There is nothing more important than a person's attitude toward humanity and their duty toward reforming the ills of society."

Lorna was taken aback at this unexpectedly lofty answer.

"I am a student of philosophy, you know," added Miles, almost smugly.

Lorna did not know. Yet, the acquisition of such knowledge did seem to add to the complexly puzzling and unfathomably intriguing singularity of this unconventional young man.

"I gather, then, that you would only fall in love with a woman who shared your philosophical attitudes and ambitions?"

Miles reflected on this for a moment. Then, "Yes, I suppose I would."

Lorna laughed a bit caustically. "That is a rather unromantic view. You'll be hard-pressed to win a girl's affections with such talk."

Miles shook his head impatiently. "But that is just what I mean. I don't intend to 'win a girl's affections'. Such superficial notions are precisely at the heart of what renders our society senseless."

Lorna sighed. "I think I'd best be going. I cannot understand why I am even discussing such topics with you. Your lofty philosophies are beyond my comprehension."

She rose from the stool. Miles jumped up, too.

"You mustn't say that. You are uncommonly perceptive, in my opinion. Next time I see you, I shall lend you one of my best books on Benthamism, and then you will have a better understanding."

Lorna bent to pick up the hamper. "The next time you see me shall be purely coincidental, as was our meeting today."

There was a twinkle in Miles's eye as he grinned at her. "It shall be soon enough, I'll wager." His impudence knew no bounds. "Shall I see you to your brother's office?"

"No, thank you," Lorna was coolly polite once more. "I can make my way there myself. Good day, Mr. Anderson."

And she walked away, determined that she should never cross the University Park on a Wednesday afternoon again.

There seemed to be some mystery surrounding Jasper's position at the bank. He never talked about his job, and whenever any member of the household inquired as to how his day had gone, or how things were coming along at the bank, he always gave a vague, rhetorical answer: "Fine", or sometimes, "Well enough, I suppose", as if he wasn't even certain himself. He was the same debonair, carelessly casual Jasper who had first stepped off the train, and his respectable employment seemed not to have dampened his breezy charisma in the least. He still flirted and socialized and won the approval of all whom he encountered, for his smile was as dazzling as ever, and his easygoing nonchalance put all at ease. He and Tom often kept extraordinarily late hours which was taking a toll on Tom, who often appeared tired and subdued at breakfast or after work, but it seemed not to affect Jasper in the least. Before leaving for the bank each morning and upon his return, he seemed as relaxed and high-spirited as ever.

Mrs. Hathaway asked Tom about it one day.

"You spend more time with Jasper than any of us. How does he fare with his position at the bank? Has he received any commendations or approval from Mr. Custis? Is he happy in his employment? I cannot extract any words from him on the subject. Your father inquires after him in his letters, and I cannot write with any certainty in my reply. I am sure when he returns to England your father will be anxious that Jasper should settle into a permanent lodging of his own if he is secure in his income."

But Tom could give her no insight on the subject, for in the hours he spent with Jasper, the topic of his relation's employment or financial situation was rarely broached, for Jasper appeared to have no interest in discussing it.

However, Mrs. Hathaway was soon to receive some enlightenment on the subject and was duly provided with some very specific information to write her husband about.

One morning, shortly after Mrs. Hathaway's conversation with Tom, she and her daughters were in the morning room writing up a guest list for an upcoming dinner party when Jasper happened to walk through the hall without. He didn't make any particular sound as he walked, but Mrs. Hathaway glanced up just as he passed the door.

"Is that you, Jasper?" she called out in surprise. Lorna and Rosamond looked up as their mother rose. Jasper paused and came to the door of the room. "Are you off to the bank at this late hour?" inquired Mrs. Hathaway with some anxiety.

Jasper looked at her blankly. "Is it so late as all that?"

"It's past ten o'clock!"

"Oh." Jasper looked as unconcerned as ever. "No, I don't think I shall be going to the bank today, or any other day for that matter." He was so calm and collected, even as the three ladies before him clearly showed their amazement at his words. "The fact of the matter is, I haven't been at the bank for quite a while. I've given up my position there. It really didn't suit me at all."

Mrs. Hathaway did not attempt to conceal her agitation. "But . . . but . . . do you mean to say you were *released* from your position there?"

Jasper cocked his head slightly, as if pondering the specificity of her words.

"I would say it was a mutual agreement between Mr. Custis and myself." He nodded in a most unconvincing manner, a flippant smile playing about his lips. "Yes, definitely a mutual agreement." And he tipped his hat to the ladies and proceeded down the hall. The front door was heard shutting a moment later.

There was silence in the morning room for a long moment before Mrs. Hathaway regained her senses. "Well!" she exclaimed. "I wish your father were here. You can be certain he'd pay a call on Mr. Custis and find out exactly what happened. As it is, I shall have to write to him — your father I mean, not Mr. Custis — and he can decide how best to handle the situation. I daresay he'll expect Jasper to find another position as soon as possible!"

As it turned out, Rosamond did attend the National Gallery exhibition with only Lorna to accompany her. In the months after its opening, Hugh Shadwell was uncommonly busy with his duties at the vicarage, and though he sent Rosamond several messages assuring her that he had not forgotten his promise to take her, she grew impatient and persuaded Lorna to go with her. She would let Hugh take her another time, she reasoned, as she would probably wish to see the exhibition more than once.

Lorna was good-natured about escorting her sister thus, but she did not possess Rosamond's appreciation for fine art and, as predicted, soon outpaced her, first moving ahead one, then two paintings, and finally ending up in the next room altogether, leaving Rosamond in the first gallery. Rosamond did not mind being left to herself, and she did not allow herself to be hurried by Lorna's indiscriminate haste. She had seen the finest works of art in Paris, Florence, and Madrid, and she could study the works of the Masters with a critical eye and an acute appreciation for their aesthetic beauty.

One painting in particular enamored her, and she spent a long while admiring it. It hung on the center wall, surrounded by other works, and was titled *Madonna and Child.*

For a girl whose years numbered only slightly over twenty, Rosamond had already seen in her life probably a hundred paintings called *Madonna and Child*, many of them painted by the Italian Masters or in their style. But this one particularly captivated her. It depicted the mother and infant in typical fashion, sitting inside a house that appeared to be entirely more picturesque than their circumstances would have realistically allowed. Yet there was something different in this work . . . the colors were warm and inviting, and the Virgin's face seemed to glow with a tenderness that one could imagine reflected the actual feelings a young mother may harbor toward her newborn babe. Rosamond loved the way a soft, golden light shone through the window behind the figures, bathing the infant in a honeyed luminosity, emphasizing the ethereal reverence of the scene, yet never detracting from its sincerity. It looked to be a world of grace and serenity, a perfect idyll where no calamity or ill-will would ever disturb its peace. Rosamond found it enchanting.

After contemplating this memorable work and reflecting on the unparalleled skill of the artist, she became conscious of the fact that Lorna must have long since outdistanced her. She sighed, knowing that she could not spend all day inspecting a single painting. But as she turned to move on to the next canvas, a rather singular occurrence came to pass.

Glancing at the far end of the room, she met the gaze of a man who happened to cast his eye upon her at the same moment.

And Rosamond, who was ever the subject of others' lingering gazes and second glances, found her own attention arrested.

The gentleman was tall and well-built, with hair nearly as black as Rosamond's own, and a handsome face with strong features and slightly sun-tanned, as one who has spent a great deal of time out of doors. He wore a smartly-tailored suit, superbly cut, and bore himself with the patrician composure of an aristocrat. But it was his eyes that held Rosamond's attention — dark and brooding, they narrowed as they beheld her, not in adversity, but in pensive contemplation.

Rosamond did not internalize any of this, for their gaze held only a fleeting moment before she blushed and turned rapidly away. Yet it made enough of an impression on her that she neglected to look at any of the other paintings in the room and instead hastened to the next gallery, where she found her sister waiting.

Lorna was seated on a bench at the opposite end of the room, having already navigated the entire gallery, which comprised the remainder of the exhibit. She smiled amiably as Rosamond approached.

"Don't be alarmed," said Lorna with benevolent complaisance. "I've already resigned myself to sitting here for another thirty minutes while you peruse the paintings in this room. So go on," she shooed her sister away. "Don't hurry on my account . . . I'm only too happy to give my feet a rest."

Rosamond threw an appreciative smile toward her understanding sister, and turning her attention toward the masterpieces of the 16th-century, she was soon immersed in their opulent beauty and studied with great admiration the products of such inimitable talent and unparalleled significance. She was sorry that she had left the first room so hastily, and she determined that she would return with Hugh another day and take in the works she had inexplicably overlooked.

Chapter IV

Jerry Flynn was as much a permanent fixture in the East End docks as the rats that swarmed off of the ships and scurried about the dank warehouses whose decrepit edifices settled like heavy monstrosities at the very edge of the wharves. There was nothing that went on in the dockyards that Jerry did not know of, or likely have a hand in, if it was a particularly sordid dealing. With his mangy, matted hair, patched secondhand garments, and blackened teeth that did not provide adequate shielding against his rancid breath, Jerry Flynn was known to all in the docks, from the lowliest common laborers to the overseers to the constables, with whom he was a favorite suspect for every misdemeanor. He had no legitimate profession to speak of, but legitimacy held no interest for him, and his means of subsistence always caused much unruly speculation amongst the dock workers at their mid-day respite. He was not by any means entirely unique, for there were others like him, denizens of the riverfront, but on a particularly overcast night, Jerry Flynn happened to be the one who lurked in the shadowy vicinity of the Bengal Tea Warehouse, which company was the chief rival of the Star of India in profiting from the Indian trade.

The East End is never deserted, even at night, but once the sun sets, activity is confined to dark corners, desolate mews, and abandoned sheds. The streets themselves would seem empty, sinister, and silent. Jerry Flynn liked it that way; it was his domain, *his* sinister silence, *his* bleak kingdom.

Which is why he was profusely perturbed to have the morbid silence broken by intruders.

There were two of them, and he heard them approaching before they came into view, for they made no attempts at subtlety as they clattered along the dockside road. They were obviously inebriated. He heard their voices: one singing noisy off-key snippets of a tavern ditty (completely unrecognizable to any who was not intimately familiar with such songs), and the other emitting low moans, as if grieved or pained or simply incoherent. Once in view, they were easily distinguished by the flickering flame of a lantern swinging loosely in the hand of the taller man and apparently pilfered from a nautical-themed alehouse. He was the one intermittently serenading, whilst the other man gave off the hollow moans.

Jerry knew well these types, and hated them, and saw far too many of them in this manner. Wealthy West End scoundrels . . . they were parasitical pariahs who crossed into the East End only under the cover of darkness and ingested its cheap liquor and easy betting with eager voracity, but who wouldn't deign to look upon the vicinity in the light of day. They took whatever earthy pleasure the neighborhoods would offer them and left nothing in return but a few coins and less concern. They were arrogant, insolent, and contemptuous, and they were trespassers — they did not belong to his world, only used it for their whimsical self-indulgences.

So, when these two drunken knaves came staggering along, noisily making their presence known with their voices, feet, and pendulant lantern, Jerry Flynn felt only contempt in his veins and sought to avoid them by ducking into the Bengal Tea Warehouse. He had picked the door's lock many times and was inside the building in a matter of seconds. He heard the footsteps and voices approaching and saw the flickering lantern light beneath the door. Then, just as they should have passed, the voices, footsteps, and swinging light suddenly halted.

He heard the familiar moaning of one of the men, then he heard the other say in his slurring, drunken dialect: "No you don't! Now see here . . . we've still a ways to go. Pull yourself together, Tom old man!"

There was some sort of response from the other man — presumably Tom — but it was unintelligible to Jerry. There was a sudden thud against the door, which caused Jerry to jump, prompting him to take refuge against the wall beside the door as opposed to behind the door itself. And he moved just in time, for the door swung slowly open, and the dim light of the lantern cast a hazy glow a few feet into the cavernously dark warehouse. He saw the shadows of the two men outlined in the open doorway. Neither was standing completely upright, but the taller one with the lantern was supporting the other man with his free arm, yet still staggering drunkenly. He raised the light a bit and seemed to be attempting to inspect the premises.

"This looks good," he slurred sleepily. "Yes, I think this will do for a bit . . . until you've regained your senses. Here, Tom, here you go," and he led Tom with some difficulty into the warehouse's interior and deposited him on the floor, with his back up against a wooden crate. Tom promptly passed out, and the taller one shook his head as if he could not believe his companion's sorry state. "That's what happens when you drink too much," he drawled, hardly sober himself.

Jerry Flynn pressed his back against the wall, intending to slip out the open door as soon as the taller man situated himself. This took some moments. The man first set the lantern upon the ground, then removed his coat and laid it upon the warehouse floor where his friend lay. By now it had grown quite silent within the cavernous building and the hurried scuffling of the rats could be heard, re-emerging from their temporary refuges and resuming their foraging amongst the wooden chests and crates. The man seemed not to be bothered by this as he sat upon his coat and moved the lantern nearer with an unsteady hand, as if this small imprisoned light would keep the rodents away from him. He laid his hat beside him, then leaned back heavily against one of the chests. Jerry still waited until the breathing he heard was fairly steady, and when he was certain that both men were asleep (or at least insensible), he slipped out the door noiselessly, as was his habit.

He had walked not ten yards away from the warehouse when he heard a sudden crash from within. It was accompanied by the sound of breaking glass. Though he was used to sudden disturbances in the night, Jerry stopped and turned back toward the Bengal Warehouse. Creeping back toward the big wooden door, which was only slightly ajar, he heard no further sounds for a moment. Then he became aware of a faint glow emanating through the cracked doorway. Peering in, he glimpsed a sight that momentarily froze his serpentine heart.

The lantern had been knocked over, presumably by the restlessly drowsy taller man, and ignited the wooden crate just behind it. The flames danced and crackled all along the edges of not only that crate, but the one adjacent to it as well. And it was spreading still. Jerry gave an involuntary chortle and dashed inside the premises. Removing his own bedraggled coat, he shouted at the sleeping man and began to beat the flames with his coat. The tall man languidly opened his drink-heavy eyelids and stared incoherently for a moment at the husky, ungroomed derelict who was zealously slapping his coat at the escalating fire.

"Get up, ye drunken bastard!" shouted Jerry Flynn with fury. "Can't ye see what ye've done? Get up, and get to work! This fire's out of control!"

The young man's dazed eyes opened wide as perception enlightened his brain. But instead of grabbing his coat and beating at the flames, he took hold of his hat, scrambled up to his feet, and ran unsteadily toward the door.

"Get back here, ye scoundrel!" called Jerry after him, but the man paid him no heed, and merely hastened out the door, leaving the vagrant and the insensible companion alone in the warehouse.

The fire was now spreading rapidly, and the voluminous warehouse, crammed full of wooden crates, wooden boxes, and wooden chests, was as vulnerable fodder waiting to be consumed by the ravenous flames. It was beyond Jerry's capacity to douse the fire with only his soot-disintegrated coat. The blaze had engulfed a sizable portion of the stock, and the heat and smoke were getting to be unbearable. Soon the burning warehouse would be noticed by passers-by, and Jerry did not wish to be discovered at the site of such calamitous destruction. He ran toward the door, still clutching his ragged coat, but gave pause before exiting the premises. His eyes brightened and his mouth turned leeringly upward at one corner as was the case whenever he had any sort of scheming inspiration.

Jerry Flynn was most definitely not an altruist, nor even marginally soft-hearted, but he was decidedly one who would firmly seize upon any opportunity for self-profit. And so it was that he turned back, hurried over to the senseless body of Tom Hathaway, and pulled him to the door and out into the dark night.

When Jerry first grasped onto him, Tom dazedly opened his eyes, then promptly let his eyelids fall again, allowing his unknown rescuer to exert the whole of his energy toward the rescue. Jerry knew nothing of compassion or benevolence, cared nothing about the life of this unknown gentleman, but saw in the situation a chance to turn indiscretion into advantageous profit. Ever and anon, that was the key to Jerry's survival and infamy.

Lorna sat up in her bed, the open book lying on the coverlet before her, and the bedside lamp providing the only illumination in the spacious room. She knew without looking at the mantel clock that the hour was very late, yet she did not extinguish the light and attempt to sleep. She was certain that she was the only person awake in the Hathaway residence.

She had intended never again to return to the University Park when there was any chance of an encounter with Mr. Miles Anderson. And she persevered in that resolve for several weeks after their meeting upon the lawn. She was quite stubborn, and the very fact that he had so arrogantly predicted her imminent return ought to have been enough to keep her away.

Yes somehow she was attracted to the boldness and eager frankness of the young man. She had never met anyone who spoke to her so freely on topics that had previously been ideas only inside her head, but that she had always longed to put forth from her tongue. Granted, she did not truly understand his philosophical theories, but she found it immeasurably refreshing to have someone with whom to engage in spirited dialogue without fear of reproval. She was never entirely at ease in polite society, unlike Rosamond, who had a natural inclination towards gentility, and Lorna felt that in the company of Mr. Anderson she could be comfortable in her candor and forthrightness. Also, she had grown somewhat discontented since Jasper rarely went out with her anymore on outings or walks. She had liked having such a steady companion and missed the comradery. For these reasons she had returned to the University and resumed her acquaintance with Miles Anderson.

And so it was that she was now in possession of a book he had lent her at their last conversation. He never had ceased since that second meeting in his insistence that she borrow one and familiarize herself with his philosophical persuasions. Although Lorna had never been particularly interested in such loftily abstract theories, she at last conceded to take the book, in part because she did have a curiosity about his ideas, and in part just to curtail his prodding.

But now, as she held the book before her in the dim glow of the lamp, she found herself unable to concentrate upon or absorb the pedantic vocabulary. The words swam before her eyes as her eyelids grew heavier. She did not want to go to sleep yet, though. She had not heard Tom come home, and it was her habit to listen for him, though he may not have known it. She could not remember him ever being so late when he was expected to be at the office in the morning. She sighed and attempted for the hundredth time to focus on the page in front of her, which was headed with the inordinately dull title of *"Utilitarianism as Applied to the Laboring Masses"*.

Her flagging concentration was abruptly interrupted, however, by a sound she heard from within the house. She glanced up from her book and strained to listen. Yes, she definitely heard footsteps ascending the staircase. That was not normally the sort of thing Lorna would hear from her bedroom, but the person climbing the stairs was making no attempt at inconspicuousness and was creating rather a din thumping up the steps. Lorna slid out of her bed, and, putting her wrapper on over her long nightgown, she opened the door leading to the hall and peered into the darkness.

By the faint light emanating from her own bedroom, Lorna discerned a figure completing his ascent of the staircase and stepping into the upstairs hall. He was carrying a hat, having apparently just come in from the street outside.

"Jasper!" she hissed. "Whatever are you doing out so late? Don't you know that Tom must be at his post in the morning?" Then she paused as something occurred to her. "Where is Tom?"

Jasper came nearer, wobbling a bit as he approached her door. Lorna peered closer and saw that his eyes were glazed and glassy. She frowned. Even with her liveliness, Lorna had been brought up amongst the well-bred and had never associated with anyone who was overtly inebriated. But she could well imagine that the glassy eyes and tremulous gait were symptoms of that vulgar state. She was disgusted.

"Where is Tom?" she demanded again, her sharp whisper betraying her repugnance.

Jasper motioned toward the darkened stairway, as if Tom were right behind him.

"He's back there," he said in a very loud whisper. "He'll be in when he wakes up."

Lorna had not the slightest idea of what Jasper was talking about, but she did not attempt to detain him further, as any rational conversation appeared to be futile.

"You'd best get straight to bed," she ordered, "and mind you, walk softly. It won't do at all in your state to wake Mother or Rosamond. Or the servants," she added.

Jasper nodded politely and ambled down the hall toward his own room, carefully picking up his feet with exaggerated elevation so as not to make a sound, until he disappeared into the darkness at the end of the corridor.

After pulling the unconscious gentleman from the burning warehouse, Jerry Flynn dragged him down a back street until he felt that they were a sufficient distance from the building so as not to be discovered by any seeking evidence of perpetrators. He then deposited the man under a dark shed, and sat down beside him to wait. It was not until the early hours of the morning that the gentleman stirred with a slight moan. Jerry, who'd had his eyes closed, but was habitually alert, was at immediate attention. He leaned in and grasped the man's arm.

"Awake now, are ye? About time, too. We'd best hurry, or it'll be gettin' light."

The gentleman was not at all fully cognizant, but he was able to look at Jerry and apparently comprehended his words.

"Where are we going?" he asked drowsily as Jerry pulled him to his feet.

"We're goin' home!" said Jerry, as if it was the most natural thing in the world. "Home, of course. Where else would we be goin'?"

The gentleman leaned quite heavily on Jerry for support, but said nothing, except to repeat the word "home".

Jerry started walking with him through the darkened mews, westward. He kept talking as they lumbered along. "Home is where you belong, where you can crawl into yer nice comfortable bed and sleep until . . . ah . . . breakfast." The gentleman merely nodded. Jerry glanced sideways at him. "Now then," he said, "I can't quite recall the exact address. Do you recollect the street?"

"What street?"

"The street where you live, of course." Jerry was speaking in his overly-polite tone. "The street where your home is."

"Home . . .," the gentleman repeated. "Grosvenor Square."

Jerry's eyes lit up. "Oh, Grosvenor Square, is it?"

The gentleman eyed him suspiciously. "Don't you know?"

"Yes, yes," said Jerry hastily. "Of course I know. And Grosvenor Square is where we're headed. It's quite a far walk from here. I'd hire a cab, but I seem to be plumb out of money."

The gentleman fumbled in his coat pocket and pulled out some coins. "Cab money," he said.

"Aye, that's fine then," said Jerry. "As soon as we come within sight of one, I'll hail it."

They walked on without much difficulty, for the gentleman seemed to be recovering as he walked. He suddenly frowned. "Why are you taking me home?" he demanded.

"Why, because I helped you out of the warehouse, and now we're going home," explained Jerry in a way that indicated no further explanation was necessary. The gentleman looked confused but pressed the vagrant no further. At last, just as day was breaking, they came upon a hansom cab and rode to Grosvenor Square in comfort.

It did not take long for news of the fire to spread. The Bengal Tea Company was well-known in London, and the fire had completely devastated the company's supply, sending its stock plummeting. Aunt Sarah came during breakfast with the news, for she knew the company to be a competitor of Mr. Hathaway's own business.

"This ought to put the Star of India Company in fine measure," she predicted, with an air of wisdom. "Won't this be something to write to Mr. Hathaway about!"

Mrs. Hathaway nodded rather disinterestedly as she sipped her tea. "Yes, I suppose his business associates here in the city will convey the news to him. I never write to him about any sort of business affairs."

"I am sure Tom can apprise him of the news. They say that everything in the entire warehouse was destroyed — at least three ships' worth. It will be a while before they can recover, I daresay, and all the better for Mr. Hathaway's company!"

Mrs. Hathaway paid scant attention to her sister's commentary, having no real interest in anything relating to the world of commerce. She did, however, attend to the mention of her son.

"I'm afraid Tom won't be writing any letters today. He did not go to the office this morning. He's sent word down with James that he's out of sorts and has kept to his bed. And you know Tom . . . he seldom complains of any ailment, so he must truly be ill, poor dear. I intend to go up to him after breakfast."

Rosamond, who was the only other partaker of the breakfast, had not thus far contributed to the conversation, for like her mother, she cared nothing for affairs of business. But she now spoke up. "James related that Tom has requested not to be disturbed."

"Yes, yes, I know," warbled Mrs. Hathaway, unconcerned. "But I am his mother, and I must look after my son, however grown he may be. At any rate, I'm sure he was referring to you and Lorna. He knows Mrs. Allerton's dinner party is tonight, and he doesn't want you contracting any illness that would prevent your going. Sir Henry will be there, and you know how attentive his son has always been to you, Rosamond."

Rosamond was quite certain that Tom's wish for privacy had little to do with preventing her from attending a dinner party. He was probably genuinely ill and truly wished to have some peace and privacy in his sickroom. However, she knew her mother would not be thus persuaded, and so she said nothing, but privately resolved to send up some rose water to her brother, for that always soothed her whenever she was feeling poorly.

It was nearly noon when Jasper appeared downstairs, looking as debonair and vigorous as ever. Upon being apprised of the day's news, he expressed only slight interest in the East End fire, but showed admirable concern for Tom's condition, declaring that he had thought "the boy" looked a bit peaked the previous evening, and that he was certain a day of rest would be exactly what was needed. Jasper seemed to be in uncommonly fine spirits and even offered to take Lorna out rowing that very afternoon.

Tom did not leave his bedchamber the entire day, but his mother did look in upon him after breakfast and subsequently informed everyone that he had no fever, but only a headache so excruciating that it rendered him horribly nauseous, and he could do nothing but lie in the darkened room and sleep. His sisters rather fretted over his discomfort, and their mother assured them that she would summon the doctor if Tom was not better by the next day.

This was not necessary, however, as Tom did appear at breakfast the following morning and, insisting that he was quite recovered, went in to the office as usual, though he still seemed to be unnaturally somber and despondent.

It was briskly chilly the following day when Tom and Rosamond stepped out of the Star of India Tea Company offices. Rosamond was concerned over her brother's continued melancholy and thought that a visit to the Shadwells' home in Hanover Square after his workday might cheer him up. So she had met him at his office in the afternoon, and the two of them set off toward the familiar square.

Tom seemed uneasy as they walked, however much Rosamond attempted to divert him, which only heightened her concern. He kept looking back behind him until at last Rosamond glanced over her own shoulder to see what was engaging his attention. She saw nothing out of the ordinary except for an elderly, husky vagrant walking about twenty meters behind them. He seemed decidedly out of place in this affluent district, but she did not deem him worth any relevance. Still, when Tom took her arm and began to walk at a brisker pace, she became disconcerted.

"Tom, why are we hurrying so?" she asked. "We will draw attention walking at this pace!"

And as she forcibly slowed her own gait, she glanced behind her once more. The tattered vagrant was still walking behind them, and to Rosamond's amazement, when Tom turned his own head, the derelict grinned and waggled his fingers.

"Why, Tom!" exclaimed Rosamond. "I believe that man is waving at you!"

"Pay him no heed," said Tom under his breath, clutching her arm once more as they crossed onto a small public green.

"But what business can he possibly have with you?" she inquired.

And then, to increase her bewilderment, the man actually called out, "Good afternoon to you, Master Hathaway!"

Tom could not very well keep walking now. He stopped, and Rosamond felt his grip on her arm involuntarily tighten. The man approached from behind, still grinning affably.

"'Afternoon, Master Hathaway," he repeated blithely, then bowed to Rosamond with a "Ma'am". The effect of his overt politeness was grotesquely comical. "Now what is that frown for?" he chided Tom. "I'd thought ye'd seen me walkin' behin' ye, but I couldn't be sure, so I thought I'd call out, as a friend ought."

"I'd thank you to leave my sister and me alone," said Tom coldly, turning as if to continue on down the street.

"Eh now, is that the way to treat such a friend as has done you a favor and talked so perlitely?" The vagrant spoke with almost cherubic innocence. Rosamond's eyes widened as she looked at her brother, who had been halted once more. But Tom would not look at her. He only stared at the man in consternation.

"A favor?"

"Eh, Master Hathaway, you know it were a favor as I rendered ye two nights ago. And now I've come to offer you another, in spite of how poorly ye received me this afternoon." Looking celestially wounded, he turned his head away.

Rosamond then saw a cloud of anger cross her brother's face. It was an emotion she had rarely seen him display.

"I have already given you ready answer to your sordid proposition. If you accost me further, I shall summon the constable," he said hotly.

The ragged man's bushy grey eyebrows shot up. "Oh, I see. It's the lady's presence, is it? Well, I can't see but that a sister so sweet and pretty as yours shouldn't want to know that her brother's in a good way. With his position in the company, I mean."

Now Tom was clearly as astounded as his sister.

"Whatever are you talking about?" he demanded, forgetting in his agitation that Rosamond was present.

The man remained calm. "Oh, I'm just referrin' to that, uh — what did you call it? — 'proposition' that I talked to you about earlier today. I told you I'd have to follow through on my word."

Rosamond thought she saw a flicker of fear in her brother's eye, but he maintained his steady stance.

After a pause, he said to the man, coolly, "I think we would be better discussing this in private. I will see my sister home first."

But the vagrant shook his head belligerently. "No sir, that I cannot do," he asserted stoutly. "I'm prepared to do you a good turn, and it's got to be here and now, or you'll just have to take th' consequences of your earlier decision."

Rosamond was truly a bit fearful of this man and his bewildering words. She would have loved to be removed from the situation and erase its memory from her mind. She could not comprehend the dialogue passing between her beloved brother and this unsavory stranger . . . only gathered from its overtones an insinuation of malevolence.

The man took the ensuing silence as a cue that he was being given allowance to continue.

"Now then," he began in an even, pleasant tone, "as I said, after our conversation this afternoon — which was so disappointin' to me; I really thought an upstanding gentleman like yourself would have been a bit wiser in matters pertainin' to yer father's business —anyway, I did have to act according to my word, as I am a man of conviction."

Tom gave an audible chortle at this, though whether it was derisive or fearful Rosamond could not tell.

"Do you mean to tell me that you actually had the audacity to go to the shareholders and repeat that fictitious tale to them?" Tom spoke incredulously.

The vagrant clucked, shaking his head. "I told you, I wished I didn't have to." He spoke as one with great regret. "'Twas yer own stubbornness as drove me to it."

Tom was clearly alarmed. "Have you no scruples?" he cried in disbelief. "How could you concoct such a falsehood?"

The man was still shaking his head. "I wish I could say it isn't true. But I am a man of business, and I've got to stay ahead, you know. It seemed best, under the circumstances, that they should know."

Rosamond, so fearful and silent throughout, could not contain herself longer.

"What does he mean, Tom?" She turned pleading, frightened eyes on her brother. "I don't understand a word of this!"

Tom was too discomposed to immediately respond, but Jerry Flynn turned to her affably.

"Eh now, don't tell me yer dear brother didn't mention as how I saved his life the other night?" Rosamond only stared in astonishment. Jerry modestly looked at his intertwining fingers. "'Tweren't nothing . . .

only I am glad I happened to be walkin' by the Bengal Tea warehouse when I was. I pulled him out just in time . . . fire had spread just inches from his head. But I am always happy to do a fellow gentleman a good turn, I am, and I only ask a fair recognition as would duly be owed in return."

Rosamond's voice betrayed her bewilderment. "Do you mean to say that Tom was inside the Bengal Tea warehouse when it caught fire? But that's absurd. He was out with our cousin Jasper all night. I heard Jasper say so."

Jerry Flynn cleared his throat. "I cannot account for another man's tale. I can only tell you what I saw. Of course, after he told me he lived in Grosvenor Square and that he was young Tom Hathaway . . . well, forgive me, Miss, but it doesn't take a man of education to make the connection . . ."

Rosamond frowned at the insinuation, but Jerry went on. "What I mean is, 'tis a well-known fact that Mr. Hathaway Senior runs the Star of India Tea Company, and, well, I figured it wouldn't look so good for that venerable institution if his son was found on the premises during the destruction of the competitor's warehouse."

Tom now broke his silence. "How dare you make such an accusation?" he cried vehemently.

"Now, now, Master Hathaway . . . I've only got yer best interest in mind." He turned back to Rosamond, who was speechless. "So," he continued, "knowin' that it would be my duty, as a loyal citizen of the Crown, to give some response to any questions the constables may be asking — for I am a prominent figure in the neighborhood of the warehouse's location — I began to worry about the consequences that your upstanding brother might suffer. So, I thought up a little . . . proposition," with a nod to Tom, "to alleviate his fear that I might divulge his name in connection with said events. I merely asked a trifle . . . enough to buy some shoes and bread fer me dear little ones . . . ." Here his eyes went piously heavenward again.

Tears of disbelief were welling in Rosamond's lovely blue eyes. "Do you mean to say," she said, her gentle voice unusually contemptuous, "that you asked my brother to give you *money* in exchange for your keeping his name from the investigators?"

Jerry Flynn shook his head. "Oh no, Miss, not from the constables. Remember . . . I had to think of my little ones. I merely asked for the smallest bit, just fer payment in saving his life, mind you. But I did attach a certain stipulation, just as a precaution, you know."

"What he's trying to say," said Tom bitterly, "is that he threatened to take this incredible tale to the company's shareholders if I refused his attempts to extort money from me."

Jerry jumped back into the tale. "I merely felt it was my duty that the company's owners ought to know, especially seeing as yer father plays such a prominent role in the Star of India's great success."

Tears of bewildered indignation were now running down Rosamond's cheeks. "Surely you didn't confront them?"

Jerry gave her a horrible smile. "Oh, remember, Miss, I only had yer brother's interest in mind. The company's, too. I just didn't want to see his name in the newspapers or be responsible for any plunge in the stock of the Star of India Tea Company. I've only just come from addressin' them — they're having a meeting over there," he pointed down the street, "in the upstairs room at Smollett's Coffeehouse. They are indeed a most distinguished, excellent group. Very responsive to my offer to keep Master Hathaway's name out of the newspapers." And Jerry Flynn produced from his shabby coat-pocket a fat wad of notes.

Rosamond and Tom both gasped in astonishment.

"But that is impossible," Rosamond exclaimed. "The owners are gentlemen of rank and honor, some of them peers — they would not be deceived by your lies! They would not condescend to such baseness!"

Jerry shrugged. "It is difficult to say what men may do when their reputations are imperiled."

Poor Rosamond! Throughout her life she had read books, viewed paintings, and seen all manner of theatrical performances depicting villains of the worst sort, but she had never encountered one herself. In her innocence she had not known that such sordid souls could possibly lurk within her own vicinity. She did not understand why Tom did not defend himself against these lies and put this knave in his place. She could only surmise that her brother was so distressed that he was not in his right senses. Indeed, it pained her to see him look so miserable, and she now cried tears of pity for him and of anger at this man's boldness. For however gentle and virtuous and well-bred she was, Rosamond had a deeply-instilled pride, and she could not bear to see her brother shamed by such libelous prevarication, nor for her father's company to partake in any sordid dealings on account of such false accusations.

"There now, Miss," clucked Jerry Flynn. "Remember as I've come to offer a favor to yer brother to set things aright." He held up the money. "This 'ere is a fair sum, but I may be able to be persuaded to go back to the gentlemen, still assembled, and recant what I told 'em . . . and return this," indicating the money, "if I could come out a bit ahead of it. Due to yer own generosity, of course."

Rosamond was sickened with horror at this man's depravity. Her usually demure and genteel demeanor was overcome by her tumult of emotions. She could not think straight; she could not conceive of any response other than to right the corruption instituted by this deplorable villain. Without a thought to logic or decorum, she snatched the notes from the man's still-extended hand. He was so taken unawares by this action that he had no opportunity to resist.

"You black-hearted miscreant!" she cried, sobbing. "How dare you threaten my brother or his employers with your reprehensible lies? This is not rightfully yours, nor shall you have the satisfaction of possessing it!"

And, still clutching the notes, she hastily departed in the direction of Smollett's Coffeehouse. She did not see the afflicted grimace on her brother's face as he relinquished to a leering Jerry Flynn a bill of exchange made out for a sizable sum.

There were near a dozen men gathered about the large table in the dim, low-raftered upstairs room of Smollett's Coffeehouse. Of assorted ages and demeanors, their affluence and prestige were the common elements that allied them. They were the principle shareholders in the flourishing Star of India Tea Company, and they spoke in low, earnest tones across the table.

One can only imagine their astonishment when into their midst burst a beautiful, raven-haired young lady, pale and tremulous, her luminous eyes brimming with tears.

"How could you?" she cried out, breathless in her emotion. "How could you allow yourselves to be so coerced? How could you believe the lies of such a low-born scoundrel?"

So ensnared by her distress was Rosamond that she was unconscious of either the environment or of the assembled, astonished individuals before her. One face made a vague impression of familiarity upon her, but she had no perception — the room, the faces, the tears were all swimming in an amalgamated blur before her. She gave no pause in her diatribe. "How could you possibly believe my brother could in any way be capable of soliciting such scandal? It is unthinkable! You must know him to be my father's son! And for you to give in to the extortive efforts of that blackguard is unpardonable! It is unbefitting and dishonorable to gentlemen of your stature and influence. It is reprehensible!" Her voice faltered with a sob. "My brother's character is flawlessly upstanding and blamelessly respectable. There is nobility in all that he does!"

With a trembling hand, she cast the stack of notes upon the table, sending them scattering across its surface. "It is an insult to him to wager this against his character! Here, take what is rightfully yours, and forfeit it not against such unfounded suspicions again! You cannot—"

Rosamond suddenly felt her shoulders grasped by strong hands. Gasping, she turned her head to look into the dark and pensive eyes she instantly recognized. The tall, dark-haired man she had seen in the gallery shook her gently, but very firmly.

"Pull yourself together, girl!" he commanded, his tone low, but unyieldingly forceful. His black eyes were severe in their intensity. "You will make yourself ill with such hysterics."

The shaking brought Rosamond back to her rightful senses. In an instant, she was filled with shame and humiliation at her immodest, presumptuous outburst. And before such strangers! She fairly went limp in her wretchedness, but that she was still in the very capable grasp of the gentleman. His black eyes softened slightly as he beheld her distress. Keeping one hand firmly upon her arm, he managed to extract his handkerchief and handed it to her.

Her angst was palpable in her gasping sobs as her shame overtook all feelings of indignation, and she flushed as some of the other men came forward. A grey-whiskered man in an admiral's coat set a chair for her, but she did not move from where she stood beside the dark-eyed gentleman.

"Here now," said another man soothingly. "You'll be all right. You mustn't worry about the money."

"That's right," put in the Admiral. "It was only a small amount — of little consequence to us or to the company."

Rosamond felt herself being led toward the proffered chair, but she could not bear the humiliation of their kindness after such an unrefined outburst as she had delivered. Rigid with remorse, she pulled free of the hand that supported her and fairly flew back down the stairs from whence she had first ascended.

The illustrious shareholders stood fixed where they were, so abrupt was Miss Hathaway's exit. The black-haired gentleman who had intervened in her declamation frowned as he gazed after her.

At last, a bespectacled middle-aged man broke the silence. "Do you think there is truth in what she said?"

"She certainly believes it to be the truth," said the Admiral.

"You were right in what you told her," said another to the Admiral. "The money is inconsequential — though to that scoundrel, I daresay it was a princely amount."

The Admiral, who seemed to be a senior member of the group, nodded. "Keeping young Tom Hathaway's name out of the papers will be easy enough. I have solid connections in that realm, as I'm sure do all of you. But I do not know him well enough to comment on his character or his trustworthiness."

"I will say this, though . . .," The well-built, black-haired gentleman turned his gaze from the stairway and spoke in a steady, deliberative tone. "I would not risk losing the father over any offense done to his son."

There were several nods.

"Lord Kendal is right," said the bespectacled man. "Mr. Hathaway may be only a minor shareholder in the company, but he has done wonders in his capacity as managing director. Any of us would be foolish to think the company would be as profitable as it is without his administration."

"As long as we have no proof that his son was in any way involved in this catastrophe, it may behoove us to simply look the other way, so to speak," suggested the Admiral quietly. "We are all men of independent wealth who do not require the profits from this enterprise to sustain us in any way. But there are others, both here and in India, whose livelihood would be shattered should this company falter. Are there any here who object to letting young Tom Hathaway keep his position? It is a minor concession to make for the continued stability of the British commerce."

There were no objections, and the men agreed that not a word would be said to the senior Mr. Hathaway on the subject.

"Damned pretty girl, Miss Hathaway," Frederick Lancaster thought to himself sullenly as he walked along the darkening quay. The young Earl of Kendal, upon leaving Smollett's Coffeehouse, had not gone directly to his residence in Belgravia, but had decided to walk along the Embankment instead. He was restless and agitated, and, wishing to avoid the throngs who would undoubtedly be promenading along The Strand at this hour, he thought a stroll along the water's edge might relieve some of his restiveness. He gazed moodily into the water, where hazy spots of light demarcated the glowing reflection of the streetlamps lining the quay.

Like so many of his fellow aristocrats, the Earl of Kendal was neither a native Londoner nor a permanent resident. His family's seat was at Stoneleigh in Cumbria, at the edge of the Lake District, and it was in that beautiful and spacious region that he had been raised. However, since inheriting the Earldom upon his father's recent demise, Frederick had taken up residence in London during the months when he attended to his parliamentary duties.

For a man of only thirty-two years, the Earl had already attained a favorable measure of renown amongst his countrymen. His reputation as a huntsman was unmatched; his skills upon the field, peerless. He was known to keep the finest stable of horses in the country at Stoneleigh, which were the envy of many an able sportsman. But his prowess was not limited to the foxes and hounds, for he had found equal success and greater adventure on the Dark Continent and in India, where he had partaken of several expeditions in pursuit of big game.

He did not revel in this renown, though. Frederick Lancaster was a man of reserve and reticence, whose pensively virile demeanor had been revealed to Rosamond Hathaway upon her first glimpse into his brooding countenance. He was ever a man of conviction, and it was widely reported that he had once killed another man in a duel. And despite his serious nature, he cut a rather dashing figure, for he had been brought up to his title and was honorable and well-bred in his bearing.

He paused for a moment, leaning against the Embankment's rail, staring at a passing barge, not really perceiving the shadowy figures moving about its deck, poling it along in the burgeoning darkness. His thoughts were still fixed upon the same matter: "Damned pretty girl. Her father ought to keep her under lock and key."

Chapter V

Tom could hear the servants still in the kitchen, the distant rattle of dishes indicating that they were finishing up their after-dinner duties before retiring for the night. The ladies had already gone upstairs, and Jasper had gone out for the evening, as usual. Tom did not accompany Jasper this night, nor had he the previous evening. He had not gone to the club. He had not much left the house, save for going to the office each morning.

Now he sat in his father's chair in the library, as he was wont to do of an evening, staring into the flickering orange flames of the blazing fire. Its cheery warmth and incandescent glow seemed at odds with the morose countenance and spiritless slump of Tom's body leaning heavily in the wing-backed chair. The bottle which Jasper had once pulled from his pocket in this very room now stood on the small table beside him. The firelight shone though the textured glass, giving its contents an amber sheen, transforming the flask into an oversized, sparkling gem. A deadly jewel, to be sure.

His eyes were distantly forlorn, despairingly troubled. He could not fathom the dismal journey that had led to this present state of gloom. He could not comprehend the demon encased in that small, innocuous bottle. But he knew that it was that demon that had led him astray, that still held him in its iniquitous clutches. He could not understand why Jasper, night after night, could partake of drinking and gambling with such excessive unrestraint and not fall victim to the demon as he had. Jasper, through no benevolent intention, had been the one to expose the depths to which Tom had sunk. And now he was here, in this present state of misery, having brought degradation upon himself and coming dangerously close to imperiling his family name. He knew he might not be so fortunate the next time. He must see that there would be no "next time". Jasper would have to carouse on his own.

Tom did not start when the door opened, for it was very softly, and he somehow knew that it would be Lorna, even before he saw her. She was in her dressing gown, her long wavy brown hair cascading down her back. She glided over to him noiselessly and perched upon the arm of his chair, putting her own arm about his shoulder and smiling down at him affectionately.

"Dear Tom." She spoke barely above a whisper. "You love to sit in here as Father does. It reminds you of him and brings his presence nearer. It has always been his habit on evenings when he is at home. I can remember, even in days of old, how he would sit in the library in Hanover Square, smoking his pipe, reading his newspaper, or just looking into the fire as you are now." She smiled again. "It is nice to think that you are carrying on his tradition."

Tom nodded, but his thoughts were plainly elsewhere, Lorna could tell. Her brows knit in concern, and she laid her head against his.

"What is it that troubles you? Do not deny it, for I can tell these past few days that you are burdened with some great care. You have hardly spoken or left the house. Even at dinner and at tea you say nothing, only seem terribly preoccupied. I was worried about Rosamond, too, for she did not leave her room all last evening after the two of you returned home, though she seems to have recovered her spirits today. But *you* . . . you are afflicted by something still. You have never kept anything from me before."

Tom gave her hand a gentle squeeze. "My sisters have always been my good angels," he whispered. "And see how I have repaid their goodness." Lorna was puzzled and concerned by this statement, but Tom did not elucidate, only gave her a wistful smile. "That will change," he said, audibly resolute. "You will see an alteration herein. I cannot explain, but trust my resolve, and I shall be back to my true self in swift duration."

Lorna still did not understand, but as he seemed satisfied in his earnestness, she did not press him further, only gave him a quick hug and rose, saying warmly, "You are the dearest brother any sister could ever hope for."

The warm, rich color of her eyes reminded him of the bottle beside him on the table, with its amber-hued contents. His attention involuntarily strayed to it. Lorna's eyes followed his gaze.

"Why Tom!" she exclaimed in surprise. "Have you been drinking? You know Father always says no man should drink alone." She paused, reflecting. "I daresay it's Jasper's influence. I know him to be reckless in that capacity. You mustn't emulate his deleterious deeds." She picked up the bottle. "I'll dispose of this so you won't be further tempted. Now come upstairs and get some sleep. You've promised recourse back to your complaisant self . . . after a good night's rest, I expect to see that transformation tomorrow!"

Tom did not immediately rise to follow her. He could have laughed aloud at the casual naivety of her simplistic solution. But he knew that Lorna was not foolish or simple-minded. He suspected that he would be under close scrutiny from this point on. And despite his best efforts to convince himself that she was correct in laying the blame on Jasper, he could not overcome the deeply instilled knowledge that his malady pre-dated Jasper's arrival.

Lorna and Rosamond had been invited by Edith Shadwell and her mother for tea in Hanover Square. Hugh was to ride over from the vicarage to meet them there, so it was bound to be a pleasant occasion, and both girls were anticipating it with eagerness. Lorna suggested to her sister that they should walk, for it was unseasonably mild and sunny, and some fresh air and exercise would do them good. Rosamond objected, for it was windy, despite the mildness, and she did not wish to arrive for tea mussed or disheveled. However, Lorna persuaded her by promising that they could stop in some shops in Bond Street on the way.

So they left Grosvenor Square early in the afternoon in order to have adequate time for browsing the shops before they were expected in Hanover Square. Lorna did not really enjoy perusing shops the way Rosamond did. But while Rosamond admired bonnets, fingered ribbons, and purchased several yards of delicate lace, Lorna was happily content to wait outside where she could stroll about, nod to passing acquaintances, and enjoy the refreshing breeze.

They had actually ambled quite a bit farther down the street than they had intended, which is easy to do when one is meandering in and out of shops, heedless of the interval covered, but putting them at considerable distance from Hanover Square. Lorna was surprised when she heard the bells toll five. She hurried into the millinery shop where Rosamond was giving the milliner instructions as to the trim on a newly-ordered bonnet.

"Rosamond, we must go," urged Lorna. "It is five o'clock, and we have walked all the way to Piccadilly! We will have to walk quickly if we are to reach Hanover Square by the appointed hour."

"Oh dear." Rosamond glanced at the milliner.

"It is no trouble, Miss Rosamond," that good woman assured her. "You can send a note over tomorrow with the details, or I can call at your home any day that suits you."

Rosamond was still reluctant to leave in the midst of a purchase, but she knew it would not do to be late for tea, nor did she wish to walk at such a pace as to be mussed upon arrival. So she bid good-day to the accommodating milliner and followed Lorna out into the street. The two young ladies walked north in the direction of Hanover Square. The streets were rather crowded at this hour, and it took quite a long time to walk only half the length of Bond Street. They were about three-quarters of the way to Hanover Square when Rosamond stopped suddenly.

"Oh no!" she exclaimed, her pretty brow creasing in dismay.

"What is it?" Lorna could not imagine what woe had caused her sister such abrupt consternation.

"I've left my sunshade at the milliner's. I picked up my parcel, but must have forgotten the sunshade in my haste." She looked nervously up at the clock tower near Brook Street. "We are expected at the Shadwells' in only twenty minutes. What shall I do?"

Lorna shrugged, relieved that no real calamity had befallen her sister. "It's not the least bit sunny anymore," she said, glancing skyward. "In fact, it has grown quite overcast, and it will soon be dusk. You certainly won't need it today. You can go back for it tomorrow."

But Rosamond shook her head. "It is the parasol Father brought me from India last year. It could not be easily replaced should anything happen to it."

Lorna did not share her sister's love of pretty things and thought it rather absurd to be so upset over an object of such trifling value. But she knew Rosamond treasured it, perhaps for sentimental reasons as it had been a gift, and would not rest easy until it was in her possession once more.

Lorna sighed. "Well, if we walked all the way back to the milliner's shop, we should be excessively late for our engagement. We must not put our hosts to any inconvenience, nor cause them any anxiety on our behalf. I supposed the best thing to do would be for you to go back and retrieve your parasol, and I shall go on to Hanover Square and explain the situation. They will be happy to wait for your arrival before serving, once apprised of your well-being."

This plan did not sit at all well with Rosamond. She wished her spirited sister were to be the one to go back and retrieve the sunshade, — she did not relish the thought of walking back through Bond Street, and she deemed it rather indecorous to walk thus unescorted, although it was perfectly safe — and she knew it was the sort of errand Lorna would not mind. But it was not Lorna's parasol which had been lost, and it apparently did not occur to Lorna that her sister should have any hesitancy about fetching it. She was already on her way toward Hanover Square before Rosamond could object, so Rosamond turned back toward Piccadilly and began her journey back to the milliner's shop.

She wished she had at least thought to give her parcel to Lorna — it would be one less thing for her to attend to. She wished, too, she had brought a maid with her, as she often did upon shopping expeditions, although it had seemed unnecessary at the outset since her sister was accompanying her and they would be ultimately destined for the Shadwell residence. The more she reflected on the circumstances that "ought to have been", the more she was convinced that this course of action had been too hastily applied. If she had had adequate time to consider, she would have gone forth to Hanover Square and persuaded Hugh to take her back to the milliner's shop. It would have been no great inconvenience to him, as he was to have just come over from his vicarage anyway. By the time Rosamond had considered all of these possibilities, she found herself at the milliner's door and in possession of her cherished sunshade. Clutching it in one hand and the parcel in the other, she turned back toward Brook Street for the second time.

She was really quite fatigued and would have liked to have stopped to rest, but she felt the need to press on, as the wind had picked up rather suddenly, and the sky seemed to grow more and more overcast until it looked uniformly ominous. Then, to Rosamond's dismay, before she had gone two blocks from the milliner's, fat raindrops began to dot the walkway around her, and by the time she had completed the second block, the precipitation was on the brink of becoming a regular London downpour. She only just managed to duck under the columned portico of the National Bank Building before the torrential rains set in, drenching the street she had so hastily abandoned.

That is not to say that the bank portico was a particularly comfortable shelter, although it was better than none, for it quickly became the refuge of the other passers-by seeking a dry haven. Rosamond was truly dismayed at her misfortune and hoped that someone at the Shadwells' would think to send a carriage after her. But even if they should, how would they ever find her, huddled under the bank portico with a mass of other shelter-seekers, some of whom were haplessly damp?

Somehow it was chilly and humid all at once, and between the dampness in the air and the soggy people milling about her, pressed into close quarters, Rosamond was having a difficult time staying dry, despite the roof overhead. She thought about seeking refuge inside the bank itself, wondering if its administrators would mind accommodating a young lady who had no business to transact, but who wished only to bide time quietly and unobtrusively until the shower passed. She picked her way carefully around some dripping loiterers and made her way in the direction of the heavy doors of the bank. Just as she neared them, she and several other bystanders were forced to step aside as the doors opened, and some men emerged from the bank. They must have just concluded a meeting of some sort, for they shook hands or nodded briskly to one another before heading out in various directions with their umbrellas, paying little heed to either the assembly under the portico or to the pouring rain without.

Rosamond sighed as she waited for the gentlemen to pass, some of whom nodded or tipped their hat to the elegant, pretty young lady who graced the dismal, crowded portico with her radiance. But one of the gentlemen who chanced to look upon her recognized her, and she him, causing them both a measure of momentary disconcertion. The man's purposeful gait was stayed before her, and Rosamond once again beheld the handsome, brooding face of the one who had inexplicably arrested her attention the first time she ever looked upon him.

As he bowed to her, she flushed, chagrined to thus encounter the man who had so forcefully brought her to her senses in Smollett's Coffeehouse. Although he seemed unsettled upon first perceiving her, the gentleman quickly regained his composure and just as promptly grasped the situation.

"Miss Hathaway," he said, "I fear you have been hindered by this unexpected downpour. You must allow me to convey you to your home in my carriage."

Rosamond paled at this suggestion. At the same time, her heartbeat accelerated. She shook her head. "Oh no, no thank you," she faltered. "I could not put you to such trouble."

"Nonsense," his voice maintained its even-toned resonance, but its slight edge betrayed his impatience at her hesitation. "It is no trouble, I assure you. The carriage is already here. We've only to cross a few meters without cover, but I've got this," and he indicated the umbrella he was holding. "Come."

Rosamond dutifully followed as he led the way out of the portico's crowded shelter, but before they left its covered protection, she touched his sleeve, giving him pause.

"I— I'm not going to my home." She was hesitantly flustered. "I'm going to tea in Hanover Square."

He gave a brief nod then led her out from the porch, sheltering her under his umbrella and not presuming to utilize any of its breadth for himself. A coachman opened the door of a handsome, well-appointed carriage bearing a crest which Rosamond did not have time to discern. She was swiftly handed up into the compartment, still grasping onto her parcel and her sunshade, which now seemed ridiculously superfluous. The gentleman climbed in, and, after giving the coachman the address, seated himself opposite Rosamond.

At the urging of the driver up top, the carriage rolled away from the bank, the rain pelting relentlessly against the windows. Leaning back against the richly upholstered bench, Rosamond kept her eyes fixed on the deluged street outside as she and her enigmatic rescuer fell into an uncomfortable silence.

Rosamond was mortified to be in such intimate proximity to one who had witnessed the only instance of her life when she had behaved with shameful boldness. To be now indebted to him for this new kindness only added to her humiliation. And for his part, he was much too chivalrous to make any mention of the shareholders gathering, knowing that it was certain to be painful for her. As it was his nature to be reticent, the silence was undoubtedly not as awkward to him as it was to Rosamond. It was she who finally spoke, and modestly.

"I . . . you have the better of me, sir. You know me to be Miss Hathaway . . . ," and here was profuse blushing at the recollection of his basis for such knowledge, "but I do not know your name — only that you are a shareholder in my father's company."

"Forgive me. I ought to have introduced myself. Frederick Lancaster, Lord Kendal."

Rosamond gave an involuntary gasp of surprise and dismay. "The Earl of Kendal!" The pink in her cheeks rose to an even deeper blush, which only enhanced her beauty. Her voice was tremulous in her disgrace. "You must think me a terribly brazen, forward girl, to have made such a shameful spectacle before such distinguished company!"

Frederick's darkly penetrating eyes scrutinized her. Clearly he was dissatisfied with her self-reproach.

"I thought nothing of the sort," he replied with such firm calmness that it was impossible to doubt his word. "I thought only that Tom Hathaway is extraordinarily fortunate to have a sister who loves him so dearly as to defend him before a group of formidable strangers."

"Oh, you must have no adverse thoughts of my brother! He is of such noble and gentle character — he would never have been involved in any sordid transgression!" The flushed crimson in Rosamond's cheek was no longer shame, but fervor; her eyes entreating the Earl to accept her position and rendering her utterly charming in her appeal. This was the side of Rosamond's character that was known only to her closest acquaintances — a warmth and glow reflecting her ardent beliefs, usually held so sedately within her refined demeanor.

"I think very highly of your father." Frederick chose his words deliberately. "He has been a tremendous asset to our corporation, and I should hesitate to think less of his son without conclusive substantiation."

These words seemed to soothe Rosamond, and she rewarded the Earl with a soft smile. He gave a slight nod of approval and murmured, "At last you would smile."

Rosamond demurely averted her eyes. She had yet to elicit such a pleasurable response from his countenance.

The carriage was brought to a halt rather abruptly as it neared Brook Street, and the coachman called back to the Earl, "We cannot go farther here, my lord! There is an obstruction in the road."

Both Rosamond and Frederick peered out the window and observed that there was, indeed, a large cart overturned in the midst of the Brook Street intersection. It seemed to have been unable to traverse an extremely sizable pool of muddy water that had accumulated in the street, and had been upset, spilling a plethora of barrels and boards into the intersection.

"I think we must turn back and go around from Savile Row," called the driver. The Earl agreed that this was the only viable alternative, and the carriage slowly made the turnabout and proceeded south once more.

"I'm afraid you will be delayed in reaching Hanover Square," said Frederick.

Rosamond nodded but did not seem concerned. She stared down at her gloved hands resting in her lap and became lost in thought. She reflected on all she had heard about the Earl of Kendal, mainly through society columns and idle chatter. She had never been particularly mindful of such talk as she had hitherto not been personally acquainted with the Earl, but certain vague images floated through her thoughts in connection with his personage: horses, . . . hunts, . . . a deadly duel. A country seat in the North. A father deceased in recent years. Somehow everything she knew of him seemed disconnected from her London society, yet she had chanced to encounter him thrice in only a month's time.

Now she looked up at him and spoke softly, tentatively shy. "I have something that belongs to you, which I must return, though I have it not on my person at present. Your handkerchief . . . it is at home. Now that I know who you are, I can send it to you."

He shook his head. "Do not trouble yourself over it. It is of no consequence."

"Even so, I do not feel right in keeping it."

But he shook his head again, and there was a note of cynicism in his voice as he said, "That set of handkerchiefs will soon be replaced, I have no doubt. My wife embroidered them and then declared that it was the shabbiest work she had ever done. She will insist upon my ordering a new set the next time I see her."

This remark was made casually, sullenly, and a bit caustically — but it interested Rosamond immensely, for she had never thought of him as having a wife. She could not recall ever hearing mention of the Countess of Kendal, although members of the nobility were usually popular subjects of drawing-room prattle.

Something in the Earl's final remark puzzled Rosamond. "Is your wife not presently in London?" she inquired.

"No. She is in the country."

"I suppose she will come later in the season, when the climate is pleasanter," suggested Rosamond.

Frederick frowned slightly. "I think not." There was a bitter edge to his tone. "She prefers to stay in the country year-round. She is very fond of the horses at Stoneleigh and does not care for London."

"Oh yes, your horses . . ." Rosamond was happy to have another topic to turn to, as the Earl's hardened tone indicated his disinclination to continue the topic at hand. "Naturally I've heard of your fine stables. You must miss the beauty and sport of the countryside when you are here in the city. Sometimes it is difficult for those of us who live here always to remember that not everyone wishes to be a permanent resident. You reside in the North, do you not? I have traveled in the Lake District . . . it is lovely there."

Her voice was soothingly gentle, and the Earl nodded, assuaged.

"Yes, my family's estates are in Cumbria. It does seem a world away from here, but I am acclimated to it. Even before I took over my father's seat, I came here fairly often on various affairs of business."

They had reached Piccadilly, and Rosamond could see the new music hall in the distance.

"I wonder when the new music hall is to be completed?" she queried. "It really is splendid to behold, isn't it? Even though the building is not yet officially opened, I've heard that the young princess is going to make her debut there, at the Founders Ball."

"Yes, they delivered something to my house the other day," Frederick said absently. "I hadn't opened it, but I expect it was an invitation. My father left some sort of bequest to the hall, so I suppose we're included on the Founders List."

He sounded apathetic, but Rosamond brightened at once. "Oh, but you ought to go!" she exclaimed. "It would be lovely to see the princess at her debut, and it's bound to be the event of the season!"

And finally Frederick gave her a smile, so engaging was her enthusiasm.

"You are much more enamored of the seasonal events than I am. It is a pity they did not send the invitation to you. It would be better appreciated."

Rosamond laughed. "Indeed! I should have a difficult time explaining whence I came by it, as my family would surely know that I had made no endowment. As it is . . .," she sobered, "I'm afraid I shall have some difficulty explaining my arrival at Hanover Street in your carriage, whose crest is easily recognizable."

They were, indeed, approaching the square from George Street.

"I would not be at ease putting you out in the rain," objected Frederick.

"But see how the rain has abated," Rosamond pointed out. "At last, something has worked in my favor this day! You could let me out at the end of George Street, and I should only have to walk across the green."

Frederick nodded and conveyed instruction to the driver. When the carriage pulled to a stop, the Earl himself helped Rosamond out onto the green. The air was still thick with dampness, but the rain had ceased.

"Thank you so very much for your kindness," Rosamond murmured demurely.

"Think not on it." Frederick was ever reserved. "And now, you'd best be on your way. I imagine you've long since been missed."

Rosamond could not deny it. With a proper curtsey, she set off across the green, taking care to stay on the path. She heard behind her the carriage door close and then the clatter of the horses' hooves upon the cobblestones as the coachman urged them on, away from Hanover Square.

The next day, a message was delivered to Miss Rosamond Hathaway. Upon breaking open the seal, she discovered, to her delight, two tickets to the Founders Ball enclosed with this note:

Miss Hathaway,
I hope you will not consider me presumptuous in sending these to you. They are not meant as a gift. I merely thought they should be given to someone who will utilize them rather than let them go to waste. I trust you will find a way to explain.

Your Servant,
F.L., L.K.

And shortly afterward, a small package was delivered to the Earl of Kendal's London residence. There was no note, simply a small box containing a single familiar handkerchief bearing the initials F.L., freshly laundered and pressed, and scented with lilac.

The following week marked a very happy occasion for all members of the Hathaway family — Mr. Thomas Hathaway, Sr., returned home from India. He had sent a letter the previous month indicating that his return was imminent, but it was ever impossible to specify exact dates when dealing with ships and business affairs. So it was with tremendous joy on the part of his wife and children when he arrived in Grosvenor Square.

As with all parents who have been long separated from their offspring, Mr. Hathaway was astute in noting changes he perceived in them. His youngest daughter, while always affectionately loving, had embraced him with an acute tenderness that bespoke of her prodigious relief at his return. And Lorna exuded a beaming radiance that surely signified some unseen happiness within and which amplified her natural effervescence. His only son gave him some concern, for Tom seemed unusually somber, even in his fond reception of his father.

Upon mentioning these observations to his wife in private, she emphatically dismissed such claims of alteration in any of their progeny with an airy reprimand.

"Don't you think I would be aware of any significant matter which would affect our children? This is what comes of your being absent for such extended periods of time . . . you forget the very complexion of your children's dispositions!"

Chapter VI

Rosamond's explanation to her mother as to how she had acquired two tickets to the Founders Ball was deliberately ambiguous. She could not be pressed into giving detail other than that they had been given her by "a very respectable acquaintance who would not be utilizing them". It was completely out of character for Rosamond to be so secretive, but she knew that divulging any details of her chance encounter with the Earl of Kendal would subsequently lead to further topics that would be distressing to her brother and discomfiting to herself.

Once Mrs. Hathaway realized that her youngest daughter would not be induced to elucidate further, she facilely moved beyond her personal curiosity — though allaying Aunt Sarah's was another matter — and rapturously embraced the notion that Rosamond would be attending the most prestigious event in London, which involved the jubilation of planning a new gown, ordering new gloves and jewelry, and seeing to a myriad of other details, which procurement occupied the doting mother for the next two weeks. (She even tried to persuade her husband to make a sizable gift to the music hall so that they might secure invitations of their own, but he did not deem the event worthy of such a hasty bequest).

Rosamond was quick to engage Tom as her escort, lest her mother should suggest Jasper, so it was that on the night of the ball, brother and sister found themselves at the Royal Music Hall presenting their names to the smartly-uniformed doorman and were accordingly announced to the guests inside, who were too diverted by music, acquaintances, and gossip to pay attention to anyone entering.

When the Founders Ball was described as being the grandest event of the season, it was presumably a reference to its size, for Rosamond, who regularly attended balls, had never been caught up in such a crush, nor seen such a tremendous ballroom as had been created within the unchristened music hall. The décor was opulent . . . from the gilded chandeliers, to the marble pillars twined with white and crimson flowers, to the sumptuous tables laden with every tempting delicacy imaginable, it was truly resplendent in the royal tradition. Rosamond's favorite part of every ball was the music, for its melodious richness never failed to fill her with a feeling of wondrous exhilaration, and the musicians here did not disappoint. They played with such majestic grandeur that the dancers could not help but be caught up in the glorious pageantry, swirling elegantly and gracefully under the magnificent chandeliers.

Rosamond dearly loved dancing, but upon first entry into the palatial hall, she felt rather overwhelmed by the immensity and the crowd and wished to find a quiet alcove where she could sit and observe unobtrusively. Her brother was very understanding and dutifully led her to a bench in a recessed niche where she could be comfortably seated. However, it is impossible to be Rosamond Hathaway and not attract some measure of attention, so exquisitely beautiful and pleasingly demure was she. She had chosen a white ball gown, as was always her preference, which provided an enchanting contrast to her black curls, and her luminous grace was perfectly offset by her modest gentility. It was not long before the quiet nook had been infiltrated with acquaintances, both old and new. There were amongst the guests several with whom the Hathaways were previously acquainted, and when they came forth with greetings, they were invariably accompanied by a friend or two, eager for an introduction.

So it was that in a fairly short span of time, Tom and Rosamond had received many introductions and were both lured to the dance-floor.

Rosamond quickly overcame her awe and was swept up in the dancing, falling under the spell of the music and the graceful progression of the steps.

There was one thing that puzzled her, however, and in an interval between dances, she put a question to her companion, who was the son of her father's friend Sir Henry Trainer.

"But where is the princess?" she asked. "I thought she was to make her debut this evening."

"Oh, that is yet to come," assured the gentleman. "You will see. The royal family adheres to its own archaic customs in these matters."

Soon enough, Rosamond's curiosity was allayed. At exactly ten o'clock, when there was a respite from the dancing and many of the guests were taking refreshment or mingling beneath the ornate sconces along the perimeter, the musicians played an imperial fanfare, suspending all other noise or conversation and capturing the guests' attention. Tom had managed to keep watch over his sister, in spite of the fact that they had both spent most of the evening dancing, and when they heard the fanfare they had just re-entered the main hall from an anteroom, where they had taken an intermission from the assembly. They joined the other guests, whose attention was focused on a stairway opposite the entrance to the hall.

A distinctive group was assembled at the top of the stairs; mostly men in military attire, along with several women who were not particularly young. More men in uniform stood at attention in two lines, facing each other, forming a walkway which led to the top step. Along this walkway processed two men: a young man in military attire, and a middle-aged man dressed in the elegant style of the Head Steward. Rosamond recognized the younger man as Prince Leopold, the youngest of the queen's sons, now representing his family at the presentation of his sister to the loyal subjects of the Crown. The ballroom grew hushed as the steward stepped forward and addressed the guests.

"Ladies and Gentlemen, Peers of the Realm, and Honored Guests, it is my duty and privilege to present to you Her Royal Highness, the Princess Beatrice Mary Victoria."

The guests assembled below clapped with dignity, and it struck Rosamond how very solemn was the atmosphere, as if the assembly was merely acknowledging a Parliamentary decree or a retiring ambassador.

After the steward's address, he and the prince bowed to one another, and the steward stepped aside, leaving the prince flanked by the regimental guardsmen. He turned to look down the walkway, and every eye in the assembly strained to look as the princess herself appeared, stepping delicately and slowly as she walked between the guardsmen.

She was slight and pale, beautifully attired, with a dainty silver crown resting on her light brown hair. She nodded to her brother in a very correct manner and, taking his arm, was escorted down the long staircase. It was all very deliberate and very rehearsed. It bore nothing of the jubilant excitement Rosamond recalled from her own debut. But she was delighted to have seen the princess and honored to have been present at such an important event in the young royal's career.

Once the prince and princess had attained the main floor, they became absorbed in the assembly, acknowledging and greeting the guests gathered at the foot of the stairs — a select group of peers and other relations who had been deliberately located in that advantageous position. Before long, the music began once more, and the little princess and her brother took their places on the dance floor as was proper, and the other guests duly accorded them a few measures before joining in the stately waltz. Soon the hall was again filled with graceful music and elegant dancers, Rosamond and Tom among them.

As the hour grew late, Rosamond felt she simply must have a rest. Her slippers were nearly worn through from so much dancing, and she was feeling warm and fatigued. Having been deposited by her last partner on a plush bench against the wall, Tom sought her out and expressed concern for her condition, suggesting that perhaps they ought to return home. But Rosamond protested. She felt fine . . . she simply needed a respite, as any lady would after having danced so many consecutive pieces. Tom insisted that he should sit with her during the next dance, but Rosamond would not have it, as Tom had already promised it to a very pretty young lady, who was even at that moment peering eagerly at him from behind her fan. So Tom stayed beside his sister merely long enough to make her excuses to several approaching gentlemen who were hopeful in securing her as a partner, then went off to the dance-floor himself, giving his arm to the coquettish young lady.

Rosamond was happy to have a rest and enjoyed watching the dancers while listening to the music. She was not long left to herself, however, for the dance had not even reached its mid-point when she was approached by none other than the Earl of Kendal. She saw him before he reached her, and she could scarce believe her eyes as his presence registered with her. She rose and curtsied as he bowed to her.

"My Lord Kendal," her voice was ever soft, but could not conceal her surprise. "I had not thought to see you here tonight. I . . . I mean, how could you when — well, I thought that . . .," She blushed, as she seemed to do very often in his presence. "I mean to say . . . thank you for the tickets."

He took pity on her. "Do not be alarmed at my presence, Miss Hathaway. There are certain advantages to holding a title, one of which is the ability to gain entrance to royal functions without the necessity of holding a ticket."

Rosamond smiled modestly. "I did not mean that your presence here was in any way unpleasant . . . merely unexpected."

"I see that your brother has escorted you here tonight," Frederick's voice implied his approval as he looked out upon the dancers. "It is well . . . he can keep an eye on you."

"It is magnificent, is it not? I have never been to a ball so grand as this!"

Frederick did not wish to dampen her enthusiasm by relating that he had been to dozens of similar affairs, none of which left him particularly impressed. Instead, he merely nodded, and Rosamond went on:

"But how is it that I have not seen you before now? I did not see you dancing." As soon as these words were out of her mouth, Rosamond regretted them. She had not in any way meant to intimate that he should ask her to dance, and she prayed he would not interpret her words to that end.

He did not. He merely said, “I only arrived a short while ago. I did not intend to dance tonight, only to stop by and wish little Beatrice well.”

“Yes, see how sweet the princess is!” Both of them shifted their gazes to the dance-floor where the princess was dancing near the stairway she had descended a few hours before. “But to be making her debut at only fifteen years old! It seems a tremendous responsibility to put on one so young. My sister and I were not permitted to come out into society until we were eighteen, and even then Mama still fretted over us.”

“I think you’ll find that her debut has quite a different purpose from your own. Most young girls come into society as a way for their parents to inform the world that their daughter is now permitted to be courted by eligible suitors, even if she isn’t expected to marry for several years afterward. I don’t imagine, though, that the princess’s mother is going to allow any young gentlemen to be wooing her. You see how she dances with none but appointed officers and relations.” He looked at Rosamond again. “You are right to say that she has tremendous responsibility for such a child. But one responsibility she will never have will be choosing a husband. She will have no choices in that matter, and it will probably be decided before she is even old enough to wed. Her debut is merely a formality.”

Rosamond’s countenance was somber as she pondered this. She shook her head. “You are right, of course. I don’t envy her. But then, who is to say that even in an arranged marriage there can be no love? It is well-known that her parents loved one another very much.”

That is what she said, but her tone and expression clearly indicated that Rosamond was not convinced that many arranged betrothals would end so happily. Frederick could only smile ruefully at her guileless romanticism.

“Miss Hathaway, in the princess’s circle you would be as one speaking a foreign language. They would not conceive of love as being in any way associated with marriage."

Rosamond would have been greatly interested to learn the Earl's own opinion on the subject, but of course she did not ask him. He was ever reticent and serious, with that underlying restless virility, all of which bewildered her, for he had likewise shown himself to be unfailingly honorable and noble in his conduct toward her. She had no doubt that there were many young ladies present who wished he would ask them to dance, without knowing that he was ineligible to court them. She wondered what sort of person his wife was, and did he ever smile at her?

These thoughts must pass through her mind in the fleetest moment, for while the two of them were content to maintain their secluded tête-à-tête, they were soon interrupted by a third party — a large woman in a lavender gown, whose slightly greying hair was pompously accented with an imposing plumage. She approached from the direction of the dancing, where neither Frederick nor Rosamond was facing, and Rosamond started in surprise upon hearing a booming voice behind her.

"Why, Lord Kendal! How splendid to see you!"

Frederick was visibly agitated by the intrusive, grating voice, his black eyes flickering irately. But, as ever, his deportment was befittingly aristocratic, and he bowed civilly to the oversized lavender-gowned woman. "Lady Ossington."

"I cannot tell you how it pleases me to see you here tonight! I shall take full credit! You must have pondered my words at Fullerton Hall last week . . . I did convince you, didn't I? But I must say, I didn't think I had persuaded you!" She turned to Rosamond, though she was not acquainted with her. "Lord Kendal seldom attends balls, you know, despite our best attempts to entice him."

Rosamond glanced up at the Earl and saw that he had become restlessly sullen. However, he made the proper introductions. "Miss Hathaway, may I present the honorable Viscountess Ossington . . . Lady Ossington, Miss Rosamond Hathaway."

Lady Ossington nodded in response to Rosamond's graceful curtsey then leaned in a bit closer to the young lady. "My husband was a great friend of Lord Kendal's father, the late Earl, God rest his soul." This last bit was embellished with excessively pious eyes cast heavenward before she continued on to Frederick: "And how is everything at Stoneleigh? We meant to stop by for a week or two last autumn when we were on our way to Edinburgh, but one thing or another came up to delay us — you understand how that goes — and we were impelled to continue straightaway to Scotland without any respite. How I should love to see the old place again . . . I haven't been there since your father's passing, but I always have such fond memories of its loveliness." And here her hand went to her heart, as if reflecting on the most cherished of memories.

"We should be delighted to have you there at any time." Frederick was coolly polite.

This invitation seemed to greatly please Lady Ossington. She waved a hand in the Earl's direction. "Oh, and you must give our regards to your gracious wife. Though I have only met the Countess on one occasion, I hope she should not have forgotten me? You really must induce her to come down to London for the rest of the season. I daresay you would be more inclined to accept invitations to balls if she were here with you."

But Frederick did not respond in kind to the woman's lighthearted intimation. Rosamond saw his dark eyes flash, and she detected the hardened edge to his tone. "I am afraid the Countess will not be persuaded to come to London this season or any. She does not care to partake of society here."

There was a pause, as Lady Ossington was visibly flustered by this statement.

"Oh . . . oh well. It is of no consequence. We would be just as pleased to see her at Stoneleigh later this year. Please do remember us to her. And now, I must take my leave . . . my husband will be overindulging at the refreshment table if I do not attend to him. Good evening, Miss Hathaway. Au revoir, Lord Kendal!"

And in a flurry of silk and feathers, she departed.

Frederick turned to Rosamond, but they would not be able to reclaim their quiet haven, for the music had ended, and before either one could utter a syllable, a very fervent young gentleman had presented himself to Rosamond, eagerly reminding her that she had promised the next dance to him.

Rosamond was rather in a daze, between the hasty departure of the overwhelming Viscountess, the sudden besetting upon by the stream of guests exiting the dance-floor, and her own irreconcilable desire to resume her sequestered discourse with the Earl; and she could only look up at him, her deep blue eyes full of helpless uncertainty, before she was whisked off to the dance-floor by her enthusiastic partner. She did not see Lord Kendal for the remainder of the evening, and as she could have no certain expectation of encountering him again, she wished that she had been able to bid him a proper good-night.

It had been many weeks now that Lorna had been regularly meeting up with Miles Anderson at the University. They usually sat on a familiar bench and conversed, or sometimes he would bring his sketchbook or watercolors and render drawings or paintings while she looked on. He never seemed to mind having an observer, as he was not in the least self-conscious about his work and really relished her approving praise, for she did admire his talent. Sometimes he let her take up the pencils or brushes and create works of her own, for Lorna was never timid at approaching new endeavors, and she was delighted to discover that she seemed to have some natural aptitude, especially in painting.

Whatever pastime they chose, their activity was always accompanied by a great deal of discussion, for Miles was full of scholastic zeal, and one could not spend a significant amount of time in his presence without igniting or absorbing his fervor. As a student of philosophy, he had a great many ideas about what was amiss in modern civilization and how to redress those injustices. As Lorna had read several of the books he lent her, she had gleaned from their pedantic pages a rudimentary idea of some of his convictions. She gained more, though, from his own discourse, for he could phrase things in a lucid, coherent manner, and it was so much more compelling to hear things from one who was earnestly impassioned rather than from a cold and sterile book.

Although she now had a better grasp of Miles Anderson's philosophies, she was not wholeheartedly approving of them. They all seemed to involve what she perceived as radical social reform, and she was certain that most of his ideas were bluntly contradictory to the standards and traditions she had been taught to uphold. Yet this did not repel her as it should. Somehow, it only piqued her interest. While Lorna had never done anything outrightly shocking or unseemly in her life, she had, at times, dabbled at the edge of indiscretion, and it was a place to which she had been inexplicably drawn, like a child standing at the door of a forbidden cupboard. So, while she had recognized Miles's notions to be unconventional, she found herself slowly beginning to form an interest in them. She came to understand some of his favorite phrases, such as "utilitarian society", "the greatest good for the greatest number", "promoting pleasure while avoiding pain", and "consequences, not intentions".

She knew her family would be shocked to know that she was discussing such radical principles with a man they knew nothing about. She was sometimes shocked herself, but Mr. Anderson had such an ardent, likeably entrancing way of explaining everything, that she could not help but be enamored by his words.

As the days wore on, and the weather turned colder, it became impossible to sit outside comfortably, so they took to walking instead — Lorna wrapped in a pretty cloak or shawl, and Miles with a scarf about his neck. They loved to meander through the Covent Garden market, carrying on their conversations amid the din of hawkers and tradesmen calling their wares. The covered market was being renovated, but the open stalls displayed all manner of enticements, both useful and exotic. Sometimes Miles would purchase for Lorna an orange or a small posy, and once she bought him a scarf, for she declared that his old one was "the unsightliest conglomeration of loose threads" that she had ever seen. She had no fear of being sighted by any familiar acquaintances, for none in her family's circle would think to appear in Covent Garden, and she did not care for any to discover that she had frequented that pedestrian square.

One day, as they were leaving the crowded market and making their way back toward the University, Miles seemed dissatisfied with the course of discussion. However much Lorna might be interested in his philosophical theories, she rarely admitted such to him, and on this particular day he seemed especially frustrated at her unwillingness to share his point of view.

"But, Lorna," he protested, "you are not applying logic to the situation. Has nothing I have spoken in the last hour registered with you?"

Lorna's eyebrows arched in surprise. "Pardon me, but did you just address me by my Christian name?"

Miles was impatient. "Yes, what of it?"

Lorna was too amazed at this blunt lack of decorum to speak for a moment.

"Don't you think that's a bit presumptuous?"

"I don't see why." His demeanor was almost sulking. "You refer to your siblings and other friends by their Christian names."

Lorna nearly laughed in astonishment. "I refer to my siblings in such a way because they are family members. And there are very few, outside of my relations, with whom I am on such terms of intimacy as to address by their given names."

Miles was still sulky. "I've heard you refer to your clergyman friend by his given name."

Now Lorna did laugh, so ridiculous was this assertion. "Hugh is such an old friend . . . we are all in the habit of referring to him and his sister as intimates. They are practically members of our family."

But Miles would not be pacified. He ran a hand through his ginger hair. "But this is absurd! I have sat with you and walked with you these many weeks now, and still we must adhere to such formalities? This is a prime example of the preposterous mannerisms that are suffocating our civilization. These prudish barriers are obstacles to the very attainment of our happiness!"

Lorna merely smiled, never one to be easily offended. "I'm afraid you are in small company with such opinions. The majority of our society is happy to uphold such proprieties."

Miles kicked a small stone on the ground before him. "Yes, that's the trouble with our world. No one is willing to progress away from obsolete tradition."

Lorna had nothing to say on the matter, and they walked in silence for a few moments before Miles looked up, his face brightened with enlightenment. "I've just had an idea!"

Lorna looked over at him, eyes widened with good-natured curiosity.

"We shall both go to Clerkenwell on Friday!"

Lorna was bemused. "Clerkenwell?"

"Yes, Clerkenwell Green . . . you shall come with me."

"What on earth would I be doing in Clerkenwell Green?"

Miles was by now so enthusiastic about this proposal that his eyes sparkled with delight. "You ought to spend more time there. It is the seat of progress. We all meet there regularly . . . my friends and I . . . anyone interested in changing society for the better." He grinned broadly at her. "You would be a fetching diversion at our meetings, to be sure. There is to be a lecture on Friday on John Stuart Mill. It would be a fine introduction for you . . . and very enlightening."

"John Stuart Mill," Lorna mused. She recognized the name as one of Miles's favorite heroes of philosophy. "I think one of those books you lent me was written by him. Is he alive still?"

Miles nodded. "He is aged . . . he has not lived in England these many years. It is not a lecture presented *by* Mr. Mill . . . merely on the topic of his philosophies."

Lorna's face betrayed her doubt. "I do not know . . . I cannot say the topic particularly interests me."

"You cannot know without hearing it whether or not it will prove worthwhile. I should be terribly disappointed if you do not attend."

He was so earnestly appealing that Lorna could not help smiling at him. "Even if I agreed to go, I cannot imagine whom I would dare ask to escort me. Certainly not my parents or siblings . . . none would approve of either the location or the topics addressed. Perhaps Jasper . . . ."

Miles was clearly resentful at her deliberations.

"Why should you require an escort? I will accompany you."

"You cannot expect me to attend a lecture in a public forum with you alone. The situation would demand a chaperone of some sort."

"That is precisely what I mean when I refer to senseless social conventions," cried Miles in consternation. "You are not a child requiring the supervision of a nurse! Why should it ill-befit you to attend a function with me, who does consider himself your friend, despite your limiting qualifications of that designation?"

He had halted his walk and, thus compelling her to stop also, now stood confronting her, his expression one of vexed indignation.

Lorna did not allow herself to be discomposed but only stared at him thoughtfully for a moment. Finally, "Very well," she said. "I shall go with you to Clerkenwell Green. But you must promise to take me away from there if at any point I feel uneasy with either the situation or the contents of the lecture."

Miles was elated at her acceptance. "Of course . . . I would never subject you to a situation that caused you any discomfort. Have no fear of that. Shall I call for you at your house, then? I could take a hansom cab."

Lorna vigorously shook her head. While Miles knew by now that she lived in Grosvenor Square, the other residents of her household knew nothing of his existence, and she preferred to keep it that way.

"No," she said, "I'll meet you at our bench on the campus, as usual.

We can always take a cab from there if we cannot walk."

Lorna disliked deceiving her family as to where she was going. Usually, when she met Mr. Anderson on Wednesdays, she told her mother that she was taking a mid-day repast to Tom, which she did indeed do (after her walk with Miles), so it was not really any dishonesty . . . only a bit of a misrepresentation as to the amount of time she spent with her brother. But the lecture in Clerkenwell Green was to be held on a Friday, late in the afternoon. She could not very well visit Tom so near to the hour when he would be departing the office to go home, and she could think of no other plausible reason as to why she would be venturing forth on her own. She thought perhaps she could say that she was going to drive out to visit Hugh, but when she thought it over, that alibi was full of impracticalities: First of all, she couldn't outrightly lie, so she would actually have to take the time after the lecture to go visit Hugh, and that was a considerable distance. Secondly, Rosamond would probably beg to go along if she found out her sister was driving out to the vicarage, and that certainly wouldn't do. And most importantly, Hugh lived at such a distance that the only way to achieve his residence would be to go in a carriage, and she definitely would not be able to arrive in Clerkenwell Green in the Hathaway carriage, or keep the coachman from revealing her destination.

In the end, Lorna simply didn't make an excuse. She told a maid that she was "going out", lest anyone should inquire after her, and slipped out the front door without mentioning a word to anyone else. The knowledge that she was going to a place of which her family would unquestioningly disapprove filled her with a mixture of trepidation, guilt, and exhilaration.

She and Miles Anderson met accordingly at the University's park and decided to walk to Clerkenwell, as the day was fine and they had an abundance of time. Upon arrival in that neighborhood where Lorna had never been before, she found that the vicinity was the location of several ancient churches, some abandoned market stalls, and some buildings near the green itself which looked as if they had been recently restored. Altogether, it did not present a very picturesque impression, but Miles seemed oblivious to that fact as he led the way to one of the newer buildings.

Lorna had imagined the lecture to be in a large hall, crowded with many listeners, as had been the case with lectures she had previously attended. But upon entering the building, she found that the "hall" was in reality a room that was only half the width of the house itself and that those attending numbered only about twenty. She also found herself to be the only female present. None of this seemed to be noticed by Miles as he led her to a chair near the door, where she had requested to be seated. Almost immediately, several acquaintances of his came over to greet him, and he duly (and proudly) introduced them to Lorna, who felt extremely self-conscious amongst such a group of men.

They were remarkably alike in their bearing . . . nearly all dressed in the common, unpretentious attire of the working class, some of them a bit scruffy, but they represented all ages — some as young as Miles and Lorna, and others grey with age. They all greeted Lorna in a friendly manner and seemed entirely unconscious of any class differences, just as Miles had the first day she met him. However, as soon as the lecture began, they became very serious, listening intently — sometimes nodding their heads in agreement, sometimes vocalizing a hearty "Hear, hear!"

Lorna was, in truth, somewhat uncomfortable listening to the content of the lecture, for it dealt with convictions that, while familiar to her from her discourse with Miles, still stood in direct opposition to her natural breeding. Such social reform and talk of "happiness as the sole end of conduct" were concepts that she knew would appall everyone she knew, yet part of her could not help but be drawn in as the lecture progressed . . . whether by its message or perhaps simply by the way her companion was so engrossed in the proceedings. His eyes were full of such zeal and his smile so enthusiastic every time he looked at her — he was plainly eager for her to share his alacrity and jubilant to have her at his side in the presence of his associates in a setting he seemed to think was hallowed ground.

It was really Lorna's first glimpse into the world of Miles Anderson . . . the liberal doctrine, the free-thinking rhetoric, the impassioned comrades. She did want to please him, and never let on that any part of the situation unsettled her; her desire to placate him overcame any feelings of trepidation. This inclination to indulge his sentiment was new to Lorna, who was usually so strong-minded and independent, and she was conscious of the aberrance. Indeed, she had thought on it before. She was very aware of the fact that she had developed feelings for the unorthodox Mr. Anderson . . . why else would she have devoted such a great deal of effort to meeting up with him so regularly, even knowing that her family would chastise her actions should they discover the nature of her sojourns?

As to why she had acquired such feelings, she did not know. Miles was neither handsome nor wealthy nor able-bodied nor debonair. Yet, none of those characteristics had ever interested Lorna . . . she had certainly known men who exhibited such traits, and none had left any impression upon her. Perhaps it was the very nature of Miles's unconventionality that attracted her, and his outright radicalism touched that part of her that was drawn to nonconformity. And she was sure that he was partial to her, and had been from the very first. She could not think where such a relationship would take her if it were to be acknowledged . . . eventually her family would expect to meet him, and bringing him into the world of Grosvenor Square was unimaginable. She could not even conceive of the scenario, so disparate was his world from theirs. She would not allow herself to think into the future, but only to concentrate on the present and on the prospect of another meeting on Wednesday afternoon.

When the lecture was over, it seemed that Miles's friends intended to recess to a nearby public-house to further discuss the issues put forth. Lorna knew her presence hindered Miles from joining them, and she suggested that he could hail a cab to take her home then proceed to join his friends. But he only grinned at her and shook his head.

"Not at all, Miss Lorna Hathaway," he remonstrated. "You are only trying to abstain from the necessity of divulging your own impressions to me. But I am heartily interested in your views and intend to discuss them in-depth all during our long walk back. However," he added, as an after-thought, "we could take a cab if you are too weary to walk. And I'm afraid you've missed your tea, so you are probably hungry as well."

Lorna beamed back at him. "You know I am never too tired to walk. And as for tea, perhaps we can find something to sustain us on the way."

It was never his custom to offer her his arm, but they walked together side-by-side as two who are in complete harmonious congruity.

Chapter VII

The opera was always a festive occasion, and never more so than during the high season. It was, in London, the place to see and be seen. Attendees at any theatrical or musical performance were bound to be a diverse group, as there was no discrimination in admittance other than the price of a ticket. The theatre or opera were places where classes could mingle, or at least observe one another, without either one feeling misplaced — for within the auditorium each class would be segregated according to their seating location, but nothing could prevent each from examining the other. The upper-classes, of course, were given to the closest scrutiny, both by the working and middle-classes, as well as (and perhaps most closely) by their fellow noblesse. The opera did tend to be more the realm of the elite classes, but there were still always throngs of bourgeoisie who occupied the upper galleries.

On a late-winter evening, Mr. Thomas Hathaway, his wife, and youngest daughter arrived at the Opera House with little time to spare before the curtain was set to rise. The entire family was to have attended the performance, but Tom decided shortly before the departure from Grosvenor Square that he did not feel up to the occasion, and Lorna declared that she would stay home with her brother. Rosamond was not long disappointed by her siblings' absence, for she loved the opera, as she loved every manner of dramatic entertainment, and had been looking forward to the performance, which was to be a London premiere.

When the Hathaways' carriage arrived at the Opera House, throngs of people were entering the building. Ladies and gentlemen arrived in carriages and cabs and proceeded through the central doors, while the middle-classes arrived mainly on foot and entered through the doors on either side of the main entrance. From the elegant gowns of the aristocratic ladies to the best suits of the bourgeois gentlemen, everyone wore their finest when they turned out at the opera, for it was invariably the scene of much speculation and exhibition. If one did not wish to be seen or appraised, one had better abstain from the pleasures of the opera, for all attending were submitting themselves to the unabashed scrutiny of the masses.

Once inside, the ladies and gentlemen would mingle in the Grand Salon or in the anterooms upstairs, while the middle-classes congregated in the central reception halls or in the opulent foyer. The Hathaways entered the foyer just as the orchestra inside the auditorium was tuning their instruments, which was the signal for the guests to make their way toward their seats. There was again an aura of pomp and pageantry as the patrons streamed into the auditorium — first up the Grand Staircase, then branching off according to their rank — the wealthy to their appointed boxes, and the others to the dress circle or up to the distant altitudes of the upper galleries.

As the Hathaways ascended the Grand Staircase, they happened upon Sir Henry Trainer and his son Douglas, who had danced with Rosamond at the Founders Ball. In the midst of the crush there was little opportunity for more than formal greetings exchanged between the two families, but young Douglas did make a point of bowing to Rosamond and asking if he might present himself at her box during the interval between acts, to which Rosamond gave him a nod of assent before following her parents up the rest of the steps.

Mr. Hathaway had been able to procure a box, but upon arrival to the anteroom Mrs. Hathaway fretted because it was a rear box and not near enough to the stage, or in good proximity for the surveillance of the other patrons, for her liking. However, as there were only three of them, they could all sit forward in the box, and Mrs. Hathaway had brought her opera glasses, so no one should have an obstructed view, no matter how distant.

As the lights were dimming and the overture began, Mrs. Hathaway leaned over to Rosamond, who was sitting between her parents, and said, "It is well that Sir Henry's son should speak to you. He is an excellent young man with very promising prospects. But, my dear girl! Why didn't you wear the lovely necklace your father brought you from India? I mentioned to you this afternoon that it would look stunning with that gown."

Rosamond's hand inadvertently went to her neck, which was bare. She had not forgotten the necklace . . . she did think it beautiful, but of late she had acquired a preference for a bare neckline with a formal gown. It was an acceptable fashion trend, but she could never convince her mother of its merit.

And as to the matter of Sir Henry's son, Rosamond was accustomed to her mother's conspicuous implications that she ought to encourage one of her ardent admirers in his pursuit so that she might settle upon a good match. Rosamond was not disdainful of most suitors, and she did think Douglas Trainer an agreeable gentleman, but such attentions must pose a constant dilemma for her, for while it was never in her nature to flirt or play the coquette, she also tremendously disliked feeling as if she was the cause of anyone's disappointment, and so the inevitable result was that her guileless sincerity only increased the ardor of her beaux and further added to her appeal.

Now, she only had opportunity to smile and give a slight nod in response to her mother's assertion, for the curtain had risen and the performance commenced. The first act proved to be enthralling . . . not just in its divine music, which always entranced Rosamond, but in its story, which had all the elements of a doomed romance, certain to foreshadow harrowing tragedy by the end of the third act. She wished she had brought her own opera glasses, for her mother retained possession of the only ones they had with them and was utilizing them as much to study the patrons in the other boxes and the parterre as to watch the performance itself. Every now and then her mother would lean over and whisper behind her fan about "So-and-so's exquisite jewelry" or "Such-and-such's horrific gown" or "Can you believe *she* arrived with so-and-so?" Rosamond would have preferred to listen to the opera without this commentary, but of course she could not say such a thing to her mother.

At the conclusion of the first act, an attendant appeared and delivered a message to Mr. Hathaway, who read it aloud to his wife and daughter:

The Earl of Kendal presents his compliments to Mr. Thomas Hathaway and cordially requests the honor of receiving him and his family at such opportunity as may be deemed favorable by all members of the party.

Rosamond hoped her parents did not notice her flushed countenance upon her initial hearing of the contents of the message, but she had no cause for concern, as her mother was fully engaged in exclaiming over the message herself.

"The Earl of Kendal!" she uttered in delighted amazement. "Why should he be inviting us to his box?"

"A business acquaintance of mine," explained Mr. Hathaway. "One of the shareholders of the company. An excellent gentleman . . . and a sharply perceptive investor for one so comparatively young. Only in his thirties, you know, but inherited his title when his father died several years ago."

"I know all about the Earl of Kendal," his wife interrupted impatiently, as if her knowledge had been acquired from the most obviously credible sources instead of from the society columns and ostentatious gossip. "How cordial of him to invite us into his box!" She was plainly exhilarated by this unexpected honor. "Oh, if only I'd known! I would have worn my new violet silk gown instead of this one. I hope I am presentable?"

"My dear, you are always presentable," assured her husband.

"Come now, let us be going."

"But would it be appropriate to bring Rosamond?" mused Mrs. Hathaway doubtfully. "We do not want to be presumptuous and impose upon his hospitality."

Rosamond suffered a moment of anxiety here, despite the fact that her father responded almost immediately.

"Well, he certainly would not wish her to be left here unattended. And the message specifies *Mr. Hathaway and his family.*"

And so Rosamond and her parents were led by an attendant down another long, mirror-lined corridor to the front boxes and shown into an anteroom. The attendant crossed the small room and stepped into the box, announcing, "Mr. Thomas Hathaway and his party."

The Hathaways were then admitted into the box, where three people rose to greet them. One, of course, was Frederick Lancaster, the Earl of Kendal, but his companions were not recognized — one was a tall and slender woman of perhaps fifty-five, and the other was a kindly-looking gentleman of about the same age. Both were impeccably dressed.

The Earl immediately stepped forward and greeted Mr. Hathaway, who in turn presented his wife. Frederick bowed to Mrs. Hathaway, who managed to be flustered and polite at the same time, dropping into a polished curtsey, head barely inclined.

"My Lord Kendal, it is truly an honor to make your acquaintance."

Mr. Hathaway then motioned to his daughter, who dutifully stepped forward. "Lord Kendal, my younger daughter, Miss Rosamond Hathaway."

Rosamond had somehow known that Lord Kendal would not reveal to her parents any prior acquaintance with her, but when he turned to her now — his face perfectly impassive except for polite acknowledgement, as would be accorded any introduction — Rosamond still felt her heart skip a beat as he bowed to her. She accordingly sank into a graceful curtsey, but as she raised her head, his serious gaze lingered on her face for the briefest moment, as if to convey an unspoken acknowledgement.

Frederick then turned toward his companions and, speaking to the Hathaways, said, "May I present Lady Abercrombie and her husband, Sir Richard Abercrombie. Lady Abercrombie is my mother's sister."

Lady Abercrombie and Sir Richard both smiled graciously, and Lady Abercrombie was quite taken with Rosamond.

"What a charming daughter you have," she said to Mrs. Hathaway, once both ladies had taken their seats at the front of the box.

"Why, thank you." Mrs. Hathaway beamed as she glanced at Rosamond who had been seated beside her. "Yes, we are quite proud of her, and she adores the opera. My, what a splendid view you have from here," Mrs. Hathaway could not help noting as she peered over the stage and orchestra below.

"It is fine, isn't it?" agreed Lady Abercrombie pleasantly. "Are your seats not as advantageous? I saw you as you were entering your box. I must confess it was I who pointed out your presence to my nephew when I remarked upon your daughter's rare beauty. He recognized your husband, of course, and then sent over the note just before the first act ended. But I heard there is to be a ballet in the second act, which would follow the French tradition, would it not?"

As the two ladies conversed, Rosamond could not help but let her gaze wander to where the three men were standing in the opening to the anteroom. She could not hear what they said, for they spoke in subtle, low tones as is typical of men. The Earl did glance over at her at one point, but made no attempt to communicate with her before reverting his attention back to the other gentlemen, and Rosamond turned back to her mother and Lady Abercrombie, though she did not participate in the conversation, only listened. The two older women were getting along famously.

At last Lady Abercrombie called out to the Earl, "Frederick! People are returning into the loggia . . . it will be nearly time for the second act to begin. You know how the first interval is always the short one. You must ask Mr. Hathaway and his family to view the remainder of the performance from here, for they are in a rear box and cannot see half as well."

"It had been my intention, I assure you." Frederick was never one to use an excess of words, but his manner was ever cordial, however reticent.

Mrs. Hathaway protested (rather feebly, it must be said), and was obviously pleased when her objections were over-ridden, and Lord Kendal ordered the attendant to bring two more chairs into the box.

There was then some difficulty determining what the seating arrangement should be, for there were four chairs already situated at the front of the box, and the two additional chairs were placed behind these.

"Rosamond, of course, must sit in the front," said her mother, "and Lady Abercrombie and Sir Richard."

"But no, that will not do," protested Lady Abercrombie. "For then you would be separated from your husband, which would be most unseemly. Sir Richard will sit behind with Frederick, then your family will all be afforded the view."

"Why, dear Lady Abercrombie," objected Mrs. Hathaway, "then you would be in the very predicament which you suggested would be unsuitable for me. You must not sit apart from your husband."

Rosamond, who had said scarcely a word since entering the box, spoke up, her voice gentle but clear. "If I sit in the front, then somebody shall be separated from their spouse. It would seem apparent that the solution would be for me to sit in the rear."

The two older women immediately protested, but Frederick put a stop to it with his firm, even tone. "There is not a poor vantage-point in this box. Even the chairs in the rear will afford excellent views, and I cannot help but agree with Miss Hathaway that the best solution would be for the two couples to take the four seats that are together. And if Miss Hathaway does not object to my company, I see no reason why she should not be comfortably situated sitting behind."

Even Mrs. Hathaway could not protest when the Earl gave directive, and as Rosamond certainly had no objection, she found herself seated beside Frederick Lancaster and suddenly feeling very shy. She opened her fan to occupy her hands and kept her eyes cast downward or frontward until the lights dimmed.

But then, when the audience fell hushed, and the beautiful music wafted up from the orchestra, she experienced what she could not reconcile or explain. There is something about sitting in a darkened theatre, with the only light emanating from a distant proscenium far below and the surrounding people sitting unnaturally still in their anticipation and attention, which makes a young girl feel indistinct, yet an integral part of the shadowy darkness. And if she happens to be sitting in close proximity to one who is broodingly handsome and who, despite his restless virility, has consistently comported himself most chivalrously, then her pulse is apt to quicken, as Rosamond's did now. For when the lights are low, one must rely on the senses of hearing and touch to convey perception, and in the darkness those sensations are unforgivingly heightened. In the shadowy stillness Rosamond was acutely aware of Lord Kendal's quiet breathing beside her, and when his arm chanced to brush against hers, she was conscious of a mercilessly fluttery stirring within her breast. She could only pray that he might be insensible to this sort of unintentional emotion, and when she dared glance over at him, his own gaze was fixed on the stage below. But when a few moments later she cast a second glance, she found herself meeting his gaze, those dark eyes fixed upon her, and, as she hastily averted her own eyes downward, she was silently grateful for the darkness that masked the rising blush upon her bare neck. She was truly bewildered by this unbidden sensation, and she resolved that there should be no more stolen glances.

Rosamond determined to keep her thoughts henceforth trained on the performance below, but this proved difficult, for there was a great deal of whispering taking place before her as her mother and Lady Abercrombie seemed to be caught up in discussing something relating to a box opposite, upon which both ladies' opera glasses were focused. In addition, it was into the second act that the ballet had been incorporated, and while it was undoubtedly lovely, and something by which Rosamond would usually be enchanted, in this instance it did little to engage her attention, as it did not in any way advance the opera's storyline, to which she had been attuned during the first act but hopelessly inattentive during the second act.

When the curtain went down and the lights rose for the interval before the third act, Lady Abercrombie declared that she wished to go downstairs and take her refreshment in the Grand Salon. She inquired if the Hathaways would care to join her, to which Mrs. Hathaway said they would, for she, too, wished to circulate amongst other acquaintances and partake of the usual chatter which promulgated both news and gossip. Everyone rose, and Sir Richard and Lady Abercrombie headed toward the anteroom, with Mr. and Mrs. Hathaway following.

"Come, Rosamond," said Mrs. Hathaway, for her daughter was hesitating. Still Rosamond lingered. "Come, come! We must not delay the others," her mother scolded.

Frederick was eyeing Rosamond and now stepped forward.

"The second act was so long, I cannot think but that Miss Hathaway is too tired to walk all the way back down to the salon. I am reluctant to make such a journey myself. She is most welcome to stay here, and I will have some refreshment brought to the anteroom for her. You need not fear for her comfort."

"Oh, but I could not put you to such trouble," avowed Mrs. Hathaway. "You have already been imposed upon enough this evening. Attending to my daughter is not your duty, and I should never place such a burden upon your hospitality."

"I would not have invited your family into my box if it had been any imposition, and I assure you there is no difficulty in attending to Miss Hathaway during the interval." Frederick was always firm, even as he was polite, and Rosamond guessed that he was used to being obeyed.

Certainly he had made his intention clear to Mrs. Hathaway, who yielded with a murmured, "Very well, my lord. Your kindness is appreciated," then scurried away, anxious lest she be left too far behind the others.

Rosamond gave Frederick a shy and grateful smile and then walked up to the balustrade and peered over its ledge into the orchestra pit.

"How fine all the instruments are, and how well the orchestra sounds tonight. I never can decide which instrument is the loveliest. The harp, I suppose. I play only the piano, as it is."

Looking out over the auditorium, she remembered how her mother and Lady Abercrombie had been interested to the point of distraction in the box directly opposite. She lifted her gaze thence, and beheld the box's inhabitants still sitting in their seats and conversing animatedly. There was a lady with red-gold hair and a bright blue gown sitting in the front with a gentleman. Another couple stood in the rear of the box.

"I wonder who she is?" Rosamond inquired aloud.

Frederick, who had remained at a slight distance, now joined Rosamond at the balustrade and looked into the box that occupied her attention.

"Mrs. Jeremy Cade," he informed her rather indifferently.

"Mrs. Jeremy Cade?" Rosamond knitted her pretty brow. "I'm sure I've heard that name, although I cannot think in what capacity. How beautiful she is, though!"

Frederick had nothing to say to that, for he clearly was not moved by the lady's comeliness.

"Why, I believe she is smiling at you!" Rosamond said in surprise, for it was very unmannerly for a lady to acknowledge a man across a public venue.

"Undoubtedly," replied Frederick dryly, turning his back toward the lady's box. "Propriety has never been Maria Cade's strength. She was a friend of my wife's from Waterford, and she seems to feel that gives her leave to include me in her circle of acquaintances, though I have never given her reason to assume any such thing." He saw Rosamond's puzzled expression, and he knew that she was perplexed at the unkindness of his words. He elaborated to her: "Mrs. Cade has acquired quite a reputation in London. And, I might add, that gentleman in her box who has escorted her here tonight is not her husband."

Rosamond's shock was apparent. "But that is scandalous!"

Frederick's own distaste was equally visible. "I assure you that a woman who so brazenly flaunts her indiscretion is invulnerable to any gossip that may follow, however ruinous to her reputation."

Rosamond fell silent, dismayed by such shameless corruption. Frederick saw her troubled countenance and stepped closer to her. His voice came low and subdued. "I am sorry. I ought not to have spoken so forthrightly."

Rosamond did not make any immediate reply, for though her thoughts had been successfully diverted, she was now lost in a different meditation, turning over distant images in her mind, which Frederick's last words had called forth. For his part, he was always content to be silent and so did not disturb her, but retained his stance at her side looking out over the balustrade.

At last Rosamond spoke . . . yet she did not look at him, keeping her eyes cast downward, though she seemed not to see any of the people milling about below. Her voice was very soft and tentative. "I . . . I had seen you once before, —before the coffeehouse, I mean."

There ensued a long silence before Rosamond heard him murmur, "I know."

His voice was barely audible, but those two words caused Rosamond to lift her eyes in wonder. He was not looking at her, but she saw that his brow was furrowed in troubled sullenness. She was amazed at his response . . . that the fleeting gaze in the art gallery should have left any impression on him . . . that he did indeed recognize her when he had grasped her by the shoulders in Smollett's Coffeehouse.

Now, breaking out of his troubled reverie, he finally turned his serious gaze upon her once more, his dark eyes gleaming moodily. And for once, Rosamond did not avert her own gaze, for in that moment there was a wordless revelation that was inordinately complex. And they lingered, thus transfixed, until their silent communion was severed by the sound of footsteps in the anteroom, followed by a muffled "ahem".

The spell broken, Rosamond and Frederick turned to see an attendant standing in the doorway of the anteroom. He bowed to Frederick.

"Pardon me, my lord. There is a gentleman who wishes to speak to

Miss Hathaway. Mr. Douglas Trainer."

Rosamond's cheeks pinkened. "Oh dear," she murmured. "I had forgotten about Mr. Trainer." She turned to Frederick. "He had asked to see me during the interval. He must have gone to our box after the first act and found us absent."

There was an apologetic reluctance in her voice, but none in Frederick's response. He immediately gave orders to the attendant.

"Show Mr. Trainer into the anteroom. Miss Hathaway will receive him there."

Rosamond followed him into the anteroom where Douglas Trainer stood inside the door. That gentleman directly stepped forward and bowed to the Earl.

"My Lord Kendal, please pardon this intrusion. I realize you do not know me, but I met with Miss Hathaway's parents in the corridor, and their companion, Lady Abercrombie, said that I could present myself here in this fashion."

Frederick could appraise this young man in an instant: courteous, well-bred, likeably friendly, and warmly sincere. Precisely as a suitor to Rosamond Hathaway ought to be. Frederick was characteristically taciturn. "Do not apologize. Miss Hathaway is most welcome to receive guests here. You may sit here in the anteroom, if you like."

Mr. Trainer gave a nod of thanks, then Frederick exited the small room, not out into the corridor, but back into the box.

Mr. Trainer greeted Rosamond, who asked him if he'd like to sit, for there was a small settee and two armchairs in the room. Once seated, Mr. Trainer lost no time in engaging Rosamond in conversation, for he was pleasantly articulate and eager to discuss with her the opera, the Founders Ball, and news of various mutual acquaintances.

Even as she politely attended to the conversation, Rosamond let her eyes stray toward the entrance into the box, for Frederick had not drawn the curtain, and she could see him standing out there, leaning against the side of the balustrade, restlessly aloof, his eyes darkly distant beneath his creased brow.

Mr. Trainer sat with her in the anteroom for about a quarter of an hour before a host of voices was heard in the corridor, laughing and chattering jovially. Sir Richard and Mr. Hathaway entered the room, followed by Lady Abercrombie and Mrs. Hathaway, all in good spirits; the women especially buoyant.

"Oh, my dear," said Mrs. Hathaway to Rosamond, who, along with Mr. Trainer, had risen upon the couples' entrance. "You really ought to have come down to the salon." She put her arm through her daughter's as they followed the others back out into the box. "Mrs. Bidwell's Harriet was there . . . she's just this week accepted Mr. Philip Preston's proposal . . . and you should see her ring! An emerald — not the largest I've ever seen, but quite sizable and in a very elegant setting." She bent her head closer to Rosamond's and lowered her voice, but lost none of her enthusiasm. "Lady Abercrombie and Sir Richard are absolutely delightful! We are all invited to their home for a dinner party in a fortnight. I've heard her gatherings are most recherché!"

All of this news did interest Rosamond, but she did not follow her mother to the seats, but instead paused as she entered the box. For she must not forget her visitor who was still standing just within the anteroom door.

Mrs. Hathaway glimpsed him as she turned toward her seat. "Oh, Mr. Trainer! You did find your way here — I'm so glad. I apologize again for the confusion. We really ought to have sent a message down to you when we left our original seats. But then, we had no way of knowing that we'd be staying here for the rest of the performance." And here she tossed a smiling nod to the Earl.

Douglas Trainer smiled affably. "It is understandable. And now it looks as if the third act is about to begin, so I'd best return to my own seat."

Rosamond saw her mother glance at Lord Kendal, and she knew her mother wondered if the Earl would invite Mr. Trainer to stay on. But he said nothing, merely nodded his head in acknowledgement of Mr. Trainer's bid of good-evening, and the young man left with a final bow and smile for Rosamond.

The party in the Earl's box resumed their seats as the curtain rose upon the third act. Rosamond wished she could have spoken to Frederick again before the others came back, but as Mr. Trainer had stayed the entire time, there was no opportunity.

Once more the audience fell silent, and although Rosamond once again fell under the spell of the darkness, she reminded herself that she must concentrate on the resolution of the story. Fortunately, the third act opened with a spectacular battle scene which would have absorbed the attention of even the most apathetic spectator, and Rosamond found herself easily engrossed. However, when the story's hero was very suddenly, and very unexpectedly, killed in the midst of the battle with a rather loud gunshot, Rosamond gasped audibly and dropped her fan, causing everyone in front of her to glance in her direction. Embarrassed to draw such attention, and distraught at the hero's untimely demise, she shrank back into her chair contritely. Frederick, beside her, easily scooped up her fan from the floor and handed it to her.

She took it with a whispered murmur of, "Thank you. I'm sorry."

"You did not expect our hero to die so soon in the third act," remarked Frederick, also in a whisper.

"No, I did not read the libretto," admitted Rosamond. "Though, I must confess that loud noises always cause me to jump."

"That gunshot was very realistic," conceded Frederick, "although the sound was actually produced by the drummer."

Rosamond was happy to be in conversation with the Earl, for she had felt somewhat awkward about Mr. Trainer's arrival, though she could not fathom why. Now, she inclined her head slightly toward him and whispered demurely behind her fan: "It was very kind of Lady Abercrombie to invite us to her dinner-party."

Frederick had likewise inclined his head toward her, and now gave a nod. "Yes, she is quite well-known for her 'dinner-parties', as she calls them. Really her excuse for cards, which is her favorite amusement. But do not put it past my aunt to have an ulterior motive, for I heard her and your mother discussing plans to invite young Mr. Trainer as well."

Rosamond's eyes widened. "But I thought she had only spoken with him momentarily tonight."

"Yes, well, other than cards, her favorite pastime is matchmaking. And she seems to have taken an avid interest in you."

Rosamond averted her eyes and righted herself, bringing her fan down slowly. "Oh, I see."

But Frederick leaned in closer. "Do not think badly of her, though," he whispered. "She means well. She really is wonderfully intelligent and sympathetic . . . one of the few truly resourceful women I know."

Rosamond knew this was high praise from one who was usually so reticent, and it did cause her to look somewhat differently upon the august Lady Abercrombie.

There was one question Rosamond should have liked to ask Lord Kendal, though modesty prevented her from putting it to him, and they did not converse again for the remainder of the act.

However, he must have read the question in her eyes, for after the curtain had fallen upon the tragic finale, and the lights had risen, and everyone was standing collecting their things, exchanging well-wishes, and preparing to go, Frederick turned to her and said simply, "I shall see you in a fortnight, then. Good evening, Miss Hathaway."

And though she said nothing, only curtsied sedately to his bow, before she inclined her head Frederick caught sight of the shining radiance illuminating her deep blue eyes.

Chapter VIII

The first race of the season was a welcome event for Londoners, both native and seasonal, for it heralded the approaching spring and its accompanying promises of fair weather and rejuvenation. It had not the air of formal pomp and celebrity as would the races later in the year at Epsom or Ascot, but it was instead a day of general convivial festivity as old friendships were renewed and new associations convened. It was also a day of keen speculative anticipation, as the nobility and gentry brought forth their most promising thoroughbreds to be tested in the day's races, thus setting the standards for wagers in the subsequent races of the season. For it was during the racing season that gambling would move out of the elite gentlemen's clubs, whose gaming-tables were the private commodity of members only, and onto the picturesque thoroughfare of the race-course, where gentlemen and commoners alike might wager openly without fear of reprobation, for horse-racing was considered to be conventionally civilized, suitable even for ladies' attendance, although ladies must only be spectators, not wagerers.

The throngs who turned out at the race-track for the first race were a mélange . . . a motley assortment ranging from the dignified aristocrats to the familial middle-classes to the rowdy working-classes, and naturally all manner of bookmakers and enterprising "artistes" in the business of securing wagers. And since the race-course was outlying, the event also attracted curious rural folk from the surrounding country villages and remote outskirts of London.

The venue itself was refreshingly pastoral for those who drove out from the city . . . its flat, broad, treeless plain a quaint novelty to the native Londoners and a comforting reminder of the delights of country life to the seasonal Londoners, who could look forward to returning to their country abodes in only a few months' time.

Several members of the Hathaway household had decided to venture forth from Grosvenor Square for the opening-race day. After staying in the city all winter, it would make a pleasant excursion, and Tom and Lorna and their cousin Jasper set forth in eager anticipation of the day's festivities, along with Hugh Shadwell, who was easily fetched from his vicarage on the way.

They could not convince Rosamond or Edith to join them, for those young ladies did not care for horse-racing itself and would only be persuaded to attend the Royal Cup races in the summer for the social aspects of such events, paying no heed to the nature of the sport.

So it was only a party of four that arrived in the Hathaways' carriage upon opening day, but such a light-hearted and mirthful group it was! For nearly as soon as they arrived, they found themselves in the company of familiar acquaintances from town and those who had come down from the country for the event, so there was a great deal of affectionate greeting and fond recollections.

Once the races actually commenced, however, and the crush began to move toward the track, the Hathaway group found themselves subdivided, for Tom and Jasper wished to place wagers at the track, while Lorna and Hugh, who naturally would not wager, desired to go to the paddock to examine the horses.

"It is very well for Mr. Shadwell to take Lorna to the paddock," said Jasper, "and Tom and I shall position ourselves at the edge of the racecourse."

But Lorna was not pleased with this plan. She looked to Tom

doubtfully. "Perhaps we could all go to the paddock together after the first race. Then we would not need to divide our party."

"Come now, Cousin Lorna . . . don't tell me you wouldn't trust the exemplary Mr. Shadwell to escort you such a short distance and amidst such a throng!" Jasper's tone was derisive, and Lorna's eyes lit up with indignation at his cavalier impudence. Her esteem for Jasper Munroe had long ago begun to wear thin, and of late she had been in possession of a strengthened assuredness that emboldened her to retain her poised stance under any condition.

"You know perfectly well that has nothing to do with it," she retorted. "I would entrust Hugh with my life and all that I treasure. I merely thought it would be best if we should all remain together." And here she looked again at her brother.

Tom interceded, never liking animosity between any, least of all his sister and cousin.

"Here now," he said soothingly. "We can agree on a plan. Let us determine a location where we can meet at an appointed time, and that way we need not fear losing one another in the crowd, and no one need tarry where they do not wish to be." He knew that losing sight of the party was not really Lorna's worry, and he sought to placate her further, for he saw her about to object again. He took her arm and said to her in a low voice, "Jasper and I shall stay trackside, only wagering and viewing the outcomes of the races. There shall be no digression on my part."

Lorna still did not look entirely complacent at separating from her brother, but she could not deny that she wished not to spend the afternoon trackside amidst the crush and would much prefer to visit the quieter paddock. And she knew that Hugh would not be in amongst the gamblers, so it seemed only befitting that she should keep him company.

They determined on a bench near the gate as a rendezvous, and the group divided into two, with Hugh and Lorna turning their backs to the race-course and heading toward the paddock. It was a slight distance and afforded them a rather pleasant walk across the long field. Only intermittently did they pass other walkers, so it provided them ample opportunity to converse.

"I am sorry if I seemed abrupt with Jasper back there," Lorna began. "His insolence will get the better of me."

"Any apology should be on his part," said Hugh. "I was taken aback by his discourteous tone, especially toward you."

Lorna tossed her head. "I think Jasper Munroe does not relinquish his flippancy for anyone, even if she be a lady or a relation."

"You did not always think of him so poorly," Hugh gently pointed out.

"No," Lorna conceded. "He has changed since he first came to us. He used to be very agreeable company . . . we'd pursue all manner of diversion and recreation together, always in the context of innocuous amusement. But then, he started leaving me behind and going off on his own during the day, and only going with Tom to the club in the evenings. And now I gather he doesn't even do that. Father goes to the club, Tom goes nowhere, and heaven only knows where Cousin Jasper idles away his time."

"You sound a bit resentful." Hugh was always remarkably insightful, and Lorna gave him a rather sheepish smile.

"I suppose I am," she admitted. "When he first arrived and knew no one, he was a willing enough companion, but once he had his bearings and made acquaintances in London, he no longer sought out my company."

"You ought not look too closely into such behavior," said Hugh. "It is only natural for such a young man to look for fellow comrades in light of his interests that a woman should not fulfill."

"And yet . . . " said Lorna thoughtfully, "there are some who would not agree that a woman is incapable of providing adequate companionship in any given diversion."

Hugh frowned. "I should not think very highly of such a claim. For to consign a woman to such indecorous pursuits as a solitary bachelor engages in would be to show a gross lack of consideration for her delicacy or for her dignity."

Lorna sighed. "You are right, of course, Hugh. What should we ever do without your honest rationality? I must sit and talk with you at least once per week so that you can constantly re-establish my sensibility."

Hugh laughed. "And why should you have need of that?"

Lorna sighed again. "I cannot say. Only lately I sometimes feel as if my sensibility, or any sense of practicality I might have once possessed, has flown away into a world of fabricated delusions."

By now they had achieved the paddock and were looking over the brick wall but paying little heed to the horses within.

Hugh looked at Lorna thoughtfully. "You say that Jasper has changed, but I wonder if it isn't you who have changed?"

"Hm? How do you mean?"

Hugh smiled. "Well, the Lorna Hathaway I once knew certainly never needed grounding on a weekly basis . . . or at least never would have acknowledged it even if she did."

Lorna smiled back. "Oh, so you think I've come into self-consciousness? Is that how I've changed?"

But Hugh shook his head. "No, I think that is only part of it. And I will say this to you: Change may not be the terrible thing you perceive it to be. I would say in recent months when I've seen you, you've been in extraordinarily good spirits. Of course, you always have been lively, but of late your ebullience is practically palpable. Why, look at you even now — there is a sparkle in your eye even as you attempt to conceal your smile from me. If this signifies a change, then it must be something favorable to you."

Lorna did not reply, but his reference to her concealed smile only caused her to smile broadly, her eyes sparkling most definitely. It was contagious, and Hugh could not help but grin back at her and say, "There! What did I tell you? This happy change is not in my imagination!"

Lorna laughed aloud, but said nothing, only turned her attention to the horses in the paddock as if she was suddenly absorbed in their inspection.

But Hugh persisted. "Come, Lorna, you cannot conceal anything!

You are in possession of some felicitous knowledge and would not share it with me." But Lorna merely shook her head, still beaming. Hugh leaned comfortably against the paddock wall where she was standing. "Ah, you will make this difficult and impel me to guess it, I see. Hmm . . . could it be that you have come into possession of something that brings you great joy? No, I do not think so. You are far too imaginative to be so exhilarated over something merely tangible . . . unless it is a gift for someone else. Now there's an idea . . . perhaps it is not a secret about yourself, but regarding someone else. Hmm . . . is it your sister? Has she finally fallen in love with one of her suitors?"

Lorna vigorously shook her head, but Hugh was not discouraged. "Ah, but I saw that glimmer in your eye. It must be about someone falling in love. Tom? Don't tell me Tom has proposed to some lovely young lady?"

"You ought to know if he did," remarked Lorna, "for I cannot imagine who that would be other than your own sister."

"Aha! Then it must be only yourself! Lorna Hathaway . . . have you gone and fallen in love?"

Lorna did not need to respond, for her rosy smile gave her away. Hugh was delighted in his successful conjecture, but never overbearing, for it was his nature to be calm. He only smiled at her with a fervent warmth. "Why, Lorna, I am amazed! How could you have become so enamored of someone without my knowledge? It is impossible! Now you must tell me who it is . . . and does he return your regard?"

But Lorna would not address either question. "You may be a brilliant guesser, but you shall get nothing more out of me. You can postulate as many names as you like, but I shall affirm nothing."

"Ah, then I must be cunning," said Hugh, "and use underhanded methods. I shall ask Rosamond or Tom, for they are dearer to you than any and would surely know with whom your affection lies."

"Oh no, no!" And Lorna truly looked so beseechingly distressed that Hugh was taken aback by the sudden change in her temperament. "You must not breathe a word to them, or to anyone! Truly you are the only one who would guess such a thing, or be observant enough to notice any change in my demeanor. I had not even been cognizant of such a change. Please do not divulge a word . . . promise me!"

"Yes, yes, of course I will honor your wishes." Hugh was soothing in his calm sincerity. "You know I would not offend you. It was thoughtless of me to tease, and I am sorry. I did not know it must be such a secret."

Lorna put her arm affectionately through Hugh's as a sign of her forgiveness. "I am not certain where my own understanding lies in this matter, and I should not like to promulgate anything when it is all so ambiguous in my own mind. Come now, let us forget about it and just focus on the races, shall we? It is such a glorious day, and look at those magnificent creatures!" She turned her focus back to the paddock. "Look at that grey colt. It must be the Duke of Norfolk's Lancer. See the star on his forehead! Norfolk's entry last year had one just like it." And from that point on, they immersed themselves in the proceedings of the event, and Lorna was in as fine of spirits as ever, for her disclosure to Hugh Shadwell had been a cathartic and truly necessary release.

Meanwhile, Tom and Jasper had situated themselves beside the pavilion that had been erected for the horse owners and members of the Jockey Club. It was a popular spot, and they had to peer over a few shoulders to observe the first race, which had just finished. As Tom had no winnings to collect, he stayed where he was, trackside, while Jasper went to collect on his wager.

When Jasper returned with his modest winnings, his animated expression and brisk step suggested a buoyant vitality. Indeed, his eyes glinted as he pulled Tom away from the edge of the thoroughfare to the side of the pavilion where the only spectators stood on the other side of the pavilion's enclosure.

"Here, I've just had an extraordinary bit of luck!" he intoned under his breath to Tom. "After I collected on my wager, I stepped around behind the pavilion to put the bills in order. As I stood there, I overheard a couple of fellows talking on the other side of the pavilion wall — they were obviously attempting to cloister themselves, for they spoke in very hushed tones, but they had no way of knowing I was on the opposite side of the wall. They must have been owners or board members or some other influential sort, else why would they have been in the pavilion? At any rate, I heard one say to the other that he had just changed his wager for the next race. He had seen the Earl of Dartmouth put a *vast* sum on Lord Cranborne's Blackmoor, and he was going to do the same. Dartmouth's head of the Jockey Club since the last board election, and he must know something to put a vast sum down."

Jasper's voice had inadvertently risen as his excitement mounted.

Tom looked at him dubiously. "Lord Cranborne's Blackmoor?" He looked up at the race order placard. "This is Cranborne's first entry, and the odds on Blackmoor are only twenty-two to one. I know nothing of the horse's pedigree."

"What does any of that matter?" Jasper frowned impatiently. "I've already determined to place my wager on Blackmoor."

"If the Earl of Dartmouth should lose his wager, it would be of little consequence to him. But if you place all you have on the same horse and lose, you would sorely feel the loss," Tom pointed out.

"I tell you, it is a certain win!" Jasper was intolerant of such cautious hesitancy. "But how much better it would be if I had an adequate sum to wager. As it is, I have only ten pounds and no credit to speak of."

Tom shrugged. "Should you bet it all and win, you would then be in possession of two hundred twenty pounds — a very tidy sum."

Jasper's eyes glinted craftily. "Ah, but if I had one hundred pounds to wager, I should come out with over two thousand pounds! A vast sum indeed. You need only lend me some money."

Tom shook his head. "It is a foolish bet on an untried horse. And I have not nearly such a sum at my disposal. I have only twenty pounds on my person."

Jasper's eyes narrowed. "But you could draw up a bank draft for the remainder of the sum. Your father has your name on his account."

Tom was astonished at Jasper's effrontery. "My father entrusts me with that privilege for reasons pertaining to his business, not for petty amusements and injudicious wagers. Your temerity knows no bounds!"

Jasper leered. "It is not temerity . . . it is astuteness! How do you suppose your father and his colleagues made their fortunes? Only by taking risks! It is the surest way to success!"

Tom nearly scoffed, but it was not in his self-conscious nature. "There is no comparison to be made between a wise, informed investment and a gambling wager. My father's experience, intelligence, and insight have served him well. None of those come into play at the bookmaker's table."

Jasper moved in closer, his usually carefree demeanor almost menacing. "And what of your father's son? Does he exercise the same prudence? Would your father be well enough acquainted with your deeds to establish an authentic judgment of your merit?"

Tom turned pale. Jasper continued: "Or perhaps you've shown your prudent nature by keeping your father in ignorance of certain indiscretions? Yet I am sure that you would subscribe to the virtue of candor, so it may be wisest to be forthcoming. Ought I to have been more forthcoming about you to the uncle who has been so benevolent to me? It is not too late."

Jasper's acerbic malevolence, so carelessly put forth, filled Tom with both fear and vexation. Jasper only smirked at such apprehension. "But only think how pleased your father would be should the results of your enterprise put into that bank account a sum considerably larger than the original principle, for naturally your munificence shall not be repaid without interest."

Tom looked at the wager ticket that Jasper was extending toward him. He was full of trepidation. "Ninety pounds is no trifling amount."

Jasper handed him the ticket. "Neither is the one hundred fifty that shall be replaced into the account."

Tom involuntarily glanced at the form. Jasper had already penciled in everything, save for Tom's signature on the line of credit. Tom looked at the document with great distaste and shook his head. "I cannot sign this, Jasper, and you are unrighteous to press me."

Jasper was outwardly calm, but his eye was cold as he regarded Tom. "It may be yourself who warrants that designation, at least in the opinion of your father, after I have a chat with him this evening."

Tom was visibly shaking as he looked over the wagering-sheet once more. "Lord Cranborne's Blackmoor," he repeated to himself, as if fixing the horse's name in his memory, then he took a deep breath and signed his name with a heavy hand, as one who signs his life away. He looked up, loathing himself, and beheld Jasper's eyes — sparkling in their old debonair way.

"There now, old fellow, that wasn't really so difficult, was it? No harm done . . . and think of the surplus you shall be in possession of by tomorrow."

Tom's broken expression betrayed the fact that he did not in any way share Jasper's easy confidence. He held out the ticket to Jasper as if it were some contaminated object of which he would rid himself, but before Jasper could grasp the paper, it was suddenly snatched from Tom's fingers by an unperceived hand. Tom gasped and whirled around to find himself in the commanding presence of the Earl of Kendal, whose black eyes flashed angrily as he crumpled the paper in his hand.

"You fool!" he growled. "Do not engage in matters of which you know nothing, or you will find yourself accountable to higher powers than this scoundrel!"

The Earl's authority was not only in his rank, but in his forceful demeanor, and though his words were directed toward Tom, his dark glare fell upon Jasper, rendering even that cavalier young man speechless. Without further word, the Earl stalked away, pocketing the crumpled wager-ticket, and entered the pavilion.

Jasper could not have known the intruder's identity, but Tom did, and his first thoughts upon regaining his bearings were of paralyzed, irrational fear . . . fear that his action would be related to his father, fear that his or his father's positions would be jeopardized, fear because he knew the Earl of Kendal was already aware of a questionable blemish upon his character, courtesy of Jerry Flynn.

But then, as the horn sounded, and the race commenced, relief began to slowly wash over Tom's soul, for it was too late for Jasper to place another wager upon Blackmoor, and he was freed of any obligation he had no wish to resurrect. And then, as Cranborne's Blackmoor placed a dismal sixth, a new feeling began to take hold of young Tom: gratitude. However much he may have angered Lord Kendal by his rash conduct, he could not help but feel that the Earl had delivered him, however unintentionally. Jasper had not much to say at such a loss by Blackmoor, but Tom knew that his own position should have been inescapably wretched if Jasper had turned in the wager with his name attached to it.

Upon further reflection, Tom could not conceive why the Earl should have taken any interest in his recklessness, except on behalf of his father, whose relationship in business the Earl must surely esteem. Of only one thing was Tom certain . . . he must not place himself in such a precarious position again. He had been avoiding Jasper's company for many weeks now, but he knew that as long as Jasper remained situated in the Hathaway residence there could be little peace in his mind, even as there had been none since almost the first day of Jasper's arrival.

The dinner parties given by Sir Richard and Lady Abercrombie were splendid affairs, given regularly, and generally attended by a core circle of established friends and relations, interspersed with a few new additions to "keep things interesting", as Lady Abercrombie was fond of saying. She liked to keep the guest list at about thirty in order that she could count on a good number for the card-tables, in case some guests chose not to play.

Unfortunately, the date that the Hathaways had been invited to attend happened to be the same night as the Shadwells' reception for a visiting relation in Hanover Square, and as Mrs. Hathaway could not bear to miss the illustrious dinner party at the Abercrombies', it was decided that Tom and Lorna should go to the Shadwells' in Hanover Square as they did not know the Abercrombies, and thereby the Hathaway family would be represented at both events.

Rosamond did not know why she should be slightly nervous as she and her parents arrived at the grand house in Kensington, whether it might be attributed to the prospect of meeting with Frederick Lancaster again, or knowing that Douglas Trainer would be in attendance as an intended favor for herself.

The format of the evening seemed to follow a precedent long since established from previous gatherings. Sir Richard and Lady Abercrombie received their guests in a stately conservatory just off the main hall, where everyone mingled until dinner was announced, at which time everyone proceeded into the dining room. After dinner, the gentlemen retreated to their brandy and cigars in the study, while the ladies convened in the drawing room until the gentlemen returned to them there. After a leisurely hour or so engaging in the comfortable diversions of mixed company, all would process into the gaming-room, which had been specially established for card-playing, where the tables and chairs were grouped for the optimum socialization of both players and observers.

The Hathaways were greeted very graciously by Sir Richard and his wife in the conservatory. Lady Abercrombie smiled warmly at Rosamond.

"My dear child, you look lovely. I'm so glad you were able to come. I think there is one here with whom you are already acquainted."

And she directed Rosamond's attention to a small grouping near the center of the room where Douglas Trainer was standing in conversation with some other guests. He spotted her almost immediately and, excusing himself from his companions, he made his way to where Rosamond was standing.

"Miss Hathaway!" He smiled at her genially as he greeted her.

"This is delightful . . . to see you again so soon after the opera. You must come and meet Mr. and Mrs. Dalrymple. They were at the opera premiere the same night we were and have much to say on the subject of the performance."

The amiable Mr. Trainer had made a favorable impression upon a good many people in the room in the short duration since his arrival, and Rosamond subsequently found herself introduced to a fair representation of the other guests.

Even as Mr. Trainer kept her by his side during that first interval, Rosamond could not help letting her eyes periodically peruse the perimeter of the room, but she saw no other familiar face amongst the guests. Indeed, Frederick Lancaster did not arrive until just before dinner, and he entered the room very unobtrusively, greeted his aunt and uncle, then joined a group of men near the fireplace.

As the guests proceeded into the dining room, he bid Rosamond a courteously concise "Good evening" in precisely the same manner as he greeted the other guests, detached and reticent as ever. During the dinner, he neither addressed Rosamond, nor even looked in her direction, which should not have troubled her, for there was no reason to think that he should; there were many people seated between them at the table, all of with whom he was doubtlessly better acquainted and to whom he was much more likely to direct his attention. His indifference did make a slight impression upon Rosamond, though, even as her own conversation continued to be monopolized by the charismatic Mr. Trainer.

After dinner, when the gentlemen had departed into the study, the ladies retired to the spaciously elegant drawing room where news and gossip could be exchanged without interference from the gentlemen's political or economic discourse. Rosamond thoroughly enjoyed this portion of the evening, for she was able to converse quietly for a time with her hostess, who sat with her before one of the fireplaces at the room's periphery. Lady Abercrombie proved to be a cultivated woman with admirable knowledge of many topics which Rosamond held dear: music, literature, travel, and art.

They sat somewhat apart from the other ladies and spent a very pleasant hour indeed.

After that time, the gentlemen returned, and the social hour commenced. Rosamond found herself the object of not only Douglas Trainer's admiration, for there were other young men present who also sought her favor.

Eventually, several of the young ladies were persuaded to play, including Rosamond, who was delighted to discover that Lady Abercrombie retained not only a pianoforte, but also a classically lovely old harpsichord, meticulously restored and in excellent tune, its painted wood case portraying a colorful pastoral tableau. Lady Abercrombie allowed her to play upon it, and Douglas Trainer would naturally turn pages for her. It was easy for Rosamond to lose herself in the beauty of the music once she began playing, and from the moment her finger touched the first key of the old harpsichord, she was caught up in the enchantment of a bygone era which its melodious sound called forth.

Except for his initial greeting, the Earl of Kendal had not spoken to or acknowledged Rosamond in any way during the entire evening, and as she played she was aware that he sat apart from the listeners, nonchalantly leaning back in his chair near the fire. However, when she chanced to look up from her playing for the briefest moment, she found herself the object of his intense and brooding gaze. Quickly averting her eyes, she was conscious of a stirring within her that was reminiscent of the fluttering sensation she had felt sitting beside him in the darkened theatre. And though she did not look in his direction again, she felt his steady dark eyes upon her, and she knew that he was not indifferent to her presence, whatever distance he may have kept.

At last the guests moved from the drawing room into the card room where they seated themselves in parties of three or four about the small, polished tables and commenced with the pleasures and strategies associated with social gaming. Those who did not wish to play found comfortably-cushioned chairs scattered about the room, and it was into one of these that

Rosamond settled, near where her parents and Mr. Trainer were playing, for she herself did not care for cards. Still Frederick did not pay her any heed, as he was seated at a table across the room with a contingent of other men and remained there the rest of the evening, winning many hands, for his reserved nature and sharp perception lent themselves to competency at the card-table.

During a respite, as the guests moved about the room mingling and regrouping their parties, Rosamond saw Frederick greet her parents and remain in conversation with her father for several moments, as would be natural between business associates. Douglas Trainer insisted that Rosamond sit beside him during the last half-hour of play, making it a point to include her in his deliberations and assessments, and although he did not win many hands, he was ever good-natured and evidently gratified to be sharing the company of such an enchanting lady.

The hour was very late when the guests began to disperse. As was often the case, there was some interval between the time Mrs. Hathaway told Rosamond they were set to depart and the actual moment they took their leave. Her parents spent a lengthy time in the card room, exchanging last-minute well-wishes and goodnights to Sir Richard and Lady Abercrombie, who vowed that the Hathaways would henceforth be amongst the regular attendees at the dinner parties, much to Mrs. Hathaway's delight.

Douglas Trainer bid his adieus to Rosamond in the hall, asking her permission to call upon her the following afternoon, which leave she gave with a modest consenting nod. His carriage was ready before Mr. Hathaway had even given the order for theirs, and after Mr. Trainer departed, Rosamond headed back toward the card room where her parents still idled. She was really quite tired, though, and instead of entering the room and facing the prospect of further expenditure of energy, she sat upon a decorative bench that had been placed in the hall opposite the elegant staircase.

As she sat there waiting for her parents to emerge from the card room, she became aware of someone entering the hall. When she looked up, she beheld Frederick Lancaster standing before her. Before she could rise, he crossed to her bench and slid onto the seat beside her. Despite his aloofness all evening, there was a glimmer of warmth in his eyes behind their pensive darkness.

He did not sever the quiet atmosphere of the hall, but merely inclined his head toward hers and said, very low, as if they were still in the hushed theatre, "Miss Hathaway, you may wish to consider attending the auction with your father next weekend. We shall be liquidating some of his Indian acquisitions on behalf of the company, but there are some excellent paintings which are to be put on the block that day that I think would be very much to your taste."

That was all he said. He rose with a nod and a quiet "Good evening, Miss Hathaway," then returned to the card room, leaving Rosamond — who had never uttered a word — with much to ponder over the ensuing hours and days.

The following day, an event occurred which had some significance to the members of the Hathaway household. Its initiation began early in the day — long before Douglas Trainer's promised visit to Miss Rosamond — and while it impacted all members of the family, none would be so relieved by its consequences as young Tom Hathaway. Lorna proved to be his inadvertent deliverer.

Ever since her conversation with Hugh Shadwell at the race-course, Lorna had turned over several issues in her mind, but only one lent itself to direct action, and it was her determination to resolve this issue that prompted her to seek out her father in his study the morning after the dinner party.

The Hathaway siblings seldom disturbed their father in his study during the morning, for even when he was at home he had, at times, various matters of business which required his attention, and when his study door was closed in the daytime, the household members knew he was occupied.

However, Lorna felt this matter should not be put off longer, as it had already been delayed long enough in her estimation.

Mr. Hathaway bid her come in when she knocked on his study door, and he smiled when he saw his eldest daughter, for his children seldom intruded, and he knew it must be a worthwhile cause for her to thus venture forth.

Lorna was always a forthright young lady, and she asserted her point almost immediately upon closing the door. "Father, I wish to speak with you regarding Jasper Munroe." She walked over to her father's desk as he bid her to take a seat.

"Jasper?" Mr. Hathaway was clearly surprised by the subject of her desired discourse. "Is there a problem?"

"I should say there is!" Lorna asserted with spirit. "It has been evident for quite some time, and I wonder that you have not addressed it prior to this."

Mr. Hathaway knit his brow in perplexion. "And what is it that I should be addressing?"

"Perhaps it is not as evident to you as to the rest of us, as you were gone from London for such a lengthy period, but I, for one, cannot help feeling that Jasper is overstaying his welcome. When you announced that he would be residing with us, we were given the impression that it would be but temporarily, and yet he has been here for many months now."

Her father frowned. "You must remember, child, that Jasper is our relation, and I cannot shirk my duty in assisting a family member."

Lorna sighed. "I understand that, Father, but I cannot help but think that Jasper is taking undue advantage of your benevolence. He does nothing of any merit, only spends his days lounging and sleeping, and his evenings gambling and drinking and who knows what else? My own brother, who could live in exceeding comfort upon your allowance, is not permitted such a life of idleness, and rightfully chooses to learn the value of work, while this relation cannot keep a job due to his indolence, and makes no effort to seek self-sufficiency."

Her father still frowned as he nodded his head thoughtfully. "I confess, these thoughts have crossed my mind at times. I had intended to speak to the boy in the near future should he fail to find another position. But the tone of your words troubles me, Lorna." He leaned forward, giving her a questioning look. "Has there been some quarrel between Jasper and yourself, daughter?"

Lorna pondered the question before giving her father answer. "I cannot say there has been any specific incident that precipitated this," she maintained steadily. "Only that our recent encounters have been somewhat . . . strained, and not entirely amicable on either of our accounts."

Her father smiled at her fondly. "My Lorna . . . always honest, even as to your own imperfections."

Lorna's face colored a bit, as she knew this praise was not entirely merited. But her father continued: "You've used the term 'we' several times. Are your siblings also at odds with Mr. Munroe?"

"I cannot speak for them. Rosamond has disliked Jasper from the beginning, although I cannot say what foundation she has for such feelings. Of course she would never broach the subject with you, although she may give you honest answer if asked. And Tom . . . " Here Lorna broke off, for she could not rightly say what Tom's opinion was. After a pause she continued. "I only know that Tom used to spend a great deal of time in Jasper's company, and now Tom only spends a great deal of time at home. I do not know if they had a falling out."

Mr. Hathaway said nothing, seemingly deep in thought. Lorna suddenly rose and impetuously crossed to her father, putting her arms about him.

"Dear Father, of course it is your home and your decision as to how you deal with Jasper. I am not trying to step out of my place. It is only that this issue has weighed on my mind of late, and I could not think that it would do any harm to bring it to your attention."

Mr. Hathaway patted his daughter's arm affectionately. "You are correct . . . it is my house and my place to make decisions. And you are my daughter, and your welfare and happiness are my chief concerns. You must be an advocate for your brother and sister as well, for they would not voice their troubles to me as you have. You have said your piece . . . now it is my job to set everything aright. I shall not delay in having discourse with our houseguest."

Lorna kissed him fondly on the top of his head. "You are truly the dearest father in the world. I know you will do what is best for everyone."

It was with a great amount of curiosity that Lorna speculated upon what passed between her father and Jasper that evening, for Mr. Hathaway called young Mr. Munroe into his study after dinner, and the two of them spent more than an hour behind the closed door. When they finally emerged, nether man said anything in the way of explanation to Lorna, but it seemed to her that both men looked satisfied, and Jasper particularly looked pleased. She refrained from pressing her father for information, but as it turned out, she had not long to wait before her curiosity was assuaged.

When she came downstairs the next morning, she was surprised to find Aunt Sarah Blakely in the front parlor at such an early hour (though past breakfast, which Lorna had missed). Rosamond, who had been ascending the stairs as Lorna came down, had given her sister an especially bright smile, but said nothing other than that Lorna ought to hasten into the parlor as their mother had some news.

So it was with a feeling of some anticipation that Lorna entered the parlor, which was cheerfully lit with the morning sunlight streaming in through the long windows. Aunt Sarah and her mother were huddled on the plush sofa, excitedly talking in hushed tones.

"Good morning, Aunt Sarah, Mother," Lorna greeted them as she entered.

Without even bothering to return the greeting, Mrs. Hathaway rose immediately and went toward her daughter. Her voice was tremulous and her eyes animated with the fever of her excitement. "Oh Lorna, you will not believe what has happened . . . Jasper has gone away to America!"

Lorna was stunned. "What? What do you mean?"

Aunt Sarah rose, also triumphant in her early knowledge of the situation. "Yes, it's true," she intoned. "Left without a word to anybody!"

Lorna was still amazed. "But how . . . so suddenly!"

Mrs. Hathaway led her back over to the sofa and sat on one side of her, Aunt Sarah on the other. Mrs. Hathaway spoke very fast in her agitation. "None of us knew! Rosamond and I finished our breakfast after your father and Tom left, and I mentioned to Agnes that she needed to leave the jam-pot out for Jasper, as she had started clearing it away. And Agnes just looked at me and said, 'But Ma'am, Mr. Jasper has gone away with his trunk before sunrise. I thought he wasn't returning today.' Can you imagine? And to hear it from Agnes! Well, naturally I sent a note to your father's office immediately, and he sent back the reply that it's true and that he will give us details when he returns this afternoon!" Mrs. Hathaway put her hand to her chest, as if to still her throbbing heart. "Your own father knew all along and never breathed a word to me!"

Aunt Sarah shook her greying locks. "Never a word!" she breathed.

Lorna was too astonished to say much at the moment. She certainly wasn't going to reveal the nature of the talk she'd had with her father only the day before . . . her mother would only reprimand her for not being forthcoming. And she certainly hadn't anticipated that Jasper would have taken such immediate action.

Later, after Aunt Sarah and her mother had gone out calling, and presumably to spread the word, Lorna went upstairs to Jasper's room. She knocked, then turned the doorknob when there was no reply. The door opened easily, and Lorna stepped inside. The maid had not yet tidied up the room, and the bed had not been made, but other than that, there was no indication of habitation within the room. There were no toiletries or accessories on the bureau, no water in the basin or pitcher — apparently Jasper had left at an excessively early hour, before anyone had even brought fresh water for the morning. As Lorna's boldness increased, she opened the wardrobe, which was entirely empty, and the bureau drawers, which were mostly empty, save for a single glove and a torn waistcoat.

Lorna stood in the middle of the vacated room and took one last look in each direction before she made her way back toward the door. Although the empty room attested to the truth of Jasper's departure, she could still scarcely believe the truth of it. It would not be like Jasper to leave for a distant territory with no money, prospects, or connections. Especially as she recalled the satisfied look upon Jasper's face as he left the study did Lorna suspect that he had not left with only his possessions. She was certain that his most valuable "possession" was probably a sizable bank note, given with her father's blessing.

Chapter IX

Rosamond had indeed pondered Frederick Lancaster's succinct words in reference to the auction. In truth, though, her meditation on the subject never had but a single disposition . . . she did have a desire to attend the event, surely due to her curiosity as to the nature of the paintings to which he had alluded. Her father had no objection to her going. As it was for him a business function, Tom would also be present and could attend to his sister, and Mr. Hathaway agreed that it would be a fine way for her to view some rare works of art that would not otherwise be publicly displayed.

Rosamond had never been to an auction and was surprised when they entered the bank's public-room at how many people were in attendance. The auction was already under way and, from the rear of the room where they entered, she could not even see the platform at the front where the auctioneer stood, so many people were crowded about. It was a refined crowd, though, and there was no sense of discomposure amongst them. The onlookers and participants stood toward the front where the auction-block dominated, but the rear of the room was arranged for the means of conducting business, with several large tables available for whatever need may arise amongst the men of commerce.

It was at one of these tables that Mr. Hathaway's business was to be conducted, and his associates had already arrived and reserved one for their purpose. Rosamond had given little thought to the nature of her father's business for the day, but as soon as she sighted the table, she stopped short just inside the door, for it suddenly occurred to her that these business associates of her father's may well be some of the very men who had been present at Smollett's Coffeehouse that day that still brought a crimson flush to her cheek whenever she thought on it. She certainly did not want to encounter any of the shareholders again, save one whom she spotted even now, deep in dialogue with another gentleman at the table and oblivious to her presence.

Tom was her greatest ally in this situation, however, for of her entire family, he alone was knowledgeable of the fact that his sister had ever encountered the principle owners of the Star of India Tea Company. He sensed her pause upon entry of the room and quickly realized her reason for reluctance. Tom stopped their father, who had immediately headed toward his associates, and informed him that he would take Rosamond up to the front where she could better watch the proceedings. So Rosamond was able to avoid any meeting that may have caused her discomfort, and she and Tom proceeded toward the auctioneer's platform. They found a place to stand at the edge of the assembled crowd, but not too far from the platform, so that Rosamond was afforded a fairly good view.

The auction's proceedings were not at all the way she had imagined. Somehow, the word "auction" conjured up a rather disorderly image in her mind . . . of cacophonous voices and the auctioneer's shouts and unruly people crowded about in a coffeehouse or tavern, as auctions were of old. This auction, however, bore little resemblance to such proceedings of yesteryear, for this was conducted by and for men of wealth and businesses of prestige. The room was actually fairly quiet, for those assembled and those conducting business spoke in moderate tones, and even the auctioneer was exceedingly decorous, standing at his polished podium.

At the moment, the items up for bid seemed to be a group of exquisite imported textiles and furnishings, some of which were amongst her father's holdings, which had necessitated his immediate attention at the table with his associates. Rosamond thought many of the items to be very beautiful and others to be not at all to her taste. One mantle clock in particular . . . garishly embellished with carvings of what appeared to be grotesquely leering monkeys was so horrendously gaudy, she could not believe anyone would bid on it, much less at the price for which it went. But when she turned to glimpse the successful bidder and saw that it was Mr. Kenneth Russell, whose wife kept the most tastelessly over-embellished drawing room in London, she conceded to herself that everyone's sense of aestheticism was unique, even if someone's inclined toward leering primates.

After about thirty minutes of observing the auction, the two siblings were joined by the Earl of Kendal, who had taken a respite from the business proceedings at the back of the room and slipped into the row of onlookers beside Rosamond, greeting both Hathaways with effortless cordiality. Tom was at once uneasy, for his hapless encounter with Lord Kendal at the race-course was foremost in his mind, but the Earl said nothing regarding Tom's indiscretion, and gave no indication that he had even seen Tom recently.

Rosamond, too, had some contradictory feelings as the Earl greeted her. Her initial, instinctive sentiments of gladness were tempered by feelings of doubt, as he had seemed to pay her little heed at the Abercrombies' dinner party, at least overtly. It was truly difficult to read the thoughts of a man who was so reserved in his speech, yet whose brooding dark eyes always seemed to draw her own. He seemed to be able to read her thoughts, however, and the easy familiarity of his next words reassured her, though she dared not acknowledge such a feeling, even to herself.

"I thought I'd come and make sure you were mindful of this next group of paintings. They are certain to be of interest to you."

Rosamond made no immediate reply, only eyed him inquisitively, for she truly wondered how he should be knowledgeable of her aesthetic preferences. She could not recall ever discussing the matter in his presence.

The auctioneer's assistants brought forward the grouping of paintings that would next be put upon the block. The first one displayed was very old and clearly in the Italian style. It was quite large and showed a mythological tableau with plump and rosy women draped in pastel linens, playing musical instruments in a white-pillared folly and virtuously oblivious to young Pan who listened without. It was quickly purchased by a foreign-looking man whom Rosamond did not recognize. The next work put upon the block was a smaller, rectangular canvas, heavily framed, and portraying a religious subject, also in the Italian style. It, too, was quickly taken up by the curator of the National Museum.

Rosamond reflected on the attributes of these two works of art as the next one — the last in the group — was brought to the platform. She smiled of a sudden, for she understood the Earl's intention. She gave a charming little laugh as she turned to him.

"They are all of the school of the Italian Masters," she declared to him. "That is why you thought of me . . . from the gallery exhibit."

He could not help smiling slightly . . . so delighted was she at her own deduction.

"Are they not to your liking?" he asked.

"Oh yes, they are magnificent, of course. I do love classical painting. There are other styles I love even more, though, than the Old Masters."

"And do you have a favorite?" he inquired complaisantly.

Rosamond smiled, coloring slightly. "I suppose you would think my artistic preferences to be somewhat démodé, but I am very fond of the artists of the last century . . . Gainsborough, Romney, Fragonard."

Frederick nodded thoughtfully and said to her, "Then perhaps this next group will appeal to you."

The piece currently on the block was a landscape — very Turner-esque — which did not particularly interest Rosamond, but as she strained to see the other paintings in the group, her face lit up.

"Oh, look! Look at that one in the gilt-edged frame. Oh yes, that one is just lovely."

Frederick turned his own head to see the painting that had so enchanted his lovely companion. It was not a large painting, but very distinctly in the style of the late 18th-century. The subject was a young lady in a morning gown, standing on a balcony of what was presumably her home, overlooking an idyllic rural setting of sylvan verdancy. The girl's long brown hair hung loose, as if she may have just awoken, and the sky reinforced this, for its hazy pink tones suggested the waning dawn.

Frederick looked back at Rosamond with interest. "And what is it that strikes you about the painting?"

Rosamond had never taken her eyes off of it, still enchanted. "Just see how she looks off into the distance . . . she is so beautiful. But it is the look in her eyes . . . far away, yet hopeful, I think. She is thinking about something that brings her happiness . . . or someone."

Frederick nodded as he observed the painting. "You see a great deal in that picture," he mused. "And I think the artist would be pleased with your interpretation of his subtleties."

Rosamond still contemplated the painting's subject. "She is drawn from life," she determined. "For no artist, however talented, could fabricate such an authentic portrayal of unfeigned, hopeful longing as is reflected in her eyes."

Frederick nodded again. "I believe you are right. It is indeed an exceptional work of artistic beauty, and executed by your George Romney, no less." He was still looking at the painting, very thoughtfully, as it was brought to the block. "I'm going to bid on it," he said.

Rosamond's heart began pounding, and her stomach was overcome with a sickening sensation at the Earl's last words. Her discomposure was not outwardly apparent, but her mind was reeling with anxiety. Surely the Earl, who had been so kind and so honorable toward her in every regard, would not presume to present her with such a costly and visible gift that she must refuse? Such a notion could not be reconciled with his gentility. The remainder of the bidding was a blur to her, but she was cognizant of the fact that at the closing of the bidding, the Earl of Kendal had procured the painting.

He remained exceedingly calm throughout, and when it was over, he leaned over to Rosamond and said, very simply, "I shall donate it to the museum. Then you can go and look at it whenever you please."

So audible was her gasp at these words that he looked at her with some consternation. But inside her mind and her heart, a wave of comfort swept over her as her anxiety gave way to joyful gladness, and she was ashamed that she should have ever doubted his intentions.

He clearly did not comprehend any of her previous misgivings or her sudden sentiments of wondrous gratification. He heard only her amazed reactive gasp and felt that she must have misunderstood his intent, and thus felt the need to elaborate. "It is too fine a work to be shut away in somebody's house. There are undoubtedly other young girls who would benefit from the opportunity of visiting this painting and may be as enchanted as you are. It should be hung where all can admire it."

If Frederick had doubted Rosamond's reception of his first words, he could have no doubt as to her feelings now. Her countenance as she looked upon him could only be described as luminous. And to be rewarded with such an engaging look of admiration as she now bestowed upon him, he would easily have given up the price of a dozen such works of art.

As it was, Frederick merely said to her, "I must go now and settle my transaction with the clerk, and then I must be back to my business associates. Good day to you, Miss Hathaway." And with a bow to her, and a nod to Tom, he disappeared into the throng of people standing near the auctioneer's platform.

Lady Abercrombie and Sir Richard were true to their word, and the Hathaways were extended an invitation to their next dinner party, their debut having been so well-met. Mrs. Hathaway insisted that Tom and Lorna accompany them, as they were included in the invitation and had been unable to attend the first evening. Neither was particularly interested, being unacquainted with the hosts, but they gamely acquiesced with their mother's wishes. So it was a group of five from Grosvenor Square who turned out to the grand house in Kensington for another social event.

As it was her second occasion to attend such a gathering, Rosamond was acquainted with several of the other guests and almost immediately found herself in conversation with a small ensemble who readily remembered the lovely and graceful young lady. She knew that Douglas Trainer had also been invited again, as he had made himself a rather frequent caller in Grosvenor Square since the last dinner party.

Sure enough, about a quarter of an hour after the Hathaways' arrival, Mr. Trainer entered the conservatory, was amicably received by his hosts, whose greeting he returned with his usual convivial affability, and promptly sought out Rosamond Hathaway. Having been so frequently in her company of late, he must have felt a confident familiarity, for several times in their subsequent conversation did he mention places "we" ought to attend or activities "we" should pursue together. This familiarity was not lost on Lorna, who had joined her sister and Mr. Trainer, and several times did she cast Rosamond a bemused, inquiring glance. Rosamond only blushed gracefully at her sister's unspoken questioning, for while she had no dislike of Mr. Trainer, she did not feel equal to the level of intimacy which he presumed.

The three of them happened to be standing near the door when the Earl of Kendal entered, and Rosamond overheard Lady Abercrombie greet her nephew.

"Frederick! You are so inconsistent in your attendance!" she scolded. "You usually appear but occasionally to my parties . . . I had not thought to set a place for you tonight as you came last time. It is not like you to attend twice in a row!"

"Shall I go then?" And Frederick turned, as if to exit.

"No, no, of course not!" His aunt extended an affectionate hand, which he took and kissed decorously. "You know how I am always pleased to see you. Nothing should delight me more than if you would appear at every dinner . . . but somehow I suspect that you shall not be bound to such consistency."

Frederick certainly saw Rosamond as he moved into the room, for she was standing so near to the Abercrombies, but once again he gave her only a polite nod of acknowledgement then crossed the room to join another group of acquaintances. Rosamond's mother, however, was not hesitant to greet him, for she wished to introduce Lorna to the dashing young Earl who had so graciously received them into his box at the opera. So it was that she took Lorna away, leaving Rosamond with Douglas Trainer, and Rosamond saw her mother at the other end of the room, presenting her sister to Lord Kendal, who appeared to greet her cordially.

In a few moments, Lorna returned to Rosamond and, squeezing her hand, whispered, "Good heavens . . . do I have to be introduced to every member of the peerage that Mother encounters!"

Rosamond could not help smiling to herself . . . it was so like her strong-willed sister to be unimpressed by titled nobility, no matter how dashing or handsome he may be. And certainly the Earl of Kendal's pensive seriousness would not interest such a vivaciously lively young woman as Lorna Hathaway.

The three of them were presently joined by some other guests who had met Rosamond and Mr. Trainer at the previous dinner, and when Rosamond glanced across the room and saw Frederick move away from his own group, she rather abruptly excused herself and crossed to meet him. When he perceived her approach, he stopped and received her sedate curtsey with a bow.

"Miss Hathaway, good evening." Despite the rhetorical politeness of the greeting, the momentary flicker of his dark eyes would disclose a warmer sentiment. "I see you are now amongst the regulars who gather here."

Rosamond smiled modestly. "Yes, Lady Abercrombie and Sir Richard have been most gracious to include us again. They are very kind."

"My aunt is quite fond of you, I believe."

"I did have some opportunity to converse with her last time," said Rosamond. "I only hope I made a favorable impression upon her. I should very much like to earn her respect."

"Have no fear of that. Your presence here tonight affirms her regard for you . . . and your family."

That was the extent of their discourse, for at that moment dinner was announced, and Douglas Trainer came to claim Rosamond in order to escort her into the dining room.

At dinner, she was seated between Tom and Mr. Trainer, but on more than one occasion her eye wandered to the end of the table where the Earl was seated near Sir Richard. She observed that he did not engage in much conversation during the meal, but seemed distracted and sullen, although those around him appeared not to notice.

When the ladies retired to the drawing room, Rosamond once again had the privilege of conversing with Lady Abercrombie, but not in private as she had previously, for on this night Mrs. Hathaway and Lorna were included, as Lady Abercrombie had not had any opportunity to speak in depth with the elder Miss Hathaway. Even as Lorna and her mother easily conversed with their hostess, Lady Abercrombie made a point in several instances to draw Rosamond out, for that august lady was indeed fond of Rosamond and was exceedingly interested in her input and preferences.

When the gentlemen entered the room, young Mr. Trainer found himself with a bit of competition for the attention of Miss Rosamond, for others could now claim a higher degree of familiarity with the young lady as she had been twice in their midst. And yet, despite her best efforts to attend to her companions' discourse, her thoughts would still invariably wander to one across the room who was neither an eligible suitor nor ostensibly attentive to her, and who seemed to be keeping much to himself this evening.

When the doors were opened into the card room, Rosamond progressed with her family and the other guests to the door, but did not herself pass though, and instead lingered in the drawing room, for she saw that Frederick Lancaster had not followed the others' departure, but remained where he had been standing near the tall windows at the opposite end of the room. As if he had not even been aware of the departure into the card room, he stood before the window, staring absently out into the dark night, his brow furrowed in brooding contemplation.

Perhaps he perceived another presence in the otherwise-deserted room, for he turned his head and beheld Rosamond standing just inside the door.

"Are you not going to play cards tonight?" she inquired. "You seemed to be quite proficient at it last time."

There was a pause before Frederick responded.

"I suppose I shall eventually. Right now I am inclined toward the tranquility to be found here."

Rosamond smiled understandingly and quietly closed the door into the card room, blocking out all the clamor from that room and rendering the drawing room silent. She took a few steps toward him.

"If you desire any company, I shall be happy to stay with you here." She paused in her step and hesitated at an afterthought. "Of course, if you prefer solitude, it is no concern of mine."

"I should like very much for you to stay. However, I believe there are others in there," he nodded toward the card room door, "who would resent your absence."

Rosamond's face flushed a shade of pink, and she instinctively raised her head and straightened her white shoulders. She spoke clearly, however soft her voice. "I am beholden to no one in there, save my parents, of course."

Frederick had once before glimpsed this regal pride in the usually demure Rosamond, and the subtle flicker of warmth in his eye betrayed his approval.

Rosamond crossed to the windows and sat upon one of the recessed window-seats near where the Earl stood. The room seemed very large and very quiet when it was emptied of the other guests, and both Rosamond and Frederick were respectful of the stillness, keeping their own voices low and thus necessitating their close proximity.

"It seems that I have now made the acquaintance of the entire Hathaway family," remarked Frederick. He looked at Rosamond. "You are very different from your sister," he mused. "Her eyes are brown . . . yet they are lighter than your blue eyes."

Rosamond laughed softly. "Yes," she said, "it is true . . . my eyes are such a deep shade of blue . . . and Lorna's are exceptionally light for brown. If you knew her better, you would see that we are different in many ways other than our appearance. She is very high-spirited and has a strength of character that I cannot help but admire. And though she may appear to be somewhat strong-willed, she has always been devoted to Tom and me."

"Both your siblings are very dear to you," observed the Earl.

"Yes . . ." Rosamond lowered her eyes and was lost in reverie for a few moments. But while Frederick would naturally surmise that she was reflecting upon the subject of her siblings, her next words indicated that her thoughts had been elsewhere. When she lifted her eyes and spoke to him, there was much sincerity in her tone, and it was plain that her sentiment was heartfelt.

"You have been so kind to me in so many ways. I cannot help but feel that my outward appreciation falls short of the gratitude I feel. I do not know how I can possibly repay such kindness as you have shown me."

Her words caught Frederick off-guard, and he stood there for a long moment, looking into those eyes whose dark hue he had only just remarked upon. When finally he stirred, he did not avert his gaze, but moved to sit beside her on the window-seat. Sitting so near, and with such a grave countenance, he looked directly into her eyes and spoke in a hushed, yet firm, tone. "Rosamond Hathaway . . . you must never say such a thing to me again. You shall not be beholden to me or to any man. And let no man ever tell you otherwise."

His face was so near her own that she could feel his soft breath upon her neck. There was no awkwardness between them — indeed, there had been none since their encounter in the rain in Bond Street — and so it was not unease that now caused Rosamond's heartbeat to quicken. The gravity of his words was not lost upon her, but she was undeniably more conscious of his presence than of the significance of his words.

As he leaned back against the recessed wall, he chanced to look upon the fan she held folded in her lap. It was the same one he had retrieved from the floor in the opera box. His eye was now caught by some lettering etched onto the fan's wooden frame. He gently lifted it from her fingers and ran his own finger under the letters.

"R . . . F . . . H." He looked back to her inquiringly. "Your Christian name?"

She smiled. "Yes. Rosamond Frances Hathaway."

"Rosamond Frances Hathaway," he repeated to himself. "Yes, that suits you."

He did not say exactly how it should suit her, but his tone and expression as he placed the fan back in her hand indicated that his reasons were favorable. Rosamond slightly shifted her position so that she could see out the window behind them.

"Oh look!" she exclaimed suddenly, brightening.

Frederick peered out the window, perplexed, for he could not imagine what she could discern in the darkness.

She laughed at his puzzled expression. "Don't you see them?" she asked. —"The fireflies!"

Now it was his turn to smile. "Yes, I suppose I do see them, now that you mention it."

They both turned their faces back to the window and looked out at the flickering little bits of illumination.

"Surely you must have chased them when you were a lad?" Rosamond asked. "Tom used to catch them for me in his hand, for I could never catch one myself."

Frederick nodded. "Yes, my brothers and I used to run about and see who could catch the most. Living in the country as we did, fireflies were plentiful." He squinted, peering into the darkness. "It is difficult to see them with the light coming off of the street lamps." He leaned back away from the window and stood up. Rosamond looked up at him inquiringly. He held out a hand to her. "Come . . . I know where you will be afforded a better display."

Rosamond took his hand, and as he helped her to her feet, she was conscious again of the fluttering within her breast, but such awareness was soon overtaken by curiosity as she followed him out of the drawing room and into the hall. He opened a door opposite, and upon passing through it Rosamond found herself in a dark-paneled library; a fairly small room, cozily illuminated by the light of the fire, and whose shelves were lined with an impressive collection of books.

But Frederick paid no heed to the amenities of the room and crossed directly to the single window on the opposite wall. Drawing the heavy curtain aside, he motioned for Rosamond to step up to the window. She did so and was delighted by what she saw. This window looked out, not to the front of the house as the drawing room window had, but rather to the side-yard, which was encompassed in a blanket of darkness as black as Rosamond's curls, and combined with the dimness of the room itself, was thus the perfect venue for the fireflies to show off their yellow-green incandescence, glimmering and sparkling like fairy lights in a sylvan wood. Rosamond stood at the window for quite a few minutes, transfixed by the visual symphony.

When at last she turned her back to the window, she was no less delighted by what she saw, for the room itself enchanted her with its dark-paneled warmth.

"What an agreeable room!" she proclaimed. "It is not much larger than our own library, but with what an extensive collection!" She peered with interest at one of the bookshelves. "Some of these books look very old. I should like to study them all," she added, a bit wistfully.

Frederick seated himself in a plush wing-backed chair near the fire. "You are welcome to read any you wish, I am sure," he said easily. "Sir Richard acquired many of them when he was the archivist at the palace years ago."

"I see." Rosamond was rather awed by this fact, for she did not know that Sir Richard had held such an exalted post.

She touched the binding of a tall, narrow volume with some reverence, then carefully pulled it from the shelf. There was no discernible title upon it, but when she opened it, the book's antiquity was ascertained, for the pages were yellowed with age, but held wonders nonetheless.

"Oh, just see this!" she exclaimed. "These illustrations . . . they are so colorful, despite the book's age. I do believe they were colored by hand." She crossed to where Frederick sat and showed him the open page whose illustrations depicted the taxonomy of an exotic flower.

He nodded. "You are right . . . it is colored by hand."

Rosamond lightly ran her finger over the illustration. "This is a book to be treasured," she murmured. Then she sat down upon the ottoman before Frederick's chair and proceeded to page through the book while he lapsed into silence.

It was a contented silence, though, and they remained thus occupied for the better part of the hour. The silence was periodically broken by Rosamond's murmurs of delight as she discovered some new enchantment in the book which she would then share with her companion, who did not seem to mind these little interruptions to his brown study.

When at last Rosamond closed her book and looked up at the Earl, he contemplated her for a moment before rising. She rose also, and Frederick took the volume from her and crossed to put it back in its place upon the shelf. When he turned from the shelf, he saw that she had followed him and was standing only a few paces away.

He spoke with quiet deliberation. "And now . . . I think you'd best be getting back to the card room."

Rosamond knew that he was right and did not state her reluctance to leave that peaceful haven, but only nodded rather absently and curtsied prettily before him, then turned toward the door. But before she passed through it, she turned back to the room, where Frederick still stood at the bookshelf looking after her, pensive once more. It seemed as if she might say something, but apparently she changed her mind and only gave him a shy wisp of a smile before exiting into the hall in the direction of the card room.

For Rosamond and the Earl of Kendal, it would become their ritual. It was never intended to be so, nor did they ever discuss or even acknowledge such an arrangement, but it became so nonetheless. At the next Kensington dinner party, Frederick left with the other gentlemen after dinner, but Rosamond noticed that he did not return to the drawing room when the other gentlemen entered. When the doors were opened into the game room, Rosamond once again did not follow the other guests to the card tables, but instead slipped across the hall to the little library, and when she tentatively opened the door, she found the Earl to be within, standing before the fire. He turned toward the door when it was opened, and Rosamond did not need to ask his permission to enter, knowing that he would not object to her company.

And so it became their custom at every gathering — taking refuge in their quiet sanctuary during the first part of the card-playing. And though neither Rosamond nor Frederick would admit to such a thing, those hours spent in the dark-paneled haven were cherished by both. Sometimes Rosamond would read aloud to the Earl from one of the volumes that she loved to examine. Sometimes they would quietly converse; more often they did not. There was always an unspoken understanding between the two … they did not require discourse to be at ease. They were content just to be in one another's presence. And deep inside, they may have feared the reality that words might call forth, and so preferred their idyllic peacefulness and hushed ambience.

Rosamond always went back into the card room alone, and Frederick usually followed within the hour.

Although Rosamond did not play at cards, it was inevitable that her absence from the card room should be noticed by those close to her. Lorna and Tom rarely attended the dinner parties, and Mr. Trainer, of course, was too polite to inquire after her consistently late entry each week, but her mother did question Rosamond after noting her absence upon several consecutive occasions. Rosamond simply stated that she did not care for cards and had found the wonderful collection in the library to be of interest. As Mrs. Hathaway knew that Rosamond never played at cards, she was satisfied with the explanation, although Rosamond herself had felt the crimson rising in her cheeks as she spoke, for even if her words were true, she knew there was an element of deception in their imprecision. No one questioned the Earl, of course, who always took up his card-playing upon his entry to the room, but Lady Abercrombie was well-pleased that her nephew should at last be constant in his attendance, and she knew then exactly how many places to set at her table.

Chapter X

Lorna was growing weary of the increasing difficulty of arranging to meet Miles Anderson in such ways that her family might suspect nothing. For such a girl who thrived upon the exhilaration of life, she found the oppressiveness of secrecy to be almost debilitating. Her deepening relationship with the zealous Mr. Anderson had also served a purpose to influence her own outlook on subjects that she had previously never given a second thought. Whenever she attended social gatherings — whether they be dinner parties, balls, or simply tea — she found herself bored and easily distracted. The conversation at such events seemed shallow and insipid to one who had grown accustomed to the spirited expostulation of her ardent friend.

Theirs was a mutual admiration, and if the word "love" had never been uttered by either, it was undoubtedly due to the fact that the pragmatical Miles would consider such pointed conventionality to be categorically unnecessary considering his long-standing, unabashed openness regarding his feelings for her.

Nothing about him was conventional, it seemed to Lorna, from his radical ideas to his renunciation of accepted social mores to his denouncement of the British class hierarchy. And whether or not she truly believed that any of his reforms would ever come to pass, she was enamored of his convictions, which were always delivered with effectively compelling intensity. And when he talked with Lorna, or even just looked at her, his pale eyes would light up, and his eager, friendly smile never failed to win one from her in return. The fact that he was not physically handsome became obsolete when he flashed that irresistible smile.

Lorna was happy, as her father had already recognized upon his homecoming so many months ago, and yet the continued need for covertness provided the one blemish in her contentment. It weighed heavily on her mind of late, as London was thrust into the glorious fairness of late spring.

It was Miles himself who broached the subject one day, though he had not suspected Lorna's consternation, for she had never discussed it with him. They were sitting on the riverbank on a promisingly sunny afternoon, having taken a picnic hamper and spread a cover upon the grass. After eating their light repast, Miles stretched out lazily upon the bank while Lorna sat slightly behind him, staring absently at the river and at some ducks floating by.

Miles squinted up at the cloudless sky. "Lorna," he began, for he still insisted upon addressing her thus, and she had given up objecting, "I cannot wonder but that I ought to feel a bit vexed that I have never been introduced to your family."

His careless tone in no way indicated that he actually felt any such resentment, but his words definitely caught Lorna's attention, and though she did not start, she shifted her focus from the river to her ginger-haired companion. As she did not immediately respond, Miles turned over on his side to where he could see her. He found her looking at him with a thoughtful frown.

"I have thought as much," she said slowly. "Lately I have thought on it a great deal," she admitted.

He did not reply, but propped his head up with an elbow upon the ground, steadily maintaining his surveyance and waiting for her to continue.

She shifted her position a bit uncomfortably under such scrutiny.

"In truth," she finally said, "I have never mentioned anything about you to anyone."

This did not surprise Miles . . . he had surmised as much. Nonetheless, he put the question to her straightforwardly, as was his way. "Are you ashamed of your acquaintance with me?"

"Oh no!" Lorna said hastily. "Of course not. It's only that . . . ." She hesitated, pondering herself what the real reason was. "Well, you're just so different."

"Ah," intoned Miles, "You fear I may not be well-received."

Lorna paused again. In truth, she was uncertain as to the exact cause of her trepidation. On one hand, she was definitely anxious about her family's reception of this rather unorthodox man. But she was equally concerned about his reception of them, knowing his beliefs and attitudes, and fearing perhaps that his attitude toward her might change after confronting her world, with its values and traditions so antithetical to his own ideology. Both reasons had contributed to her continued inclination toward clandestineness. She could not reconcile the juxtaposition of Miles Anderson and Grosvenor Square. Yet now the weariness of the burden overcame her apprehension. She suddenly determined to put an end to this ambivalence.

She looked Miles straight in the eye and said with assurance, "Miles, I should like very much for you to meet my family. Will you come to dinner one night . . . perhaps next week?"

His pale blue eyes sparkled at her, though not for the reason she at first imagined.

"If I do, will you promise always to call me Miles, and not Mr. Anderson?"

"Oh!" She feigned exasperation even as she smiled. "I certainly shan't before my family! I wasn't thinking when I said it."

"Yet, you must have been thinking it inside your head," Miles persisted as he sat up. He cocked his head as he grinned at her. "When you think of me, do you think of me as 'Mr. Anderson' or just as 'Miles'?"

She laughed, a light pealing laughter. "That you shall never know!

I should like to neither inflate nor deflate your self-perception, although I daresay it could use some deflation," she added wickedly, for it was true that humility had never been his downfall.

He laughed aloud. "Very well then. For that, I shall arrive at your house with mismatched shoes and a turban."

Lorna drew herself up, affecting haughty disdain. "You shall never get the best of me there, sir," she said with exaggerated pomposity. "You must be confusing me with my sister, for such issues of fashion never concerned me."

Miles sat completely upright, suddenly alert by her words, and shook off all vestiges of jocularity, although his enthusiasm was still apparent. "Your sister . . .," he said thoughtfully. "You must remind me about your siblings and your parents, so I am prepared to meet them. Shall I like them all?

"Goodness!" exclaimed Lorna. "What an impertinent question! Oughtn't you to be more concerned about whether they take a liking to you?"

Miles shrugged. "I cannot command their feelings. I can only regulate my own."

Lorna sniffed. "Well, I think we had better not discuss it then. I should not like to give you any preconceptions which might prejudice you against them."

Miles waggled a finger before her face. "You are a very stubborn woman."

Lorna carelessly pushed his hand away and sighed. "Besides," she said, "I have already told you about them. I remember."

Miles would not be put off . . . his mood was too mirthful. "That was long ago . . . I could not know then that your family should figure prominently in my future."

Lorna raised her eyebrows. "Figure prominently? Are you planning on seeing them regularly?"

Miles shrugged again. "They are important to you, and it seems only fitting that I should endeavor to establish some sort of rapport with those you love best."

Lorna stared at him, though she showed no signs of disapproval. "Really? I know of no such requirement. Do you aspire to love all whom your friends love?"

Miles was impatient. "Of course not, Lorna. You know ours is no common friendship, and do not allege that you think otherwise. You know that I cannot abide artificiality."

Lorna knew that this unromantic statement was the closest that Miles would come to professing love, for it was not his way to be sentimental. It delighted her, nonetheless, though she showed nothing outwardly.

Miles went on: "I shall have completed my studies at the end of this term. We must think about our future together."

Lorna no longer pretended to be shocked by Miles's boldness, but this presumptuous statement did surprise her. She looked at him steadily and said in a clear voice, "I cannot think what you mean by that. I have heard you say on several occasions that you consider marriage to be an oppressive institution that ought to be obliterated."

Miles snorted in disdain. "It is indeed — a legal means of promoting the bondage of women. Thoroughly medieval in its very structure. I should think that you, as a woman, would be the first to understand its oppressive implications."

Lorna looked at him rather coldly. "I think that is one reform you will never see realized. Most people would think the commitment of spouses is not something to be undermined."

Miles was frustrated by her coldness and inability to agree on this point and became defensive. "Now, Lorna, you know I would never disdain such commitment between those who truly love one another. That is exactly my point in this matter: Why should any woman have to sacrifice her independence and identity simply to fulfill an outdated legal prescription? It is absurd!"

As shocking as this philosophy was, it was not new to Lorna who had heard Miles and his Clerkenwell friends debate the matter before. It was, however, a point with which she could not bring herself to agree, however ardent his persuasion. But she would not argue with him now. She merely sighed and said, "Well, at any rate, please do not bring up such a subject before my family. I would most certainly be forbidden from ever meeting with you again."

To that Miles only grinned at her and said, "Knowing you as I do, I cannot imagine that would prevent you from doing it anyway."

Lorna informed her mother that evening that she had invited a friend to dinner the following week. Her mother was most accommodating, as Lorna knew she would be, for Mrs. Hathaway loved entertaining, and a new face at the dinner-table was always a welcome prospect.

Tom and Rosamond were much more attentive to this news, however, although Lorna mentioned it to them in the most cursory manner she could affect. But they knew their vibrant sister well, and though she had many friends, it was not entirely typical of her to invite to dinner a single gentleman whose name they had never even heard. The three of them were gathered in the parlor when she told them, and Tom and Rosamond pressed Lorna for further information regarding her dinner guest, for it was not like Lorna to blush ever, and her disclosure was accompanied by some rouging of the cheeks which was observed by both siblings.

"I have known him for quite some time," she confided, for now that she could talk openly, she found alleviation in confession to those from whom she had never kept anything. "Since the autumn."

"That is a long while," said Rosamond, surprised that her sister should have developed a relationship over such an extended period without uttering a word about it. She was pleased, though, for she could see that Lorna considered the young man in question to be significant, and she had long wondered whether her independent sister should ever find a gentleman worthy of her admiration. Rosamond said as much, slipping her arm through Lorna's. "Mr. Anderson must be a worthy gentleman, indeed, to have sustained your interest over such a period of time," she asserted warmly.

Lorna smiled at her sister and did not deny that her interest had been sustained, which indicated to Rosamond that Lorna was very much in earnest, as she was usually quick to make light of any man who showed preference toward her.

"He is rather different," admitted Lorna. "But I do hope you'll approve of him."

Tom, who had thus far been silent, now grinned fondly at his sister. "Oh, we're to sit in judgment, are we?" He straightened himself and looked at her with a mockingly serious eye. "I shall be certain to appraise him against impossibly high standards, for, as your brother, it falls to my duty to ensure that my sister is carried off by no less than a prince upon a white steed."

Lorna gave him a wry smile, accompanied by an incredulous laugh. "Despite your noble intentions, dear brother, I do not think I desire to be carried off by a prince, or even a knight, however fair his steed."

"I suppose I cannot persuade you otherwise," agreed Tom good-naturedly, "for I know you too well. You would probably insist upon taking the reins yourself, and there would be an end to my conjured romance."

Rosamond, who had seated herself upon a small upholstered chair, had been scrutinizing her sister thoughtfully during this exchange. "What do you mean when you say he is 'different'?" she asked with interest. "Do you mean he is different from us in some way, or different from other men?"

"Both." Lorna turned back toward her sister. "He is not like anyone I have ever met. Certainly he is not like our other gentleman callers, for he is neither rich nor handsome nor particularly refined."

Rosamond felt this statement was somewhat unnecessarily directed toward herself, as if she had shown a preference for callers bearing such attributes, when instead she had never shown undue preference to any of her suitors who called regularly in Grosvenor Square. But she did not point this out, and let Lorna continue with her description of Mr. Anderson, which Rosamond was truly interested in hearing.

"He is very genial and kindly and attentive — though in no way fawning. And he is very well-learned on . . . a variety of subjects."

This was truthfully a very unsatisfactory description in the opinions of both siblings, and shed little light on Lorna's esteemed acquaintance, for it was very vague, but it must have seemed adequate to her, for her amber eyes were glowing as she put forth his merits, doubtlessly calling up clearer-cut characteristics within her own mind.

"Wherever did you meet him?" asked Tom with curiosity.

Lorna turned back to her brother. "At the University. Do you remember how we always used to meet you there, Tom, and all your friends? I still like to walk there sometimes, or sit on the lawn. He is a student there himself, and was when you were there, too, although he does not remember ever having met you, as he was ahead of you."

"He has been there a long while, then," said Tom rather dubiously.

"Yes, he is completing his second degree. This shall be his last term."

"And just what does this paragon intend to do with himself once his days at the University are ended? What is he studying?" inquired Tom.

"He is a student of philosophy," Lorna responded with utmost gravity. "And an artist."

These revelations were met with a rather prominent pause, during which Tom and Rosamond unwittingly exchanged glances. Lorna noticed but maintained her staunch stance. Rosamond was the first to find her tongue.

"Indeed?" she put forth. "Is he not required to earn his living then? Has he other means of support?" Lorna did not readily respond, and Rosamond was puzzled. "Has he given no thought to establishing himself beyond the University?"

Rosamond's questions were not intended to give offense, but Lorna's reaction was defensively vehement. She turned upon her sister with unexpected intensity.

"He has a brilliant mind!" she retorted. "And an uncommon talent. He will go far on his own! He has the foresight to see beyond the petty parameters of the current tide. You will see . . . he will be a leader in the changes that will come upon our society!"

"Now, now," Tom allayed her with a hand upon her arm, for she truly seemed prepared to launch into a speech that would rival Friends, Romans, Countrymen. "We do not seek a diatribe here. Evidently this is a weighty matter, and we shall treat it accordingly."

Lorna, calmed though still enraptured, squeezed her brother's hand. "Oh, if you could but hear him speak on worldly subjects! You would be astounded at his genius!"

Rosamond did regret that her sister had misconstrued her words and spoke her next thoughts with some hesitance. "But surely there is some tenderness on his part also?" she asked. "For a brilliant intellect cannot be enough to win your affection."

Lorna nodded with a slight smile, which was more to herself than outward. "I believe so. He has given me cause to believe it. I have given it some thought, though," she went on, "and I think it would be well to invite another guest . . . to help alleviate any awkwardness he may feel, being the only one present who is not of our household." She turned to Rosamond. "Perhaps you could ask Edith to come?"

Lorna had truly pondered in advance the question of whom to invite, and Edith Shadwell seemed a wise choice; she was quiet and polite and never sought attention . . . and would not be inclined to say anything that might provoke Miles, which was one of Lorna's fears — that Miles should somehow be induced to proclaim his controversial philosophical theories and be immediately ostracized by her family. Also, Edith would be a good source of diversion for both Tom and Rosamond, whom Lorna felt would find few commonalities to discuss with Miles Anderson.

Unaware of these intentions, Rosamond readily agreed to invite her friend, and Lorna felt reassured that all was in place for the occasion to progress smoothly.

Her peace of mine was not to last long, however, for the next day Rosamond knocked on her bedroom door as Lorna was dressing to go out calling.

Rosamond was smiling brightly as she entered and said, "I've just received a note from Edith. She will be able to come to dinner next week and Hugh also, for I invited him as well. We haven't seen him in quite a long while, and it seemed a fitting opportunity as long as we were inviting his sister. I knew you wouldn't object, as you prefer larger circles for socializing."

"Oh, that is fine then." Outwardly, Lorna returned Rosamond's smile, but inside, her stomach gave a jolting lurch, for this development was unexpected and not well-met. As dearly as Lorna loved Hugh Shadwell, she could not wish him to be present when Miles was in Grosvenor Square. Knowing Miles's beliefs, she could not assume that the presence of the clergyman would promote harmony, however good-natured both men may be. Miles was generally only good-natured until his principles were challenged.

Lorna's anxiety increased several days later. She was passing by the morning room in the lower hall when her mother called out to her from within the room.

"Oh, Lorna! Come here for a moment, won't you?"

Lorna paused in the doorway as her mother came forward.

"I forgot to mention that Aunt Sarah will be at dinner with us when your Mr. Anderson comes. When I mentioned that you had invited a young man, she expressed interest in making his acquaintance, so naturally she shall be included."

Lorna was certain that Aunt Sarah Blakely was *most* interested in making the acquaintance of any young man whom Lorna would invite to dinner, which is why Lorna had taken care not to mention the subject to her aunt. Officious Aunt Sarah relished any first-hand knowledge she could acquire regarding every member of the Hathaway household. She did not like to miss out on a thing. Fortunately, since taking up residence in Primrose Hill, Aunt Sarah had not been so frequently present in Grosvenor Square, but this auspicious circumstance seemed as if it would not apply to the dinner for Lorna's guest. One thing was certain: Aunt Sarah always put forth exactly what she thought, and should she take issue with anything Miles Anderson said, she would not hesitate to call him to task.

Mrs. Hathaway had not yet revealed all to Lorna, though. She must have noticed the look of apprehension on her daughter's face, for she was quick to add, "Oh, I know what you're thinking, my dear. I, too, was concerned when I realized that, with Aunt Sarah coming, we should have an odd number at dinner. But do not be perturbed; I have already rectified the situation. I took the liberty of inviting Mr. Douglas Trainer . . . he is such pleasant company and always so attentive to Rosamond. I knew he would be certain to accept. So, we shall be an even ten . . . and you shall have nothing to worry about!"

If only Mrs. Hathaway's words were true! Instead, Lorna spent the remaining days before the dinner-gathering worrying a great deal, although she tried to allay such concerns. She reminded herself that small dinner-parties were given frequently in her household, and there was no reason to suppose that this one should be more eventful than any other. And the additional guests would surely be a boon, as it would guarantee that all attention would not be upon Mr. Anderson.

When the evening finally arrived, Lorna found herself in a state of mixed emotions: anxiety and excitement contested for predominance within her. Her siblings noticed, despite Lorna's attempts at outward conviviality, and were only reinforced in their beliefs that her gentleman was indeed held in high regard.

Aunt Sarah was the first to arrive, as was to be expected. Both Mrs. Hathaway and Rosamond were still upstairs dressing when the officious aunt was shown into the drawing room, but she was very cordially greeted by Mr. Hathaway and his two eldest children. She fretted, as always, that it had been too long since she was last in Grosvenor Square, and while they only politely nodded, all three Hathaways were certain that it had been less than a fortnight since they last had the pleasure of their aunt's company.

Rosamond and her mother came down just as Hugh Shadwell arrived with his sister Edith. These two were always welcomed warmly, and there was such an easy familiarity to the conversation once they sat down that Lorna began to relax, for she could see that all present were in good spirits. Douglas Trainer arrived promptly at the appointed hour, as was his impeccable custom, and once again all fell into comfortable discourse, for Mr. Trainer had of late been such a regular visitor that all were at ease in his company. Even Hugh and Edith were familiar with that gentleman, and duly left open the seat beside Rosamond, which he naturally, and very willingly, accepted.

Lorna began to be nervous again as the clock ticked first five, then ten past the hour. It was still too early for anyone else to take note of one guest's absence, but Lorna could not help wishing that the drawing room windows looked onto the street so that she could watch for Mr. Anderson's approach. As it was, she kept her focus more on the clock than on the conversation until, at quarter past the hour, Agnes announced Mr. Anderson's arrival, and that young man presented himself into their midst.

Lorna was relieved that there was nothing remarkable about his appearance — save the usual brightness of his ginger hair — or his attire, for it had occurred to her that she had never seen him in the evening, and rarely indoors, and she hoped that he possessed suitable evening attire, as she knew that he paid little heed to fashion trends. She need not have fretted, though, for all was quite appropriate and inconspicuous in his appearance.

Lorna went forward to greet him and accordingly introduced him to her parents, siblings, aunt, and guests. She recognized at once that Miles was not entirely at ease, due certainly to the formality of the occasion and the surroundings, and there was a certain stiffness in his bows and greetings which was not characteristic of his usually easygoing demeanor. Only when he had been seated beside her on the sofa did she sense that he was somewhat more relaxed, for when he looked to her and smiled, she saw the familiar warmth in his eye, which was just for her.

As was typical in the presence of an unknown guest, conversation tended toward topics of general interest, to which Miles willingly contributed, for he was never hesitant or reticent, however unfamiliar the environment. Before long, dinner was announced, and in the dining room, too, all went smoothly. Miles broached the subject of the University, as it was a common point for both Tom and himself, which proved a good topic, as many of the others at the table could also contribute, for most had spent some amount of time on the campus. Aunt Sarah was the only exception, having never even visited the University, and was thus inadvertently forced into uncharacteristic silence as the meal progressed.

It was the time after dinner which Lorna dreaded most. She would be left alone in the drawing room with the other women, and there would doubtlessly be comments and remarks sent her way as means of reactive judgment upon making the acquaintance of Mr. Anderson. She was to be pleasantly surprised in that regard, though, as the only one who mentioned him was Rosamond, who gave her hand a squeeze and whispered in her ear: "Your Mr. Anderson seems most agreeable."

It was meager praise, but Lorna could imagine that a girl like Rosamond would find Miles Anderson to be of little appeal on the surface. However, Lorna was content that Rosamond should not see deeper into his character, for the beliefs of her sister and her guest should certainly be discovered to be so opposite as to shock Rosamond and put off Miles, for though he had professed to be interested in a woman's intellect, Lorna knew he would scorn those who did not agree with his ideology.

The truth of the matter was that Lorna was more concerned about what ensued in her father's study, where the gentlemen adjourned after dinner and where she would not be present to interpose or moderate. While no lady could ever be certain as to precisely what gentlemen discussed over their brandy and cigars, she knew that politics and economics were likely topics, and both were areas where she would prefer that Miles should not share his very radical points of view. On the other hand, they may discuss nothing except sporting or racing or travel, which would be harmless enough as Miles would be able to contribute little input on such subjects.

The next hour ticked by slowly for Lorna in the drawing room. Edith and Rosamond, who always had a great deal to say to one another, had cloistered themselves in an alcove, so Lorna and her mother were left to listen to Aunt Sarah who, having been compelled into silence during dinner, compensated by giving free reign to her tongue once bereft of the men's presence. She talked mostly about her front parlor, which she was in the process of redecorating, and about her dissatisfaction with the ability of the London merchants to transport her new furnishings intact to Primrose Hill. This led to a reminiscence, shared by Mrs. Hathaway, of an incident from their childhood, which Lorna had heard a hundred times before, and to which she only half-listened.

At long last, footsteps were heard in the hallway, and the gentlemen appeared in the drawing room. Lorna was instantly aware of the quietness of the group, although she could not attribute this necessarily to anything Miles may have interposed, for no one else amongst the men was particularly garrulous upon any occasion, especially her father and Tom. She did experience some uneasiness, however, when she observed a great deal of whispering commencing in the alcove where Douglas Trainer had replaced Edith at Rosamond's side. He seemed to be doing all of the relating, while she received the information with wide and apprehensive eyes. If there was any unnatural discomposure amongst the gentlemen, though, Miles seemed oblivious to it as he joined Lorna and her companions, for his manner was as genial as ever, and when he gave Lorna such a disarming smile, she could not help but feel a tender warmth stir within her.

Rather than allow the situation to open itself to further discourse, Lorna immediately suggested a round of tableaux, which was very well-received amongst the young people, for it was a game in which all could partake with equal enjoyment. However, neither Lorna's parents nor her aunt wished to participate, contenting themselves with looking on and thus creating an odd number for the remaining participants, which made the groupings difficult to negotiate. At last it was decided that Hugh Shadwell, Douglas Trainer, and Rosamond should constitute a group of only three, while Lorna, Miles, Tom, and Edith should form the remaining party.

"I don't see how we shall possibly create a successful tableau with only three," fretted Rosamond when she was gathered with her group in one corner of the room.

"Why, it is simple enough," countered Mr. Trainer enthusiastically. "We shall make a perfect presentation of *Francesca Da Rimini*, for Rosamond surely looks just as Francesca must have, with her raven hair, and Mr. Shadwell will make a stalwart Giovanni, and I shall be Paolo!"

"Indeed?" Rosamond was unconvinced. "And why should not Hugh play Paolo? It seems hardly appropriate for a clergyman to play such a violent warrior as Giovanni." Her reasoning, in reality, had less to do with any opposition to Hugh portraying Giovanni as it did to her resistance to Douglas Trainer playing Paolo opposite her Francesca. But Hugh frustrated her effort, however unwittingly.

"Nonsense!" he cried. "That is the joy of play-acting . . . to portray a character against type. Nothing shall give me greater pleasure than to inhabit the role of the vengeful Giovanni!"

So the trio commenced their plans, and nothing is more assured than the joy Mr. Trainer received from portraying Francesca's ardent paramour.

Meanwhile, in the opposite corner of the room, the other young people were having difficulty in agreeing upon a subject for their tableau.

"Why not do *A Midsummer Night's Dream*?" suggested Tom. "We could easily portray the two pairs of lovers."

"Oh no," protested Lorna. "That would be too obvious." She immediately blushed, not intending her words to indicate that it was obvious that they should be two pairs of lovers in reality. But if anyone interpreted such a connotation it must only be Edith, whose cheek was also a bit crimsoned.

Neither gentleman seemed to take any meaning from her words, for Miles immediately interjected, "I've got it! If we're set upon Shakespeare, let us do *The Tempest*. Your brother and Miss Shadwell could be Ferdinand and Miranda, and you and I shall be Prospero and Ariel."

"Oh, I see," Lorna sniffed. "You have set me out to be your slave."

"Not at all," protested Miles. "It is only secondary that Ariel does Prospero's bidding."

"Indeed, Lorna," Tom persuaded, "most of us think of Ariel as only a beguiling spirit with an exceptionally clever mind who wants nothing more than to be free of Prospero's subjugation. The role suits you perfectly."

Edith was nodding her head, and it was clear that the whole party was enamored of the plan. Lorna sighed. "Very well then," she agreed. "I can see that I am outnumbered on this issue."

"Aha! This is a landmark day, indeed!" cried Miles jubilantly. "That Lorna should give in so readily. I have usually found her to be uncompromisingly set in her ways."

Even as Lorna laughed with him, she was conscious of the raised eyebrows opposite, and knew that Tom and Edith had not been unmindful of the familiar reference to herself. She quickly prodded the discourse on to the decision as to which scene they should portray.

Some ten minutes later, both groups were ready to present their tableaux. The smaller group's was guessed quite readily, for no one could mistake the look of doting admiration upon Paolo's face as he recited poetry to his Francesca (though it must be noted that her look was not nearly so convincing), nor the fiendish glare of Hugh's Giovanni as he beheld them from behind some "bushes" which were represented by two chairs pushed together.

The quartet's tableau proved a bit more difficult, for Ariel's eye kept wandering to her master, but the young lovers were quite credible playing chess and seemingly oblivious to the old sorcerer's observation.

All in all, Lorna was pleased at how the evening flowed, although she was still uncertain as to what had passed in the study after dinner. Before she knew it, the clock was intoning twelve chimes, and Hugh rose from his seat beside Aunt Sarah.

"Well, I must be off, I'm afraid," he announced. "I have to be up quite early tomorrow for an errand I'm not much looking forward to and will need to be well-rested before then."

"Really? Not a burial, I hope." That was Lorna, who would come to regret such pressing for information.

Hugh shook his head. "No, quite the opposite. One of the church council members has been remiss in getting his newest family member christened. The infant is a year old, and the wife appears regularly with the child, so you can imagine the reports I'm hearing from members of the congregation. I admit, I have rather put the issue off, as I was always hoping they would approach me to initiate the christening, but as they haven't, the time has come for me to broach the subject."

"I can see where that would be awkward," sympathized Rosamond.

"Especially on account of the father being a council member," added Mrs. Hathaway.

It was then that Miles chose to interject. "How can you be certain that the parents wish to have the infant baptized at all?"

Lorna's heart skipped a beat as she realized that Miles was going to be called on to elaborate upon one of his avid beliefs.

Hugh, and everyone else, seemed perplexed at this question.

"I beg your pardon?"

"Perhaps the parents have never approached you on the subject because they don't wish for their child to be christened." Miles rephrased his insinuation.

Aunt Sarah clucked her consternation. "Whatever are you talking about? Of course the parents would wish to baptize their child in the church!"

Miles shrugged. "Oh, I admit, most people seem to find it meaningful to have their young ones christened, but surely not all find pleasure in the rite."

There was a very significant silence during which Lorna observed the shocked expressions upon the faces of the circle gathered in the room. Her own pulse had so accelerated that she was feeling light-headed.

It was Douglas Trainer who finally broke the silence. "I hardly think 'pleasure' is the appropriate term to use in referring to the merits of baptism."

Miles turned a rather supercilious eye upon Mr. Trainer. "Then why would anyone engage in it?" he asked forthrightly.

Rosamond spoke up, her voice filled with incredulity. "People do not make decisions solely on the basis of whether or not they shall receive pleasure from the consequences."

Miles continued to be nonchalant. "Then they are fools. The amount of pleasure one receives should be the sole basis of all decisions."

Douglas Trainer, still at Rosamond's side, spoke again. "But that is absurd! Surely you cannot take such an unethical view. There are many decisions that people make based on their principles and what is morally correct, and which may bring them no pleasure, but instead the satisfaction that they have acted in a conscientious and ethical manner."

Miles remained calm, as one who is explaining something simplistically basic to a small child. "There are only two measures by which to judge conduct, and that is by the amount of pleasure or pain which results from the conduct. That which increases one's pleasure must be deemed as right conduct, that which brings pain is wrong. This is, of course, independent of one's intentions, which are meaningless. Only consequences can be judged, regardless of the intentions."

There was another long and uncomfortable silence as the others stared at Lorna's guest in disbelief. Lorna's worst fears had been realized. When she saw that Aunt Sarah, Mr. Trainer, her father, and Hugh were all ready to voice their disapproval, she jumped in first.

"Miles, please," she entreated, forgetting to address him formally. "Do not press this issue. This is not the appropriate forum."

Miles turned to her, frowning. "Do not forbid me to speak, Lorna.

There is nothing to gain by keeping one's ideas to oneself. How else shall new ideas come into the world? If you wished me to speak or act in ways which are not my custom, you should have rehearsed me before I entered this house tonight, for you know well enough my convictions. I can see that I have put you ill at ease, though, so I shall readily take my leave, as you know it is never my intention to discomfit you."

And yet he would not have the opportunity to depart first, for Lorna put her hand to her mouth to stifle a sob and abruptly ran out of the room and up the stairs, leaving a room full of people in the most awkward of situations, now heightened by her hasty withdrawal. Miles did not allow aggravation of the discomfort, though, for he followed her exit by giving an expedient bow to Mr. and Mrs. Hathaway, then departed without even retrieving his hat and coat.

Hugh and Edith ended up not leaving immediately after all, for the party that remained engaged in some earnest conversation, and by the time Rosamond went upstairs to look in on her sister, all were quite convinced that they had seen the last of Miles Anderson.

Lorna was the only one who did not share their postulation. For as the days went by, she found she could not be angry with him, and only affirmed in her own mind her love for him, though she never spoke of him, nor did her family ever mention his name in her presence. At the end of the week she was convinced of only one thing: that she must never again bring together Miles Anderson and Grosvenor Square.

Unlike her sister, Rosamond did not allow herself to dwell on her own feelings or convictions in matters of the heart, for doing so was far too dangerous. Certainly, the time she spent in the company of Frederick Lancaster was the sweetest happiness she had known; shut off from the world in the hushed and peaceful library of the Abercrombies' residence, indulging in nothing more harmful than the occasional shared gaze or unpretentious words. While they never spoke of anything personal during those quiet evenings, the words they left unspoken were far more eloquent than any they could have given voice to. Yet ever in the midst of this tranquil Arcadia was there projected a certain tragic quality which must necessarily accompany every endeavor where hope is futile, but clung to nonetheless. And enshrouding all of this — the beauty, the serenity, the tragedy — was one whose name was never uttered or acknowledged, but of whose invisible presence, hanging over them like a shadow, they were acutely aware.

It was only a few weeks after Lorna's unfortunate dinner party, on a warm and mild evening in mid-summer, that Rosamond sensed something was amiss. She and her parents were in attendance at one of the Abercrombies' gatherings, as usual, and when the guests began to move from the conservatory into the dining room, Rosamond took notice of the fact that the Earl of Kendal had not arrived. He never arrived very early, to be sure, and while he always made a point of greeting Rosamond, he rarely had any regular discourse with her until they were alone.

He had never arrived so late as to miss dinner. All throughout the meal, despite her attempts to appear engaged in the conversation going on around her, she could not help but think on the absent Earl. She chided herself for such presumptuous thoughts . . . surely there were a thousand reasons why he should be late, or why he should appear not at all. She had once heard Lady Abercrombie mention that Frederick was seldom consistent in his appearances. There was no reason to think he should continue on in the regular manner as had become his habit over the last months. Surely she could not flatter herself that he would attend merely to see her. That is what she told herself, but she found no consolation in such thoughts.

As she sat with the other ladies in the drawing room after dinner, she purposely kept close to her mother, for her mother's chattering would free her of the necessity of conversing. Even then, her thoughts strayed to the study where the gentlemen gathered, and she could not help wondering if Frederick was amongst them. However, when the gentlemen appeared in the drawing room, she saw immediately that it was only the same group as had been seated at the dinner table. It was somewhat easier to distract herself once the gentlemen joined them, for Douglas Trainer was an excellent conversationalist and managed to keep her mostly engaged.

When the doors to the card room were opened, Rosamond started to follow the other guests, but once again hesitated at the door, as she had that second evening. She could not dispel one notion which kept tugging at her mind. She must resolve the nagging question which had passed through her thoughts many times since the gentlemen returned from the study. So Rosamond did as she was accustomed; she turned away from the card room and crossed the wide hall to the library door. She felt her heart flutter with the trepidation of uncertainty as she took hold of the knob, but no fluttering could compare with the swelling of her heart as she opened the door and saw Frederick sitting in his usual chair in the dimly-lit room.

He rose as she entered and approached him, and said to her simply and gently, "I thought you would come."

"I almost did not," she admitted. "I was not certain you would be here. You . . . you were not at dinner, nor in the drawing room."

"No." He turned from her and walked to the window, which was open to try to catch any slight breeze that might penetrate the warm night. "No, I am in no mood for such a congregation."

Rosamond did not press him to elaborate, as she perceived that he was not disposed to do so. Instead, she took up a volume which she had begun to peruse last time and settled herself upon a sofa. But she could not maintain her focus, for she sensed from almost the first that something was amiss. Frederick was unusually restless, his darkly brooding countenance and pensive frown betrayed a disquietude that went beyond his habitual reticence. Whenever she spoke to him, he seemed only partially to listen, although nearly every time she looked up at him, she found his distracted gaze fixed upon her.

Yet, it was nothing Frederick did that brought Rosamond the greatest anxiety, but rather what he did not do, for he did not send her back out to the card room as he usually did after an hour or so. She had no wish to go — indeed, she never did — but the very fact of this aberrance led her to believe that her concern was warranted. Closing her volume, she quietly stole over to his chair and perched upon the ottoman at his knee, which she was wont to do.

"My lord," she said, looking up at him, "I cannot help but think that there is some weighty matter pressing upon you which is causing you grief."

Frederick frowned and rose, extending his hand to her, and as he gently pulled her to her feet he murmured, "I always dislike you sitting there in such a subservient manner. It seems ill-fitting a lady of your . . . refinement." He turned and walked restlessly over to the window, pulling shut one of its panels. When he turned back, Rosamond was still standing beside the ottoman, her countenance plainly dissatisfied at his evasion. Seeing this, he returned to her and said only, "Think not on it more. Such matters should never trouble you."

Rosamond knew that he was angry at himself for causing her consternation. She said no more, but glanced at the clock on the mantle, which was quietly chiming an hour long past her usual departure into the card room. Frederick looked at it, too, and said nothing, but only went back to the window and slipped again into his melancholy reverie.

Rosamond did not go into the card room that night, for despite his sullen moodiness, Frederick wanted her to stay, and she only left the library when she heard voices in the hall, indicating that the guests were departing. And afterwards, in spite of the Earl's bidding her to speculate not on his cares, her mind would not allow her such peace, for she had seen his troubled eyes.

Two days later, Rosamond received a note, which only increased her unease. She recognized the script, though she had seen it only once before. In keeping with the Earl's reticence, the message was brief — only one line:

I must see you before the week is out.

And yet in reading that one sentence, Rosamond's heart skipped a beat in apprehension. It was not like the Earl of Kendal to make such a request . . . he had never asked to see her before, and she knew that he would not have done so unless there was substantial cause.

She reflected on how such a meeting could be arranged. Often, on Sundays, she and Edith would walk in the park after church if the weather was fair. Edith had already told Rosamond that she had another obligation this week, but her family did not know that. They would not think it remarkable should she head in the direction of the park after church. She hastily scrawled a message to the Earl, indicating the time and location and sent it off to Belgravia, but she could not send off the feeling of foreboding that overshadowed her heart.

The winter garden was to be their meeting-point, as it was certain to be peaceful and unoccupied at this time of year, and as Rosamond approached it from the old Elm Path, she saw that Frederick was already there, waiting at the gate. She quickened her pace as he came forth to meet her.

"I am sorry if I am late," she apologized. "The sermon was unusually lengthy today. I came as quickly as I could, though I did forget my gloves in my haste."

Her endeavor to keep her tone light and ordinary did not deceive him. He gave her a fondly abstracted smile, even as his eyes retained their somber contemplation.

"You need not apologize," he assured her. "I have only just arrived.

Come," he nodded toward the garden gate, "let us walk."

They passed together through the gate into the winter garden, now barren and deserted and empty of foliage in the summer's heat, and made their way along the path toward the distant arbor.

"I shall not keep you long. I daresay you have things of more importance to attend to today." His tone was thus far even, but the calm terseness of his next words seemed affected. "I did not want to leave London without bidding you goodbye."

Rosamond halted rather abruptly, and Frederick's attempted brusqueness faltered as he turned to her and beheld her face — so grave and serious. Seeing her thus, his own eyes blazed with that familiar dark flame which must always reveal what words would mask. Such was the end of their walk, for neither seemed inclined to take further step, and instead stood where Rosamond had paused upon hearing his words, confronting one another.

"You . . . you are leaving the city?"

"I only stay in London for the Sessions. Once the season is over, I must return to my—," He broke off. "To my home in Cumbria," he finished with a falter. "As it is, the season is already well past."

In his typically reticent fashion, he did not elaborate as to why he had stayed longer, and Rosamond did not allow herself to conjecture any reason.

"And will you not return to London?" Her own futile attempt at nonchalance was offset by her beseeching eyes, searchingly trained upon him.

Frederick looked away and, after a pause, said, "By the time I return, I expect you will have married and be well established in a home of your own." He looked at her once again, his black eyes sullen in their gaze. "You ought to marry Douglas Trainer. He is a good man . . . and he is very much in love with you."

But the severity of his gaze gave way to a softer distraction as he saw her deep blue eyes cloud. He bent his head close to hers.

"Poor Rosamond," he whispered. "No one ever regards your own feelings in such matters of the heart. Someday you will find one, though, whom you shall love well."

He did not dare let her utter the words which she would have next spoken, but instead shushed her with a finger upon her lips and a slight shake of his head. "Do not give yourself to one you do not love. Wait until you find one who is worthy of your affection."

And in that brief moment, they two were alone in the world, and their defenses were utterly abandoned. There was no more pretense of indifference or decorum. The anguished torment reflected in their eyes was apparent, and bound them in ways that rendered words inadequate.

Finally Frederick took a step back. "And now," his tone was quietly firm, though not unkind, "Now, I shall send you home, and you shall obey, just as if I was sending you into the card room from our little library."

Rosamond did not move, despite his command. Frederick reached out and took hold of her hand. He pressed his lips softly against her fingertips.

"Good-bye, Rosamond," he murmured, and released her hand only very reluctantly. "Now go."

And she did. She left the winter garden before she could say or feel or think more. She left as if she feared that staying a moment longer would cause her to leave behind that which he had directed her to retain. Rosamond knew it was best that she should never see the Earl of Kendal again, but she knew not how to reconcile her heart to such a prospect.

Chapter XI

During the course of the next few weeks, Rosamond did her best to focus her attention upon those occupations which had always engaged her. If she nurtured within her heart any sadness or poignancy, she made effort to conceal it from her family and friends. There was little to cheer her, though, in the events that unfolded in the following months. Douglas Trainer did indeed propose to her, but her rejection, delivered in the most compassionate manner, did nothing to deter his suit or dampen his admiration for her.

Rosamond was not the only member of her family to face some inner turmoil during those months, as the warm summer days gave way to early autumn. Tom also contended with his own tribulations. Still in the grasp of the dolorous iniquity which had gripped him for so long and which he had strived in vain to overcome, he must wage a silent war upon himself, though what a covert battle it must be for him. The best days were those when he thought not on it; the worst when his shame and self-loathing overtook his senses. The latter scenario was becoming the more frequent and was brought into its fullest fruition as the result of a situation, made known to him by none other than Rosamond, who, while not unsympathetic herself, could not have realized the extent of her brother's grief.

It was an unusually cool autumn evening, and Tom had stayed at the club a bit later than his father. He decided to take a cab back to Grosvenor Square as the hour was late, but when he arrived home, he saw that there was light emitting from the parlor, although it was past the hour when any of his household were usually still downstairs. He guessed it must be Lorna, for she sometimes stayed up longer than the others, though she had been much absent of late. However, when he entered the hall, it was not Lorna but his younger sister who came to the door of the parlor and greeted him. Tom expressed his surprise that she should be sitting up so late.

"I was waiting for you," Rosamond replied. "Come into the parlor, Tom. There is something I must tell you."

He could see by his sister's countenance that this was a matter of importance, and leaving his hat upon the hall table, he followed her into the parlor. They took seats upon the little matched chairs before the fireplace, but no sooner had they sat down than Rosamond stood again, apparently too agitated to rest. She did not keep him in suspense, but went straight to her purpose.

"You know I went to the Elgars' for tea today?"

Tom nodded, though he'd really no idea of where she took her tea, as he had been out himself.

She went on, distractedly fidgeting with her handkerchief as she talked. "There were a great many people there, including Edith and her parents. I spoke with them, of course, but only very generally as there were so many other people about. But after the tea had been cleared away, and everyone went to go look at Mr. Elgar's new billiard table, Edith asked me to stay a moment in the parlor, as she had some news which could not be shared before the other guests." Rosamond paused, still wringing her handkerchief.

Tom knit his brow in puzzlement. "Why should she not? Edith often confides in you."

"Yes, I know, but—," Rosamond turned to her brother. Seeing her consternation, he rose from his chair and walked over to her. She spoke gently to him, as one who must relate tidings which are bound to bring unhappiness. "Oh, Tom . . . Edith has accepted a proposal. She is going to be married."

Tom stared at his sister as if he did not comprehend her words. "Edith….married? To whom?"

Rosamond hesitated, then said, "To Mr. Charles Byrd."

"Mr. Charles Byrd? Who the devil is that?"

Rosamond shook her head. "I know so little about him. I only met him on one occasion . . . at the Shadwells' several months ago, and I had no idea he was to make a declaration."

Tom said nothing, but turned away and walked slowly toward the gilt-edge cabinet on the far wall, where he paused, still with his back to her. Rosamond took a few steps toward him.

"I'm rather confused about it all myself. I was so shocked when she told me . . . I . . . I just didn't think to ask for many details. I really am uncertain as to how and when it all came about."

Tom still did not face her, but said, "I thought you were her dearest friend. It is strange that you would know nothing about such a significant relationship."

Rosamond sighed. "I know. Yet as much as Edith and I confide in one another, some things must always remain private. And she is so gentle and mild-mannered, she may have been too bashful to confess such a thing, especially to me, as you are my brother." Rosamond's face flushed as soon as she uttered the last words, and Tom glanced back at her rather sharply. Rosamond took a few more tentative steps toward him. "How is it that *you* had no idea?"

Tom shrugged and turned back to the cabinet again. "I have not seen her much of late," he muttered. "It seems we see more of Hugh than his sister."

Rosamond nodded thoughtfully. "Yes, and since he is residing at the vicarage, I suppose the happenings in Hanover Square are not so prevalent in his conversation. Now that she is engaged, though, I daresay he will relate it more freely."

"And why should he not?" Tom turned abruptly and walked back toward the windows. "After all, an engagement is a felicitous occasion and should rightfully be shared." He paused in his step. "When are they publishing the banns?"

"Next week, I believe. Tom — I . . . I am sorry."

Now it was Tom who flushed, then shook his head. "You should not be. She is your friend . . . you ought to be happy for her. I'm sure she is counting on you to share in her joy and preparations."

There was a brief silence as brother and sister were each lost in their own meditations. Finally, Rosamond stirred and crossed to Tom. She kissed him tenderly on the cheek, saying simply, "Good-night, dear Tom." And she crossed to the door, leaving her brother to the silence and peace of blessed solitude.

It was quite early the following day when Tom was admitted into the Shadwells' parlor with a servant's promise that Miss Edith would be right in. Although he had sat in their parlor dozens of times in his life since his earliest childhood, on this day he felt none of its familiar comfort and did not even notice the new tapestried carpet before the fireplace.

Edith entered from the dining room, unobtrusive as always, still in her morning-cap, and she, too, seemed a trifle uneasy as she greeted him, even in her own home. They sat opposite one another, she on the sofa and he in the armchair, still clutching his hat, as he intended this interview to be but brief.

"I hope it is no inconvenience to you, my calling so early," began Tom.

"Of course not . . . you know you are welcome here at any hour." Edith's soft voice was warm, despite her unusual peakedness, but somehow such warmth did little to bring Tom comfort.

He glanced down for a moment at his hat in his hand before continuing. "I . . . Rosamond told me of your news . . . your engagement, that is." Edith blushed, and not only due to modesty. Tom went on. "I . . . I just wanted to come and offer my congratulations. You know that I would always wish you the greatest happiness."

Neither his tone nor his look seemed to mirror his sentiment, and upon observing her reception of these words, he was only grieved more. She gave a little smile, and with an inclination of her fair head, politely acknowledged his convictions. But there was a certain wistfulness in her eye that cut him to the core.

He knew he had no rightful claim upon her affections. There had been no professions of love, no smoldering glances, no rapturous embraces. No mention of devotion. No promises, ever. There had been nothing of substance other than a quietly understood affection, a warmhearted fondness between two bashful souls and the expectation of others that an attachment was impending. And yet, he had given her no reason to believe that any such declaration was forthcoming. He had, of late, sorely neglected their friendship, as he had neglected much that had once been dear to him; sacrificed to that vice which seduced him still, and whose agent rested even now within easy reach. He knew that he should have been the one to make her a proposal, and glimpsing her wistfulness, he knew equally well what her answer would have been. But in his negligence, she had continued on with her life and taken new acquaintances and new interests to heart, of which he had not even been cognizant.

Pondering all of this, now all he could do was look at her helplessly and say, "Edith . . . I . . . I wish it was me. I wish it could have been me."

And as he beheld her plaintive sorrow, Tom hated himself. He hated his powerlessness, he hated his flawed judgment, and most of all he hated that weakness which prevented him even now from saying what she would have liked to hear.

He rose, overcome with emotion, his brain swelling with self-loathing, and, choking on his words, voiced what needed to be said. "I am so sorry . . . I am sorry for everything. Sorry for the wrongs I have done you.

There was a time—," He stopped himself. Tears had sprung into Edith's eyes, which only increased his vexation. His voice heightened as he went on. "But that time is past. I cannot will it back. I cannot ask you to marry me, even were you not promised to another. You will not understand, but have no doubts upon what you are entering into. It is for the best. I can say no more, except to reassure you that it is for the best. You may enter into this engagement with a free heart and no regrets."

His voice had grown uncharacteristically loud and hardened, and he despised himself all the more for the startled alarm he had provoked upon her countenance. He would not prolong this. There could be no fitting closure now. His mind groped for something to say that would provide a means of departure. Striving to regain some composure, and to end with at least the semblance of dignity, he donned his hat and said, "Do not think ill of Rosamond for revealing to me what has not yet been publicized. She is ever your devoted friend and intended no disloyalty."

And with a curt nod, he made as to exit, but was halted by Edith's voice.

"Tom!"

He turned. Edith had risen and now took a step nearer, her eyes no longer misty with tears, but soft with affection. She smiled that same shy smile that was familiar to him, and spoke words which exemplified her goodness.

"I should never think ill of her, or of anyone in the Hathaway family. They have been my dearest friends since my youth and provided me with my fondest memories, and I shall not love them less once I am married."

Tom walked briskly along the quay, his hands thrust deep into his pockets, the bright sunlight forcing his eyes downward. It was not yet noon, and there were many other people about — men and women, nurses and children, vendors, river workers — all enjoying the warm brightness and pleasantness of the views, but he was oblivious to them all. He was numb with anger at himself, disgusted with his consciousness. It was an emotion he was unfamiliar with, and thus uncomfortable in its expression. And so he walked. On and on, he traversed the entire quay, then turned around and reversed his path.

Not only plagued by anger, he was frightened also. Frightened of himself . . . frightened of his inability to discipline his intemperance. Frightened at the power such a demon held over him. Neither Jasper's nor Lorna's words had been enough to persuade him to shed his vice . . . only to redirect it to a further degree of covertness. And it had brought him only misery and shame, while robbing him of life and hope.

He fingered the little glass vessel within his pocket, then clutched it tighter as his anger and fright increased. How many more friends must be hurt? How many more family members disappointed? How many more dreams deferred? Tom concluded that it could come to only one happening: Either the consuming fire must be eradicated, or he must be consumed.

Still fingering the flask, he thought on their faces: Edith's sadness . . . Lorna's concern . . . Rosamond's bewilderment . . . Jasper's sneer. How he had inadvertently touched all of their lives, and none for the better!

As these images came to him, he was filled with a new resolution. There would be an end to it. It would end this day, this very moment. There would be no more secrecy, no more deception, no more guilt, no more grief. How he would cope, he did not know, but he would sustain himself somehow.

Slowing his pace, he pulled the bottle from concealment, eyeing it with hatred. The wickedness contained therein would hold him captive no more. Stepping up to the quay's rail, he surveyed the river below. Then, propelled by his emotion, he hurled the bottle with all his might onto the rocky bank below and walked away with never a backward glance.

It must not be thought that all of the young Hathaways were struggling with matters of the heart. Lorna had no such conflicts. She was very certain as to whom she loved, and she had the satisfaction of knowing that he loved her in return. She had struggles of a different nature, though, yet hers were bound to induce the greatest repercussions.

Lorna's conflict was made apparent to her as she sat with her family in church one Sunday morning. It was no different than any other Sunday: the family filed into their pew, the organ played, the hymn was sung. Lorna's father would give her a stern look if she did not sing, which was the case this day. The vicar ascended his pulpit, the congregation sat, and the sermon commenced. It was all very familiar, yet Lorna felt a difference in herself.

True, she harbored a secret knowledge . . . a decision which filled her with both exhilaration and dread. Yet this decision was not the source of her present misgiving, for she had no doubts upon its justification. No, the uneasy discrepancy she felt had to do only with the church itself, or perhaps the congregation, or — her brow wrinkled as the possibility came to her — the family seated beside her.

She had loved them always — father, mother, brother, sister. Yet something had changed of late . . . not the love itself, perhaps, but something more ambiguous, something below the surface of love. She glanced sidelong at them now, and, as they were intent upon listening to the sermon, so did she intently study each face.

First her father . . . sitting so tall and upright, so masterfully competent in securing wealth, yet always so fondly proud of his family. Lorna loved her father tremendously; had always felt they had a special bond, in spite of his immersion in his business affairs. And her mother . . . of course, she loved her mother, too, and she knew how much her mother doted on and adored her children. Yet Lorna could not deny that, even from her childhood, she and her mother had divergent sensibilities, which must necessarily put up some impediment to unmitigated closeness. Lorna knew that her mother sometimes found her puzzling, and that good woman, no doubt, could better relate to her younger daughter, upon whose face Lorna next turned her focus. The bond between sisters must ever be strong, however discrepant their interests, and Lorna and Rosamond duly shared a deep affection. Rosamond was indisputably bright and virtuous — even now was she earnestly attentive to the parson's words, as Lorna's own thoughts strayed. Yet, Rosamond's charm also encompassed an intrinsic seriousness which sometimes unsettled Lorna's free spirit. And Tom . . . dearest to her of all. Who could help but love Tom, with his quiet sincerity and unaffected goodness? Yet Lorna, more than any, knew that her kind-hearted brother was not invulnerable to such temptations as would be repulsed by a stouter will. Even so, he had been her closest companion in childhood and her dearest friend in youth.

Yet now, as she beheld and reflected upon her closest relations, she perceived the disconnectedness that had made her feel disparate. Between herself and each of them was there now a distance, not put there by choice, but by necessity. Ever since that night when Miles Anderson was brought into Grosvenor Square did there begin to be such a distance, which she had unconsciously built as a sort of primordial defense against the decision she had made. And now there was a chasm between them; a chasm where her family was ranged together on one precipice, while she herself was alone on the opposite one. But was there a bridge? Would there be a bridge after her decision was made known? Therein lay the quandary which now caused her some consternation. It never occurred to her to doubt her decision; she only doubted her family.

And as she sat there pondering this, she became more and more agitated. Her insides felt tense, her face grew hot. She could not be there, beside them. They did not understand. They would not comprehend. She looked about her. Everyone was engrossed and entranced in the sermon

— a hundred pairs of eyes focused on the promises of God, the merits of virtue. The vicar's words were not for her. They were for her parents, for Tom, for Rosamond. For those who wanted to believe them. Not for her, who wanted to shut them out. The words touched a part of her she did not want to confront . . . she would not confront. Here was evidence of a new influence: She was not there by choice, therefore she did not belong.

It was then that Lorna Hathaway, who had always resisted her deepest impulses, at last gave in. In the midst of the sermon, she rose from the pew and, without hesitation, walked straight down the aisle and out of the church. She could not stay.

As the ancient seat of the Earls of Kendal, the manor house at Stoneleigh was befittingly magnificent and imposing. For almost 300 years it had awed and impressed all who had the fortune of resting within its grey-stone walls, and the passage of time had only increased its inspiring grandeur. Its idyllic rural location at the edge of the Lake District in Cumbria made it the perfect setting for country gatherings and hunting-parties, of which it hosted many. And in the autumn and winter months, when the wind blows cold through northern England, its immense fireplaces provided abundant warmth and comfort across its vast interior.

It was just such a day — gusty and grey and on the threshold of a rain-shower — when the present Earl of Kendal withdrew into his study and situated himself in his favorite armchair before the roaring fire. Every room at Stoneleigh was immense, but this one appealed to him on such a blustery day, for there was only one door which, when closed, provided ample solitude for one inclined to ponder. And if his countenance was telling, Frederick Lancaster was in no humor for idle pleasantries.

He sat for a very long while, leaning back in his chair, staring into the fire, his sullen dark eyes seeing not the bright flames, but brooding upon some inward predicament. Every now and then he would shift restlessly, but for the most part he remained still, his eyes fixed on the fire, his mind deep in reverie.

He gave only a cursory glance upward when the study door opened and a woman stepped into the room. She was tall and thin, wearing an elegantly stylish riding habit, her yellow hair pulled up into a loose knot atop her head. She paused just inside the door, with her hand still upon the latch.

"Duncan said you wished to see me." Her voice was as cool as her blue eyes.

Frederick still kept his eyes upon the fire. "Yes, come in."

"I really don't have time right now." The woman's tone was proud. "Can't it wait? I've only just come in from riding and have to dress for dinner."

"No, it cannot wait. Come in, and shut the door." Frederick's voice was very firm, even as his tone remained calm. The woman obeyed with markedly resentful demeanor. He eyed her somewhat critically. "It's rather nasty weather for a ride, isn't it?"

"You know perfectly well I ride every day. Besides, I've seen you ride out often enough in gales worse than this." She was clearly impatient. "Is your purpose in commanding my presence here merely idle chatter? I would not think it, knowing you."

Frederick remained unfazed by her impatience. He paused, looking back toward the fire, before he responded. "It may be a fine idea, that. Would you object to such discourse? It would surely benefit us both."

"I cannot think what you mean."

Frederick looked directly at her. "What I mean, Cassandra, is that in the four months since I have left London, I have seen you but little and had meaningful discourse with you even less."

"What are you talking about?" Her tone was brusque. "Two of those months you spent with your brothers, traipsing off to the other side of the world on a hunting expedition."

"And the other two months?"

The Countess frowned. "I see you and speak with you every day . . . at meals . . . in the evenings . . . it is no different than usual."

Frederick rose. "Neither do you attend social events. I find I am constantly making excuses for your absence. It makes a rather poor impression upon our tenants and friends, don't you think?"

"I have many duties which occupy my time," she said irritably. "I cannot attend every dinner party or christening in the region. Now if you will kindly permit me to go and prepare—,"

"No, I will not." His command was abrupt and silenced her. "In fact," he continued calmly, gesturing toward a chair, "I would prefer if you would be seated."

She looked at him a moment with those icy blue eyes, then took the seat indicated. He sat again in his armchair.

"I am curious to know . . ." he went on, "what is it that so occupies your time?"

For the first time, the Countess looked a trifle nonplussed. "I — I'm sure that you must know. The servants, correspondence, the horses . . . ."

"Ah yes, the horses. Your favorite pastime. You are fortunate to have the finest stable in England at your disposal. I would almost have deduced that they were your reason for marrying me, except that I had not yet acquired most of them at that time." He turned his eye upon her again. "You are somewhat disheveled after your ride. I wonder what should have caused such disarray? The wind? The horse? The groom?"

With his dark eyes still trained intently upon her, her face turned ashen. She held her head erect, even as her voice wavered. "What are you implying?"

Frederick shrugged, ever composed. "A ruddier man I never saw. It is well that you are so attentive to your duties in my absence as to keep the servants happy. Our groom truly takes excellent care of my horses — the best I've had, in fact — so I suppose we must do what it takes to keep him on, mustn't we?"

The Countess rose abruptly, her eyes livid. "If you are insinuating that I—,"

But Frederick waved a hand that she should be seated again. His own eyes gleamed their black intensity, even as his tone remained careless. "Oh, you need not deny it. I would advise you, however, to take better care in selecting your friends. You did not mention in your letters that Maria Cade was here to visit you in the spring."

The Countess's haughty anger seemed to have turned to some trepidation, but she strove to maintain her composure. "Maria Cade?"

Frederick nodded. "Yes, that woman had the audacity to appear at my house in London after she had seen you." He was clearly displeased and frowned at the recollection. "At any rate, if you must choose such disreputable friends, you ought to be more discreet in what you confide to them. A woman like that has no notion of loyalty, although I cannot think what favor she hoped to have gained by such a revelation. By the way . . . I have forbidden her to ever cross my threshold again, either here or in London, so there may be some awkwardness there for you."

The Countess started to interject, but again Frederick waved her off. "Oh, have no fear. Your indiscretions are no concern of mine. I'm afraid I cannot guarantee as much for our hapless groom, though. Naturally, I shall be obliged to dismiss him, which is a pity."

The Countess said nothing, merely glared.

Frederick observed her, his own eyes narrowing. "It is correct what you say, Cassandra." He spoke in a somewhat softer tone. "There is nothing unusual in our lack of communication or in the negligible time we spend together. It has always been our way, hasn't it? Yet, it is only recently that I have become aware of such deficiency." He rose, and moved toward the fireplace. "No, I have not requested your presence here for mere idle discourse, nor to humiliate or shame you. The truth is, I would ask something of you."

Still the Countess remained silent, eyeing him coldly.

Frederick continued. "I shall be returning to London soon and should like you to come with me."

"Is that what you would ask of me?" Her tone was scornful. "You know I never go to London. I cannot abide the place, especially during the season." She rose. "So, you have your answer . . . now may I go?"

Frederick looked at her for a long moment. She averted her eyes uncomfortably, for despite her disdain, she had sense enough to know that she lacked any power or authority.

Frederick at last spoke, very low and very firm. "I think it would be best if you came."

Her icy blue eyes looked directly into his. "Is that a command?"

"I would not command you, though it is my right to do so. I would much prefer that you came of your own choosing."

"I have already told you that I do not care for the city. Is that not reason enough for me to stay here?"

Frederick looked at her with some contempt. "It would be seemlier were your choices made in accordance with your duties, which may not always accommodate your preferences. It is only fitting that a wife should be at her husband's side, though it has never been your custom. Now, I shall ask you one last time . . . will you accompany me to London?"

She glared defiantly. "No."

After a pause, Frederick turned back to the fireplace. His tone was gravely steady. "Then I think it is time we put this pretense behind us. I am going to set you free, Cassandra."

Her next words pierced the silence like a steely cutlass. *"What do you mean by that?"*

He turned back to face her. She had turned bloodlessly white.

Frederick did not mince words. "I mean that I am going to divorce you."

Cassandra stood there, fixed, staring at him in disbelief, her eyes wide with fear. She could barely utter the words: "Divorce . . . you wouldn't!"

Frederick did not reply, only stood where he was, easily meeting her gaze with his unyielding black eyes. Her arrogant voice heightened feverishly in her agitation as she advanced to where he stood.

"You are the Earl of Kendal! You cannot just divorce your wife as if you were merely ridding yourself of a simple nuisance! We are people of rank and responsibility with ties that bind!" By now, her seething countenance was directly confronting his own. "You would not dare!"

"I'm afraid I would dare, and I am going to." His tone remained steadfastly even, but his unrelenting stance and forceful gaze caused her to back a step away. He continued in a more subdued voice. "We have never loved one another, you and I, not from the beginning. There has never been any affectation of love between us."

"Then why did you marry me?" she asked bitterly. "You could have had any girl in the realm easily enough."

"You well know that it was our families made the match, as is the custom of our pedigree."

"You could have objected to the match."

Frederick contemplated a moment before he replied. "I was an ignorant young fool then. I knew nothing of life or of love. I thought love existed merely in the imaginations of poets and novelists. My impression of marital happiness was that if spouses were fortunate, as the years passed they would develop a respect for one another that was termed 'love'. If they were not so fortunate, the respect would not grow between them, and they would sustain toleration of one another. In my mind, when one entered a marital contract, it was purely chance as to whether it would end in respect or tolerance. But I have since been enlightened. I know now that love is not analogous to mere respect. We have never loved one another . . . we have not even fostered that deeper respect that I imagined. We never should have married."

"A pretty speech!" Cassandra's voice was contemptuous. "You are the last person on earth I would expect to hear utter such words, speaking so freely of love. What has love to do with it? People of our kind do not marry for love! We marry because it is our duty, our responsibility to maintain our birthright and heritage. The peace and stability of our country relies on alliances between houses such as ours!" She stopped suddenly as a thought occurred to her, then turned to the Earl. "Do not tell me you have fallen in love? It must be, else why would you speak of it so?"

Her words were bold, and he would not condescend to her conceit. He simply said, quietly, "It was a mistake that we should have ever married. I am sorry."

His resolute composure only served to fuel her hysteria.

"And what if you are in love?" she cried out, ignoring his words. "Is that reason to sever your marriage contract? Men of your rank regularly engage in such liaisons while their wives look the other way. I am willing to do as much!"

In hearing her pathetic appeal, he could only frown and shake his head. "No." He averted his steady gaze and murmured, "I would not dishonor her so."

Cassandra's response was caustically accusing. "You *do* love another! You would willingly accept the scandal of divorce and put another in my place!"

Frederick's ominous lower revealed to the Countess that she had touched on a precarious subject. But once again he would not condescend to her contemptibility. His dark eyes blazed, but his voice betrayed some pain. "No, Cassandra. I have no reason to believe she would accept such a proposal . . . especially not now."

"Then it would be all for nothing!" Cassandra seethed in her rage and desperation. "You would disrupt our lives . . . *my* life . . . all to no purpose! You cannot do it!" She approached him again, her voice trembling in her panic. "You would frame it as giving me freedom, but you know such a divorce would be condemnation. Would you ruin me?"

Frederick was not entirely unmoved, though he remained firm. "I realize that the repercussions of such a situation are invariably harder upon a woman, and I shall defend your honor to the last if that would mollify you. And while I cannot deny that it will bring unwanted attention upon both of us, I would hardly think that it would bring about your ruination." His tone became harder. "Such terminology applies to those seeking husbands, and I think that you shall no longer be burdened with that life-task. I will give you a handsome settlement . . . that should ease any concerns you may have as to your fortune or comfort. I should think such an arrangement would suit you . . . you can return to your family and friends in Waterford, where, as you have reminded me on several occasions, you were much happier than here in Cumbria. And you will have no obligations. You may take whatever you want . . . take the horses if it will make you happy . . . take the groom. I do not care," he ended restlessly, weary of discussion and moodily pensive once more.

He sat again before the fire as the Countess stood near the center of the room, her face pale, her eyes full of cold hatred. Neither one spoke again, and after a few moments of silence, the Countess swept out of the room, taking her bitterness with her.

Chapter XII

Tom's desk was situated directly outside his father's office door, and when a young man entered Mr. Hathaway's office bearing a message, Tom took no notice of it, as messages were delivered to his father a dozen times a week. This particular message, though, elicited a response that necessarily distinguished it from the others. Nearly upon the heels of the departing messenger, Mr. Hathaway hurried from his office, still clutching the note in his hand. He paused only a moment at his son's desk, and Tom was taken aback at his father's grim visage.

"I'm going home," Mr. Hathaway said abruptly. "Tell Mr. Bates I will not be able to meet with him today. I don't know when I shall return. If I am not back by twelve, have Cadogan cancel my afternoon meeting as well." And before Tom could utter a response, his father had hurried away.

Mr. Hathaway did not return to his office for the remainder of the day, and Tom went home at tea-time to allay his curiosity on the matter. However, upon his arrival in Grosvenor Square, he found nothing to satisfy his curiosity, and only such anomaly as must pique it further. For the house was unusually quiet, and no table had been laid out for tea in the parlor. The only faint sound he heard came from the distant kitchen, and the only person to be found was a disconsolate Rosamond, sitting forlornly in the morning room, idly watching the grains of sand pass through the hourglass she held in her hand, though her abstracted gaze indicated that her mind was not set upon those particles.

When she saw her brother, Rosamond jumped up, setting the hourglass back upon the side-table, and hurried over to him. "Oh, Tom! I'm so glad you're home! Where has Father gone?"

Tom knit his brow in puzzlement. "You would know better than I. He said he was coming here. Did he not?"

Rosamond nodded, her eyes troubled. "He did come home just about eleven o'clock, but he and Mother went directly into his study and stayed shut up in there for more than an hour. I cannot think what they were discussing . . . surely it must be a matter of great importance for Father to come home in the middle of the day!"

"Did our mother say nothing to you before he came home?"

Rosamond shook her head. "I was at Aunt Sarah's most of the morning. I only just arrived back here right before Father."

Tom was still standing in the doorway of the room, and he now glanced into the hall. "The door to the study is open," he observed. "Where are they now?"

Rosamond shrugged in perplexity. "Father left the house almost as soon as they emerged. He said not a word to me . . . but his face, Tom, if you could have seen it!" She shuddered at the recollection. "I should not have crossed him then for the world!"

Tom frowned. "And our mother?"

"She went directly upstairs . . . saying only that she didn't feel well. I have not seen her since. She did not even come down for tea, so it seemed senseless to have Agnes set it up as no guests were expected. I did not know you were coming," she added apologetically.

Tom smiled absently at his sister and patted her arm. "Where is our sister?"

"Who can say where Lorna is? She rarely comes down to breakfast, and I left before she appeared. She was already out when I came back. But now that you're here, let's have tea in here or in the library. It doesn't seem right in the parlor without Mother presiding over the tea table."

It was a rather strangely stagnant afternoon for the two siblings, for there was a hushed tension pervading the house caused by anxiety of the unknown. They both tried to occupy themselves, but neither expressed a desire to go out anywhere . . . their mixed curiosity and sense of foreboding compelled them to stay within the house. Neither their father nor Lorna returned, and as dusk fell, a servant brought word from Mrs. Hathaway that Tom was to escort Rosamond to dinner at the Shipleys', as she herself was still indisposed.

There was little relief for Tom and Rosamond's apprehension the next morning. Tom found his mother in the breakfast room, still in her wrapper, and looking quite peaked. She greeted him, nonetheless, with a weak smile and her usual, "Good morning, my dear."

As Tom sipped his coffee, he wondered if he should ask about the proceedings of the previous day, and decided to wait until one or both of his sisters appeared. If Lorna came down, she would be certain to make inquiries, if she knew of the situation. However, only Rosamond appeared, and breakfast was a fairly awkward affair . . . with only feeble attempts at conversation. Both siblings were waiting for their mother to speak, and their mother seemed just as interested in keeping the topic directed away from any family matters.

As the plates were cleared away, she rose from her chair and said, as if an afterthought, "Oh, my dears, just so you know . . . your father has been called away on some business, and Lorna has gone to stay with some friends in the country, so you are not likely to see either one today." She pressed her fingers to her temple. "I am still feeling poorly, so I am going to lie down." And she left the room, looking poorly indeed.

Her explanation had been entirely unsatisfactory and left Tom and Rosamond with many unanswered questions and no comfort.

At the office, Tom found that his father's secretary, Mr. Cadogan, had been apprised of Mr. Hathaway's absence, but could not — or would not — provide Tom with any elucidation as to his father's whereabouts or expected return. And Rosamond had as much uncertainty at home, for Aunt Sarah Blakely arrived shortly after breakfast, complete with a small valise, and established herself in one of the guest bedrooms, citing that she "had come to look after dear Sister, who is ailing, in her husband's absence."

Rosamond was highly skeptical of this explanation, for her mother's malaise could hardly be so dramatically termed as "ailing" or necessitate the care of Aunt Sarah, who had given no prior demonstration of any nursing expertise. But Rosamond's subtle inquiries of her aunt produced no explanations, and the senior lady spent the remainder of the day sequestered in Mrs. Hathaway's room, although Rosamond herself had been told that her mother was not to be disturbed.

Neither Tom nor Rosamond went out that night, and only Aunt Sarah sat down with them to dinner, her thin lips pinched in the kind of grim disapproval in which she reveled, but upon the causation of such relished disfavor she would not elaborate.

The next day, Tom came home to find that Mr. Hathaway had returned, though he had not made his appearance at the office. He did not see his father immediately, however, and had only Rosamond's word that he had come home about an hour earlier and seemed troubled, but had gone directly upstairs and was now conversing again with their mother. Aunt Sarah was simultaneously taking her leave, no doubt a bit miffed that she was not included in the conference, but shaking her head and clucking to her heart's content.

Even as the family sat down together at the dinner table that evening, there remained a tautness in the parents' demeanor that bespoke of a grave weight upon their consciousness. Both Tom and Rosamond wished their sister were there, for Lorna would surely be able to elicit some explanation from their father, but when Rosamond pressed her mother about Lorna's return from the country, Mrs. Hathaway would only shake her head and declare that she did not know when to expect her, then turned the strained conversation to other matters of general interest.

Despite their father's return, the household did not return to its usual easy pleasantness in the next few days; the parents being morosely silent, the young people filled with unease at such rigid ambiguity. And Rosamond soon discovered that she was to have no peace as she awaited her sister's return, for it was only four days after Lorna's departure to the country that Rosamond received a message which sent her very being into tumult.

The missive was delivered one afternoon as she sat with Edith — now Mrs. Charles Byrd — and some other young ladies in the parlor, discussing plans for the upcoming Winter Promenade. Rosamond was, truthfully, only half-participating in the discussion, as the weight of her household's problems was still upon her. When the maid walked in and, bobbing a curtsey, handed Rosamond the note, Rosamond was only too glad to have some distraction. However, as soon as she opened the message, she gave such a gasp and turned so suddenly pale that her friends took immediate notice.

"Rosamond! What is it?" cried Edith, with great concern.

Rosamond would not give her friend proper answer, but only rose, hastily excusing herself, and exited the room, leaving behind her perplexed and troubled companions. She went all the way upstairs into her bedroom, where, trembling, she shut the door behind her before she looked at the note once more.

She had not read it at all in the parlor — only perceived the author's penmanship, written in a hand she well-recognized even after so many months. Certainly it was a script she had not expected to ever encounter again, and seeing it thus unexpectedly had been enough to give her start.

The paper quivered in her unsteady hand as she read:

Miss Hathaway,

It is urgent that I speak with you. I am returned to Belgravia. Please come at your earliest possible opportunity. While I realize that such a request may be viewed as untoward, the gravity of the situation must serve to warrant its merit.

F. L.

Rosamond's brow wrinkled in consternation even as she trembled. What ought she to do? Certainly her inclination was to fly to Belgravia without hesitance. Yet at their parting it had been understood that they would never see one another again, and she had spent the ensuing months reconciling herself to that resolve, however unconvincing the results of her effort. She knew that it was for good reason that they had parted, and that the justification for that separation far outweighed their unvoiced personal feelings. And yet — the urgency of this message could not be ignored, any more than could the pounding of her heart. She must go. She must go with courage and resolve to maintain a steadfast indifference, and not let her weaknesses surface to reveal anything other than polite passivity.

She said a silent prayer then and there, for such courage as she needed must only come from a higher source than her own fragile stoicism.

Rosamond repeated her silent supplication as she approached the door of the Earl's Belgravia residence. She did not need to ring, for the door was immediately opened, as no doubt the Earl's excellent butler had been instructed to keep watch for Miss Hathaway in order that she should not be kept standing upon the doorstep. She was shown, not into the parlor, but into a small sitting-room, where the butler smiled very kindly at her and informed her that his lordship would be in directly. The man's kindness did her some good, giving her a momentary reassurance that allowed her to study the room, though she did not sit.

The room was very tastefully furnished and, despite its modest size, retained the elegance that would befit such a fashionable neighborhood. There was an ensemble of miniature portraits hanging on the far wall, and these she inspected with interest. The largest one, at the top, portrayed Frederick's father, the previous Earl of Kendal, in his young-adulthood. The dark-haired young woman whose portrait hung beside the Senior Earl's was undoubtedly Frederick's mother. And beneath were likenesses of three boys, all younger than ten, all dark-haired and dark-eyed. Even in such a rendition of childhood, Rosamond was easily able to pick out which was the eldest, for Frederick's enigmatic handsomeness was already apparent at such a tender age. She could not help smiling to herself, despite her anxiety, as her attention lingered on the familiar dark eyes.

The wisp of a smile was quick to dissolve as she heard a footstep in the hall. Rosamond turned toward the door just as Frederick Lancaster stepped into the room. And whatever resolve each may have determined upon was surely flown in that instant as they beheld one another. Neither one stirred for a long and silent while, until Rosamond, dismayed at her inability to master her heart's weakness, lowered her eyes and dropped a curtsey, murmuring a demure, "My Lord Kendal."

He nodded in acknowledgement of her greeting and came forward to meet her. How unchanged he was!

"Miss Hathaway," he began, "it was good of you to come at such short notice. I truly hope it did not put you to unnecessary trouble, for I must confess my motive for summoning you here may only be construed as selfish in nature."

"My lord, I pray you do not speak so!" interposed Rosamond earnestly. "You have ever been a friend to me, and nothing in your disposition could reasonably be deemed as anything less than noble. There was no inconvenience at all in my presenting myself here today, so put such thoughts to rest."

She, too, was unchanged from his perspective, unless it was possible she had grown even lovelier. The crimson rose in her cheeks with her sincerity.

"Nevertheless," Frederick said, motioning for her to be seated, "I'm afraid what I must tell you is not pleasant, but I cannot spare you, for you would hear it yourself soon enough . . . maybe on the morrow. And . . . ," he hesitated, frowning, "I would rather you hear it from me than elsewhere. That is my selfishness." Rosamond said nothing, only remained solemnly attentive and heedful of his word. He continued. "There is no easy or genteel way of putting it, so I shall just set it before you plainly. It will be final before the week is out, and then all shall know . . . that I have divorced my wife."

Rosamond's eyes widened in stunned astonishment which Frederick readily observed.

"Yes, you are unaffectedly shocked, as is fitting. And yet, would you have been less daunted to have heard it casually mentioned across your breakfast table, or to have read it in the newspapers? There will be much talk . . . probably most of it directed against her, which is unfortunate, for I am as guilty as she in the folly of ever entering into our marriage vows. Even so, I will neither escape scrutiny nor speculation. It is the speculation which shall be the most loathsome."

Rosamond, still dazed, looked to him with troubled eyes. "You ought to have stayed away," she said. "You ought not to have come back to London, for it is only here that such talk would culminate."

Frederick gave her half a smile. "How like you — you have not changed, Miss Hathaway. Even under the duress of such harsh controversy, you would be concerned for my welfare. But no, it would cause sensation whether I was here or not. I must stay in London, for here lies my duty."

"But surely every member of the House of Lords does not sit for the entire season! You could stay away until such talk dies down, for it never takes long for a new scandal to surface and the old ones to be forgotten." She could see that such talk was futile, as Frederick was ever steadfast in his purpose. She gave one more appeal in her concern. "Can you not sway the journalists against putting the matter into print? Surely a man of your rank and connections must have some influence with the papers."

But Frederick only shook his head, glowering sullenly. "It would make no difference . . . word would get out one way or another. You put emphasis on matters that do not concern me — I care nothing about what people think, excepting only yourself. I am imparting this to you in the foolish hope that in hearing it from my own lips, your judgment might be softened, if only slightly."

Rosamond did not look at him, her eyes sorrowful as she gazed abstractedly at the floor, reflecting upon his words. Without lifting her eyes, she murmured, "You do me a grave disservice, my lord, to relegate me to such heartlessness, or to suppose that I should be so easily swayed by the opinions of those who have no knowledge of your character."

Frederick's dark eyes were upon her as he crossed to the sofa and sat beside her.

Rosamond went on. "You are right . . . there will be much talk. It is inevitable. But I hope you know that I should turn a deaf ear to such hearsay, nor should I be guilty of contributing to such gossip, nor allow it to exert influence upon my esteem for you. I pray that I may never be such a faithless friend."

On only one other occasion had Rosamond ever seen Frederick's penetrating dark gaze falter, and that was at their last parting when he had put his lips to her fingertips and relinquished her hand so unwillingly. Such a falter in the gaze of one so usually steadfast must indicate to her where his own weaknesses lie — must they be so aligned with her own? Even now did she feel that same swelling sensation within her heart that she had felt that day in the winter garden — that feeling she had meant to put behind her forever. Must he sit so close beside her now?

This would not do — she must not let him take her hand again, or all remnants of her resolve would be lost. She stood hastily, though she felt no joy in thus conquering her senses. She crossed toward the clock-case, putting some distance, and thereby a measure of safety, between herself and the Earl.

And of course there must still be a question in her mind . . . always an unanswered question. The subject that would be foremost on everyone's tongue had never been mentioned by him and could not be expected to be, for it was overtly personal in nature. And yet there did he now give her some insight, touching upon the very subject while not elaborating upon it.

He had risen when she crossed to the clock, though he made no attempt to move toward her. "Miss Hathaway—,"

Rosamond turned back toward him.

"You must know . . . however little others will look for the truth in such a matter . . . there is no dishonor in this divorce. There is no love lost, for it was never there to begin with. Never."

Though fully cognizant of the significance of such words, Rosamond could only give him a softly sad smile as she nodded. She prayed that such would bring him assurance, for she could not stay longer. She could not depend on her ability to retain composure in light of the gravity of the situation which had been revealed to her, and even more at the re-awakening of those emotions which, while never dead within her, could at least perhaps have been laid dormant if left undisturbed. She did not need to explain . . . he always comprehended, though it was perhaps not so much comprehension of her feelings as awareness of his own, that compelled him to cross to the door and hold it open for her, providing her the ready escape she needed (which is not the same as *desired*).

Rosamond afterwards could not even recall if she had bid him good-day as she departed, so overcome was she with the complex sentiments which were besieging her emotions from without and within.

When word got out that the Earl of Kendal had divorced his wife, there was no stopping the wagging tongues of the Londoners who delighted in such a scandal. As would be expected, the most detrimental prattle concerned the ex-Countess, but as the Earl had predicted, he himself was not to be spared in the arena of whispered speculations nor gossipers' suppositions, for as delectable as such scandal must be, it holds twice the pleasure should it involve members of the nobility. And Rosamond could neither be unmindful of such chatter, for it must emanate from every mouth in the drawing room, ballroom, and card room alike. And while she was true to her word and never participated in the prate of her associates, it still pained her to hear such speculation upon the matter, and she may indeed have unwittingly induced the dampening of several conversations, so downcast did she become whenever the topic was broached.

As sure as the seasons cycle from fair to bleak within their natural course, so must all calamities appear to befall at once. And it was only a few days following Rosamond's visit to Belgravia that she and Tom both would realize the extent of their afflictions.

Mr. Hathaway had been absent from the office all day, and Tom stayed there rather late, as had been his habit recently, perhaps due to an unconscious desire to provide excuse for avoiding the nervous tension which had fallen over his household in recent weeks. On this particular evening, however, avoidance would appear to be unattainable. As soon as he had entered the hall and handed his hat and coat to Agnes, she relayed a message which must anticipate certain unpleasantness.

"Good evening, Mr. Tom," the amiable maid greeted him. "Your father says he'd like to see you in his study before dinner. Miss Rosamond, too."

Tom trudged up the stairs to his room, thinking that this request did not bode well. To summon both himself and his sister into the study must indicate that whatever was to be imparted to them was not, in his father's opinion, suitable for communicating at the dinner table. He glanced at the clock in the upstairs hall. It was nearly the dinner hour now. Whatever his father wished to say must be compelling indeed if it could not even wait until after dinner.

It was already eight o'clock when Tom fetched Rosamond from her room, and the two of them proceeded back downstairs. Tom knocked on the study door, and when they were bid to enter, they did so solemnly. Their father was seated at his handsome mahogany desk; their mother was sitting near him in a chair which had been drawn up for her purpose. Both parents looked as somber as their children, though not from the fear of uncertainty that afflicted the brother and sister.

"Good evening, my children," Mr. Hathaway rose and greeted them as Tom closed the door behind Rosamond. Mr. Hathaway indicated two chairs opposite his own. "Please be seated, for what I have to tell you is no trivial matter."

Tom heard Rosamond sigh unwittingly, as one who is already burdened by great care and must take on more as a matter of course. They sat, even as their father remained standing. Their mother was unusually silent and seemed content to let her husband convey his speech.

"This will not be easy for any of us, what I am about to impart to you, but we must take strength and comfort from one another, as must all who are kindred when faced with adversity of any kind." He paused after this ominous beginning, glancing down at his desk while he collected his thoughts. "You have doubtlessly been aware of the unprecedented length of your sister's absence. You are dutiful children, both, and have never pressed your mother or myself for further elaboration as to her situation, but it cannot be longer kept from you. Although you are both of consenting age, we have kept you unenlightened in this matter, hoping that it would be rectified without delay, but that appears not to be the case. Whether we made a wise decision in keeping you in ignorance must be left to your own judgment. At any rate—," he seemed grimly braced to lay the truth before them, "your sister has left us of her own accord . . . gone away to be with that man — I cannot call him a gentleman, as it would neither fit his rank nor character — and has thus left behind all imprints of the morals and standards that have been associated with her upbringing. And—," here his stern countenance turned sadder, "to say that such a base act is entirely out of character for the daughter and sister we loved must only attest to our ignorance and her lofty deception."

When he finished speaking, there was such a profound silence that the slightest stirring from without could be heard. It took Tom and Rosamond a very long while to process and internalize what their father had spoken, though their faces would reflect their alarmed shock.

Rosamond at last found her tongue and was much bewildered. "Do . . . do you mean to say that Lorna has run away to marry that . . . that Mr. Anderson?"

All attention was drawn by a sob emanating from their mother at Rosamond's question, but it was Mr. Hathaway who gave answer, and how sternly. "It is Mr. Anderson, but there is no talk of marriage."

Both siblings' eyes grew wide in disbelief and confusion.

"But why? I . . . I just don't understand," Rosamond persisted, much distressed. "How could she have done such a thing?"

"I cannot say, my child," said her father. "It is a terrible burden for us to bear, and it only exacerbates the ugliness of her deed to realize the grief which must now be endured by those she has left behind."

Tom glanced over at his younger sister, whose breathing was growing more audible as her distress mounted.

"But is she lost to us then?" Rosamond stood, appealing to her father. "Can you not reclaim her?"

Mr. Hathaway shook his head. "It is no easy thing, to reclaim one so headstrong, and who is past the age of consent. The only true authority I can wield is her inheritance, which she has most emphatically renounced. In one thing only has she spared us . . . she has taken her transgression far from London, and we may thus be exempted from any stain of disgrace or dishonor upon our family name."

Tom at last spoke up, though still overcome with disbelief. "Where is she?"

"They have taken up residence in Holland Cove . . . it is a very small community, from what I could tell, and on the coast. Very far from here . . . we need not fear any Londoners sighting her there. She left a note in her room before departing and made no secret of her destination. Naturally, I went after her immediately . . . as you know, I was gone for several days. But neither appeals nor remonstrance could persuade her. I went again today, hoping that the course of time would have altered her stance, but she remained fixed as ever."

Tom spoke again, his voice still somber. "And shall we never see our sister again?"

"We shall!" It was their mother who interjected this determined outburst. Her tear-stained face was contorted with both pain and adamance. "She will come back to us!"

Mr. Hathaway glanced at his wife with some pity, then turned back to Tom and Rosamond. "We can only pray that she will come to see the error of her ways and return to us in remorse and penitence. And then we shall receive her with warmth and forgiveness, for compassion prescribes that the wayward child shall be welcomed with open arms upon repentance of her misdeeds. But until then, she must be lost to us."

There followed another long, grim interval of silence as brother and sister pondered the significance of their father's words.

Rosamond finally broke the silence, her tone weary and despondent. "And what shall we say? For others will surely notice her absence."

"We shall say that she has grown discontented with the city and has gone to stay near the seashore. It is only a vague truth, but those who knew her will readily believe her discontent, knowing her high spirits."

In spite of her dismay, Rosamond had thus far shed no tears, though they would come soon enough. For now, she could do little more than shake her head weakly, her voice distant: "I cannot understand how she could do such a thing — how she could lower herself to such illicit degradation. I never would have believed her capable of it, in spite of her independent ways."

Her father crossed to where she stood and put his arm about her shoulder. "There, there, my child," he intoned, his sternness giving way to reassurance. "It will take time for all of us to come to terms with this misfortune. It may take many days, or even weeks, for your heart to lift from its heaviness, but let us always remain hopeful, even as we may renounce her conduct, that she will soon recognize anew the importance of the values of her breeding which must still be within her."

Rosamond contemplated his words. "Yes, but will those instilled principles be able to emerge under the weight of such influence as she has allowed herself to submit to?"

Mr. Hathaway could only shake his head. "The answer to that, my dear, shall be the true test of the merit of her upbringing. Come — let us go into dinner and not touch again on this subject tonight, however heavily it will weigh upon our minds."

And, with his arm still about her shoulder, he led Rosamond out of the room, and their grief-stricken mother followed. Tom lingered a moment in his chair, for he had perhaps known Lorna better than anyone, and the love he had for her could not come to terms with her departure and must leave him wretchedly sorrowful with an emptiness that would not soon be diminished.

Chapter XIII

One can only imagine the feelings that crept through the members of the Hathaway family in the following weeks: sadness, anger, disbelief, anxiety, betrayal. For Rosamond, who experienced all such emotions acutely, the sorrow and disappointment in her sister's conduct struck her to the core, and she most fervently embraced her father's appeal for prayers that Lorna would return to them with speed and attrition. Tom's reaction was less purposeful, for the sudden, grievous change of circumstance, coupled with the inner-strife of his own tainted conscience, had left him without the fortitude to ponder deeply new afflictions, nor to think beyond the present moment.

It was several weeks later that Lady Abercrombie and Sir Richard hosted a ball in celebration of their wedding anniversary, and the Hathaways were to attend, for Mrs. Hathaway insisted that they maintain their social obligations, both for their own wellness and diversion, and so that others would never suspect that there was aught amiss within their family. For Rosamond, who must contend with multiple heartaches, such diversions were well-met, for the ballroom had always brought her pleasure, and maintaining some social pursuits did indeed bring her some degree of digression from more painful thoughts which were felt very poignantly in her solitude.

For Tom, though, whose struggles were brought on from within, such activity only increased his unhappiness, and he found better comfort in the quiet peacefulness of his own hearthside and so elected to remain at home, despite his mother's entreaties.

While Rosamond still regularly attended dinner parties at the Abercrombies', this was the first time she had been invited to a ball at their home. It seemed strange to see the drawing room cleared of most of its furnishings except for a few chairs and sofas which now lined the walls, but the room was ideally appointed for a dance, with its impressive length and tastefully elegant adornments.

Despite Rosamond's best attempt to project her usual engaging brightness, Lady Abercrombie must have suspected her heart's heaviness, for as she greeted her, that worthy lady narrowed her eyes in scrutiny, and said with dissatisfied concern, "You have grown quite pale, my dear, since last I saw you. I fear you are unwell."

"Oh no!" Rosamond ascertained a bit too quickly. "I am quite well. 'Tis just this frightful cold spell has kept me too much indoors." And she smiled her charming smile at her kind hostess, who was not fooled.

She patted Rosamond's hand warm-heartedly. "Go in now and enjoy yourself," she said, nodding toward the drawing room. "But you must come and see me this week and talk to me of your worldly cares."

As she passed into the drawing room, Rosamond could not help but think affectionately upon the woman who had so befriended her, but she was not inclined to confide in her any of the troubles which now pressed upon her. She did determine, though, to heed Lady Abercrombie's words and attempt to enjoy herself, for there would be enough time for melancholy at home.

The drawing room, usually the gathering place of the select circle of acquaintances after dinner, was on this night crowded with guests, colorfully and elegantly outfitted in their finery. The musicians played at one end of the room, near the doors into the game room, thus leaving the opposite windows with their recessed benches available for the guests' respite. Rosamond had already lost sight of her parents who had gone in before her but was quickly spotted by Douglas Trainer, who always appointed himself her guardian and escort, even where no such formality existed.

She was given no time for acclimation as Mr. Trainer immediately swept her off to the dance-floor, but after dancing two consecutive sets with her, he graciously conceded to allow another gentleman to dance the next, although he contracted Rosamond's promise for future dances before relinquishing her to the next partner.

While Rosamond did comply and give her word, this would ultimately prove problematic. About a half-hour later, after taking a rest at the perimeter, she was about to head back to the dance-floor with the gentleman who had been in her company during the respite, when Douglas Trainer approached and insisted that he had already secured Miss Rosamond for this dance.

Rosamond did not recall promising him any particular set, having given only a very general assurance, but she felt herself to be in a dilemma, for she did not wish to cause any scene which may be construed as unpleasant in nature. Both men were looking to her to give her word, and the predicament made her very uncomfortable, giving rise to a heightening of crimson in her cheeks. Before she could utter a word, the situation was worsened when a third gentleman approached, an acquaintance of Rosamond's, and greeted her, inquiring if she was engaged for the current dance. She had no chance to reply, for both men flanking her gave a sharp, "Yes, she is!" in her stead, which of course caused the new gentleman to raise his eyebrows. It seemed as if all three men started talking at once then, in tones which were only very tautly polite at best.

Rosamond sighed, though none were truly paying her any heed at that instant, and could not help thinking herself the victim of most infelicitous circumstances. But as she looked out toward the dance-floor — the present site of much delightful activity of which she ought to have been partaking — she discerned at that moment coming toward her the one person in the world she would have wished to seek her out, had she allowed her mind to wander upon such channels of thought. Indeed, he was the only person in the world whose mere presence could awaken such a stirring within her breast that she was cognizant of it even now, in the midst of such company. Those penetrating dark eyes were fixed intently upon her, and from the moment she met their forthcoming gaze, she was oblivious to the gentlemen surrounding her, who were still caught up in their deferential squabbling. Rosamond wanted to break free of their banal triteness and hasten forth to meet the Earl of Kendal, but she managed to sustain her bearing until he reached her.

Frederick Lancaster paid no heed to the other men; his eyes were for Rosamond alone. And as he bowed to her, she knew that however unsettling their last sorrowful meeting had been, it would not be dwelt upon now, for that intense dark blaze in his eyes was the one she knew of old. Equally disregardful of the other company, Rosamond curtsied and took the hand he proffered, neither one mindful that such an unconstrained gesture was not the accepted norm, and that a gentleman ought to instead offer a lady his arm in polite society.

So taking Rosamond's willing hand, Frederick led her away toward the dance-floor, leaving behind a disconcerted and indignant trio of would-be admirers. But Rosamond cared nothing about what they thought . . . for it was a waltz, and she had the only partner that would truly befit her most favored of dances.

Still without a word spoken between them, Frederick put his arm about her slender waist, and having never released her hand, they were in the waltz position, but took the very slightest delay in any movement, as if there was a mutual desire to savor that moment, with his arm about her and her hand in his.

And when they began to dance, Rosamond felt an uplifting serenity that she had not known in all the weeks that had passed since she had seen him last, or perhaps since she had ever known him. At last there was no need to think or speak on topics that brought pain or sorrow. They did not need to speak at all . . . it was enough only to look and feel and touch and exist, for that had ever been their way: content just to be with one another.

When Frederick finally spoke, it was plain that, while no formal greeting had been exchanged between them, his thoughts had ever been on his amiable partner. "You ought always to wear white," he murmured, his subdued voice conveying his approval of her gown. "You wore white also to the opera . . . and to the Royal Ball."

Rosamond smiled, pleased at his approbation. "You did not dance with me then . . . at that ball."

"No," he acknowledged. "Perhaps I should have."

"I . . . I am glad that tonight—," Rosamond broke off, blushing, too modest to admit that she was pleased he was dancing with her now.

But she had no need to finish — he understood, as was evidenced by the enigmatic gleam in his dark eyes. They did not speak more, but lost themselves again in the spell of the graceful dance.

However oblivious they may have been to the presence of others in the room or upon the dance-floor, others in the room were most assuredly not indifferent to them. Indeed, there were many there who took note of the dashing Earl of Kendal — only recently the subject of such scrutiny upon the audacious divorce of his wife — and the luminous Rosamond Hathaway, for their attitude and proximity as they danced could never be mistaken for the detached formality conveyed by the other pairs upon the dance-floor. Lady Abercrombie, in particular, was most heedful of this, her keen bright eyes glinting shrewdly, but not in any approval. Neither had she been entirely ignorant of their concurrent absences from the card room at her dinner gatherings last year, but while she had never expressed a word upon the subject, she seemed determined to speak tonight, for as soon as the waltz had ended, she took her nephew aside.

Rosamond was immediately taken up by Mr. Trainer, who was likewise determined to have his dance with her, but as they began the next set, she kept glancing over to the corner where her hostess and the Earl were having discourse. Truly, it looked not to be a dialogue, for Lady Abercrombie seemed to be doing most of the talking, and with what telling admonition etched upon her brow! Rosamond knew that Frederick loved and respected his aunt, but whatever it was she now spoke to him he was not taking kindly. He said little, but only scowled and shook his head, then turned upon his heel and walked away toward the door, his countenance darkly irate. Rosamond watched him, amazed that Lady Abercrombie would have provoked such antagonism, and dismayed that he was so suddenly departing. He did turn back and cast one final look in her direction before exiting the room, but Rosamond could discern nothing from the glance, and as she could not break away from her dance-partner, was thus left mystified as to the basis of such contention.

But, however disconcerted Lady Abercrombie may have been, she appeared to harbor no animosity toward Rosamond and was, in fact, eminently gracious and attentive to her for the rest of the evening.

The members of the Hathaway household seldom spoke of Lorna amongst themselves. It would invariably call up only sentiments of sorrow or vexation — both unwelcome emotions in a household which strove to maintain its propriety above all else. But that is not to say that no thoughts were cast upon the wayward daughter, for each family member most assuredly felt some grief or pain upon reflection of her errant conduct.

Rosamond received a letter from her sister one day. It was brief and uninformative, but no doubt well-intended. It ran thus:

My Dear Sister,

I pray this letter finds you well and happy. I truly hope that my departure, sudden as it may have seemed, has caused you no excess of uneasiness. I would never wish you to suffer any grief on my account. It is not my wish to sever relations with you, and I hope that you will respond with haste to this message so that I may have assurance of your continued love, as I send you an abundance of my own.

Yours ever,
Lorna

Rosamond was rather disappointed in the contents of this letter and took some time to reflect before she endeavored to pen a response. Her note was somewhat lengthier than her sister's:

Dear Lorna,

How happy I was to receive your letter, and how much happier still shall I be when I see you again! Know that our Father and Mother, and indeed all of us, are readily prepared to welcome you back into our midst, so do not delay in putting this sordid chapter behind you and hasten home to us. We shall then never speak nor think on this grave matter again, and it shall be as if it never happened. You need not fear facing any repercussion in society, for word has never spread, not even amongst the servants. And Father will most assuredly give generous restitution to him who led you astray, so you need not heed any threat or intimidation from that party upon your withdrawal from his company.

Pray, Dear Sister, put this grievous misdeed to rest, and thus remove the wretched barricade that must necessarily exist between us until your return. Our thoughts and prayers are ever turned to that hopeful end.

Your Loving Sister,
Rosamond

Rosamond re-read the note several times to ensure that its well-meaning content should not be misconstrued as either abrasive or condoning, then posted it to the seaside address Lorna had provided.

She did not hear from Lorna again and could only conclude that her sister did not intend to hastily renounce her current situation or yet put her indiscretion behind her. And while this greatly saddened Rosamond, she knew that there was nothing else to be done until such time as her sister may take it upon herself to amend her wrongdoings.

Rosamond soon discovered that there was one in her household who did not concur with the merit of such biding.

It was late afternoon one day shortly after the anniversary ball, and Rosamond had decided to add a new silk ribbon to her fan cord, having just procured an exquisite bit of rose ribbon in Bond Street. Upon searching in her sewing box, however, she could not find her scissors and so set off downstairs to look into her mother's desk where there was sure to be a pair.

Upon entering the morning room, Rosamond was surprised to see her mother's writing tray set out upon the desk, for Mrs. Hathaway usually worked on her correspondence only in the morning hours. However, it appeared as if she had left in the midst of writing a letter as evidenced by the pen lying beside a half-written page on the desktop. Presuming that her mother had stepped out for only a moment, Rosamond proceeded to search within the desk for the scissors. Unable to find them within any of the desk's compartments, she bent to open the slim drawer which was inset below the writing surface, and as she did so, her eye chanced to fall upon the salutation of the letter her mother had been writing.

Dearest Daughter,

Rosamond's heart skipped a beat, and while she was much too well-mannered to read any of the letter's content, she could not help but take notice of a small stack of bank-notes folded into the bottom of the letter.

At that moment, she heard a shrill voice behind her. *"What are you about in here?"*

Gasping, Rosamond whirled around to find her mother coming toward the desk, clutching the ink blotter from Mr. Hathaway's study and looking stern.

Poor Rosamond, disconcerted by her mother's sharp tone, as well as what she had inadvertently seen upon the desktop, faltered as she spoke. "I . . . I was just looking for some scissors." She gestured toward the drawer in which she had been searching.

Her mother, meanwhile, had stridden over to the desk and very deliberately laid her hand atop the unfinished letter. Having done so, she collected herself as she regarded her younger daughter.

"Very well then," Mrs. Hathaway said, with somewhat stilted composure and an even more pretentious smile. "Did you find them? I thought you had your own in your sewing box."

"I cannot seem to find them there."

Mrs. Hathaway still did not remove her hand that was covering the letter, but she glanced down at the open drawer that Rosamond had indicated. "They should be in there," she said. "I used them the other day for something or another."

Rosamond did not search further in the drawer, though, so overcome by guilt and bewilderment was she as she met her mother's unwavering eye. "You are writing to Lorna," she said quietly.

Mrs. Hathaway was not particularly adept at concealing her emotions, and despite her firm stance, the color unmistakably rose in her cheeks. Her voice remained quite steady, though. "What if I was?" she said rather lightly. "Is it unusual that a mother should correspond with her child?"

Rosamond glanced again at the desktop. "You are sending her money," she said, quieter still, yet plain in her assertion.

Mrs. Hathaway made no denial, only maintained her resolute bearing.

Rosamond was troubled and perplexed. "Does Father know? I cannot think that he would condone such a gesture. It doesn't seem—,"

"No," Mrs. Hathaway interrupted firmly, "he does not know, and you shall not tell him."

Removing her hand from the desktop, she began to fumble agitatedly in the drawer.

Rosamond remained unmoved, her brow knit in doubtful dissatisfaction, her voice gentle and troubled. "But our father has made it clear, and rightly so, that she has separated herself from our family and must abide by such consequences as that must entail."

"This is no concern of yours." Mrs. Hathaway's compressed tone remained steadily rigid as she produced the scissors-sheath from the drawer and handed it to her daughter. "Remember your place, child, and to whom you are speaking. It is most unbecoming for a young girl to go rummaging unbidden through her mother's desk or to repeat tales of things which do not concern her."

Rosamond did not press the issue further and retreated with the scissors-sheath. She understood her mother's point very well, that she was not to mention a word of this to her father, but as she climbed the stairs back to her room, she could not help but feel disconcerted — assuredly over her mother's uncommonly severe brusqueness, but more so over her mother's covert dealings with her sister. Certainly Lorna's conduct was wrong and it could not be right for her mother to give aid to such a dishonorable enterprise, thereby assisting in its advancement.

This sordid undertaking on the part of her mother greatly disturbed Rosamond, and she stayed up in her room for the rest of the afternoon, wishing to avoid any encounter with her mother until the awkwardness of the situation had passed.

Mr. and Mrs. Hathaway went out quite early that evening. Rosamond heard them go, for their voices in their hurried preparation carried through her door, but she could not discern if Tom had come home yet, and once her parents left, she emerged from her room to go in search of her brother downstairs.

As she descended the stairway, she saw that Agnes was just admitting someone at the front door. It was not Tom, however, but one who was definitely not expected: the Earl of Kendal. For the second time that day, Rosamond felt a sudden and unexpected pang in her heart. What could the Earl be about, presenting himself at her home?

Before he had even given his name to Agnes, he caught sight of Rosamond on the staircase, and she hastened down to the hall.

"It is quite all right, Agnes. I shall see the gentleman in the parlor."

Agnes curtsied, looking duly impressed at the handsome and aristocratic caller, then retreated toward the kitchen.

Rosamond did not immediately lead the way into the parlor, having realized that she may have intervened too hastily. She felt the heat rise upon her neck.

"I — I'm sorry. I just assumed . . . I mean, you may well be here to speak with my father on matters of business?"

Her tone must have betrayed her hope that such was not the case, for he gave her a fleeting smile and shook his head.

"No," he said, "I came to see you. I am sorry for turning up so unannounced."

Despite the wisp of a smile which had departed from his lips almost as soon as it appeared, Rosamond could see that his mood was somber and restless. She wondered if his purpose had aught to do with his discordant interview with Lady Abercrombie at the anniversary ball, or his bitterly hasty departure there from. She had never seen him so unsettled as he now appeared as he moodily followed her into the parlor. She closed the door then turned up the lamp, as the long shadows of evening had begun to fall across the room. He would not sit, but instead stationed himself near the fire at the front of the room. Rosamond stood near him and waited for him to speak, for clearly he had something to say, however much he hesitated to put it to her.

It was not in Frederick's nature to be either loquacious or poetic. For one who was boldly fearless confronting all manner of dangers in distant lands, and who was honorably noble in character, his quietly virile strength and pensive nature must emerge as the defining attributes of his inherent disposition. Yet now he was clearly agitated, as would necessarily precipitate an oration by one who is ill-at-ease in giving speeches before a female constituency, even when such company numbered only one.

Rosamond sensed this agitation, and her own pulse quickened as he paced restlessly. He looked at her a moment, perhaps noting the heightened color in her cheeks, then averted his eyes, looking absently into the fire as he spoke.

"Rosamond . . . you must know that I love you."

As her heartbeat accelerated, Rosamond involuntarily drew in an audible breath. Frederick glanced at her, his eyes dark and flashing, with the brooding alertness that she knew so well. She longed to reach out to him in that moment, but she sensed that he must proceed without interruption, to give voice to words that needed to be spoken.

He frowned to himself as she averted her eyes. "I would never wish to distress you," he went on, "But I . . . I would ask that you would consider . . . that is to say . . . I cannot hope that . . . ." He frowned again, cursing under his breath. This was torment.

The tension between them was almost tangible, and Rosamond trembled slightly. He saw this, and his voice softened a bit. "What I'm trying to say is . . . I love you, and I . . . I want to marry you, if you will have me."

A flood of emotion passed through Rosamond, though not visible to her ardent lover, and she felt as if her heart would burst.

The tension and anxiety of the moment would certainly have required a compassionate and immediate response, but her emotional state obscured her senses, and she could not account for what she said next. She smiled primly, and her tone was remarkably even, considering her lightheadedness. "I do not know what my parents would say to my marrying a man who has so boldly divorced his wife."

It was not in Rosamond's nature to jest, and this was inexplicable, even to herself, as the words were uttered. Certainly Frederick was in no mood for flippancy.

There was a terrible silence during which a shadow like a thundercloud seemed to engulf the room.

Frederick scowled darkly at her. "Do not trifle with me, girl!" And taking her in his arms, he kissed her with a passion that nearly took her breath away.

And then he was gone. Before she could make reply or recover her breath, he was gone.

Frederick Lancaster did not return that day, or the next, or the next. He did not make any attempt to contact Rosamond at all, and she was thus plunged into such gloom as she had never known. To have so ill-treated the man she truly loved, and to know the misery that she herself was to blame for the forfeiture of all that could bring them both happiness was more than she could bear. She was wretchedly ashamed of herself, and the fact that she had no word from him, no knowledge of where he was or what he thought, greatly increased her distress, for uncertainty must always compound torment. She spent many long and dolorous hours in the solitude of her room during the day, while bitterly sorrowful tears fell upon her pillow at night.

Her mother, having no knowledge of what should be afflicting her daughter, grew increasingly concerned as the days wore on, and after several days of observing her withdrawal from all activity, entreated Tom to persuade his sister to emerge from her isolation.

She did so only dutifully, for she did not wish to inflict further pain on anyone else she loved, but she was none the better for it. She was melancholy and forlorn and sometimes appeared at tea or dinner with such a freshly-washed face that it was evident to close observers that she must have splashed water upon her cheeks to cover the tell-tale traces which had been left imprinted by tears. She took but little sustenance, and as the days progressed, she grew pale and listless, as must all who are suffering such doleful heartache.

She was not unconscious of this outwardly aberrant behavior on her part and, after a time, did her best to resume her customary habits so as not to give undue concern to those near her who daily commented on her alteration, thereby only reinforcing her grief, however well-intentioned their concern. But she could not alleviate their worry, for even in the resumption of social activities, she could not completely hide her despondency.

There were, now and again, some few moments of happiness that would penetrate her pain. These would occur when she was alone and allowed herself to reflect upon the occasion of their last meeting — which she did numerous time a day, but which usually brought to her fresh tears as she dwelt on only the miserable and shameful segment, replaying over and over in her mind the careless words she had spoken which she had so immediately regretted and which had resulted in her present state. But intermittently would she allow herself to remember the other details of the episode — the parts that filled her with vivid exhilaration, which, though it may last for only a few moments, was enough to sustain her and bring her some measure of hope in her uncertainty. For he had made a declaration of his love, and he had kissed her. And she could not think upon his kiss without feeling a thrilling surge within her breast, and its memory would sustain her through the darkest nights, even when her fleeting joy would give way once more to despondency.

She took to walking in the park with Edith again, as they had done frequently before Edith had become Mrs. Charles Byrd, and that gentle lady was only too happy to supply such companionship to Rosamond, for she was as dear a friend as ever, and marriage had not changed her sweet-tempered nature. But Edith was also cognizant of some change in her friend, though she could not guess what may have caused it. She only knew that in the midst of their conversations, Rosamond, who had always been so bright and engaging, was now often distant and distracted, with a faraway sadness in her once-glowing countenance. As much as this perplexed Edith, she could not induce Rosamond to divulge what lay so heavily upon her heart, and so felt helpless in her ability to render her friend any comfort. But this was not entirely the case, for Rosamond did indeed take comfort in the familiar companionship of her dedicated friend, and would undoubtedly have fallen to greater depths without such solace.

Rosamond did still attend the dinner-parties at the Abercrombies', although Frederick never presented himself there more. It was just as well, for Rosamond certainly could not have kept up her composure in his company, but the heartbreaking pain of having to appear to enjoy herself in such a place as held so many memories of cherished hours spent together, compounded by the knowledge that she herself was the probable cause of his absence, somehow rendered just as deep a wound.

Though it is natural for all persons to avoid what must bring them grief, and Rosamond was no exception, there was one place where she would seem to seek it out. She found herself haunting the corridors of the National Gallery . . . drawn like a wayfarer to the siren's song, she was lured again and again to the same room; to the same painting. The painting that he had purchased because she had loved it.

The girl on the balcony had ever charmed her, but now she positively captivated Rosamond, who spent countless hours entranced by the girl's subtle, distant gaze. The longing in her eyes held new meaning for Rosamond, and somehow the girl's placid hopefulness brought her some consolation. How wonderful it would be to step into the idyllic world! To be standing upon that balcony, looking out across the landscape, knowing that one whom you were awaiting would soon ride forth from the forest and claim you for his own. It was the hope that drew Rosamond in. So dreamily reverent was the girl's yearning that Rosamond could not doubt in her own mind that the girl's fondest desires must be achieved — it would be too heartbreaking to conceive that she should be disappointed.

It must not be thought that, in the midst of such romantic ordeals, Rosamond had forgotten about her sister. She remained duly distraught over Lorna's misconduct, and while she did not think about it as often as she once may have, the disillusionment and chagrin she felt in regard to her sister only added to her oppression.

One circumstance that arose as a result of Lorna's defection was a growing bond between Rosamond and Tom. Certainly, they had ever loved one another, but Lorna and Tom had somehow always been closer companions to one another than Rosamond had been to either of them. But now, in light of the misfortune which Lorna had brought upon the family, Rosamond and Tom took some comfort in one another, and while the members of the household in general never uttered Lorna's name in conversation, the two younger siblings found an outlet in private moments together when they could freely give expression on the matter.

Indeed, Rosamond had confided to her brother her encounter with their mother and her discovery of her mother's correspondence with and enclosure of monetary aid to their sister. This perplexed Tom as much as it had Rosamond . . . and when asked his opinion of such deception and abetment, he could only shake his head and admit his amazement at their mother's tactics.

Rosamond truly felt guilty at the possession of such knowledge and would have liked to apprise their father, for she knew what her mother undertook was wrong and was without his approval, but that she feared her mother's reproach after having been told so forcibly that she was not to make mention of the matter. Tom advised her to heed that injunction, for it truly was not her place, although he agreed with her that their mother's activity was certainly questionable and seemingly even unscrupulous.

A weakness is not easily overcome. And if that weakness is deeply instilled, it shall assuredly not be vanquished in an instant of smashed glass upon a rocky embankment.

Despite his resolve on that day, Tom had not so easily put his infirmity behind him. It was true that his self-reproach had prevented him from replacing the little flask, but he had another.

He had always had two. The other one was at the offices of the Star of India Tea Company, tucked safely away in the bottom drawer of his desk. He had never taken much opportunity to make any use of it, and certainly had never touched it since his renunciation of that temptation, but neither had he discarded it. Somehow, even as he abhorred its continued presence, hidden though it was, he concurrently found gratification in the knowledge that it was there.

As the weeks progressed, though, and his troubles seemed to compound, he began to think on it more and more. He found himself periodically opening the drawer during his working day and stealing a glance at the little bottle, sometimes even fingering it, as if finding solace in its mere tangibility, though he never removed it from its place of concealment. It became a distraction of which he was fully cognizant until one day he determined to remove it. Not destroy it, as he had the other, but just to put it beyond proximity.

There was a cabinet in the box-room that had been assigned to him for the purpose of storing papers and other miscellaneous articles. That would do.

Discreetly slipping the little bottle into his pocket, he made his way to the box-room at the rear of the building, his long strides reflecting the confidence of one who is determined to make a change for the better. The door was already slightly ajar when he approached, and before he pushed it open further, he stopped, for he heard voices on the other side of the door. Hearing his own surname mentioned, he gave pause, attentive to the conversation within the room. He recognized the voices as belonging to a senior and junior clerk of the company.

"See that you help Mr. Bryant move his belongings before you leave tonight. He's taking the desk opposite Mr. Tom Hathaway's." That was the senior clerk.

"Moving closer to Mr. Hathaway, Senior, eh? "

"Yes, at Mr. Hathaway's own request. He sees a lot of potential in young Bryant, I know for a fact. I overheard him tell Bryant that if he perseveres as he has been, he wouldn't be surprised to see him made Director of the company one day!"

"What? Wouldn't he want his son to follow after him?"

Tom heard the senior clerk give a rather derisive grunt at this.

"Nay, Mr. Hathaway's sharp as a tack, he is. He knows that Mr. Tom's here only on account of his own position in the company. The investors would bend over backwards to please Mr. Hathaway, that's how much they value him. They'll give his son an easy enough position, but Mr. Tom's got none of his father's head for business. Anyone can see that. —Mind what you're doing now! You nearly dropped that carton!"

As the two men within continued upon other topics, Tom took a step back, away from the door. His demeanor was utterly changed from what it had been only a few minutes before.

Abashed, flustered, chagrined.

Truthfully, he had overheard nothing that he hadn't innately known. But to hear the words spoken aloud, and in such matter-of-fact fashion, was inordinately disconcerting.

He slowly retraced his steps back to his desk and, opening the bottom drawer, replaced the bottle in its familiar location.

Rosamond endured the passage of time as well as she could, silently bearing the secret of her heart's sadness. To further complicate matters, Douglas Trainer proposed to her again. He could not have known how ill-timed was his overture, but he was left with little doubt upon receiving her reply. His previous suit had been gently declined, but on this occasion, his declaration was refused with such emotive distress, that he could not help but be taken aback, and even slightly offended. He subsequently informed her with a degree of coldness that he should not impose upon her again and was disappointed that she did not entreat him to pardon her hastiness and stay the course. In truth, once he had taken his leave, Rosamond felt equal measures of guilt and relief, and could not help wondering if Mr. Trainer would really leave off his endeavors.

Chapter XIV

It appeared that Douglas Trainer would follow through upon his resolve, for at the next Abercrombie dinner party, he did not appear. Even with his absence, though, it was a sizable gathering, being the height of the season.

Rosamond was quiet at dinner, as had been her custom of late, and when the men went to their cigars, she took her place amongst a sizable circle of ladies in the drawing room, for her preference was now to be part of a larger ensemble where it would not be noticed if she did not readily attend or contribute to the discourse. She only half-listened to their gossip, finding it an arduous task to keep her mind from wandering amidst such insubstantial dialogue.

Circumstances improved once the gentlemen re-appeared in the drawing room, for they usually brought with them the fragmentary remains of their own discourse from the study, where the conversation seemed to be weightier and of greater interest to one looking to divert and engage her thoughts. When the men entered, the ladies always rose and re-situated themselves in accommodation of the gentlemen, creating new parties which were dispersed throughout the long room.

Douglas Trainer's absence did not in any way consign Rosamond to solitude, for there were always a handful of young men eager to seek her favor, and the absence of her most conspicuous suitor seemed to bolster their optimism, motivating them to enliven their efforts at distinguishing themselves before her. She thus found herself sitting on the ornate velvet sofa quite encircled by a half-dozen companions who, happily, provided much earnest and enthusiastic discussion.

Such complacency would not last, though. During the course of the conversation, the gentleman opposite Rosamond casually glanced up at the doorway as if his eye was caught by something there, and when Rosamond turned her own head in that direction, what she beheld caused an instant transformation of her mien. Her heart began to pound within her as the color drained from her face with alarming swiftness, and her hand instinctively went to her mouth, stifling the startled gasp which would have otherwise been perceptible. Naturally this caused some alarm amongst her company, who beseeched to know if Miss Rosamond was quite well, to which she merely nodded her head. She prayed they would not see her heart still throbbing and know her consternation; for how could they comprehend that the entrance of the Earl of Kendal would affect her so?

He did not see her, or at least he did not look in her direction, but was met by Lady Abercrombie who promptly scolded him for arriving so late, though her admonishment was affectionate in nature — any antipathy harbored since the anniversary ball apparently erased. He then made his way to where Sir Richard stood with some other gentlemen near the windows, though he stopped to acknowledge several acquaintances on the way. When he passed Rosamond's coterie, he gave the group a general nod, which was returned very amicably by the other men who could not know how their young lady's heart was breaking as the Earl continued on with hardly a pause and no communication to her.

The men about Rosamond continued their lively discourse, and while she tried to at least appear attentive, it was really only an indifferent effort, for her mind and her heart were reeling in plaintive despair. Despite the vibrancy surrounding her, Rosamond's eye was drawn again and again to the Earl, who stood directly in her line of sight, though at the far end of the room, and apparently unmindful of her presence, for he was engaged in discussion with Sir Richard. But what grief pierced Rosamond's heart as she looked upon him . . . for she could not see him thus unchanged without calling forth such memories which must, in the sweetness of their sentiment, render now the stinging pain of an aching heart.

As her inner-turmoil escalated, a light-headed feverishness began to overwhelm her senses, and she began to tremble slightly. The gentleman sitting beside her took note of her condition.

"Miss Hathaway, I truly fear you are not well."

Rosamond knew she could not remain longer. She put her hand to her temple and averted her eyes. "I . . . I am quite warm. I think I must only step outside for a moment." She stood, and her companions followed suit. "No, please." She raised a tremulous hand. "Stay here. I shall be all right." And before any could protest, she stole away from them and made her way toward the door.

She tried to stay composed as she left the room, for she did not want to draw attention, but as she crossed the hall into the library, she knew that Frederick Lancaster had followed her. The room was illuminated only by the glow of the fire which cast dancing shadows onto the somber walls and furnishings.

She crossed straightaway to the fireplace and pressed her forehead against the warm mantelpiece, keeping her back to him and attempting to steady her trembling. She could not deceive him, though . . . he knew her well. She heard him at her shoulder, his voice subdued and low.

"Rosamond . . . ," he whispered. "You are trying so hard not to cry."

Naturally, that sent the tears streaming from her eyes, though she made not a sound. He gently turned her around, sending her heart into rapid flight as must always occur when he touched her.

"You are so lovely . . . no one should ever make you cry." His voice was still hushed, but as he lifted her chin, and she looked into his face, she saw that his brow was furrowed in concern, his dark eyes troubled. "I fear I have brought you great distress. See how you tremble when I touch you."

His hand had brushed against her shoulder as he pushed back one of her black curls, causing her to tremble indeed, though how could he ever know the reason?

He took a step back. "It would be better if I should leave, and never trouble you more."

"No!" It was more of a sob than a discernible utterance. She clasped his hand in both of hers and held it to her cheek, the tears now flowing without any attempt at restraint. "Do not leave. Do not ever leave me. I cannot endure being apart from you again! I am a foolish, senseless girl, who is unworthy of whatever affection you may bear toward me, but I love you! I love you so." Any further words were lost in sobs as the emotions she had kept pent-up for so many days came pouring forth.

She would have fallen to her knees before him but that he caught her up in his strong embrace.

"I have not been able to put you from my mind for one hour," he murmured. "These weeks without you have been torment."

Rosamond clung to him as one whose very soul might be imperiled upon separation. Her words came between breathless sobs. "Would you still have me for your wife?"

He gently pulled her away so that he might look into her eyes. His voice was ever low. "I cannot rest unless you are at my side, my dearest love."

And though her eyes once more filled with tears, they were not tears of despair, but rather of joy, for these two hearts who had loved so long in anguished silence could now give full expression to their longing.

They sat together on the sofa before the fire for a long while, until Rosamond's tears had subsided. They were accustomed to the silence, but how much was it enhanced with her head resting upon his shoulder and the shared knowledge that their love need never again be concealed from one another. Frederick seemed to be lost in reverie, and there was a considerable passage of time before he spoke. Rosamond knew well the frown that creased his brow.

"I cannot think but that you may regret this decision, Rosamond. It will not be easy for you, who so loves society. The scandal-mongers were heartless after the divorce. They will be merciless when I marry you. We should wait a long while, or I fear that you will be hurt by their gossip."

But Rosamond could not abide this. "We have done nothing wrong! They are so quick to judge what they know nothing about. There has been no cause for scandal."

Frederick's dark eyes flashed. "They delight in creating scandal where there is none. We might journey to the Continent for a length of time — it would seem natural enough after a wedding — and give the gossip time to die down."

Rosamond's regal pride surged within her. "That would be tantamount to admitting that we have done wrong! We have done nothing to warrant any shame, and we should not give them cause to think otherwise!"

There was another lengthy silence. "I shall take you into Cumbria, to Stoneleigh," Frederick mused absently. "We can be married there, and we will be far from the London newspapers and drawing room gossip. You will be charming in the countryside, and I can have you all to myself for a time."

Rosamond smiled as he took her hand.

"And how shall you like being the Countess of Kendal?"

Rosamond's heart gave a flutter as she took in his words. She paused as she contemplated such a station.

"I want only to be your wife," she said simply and modestly. "I will do my best to take on whatever responsibilities that would entail, though you may be disappointed in me by and by."

And Frederick's lips parted into that rare and wonderful smile, which was all the more to be treasured by his adoring beloved, as he kissed her atop her black curls. "Have no fears there, you bewitching girl. You shall be the most delightful countess in England. Certainly the most beautiful and enamoring."

Rosamond blushed accordingly and looked down at her lap.

Frederick scrutinized her for several moments before speaking.

"What is it?" he prodded gently. "What is it that is upon your mind?"

Rosamond blushed even deeper. "It is only that I . . . I cannot help but think . . . ." She looked into his face, her eyes searching for truth, yet perhaps fearing what she might find. "Did your divorce have ought to do with me?"

Frederick turned his face toward the fire, reflecting as he gazed distractedly into its flames.

"No," he said at last. "Only in that you had opened my eyes to the fact that there are deeper truths in life than we can comprehend. And if we cannot, or will not, acknowledge those truths, our life will be but a shallow existence, meaningless and desolate."

Rosamond gave him a rather shy smile, then said with some regret, "I fear Lady Abercrombie shall not be pleased with your marrying me." Frederick looked intently perplexed at such a statement, so she added: "I saw her speaking to you after we — after you danced with me at the ball."

"Ah," he nodded in understanding. "I think you are wrong. I think she shall be greatly pleased indeed. I told you once how fond she is of you . . . you must have determined as much by now. No, she had nothing ill to say about you. It was me she was taking to task." His eyes narrowed moodily as he reflected upon the incident. "She had watched us dancing. She could see that you loved me." Here he glanced at Rosamond who was filled with a surging warmth, for she did indeed love him. He went on: "She did not want to see your heart broken. She could not know that I meant to ask for your hand, and I did not tell her . . . I was too proud and too stubborn. But . . . you can see how quickly she has forgiven me." Here he gave a rueful smile. "She is fond of me, too, and cannot long harbor ill-will toward me any more than I can against her. No, she will be very pleased that you should be my wife, and you will no doubt take great comfort in her understanding." His voice took on a serious tone. "She will be your greatest advocate in London when people start to talk."

Rosamond was delighted and relieved that Lady Abercrombie would not begrudge the match, for she did truly value that lady's friendship.

She felt as if her whole world had been turned upside-down from what it had been at the start of the evening . . . indeed, from what it had been in recent weeks. Where there had once been only darkness and sorrow, there now existed radiant joy and merciful serenity. Frederick, too, found delight not just in Rosamond's love, but in her glowing happiness, and he communicated this contentment in his quiet tenderness toward her.

After sitting together for a time, Frederick at last rose, still holding her by the hand. Rising also, Rosamond's blue eyes were apprehensive as she looked at him.

"They will have gone into the card room by now," he said softly, leading her toward the door. "You must go back, or they will come looking for you."

But Rosamond seemed distressed at this suggestion. Having just reclaimed her love after such tribulation, she could not abide the thought of another parting. Frederick, turning to her when they reached the door, saw her stricken face and understood. He smiled at her fondly and, releasing her hand, placed his own hand upon her cheek.

"I shall come and see you tomorrow," he promised. "I will bring you a present." Her eyes still reflected her unwillingness to leave him. He spoke to her very tenderly. "My darling . . . I promise you that soon there shall be no more good-byes."

Yet, despite being the initiator, Frederick was equally reluctant to let her go, having suffered the anguish of heartache himself. Letting his hand fall from her cheek, his fingers lightly caressed her graceful neck before coming to rest softly upon her lily-white shoulder and thus drawing her gently toward him for one kiss before parting.

It necessarily followed that Rosamond spent another sleepless night, though not because of grievous thoughts or restless dreams, as had been the former cause of such wakefulness, but rather because the fervid exhilaration within her heart would not allow her to rest. Yet even with such fitful slumber, she rose the next morning feeling not weary in the least, although some of her elated joy had given way to a bit of anxiety, as must often be the case when myriad thoughts are left pondered throughout a long night. She somehow feared that the events of the previous evening had been nothing but a dream, and that she would discover her tremulous heart should be devastated by the shock of reality.

So it was that all morning she kept a very agitated vigil at the window overlooking the street, whilst trying to look occupied and composed whenever her mother passed through the room. Every carriage that appeared in the distance brought her first hope then disappointment as it passed through the square without stopping. She was truly growing distraught by the time luncheon was laid out in the dining room, and after hastily ingesting only a very meager portion, she resumed her window-side post in the parlor. She repeated the Earl's words over and over in her head — "I shall come and see you tomorrow." Surely, surely it was not just a dream after all? If only he would appear and confirm the reality . . . it would alleviate her anxiety in an instant, and yet while that did not occur, she must ever be in such a state of insecurity. It is such a fine line which separates the wide chasm of elation and despair!

Then, just as she was beginning to give in to her former disheartenment, her fears were vanquished in a moment of rapturous joy as she perceived a familiar carriage coming to a halt before the house. Without giving pause or hesitation, Rosamond made her way out the front door and flew down the steps to the street just as the Earl of Kendal alighted from his carriage.

"Oh, you *did* come!" she cried, reaching out both her hands to him, which he took with an affectionate and amused smile at her rosy breathlessness.

"Of course . . . I told you I would," he said as he handed her up into the carriage, then took his seat beside her. "Did you think I would not?"

"You were so long in coming!" Rosamond declared as the carriage started moving up the street. "I began to be uncertain that anything last night had been real!"

Frederick laughed. "My impatient Rosamond! I ought to have told you that I had some things to attend to in the morning." He then proceeded to tell her what he had been about. "I had to pay a call at the offices of the Star of India Tea Company to speak with Mr. Thomas Hathaway, Sr."

Rosamond gave a little gasp, and Frederick gave her hand a reassuring squeeze. "Which meeting was relatively brief and very amicable. But, before that, I had to retrieve this and see that it was properly cleaned and polished." And, opening his other hand, he held up for Rosamond's inspection a beautifully exquisite ring.

She gasped again, this time in delight, and took the ring from his hand. It was very delicate; a slender band of gold on which was mounted a single sapphire — not large, but brilliant — its deep hue the exact shade as Rosamond's eyes. It was encircled by tiny diamonds, creating a simple and elegant effect.

"Oh, how lovely," Rosamond breathed, as Frederick gently slid the ring onto her finger. "It is so beautiful!"

"It has been in my family for a long time," explained Frederick. "The first Earl of Kendal gave it to his bride when they were betrothed. The second Earl also presented it to his Countess. Of course, diamonds were rarer then, and its value would have been much greater than it is today. The third Countess of Kendal apparently had loftier visions of grandeur for herself and thought it too small and insignificant and insisted upon a grander and more elaborate ring. Since then, it has languished in the family treasury, I'm afraid. But . . . ," he looked at her, his serious black eyes flashing their intensity, "I could not help thinking of this ring when I saw your blue eyes, and thought perhaps you would like it. Of course, you may have whatever you like. I realize it's rather simple and—"

"It's perfect!" cried Rosamond rapturously, reverently stroking the ring's stones as if contemplating the elegant ladies of so long ago whose fingers the ring had graced. "I should not like any other ring half so well. Please don't get me anything different."

And Frederick's countenance showed his happiness at having such a bride who appreciated not only beauty and simplicity, but tradition and heritage as well.

"I am sorry, though," Frederick added somberly, "that you cannot wear it openly until we are married . . . or at least out of London."

Rosamond was very eager for that event to occur, and Frederick promised her that they would not delay their marriage. He needed only a few days to settle affairs in London before he could take her away to Cumbria where they would be married.

They drove to Kensington, to apprise Lady Abercrombie of their plans, for they both wished very much that she should lay to rest any misgiving which may exist in her mind over the nature of their relationship, and they knew that she would keep their secret.

Informing the other members of the Hathaway household was another matter, though. As much as Rosamond would have liked the Earl's strong presence at her side, she knew it was best that she tell her mother by herself, and without delay, for Mr. Hathaway would most definitely reveal it once he returned home that evening.

Alas for Mrs. Hathaway! Understandably elated and inconsolable at once! For what mother does not wish her daughter to wed a titled aristocrat? And yet to choose such a one as must ensure that the marriage's consummation would be met with inescapable controversy and scandal was a woeful burden for a mother to bear, and she lamented quite vocally to Rosamond. Rosamond's quiet insistence that there was nothing worthy of such insinuations did nothing to pacify her mother, who declared she felt faint upon the shock of such a revelation. She took to her bed for the remainder of the day, but once her husband came home and discussed the issue with her, the trauma seemed to pass in favor of the realization that her daughter was to be a countess, with not only a lofty social status, but the wealth and property to substantiate it. And after all, she herself had remarked on more than one occasion of the Earl's refined cordiality and handsome figure.

One area in which Mrs. Hathaway had no ambivalence was in comprehending the necessity of keeping the impending union undisclosed to any. Indeed, she should have preferred that it would remain unrevealed until long past its occurrence . . . until that time when the controversy should be somewhat diminished, though it would bring unwanted attention even should it occur five years hence.

The servants knew only that Miss Rosamond was going away, for they were assiduously employed in assisting her with such preparations as that entailed, but they knew not where or with whom, although this ignorance did not in any way curtail speculations or chatter in the kitchen or in their apartments after-hours.

For her part, Rosamond had no difficulty about displaying her ring in public, for she went nowhere, keeping diligently occupied with her own preparations and correspondence within the house. She did take great comfort in the lovely little ring, though — pulling it out of her jewelry-box and slipping it lovingly onto her finger whenever she had some moments to herself, finding immeasurable solace and happiness in the promise the ring represented.

It was well that she had such a tangible token of Frederick's love, for she had not the consolation of seeing the Earl himself for the next three days as he attended to the completion of his affairs of business in preparation for his immediate withdrawal from the city. Due partially to this enterprise, and even more so to his own cautious wisdom, he must necessarily refrain from presenting himself in Grosvenor Square, but he sent Rosamond a note each day, reassuring her that she was ever in his thoughts.

And then, on the evening of the fourth day, he sent a message saying that he would come for her the following morning, very early, as they had such a lengthy journey ahead of them.

There was very little time for good-byes, but whatever sorrow Rosamond's parents or brother may have had upon seeing her go was soon tempered by deferential acceptance as they saw how happy she was, and how tender was the Earl's manner toward her as he helped her into his carriage.

And so, even as Paris and his very willing Helen stole away in the night, so did these two lovers depart under the cover of darkness, for the sun had not begun to appear at the horizon, nor had the scullery maid even been about her scrubbing when they left behind them the city boundary.

It was a long journey north, though they traveled in a light carriage that made excellent time, and it was not an unpleasant journey, for there were many picturesque vistas to behold in passing. They put up that night at an inn whose proprietors were familiar to the Earl, for he stayed there frequently on his journeys between Stoneleigh and London. He assured Rosamond that the inn was most comfortable and the owners exemplary in their hospitality and discretion.

Indeed, the husband and wife who were the inn's proprietors went to great lengths to provide all manner of comforts to the Earl and his pretty companion, setting out a savory meal for them in a private anteroom and doing the serving themselves. Rosamond was then shown to an ample and comfortable room ("Our best," as the proprietor's wife pointed out with some pride), and given the services of their maid to attend to her needs. Frederick did not utilize the room opposite which he had been given, but instead sat up through the night in the public-room with the proprietor, perhaps to partake of that good man's conversation, but more likely to keep watch over the safety of his betrothed, whose door he kept in his view.

When Rosamond emerged early in the morning and saw that he had not slept, she implored him to utilize the first part of the day's journey for that purpose, for they had another long drive ahead of them, and she was happy enough to watch the passing landscapes through the window. She finally convinced him upon the appeal that she "couldn't bear for him to be weary and spent upon their wedding day."

The second day's journey went even faster than the first, and indeed the distance was shorter. It was mid-day when they passed into the regions of Cumbria and Westmoreland, and when Frederick remarked upon this, Rosamond felt anew the fluttery nervousness which had recurred throughout the previous days and was not uncommon to young brides contemplating their forthcoming nuptials. But Frederick held her hand, and his calm and steady presence ever reassured her, even as the ubiquitous fluttering prevailed.

They did not go to the Earl's residence at Stoneleigh, but instead went directly to the little parish church there, for Frederick had sent word from London to the vicar, who held long-established ties with the family of the Earl of Kendal, and whose living was under the jurisdiction of that estate. And there in that ancient rural church were they married in a simple, quiet ceremony, with only the curate and verger for their witnesses. And Rosamond had no wedding gown, but she picked some white blossoms which were growing wild in the churchyard and intertwined them amongst her black curls, for she knew Frederick loved to see her in white. But truly he loved her in any shade, and she required no adornments, even on her wedding day, for the luminous joy in her eyes shone brighter than any jeweled trinkets could have, and the happiness felt in these lovers' hearts as they were united was easily perceived in the glowing warmth of their countenances as they left the little church.

And so it befell that in such modest and unassuming circumstances, Miss Rosamond Hathaway became the Countess of Kendal. Far more important than any title, though, was the enduring bond represented by the simple band of gold that now encircled her finger beneath the little sapphire ring.

Although it was just beginning to grow dark when they drove through the imposing gates of Stoneleigh, Rosamond kept her face pressed up against the carriage's window, for she was eager to see the estate that she had heard so much about. And even in the dim light, she was not disappointed, for the park at Stoneleigh was impressive in beauty and size. Indeed, it seemed an age from the time they passed through the gate until she could discern the house itself looming in the distance. Again, she was delighted and awed, for a moment even forgetting her newly-acquired marital status, as she beheld the stately splendor of the immense lodge. It was more beautiful than she had imagined, and its charm was only enhanced by the warm glow emanating from the downstairs windows against the dimming light outside.

And here, upon entering the house, was Rosamond able to see Frederick in his truest role: as Master of Stoneleigh, master of a dominion in which he had grown and flourished since childhood; a genteel, unspoiled world he loved far better than the bustle and business of London. And judging by the efficiency and cheerfulness of the servants who greeted them, it was a role he executed with great adeptness. The household had, of course, been notified that their master was returning home with a new bride, and whatever their feelings or expectations may have been regarding their new mistress, Rosamond was taken by the sincerity of their smiles and simple greetings, and it occurred to her that here was none of the coldness and curtness of the city, but rather a warmth and genuineness that can be found only in country settings.

She stayed very close to her husband as they entered the main hall and were met by the head servants who had turned out to greet the Earl and his Lady, and to whom the Earl gave various directives. But once they were all about their duties, Rosamond was given over to the housekeeper, who was instructed to take her upstairs so that she could rest and get situated while the Earl met with his steward to review any pressing matters of the estate which had arisen since their last correspondence.

The housekeeper proved to be an amiable older woman with hair so white that it seemed to glisten like the tiny diamonds in Rosamond's ring. She was a kindly woman, almost motherly, who conversed pleasantly with Rosamond as they ascended the great staircase. She told her new mistress that she had been employed at Stoneleigh since she was ten years old, her father being the Head Footman and her mother a lady's maid. She remembered the day Frederick was born ("the most joyous day Stoneleigh had ever seen"), and had watched him grow ("always the handsomest and sturdiest amongst his brothers"). Rosamond smiled as she remembered the miniature portraits she had seen in the Earl's Belgravia house, and she thought to herself that she should like to sit down with this woman sometime and hear tales of Frederick's youth. Despite the housekeeper's amiability, there was nothing indecorous or overly-familiar in her manner, and her efficiency was apparent.

Due to the advancing darkness outside, the staircase itself was a bit shadowy, but the upstairs hall into which they ascended was illuminated by sconces which lined its walls, as were the subsequent corridors they traversed before coming to a halt before a set of dark-paneled, handsomely-inlaid doors. The housekeeper opened the door, then allowed Rosamond to enter the room before her. The lamps in the room had already been lighted, and there was a fire blazing in the fireplace. Rosamond did not enter far into the room . . . only a few steps, then she stood where she was and took it in.

"This has been the Countess's apartment since this house was first built," explained the housekeeper. "All the way back to the first Earl's wife."

Somehow this knowledge did not comfort Rosamond, for she could think only of her predecessor, so recently departed.

The housekeeper may have sensed this misgiving, for she added apologetically, "I would have liked to have had the room completely made over for your coming, but we had so little time to prepare." She smiled encouragingly at Rosamond. "I did have new curtains hung, though, and put new coverings on the bed. And of course, you'll be wanting to order new appointments and furnishings for yourself."

Rosamond knew the woman meant kindly, and she nodded a polite thank-you, but she could not rid herself of the tightened knot which had formed in her stomach upon realization that this was to be her abode.

A footman entered with Rosamond's small trunk and set it on the floor near the wardrobe, then, with a bow and a curtsey to the new Countess, both servants departed.

Rosamond had never moved from the spot in which she had initially paused. And now that she was by herself, she took only a couple of halting steps farther into the room. It was a vast apartment, with a very ornate marble fireplace at one end and a door at the other which presumably led to a dressing-room. The furnishings and effects were very tasteful, and the bed was elaborately carved on both posts and headboard. There was nothing sterile or unfriendly in the room's appearance, but Rosamond felt a coldness inside her that surely coincided with the knot in her stomach. She ventured over to the bed and mindlessly ran her hand over the pretty bedspread, only slowly grasping the reality of the situation.

These were to be her quarters — it had been the Countess's apartment since the time of the First Earl of Kendal, designed purposefully for the mistress of the household, which she was now. But it was not long ago that Stoneleigh had had another mistress, and she, too, must have occupied this room, utilized these very furnishings. And the room itself, while very attractive, was so immense — much larger than her room in Grosvenor Square, which had been sufficiently ample in its own right. Rosamond had not thought upon such a living situation when she had contemplated her new position. She stood in the middle of the immense room feeling suddenly very alone and very isolated. A sickly feeling took hold where the knot had been in her stomach, and she managed to make her way to the dressing-table where a little chair provided her disheartened body with support.

It was three-quarters of an hour later when Frederick emerged from his study with the steward, their business having concluded. The steward went on his way, but Frederick stopped the housekeeper as she passed in the hall.

"I trust you have seen adequately to the Countess's comfort?"

"I hope so, my lord. She did not ask for anything, and I was just on my way up to see if she required anything now." The good housekeeper hesitated, then added, "If it is not out of place to say so, my lord, she seemed rather —," she hesitated again, "rather reluctant is the only word I can think of." The Earl frowned and the housekeeper added, "I did encourage her to think about how she should like to have the room done over to suit her own tastes. I hope she should find it comfortable enough until then."

"You put her in the Countess's apartment?" the Earl asked a bit sharply.

"Why yes, my lord, of course."

"Of course," Frederick repeated rather absently, still frowning as he looked thoughtfully up the stairway. Then, "Do not worry about looking in on her," he said. "I will go myself."

Rosamond had been sitting at the daintily elegant dressing table for nearly an hour. At first, she had laid her head wearily upon the table's surface. But then, raising her head, she had only been staring absently into the mirror, unmindful of the face reflected there.

Presently, there was a knock at the door, and she rose as the Earl entered. He stood in the doorway, seeing at once that the radiance which had formerly shone in Rosamond's eye was gone. She herself said nothing, but was contritely conscious of his scrutiny, and cast her eyes downward.

After a moment, Frederick spoke. "You are not resting," he observed gently.

She looked up and met his pensive dark eyes. He glanced over at her small traveling trunk which had clearly been left untouched.

"You have neither situated your things."

Rosamond averted her eyes again and turned away, chagrined and self-conscious. "No, my lord," she murmured. "I . . . I just thought . . . I mean, I—," She broke off, unable to think of any plausible excuse. She never could deceive him. She suddenly turned back to where he stood and crossed to him, her eyes wide and beseeching. "My lord, I — this room, it's so — I mean, did she . . . did she . . . she must have . . . ," she stammered in her unhappy shame.

But Frederick only shook his head. She did not need to speak more. He understood.

"My dear girl," he said quietly, taking her hand, his black eyes gleaming. "This is not where you belong. Come."

And leading her away from the Countess's chamber, he brought her into his own apartment and assured her that he would have it no other way but that she should remain there. He brought in her small trunk himself and gave orders to the footman that when the Countess's other possessions arrived, they should be brought directly to his apartment, as she would not be utilizing the former Countess's room.

Rosamond's heart overflowed with love and gratitude toward her husband who thought nothing of disregarding conventions of formality in order that she need not be parted from him more. And so the vows they had taken but hours before were most fervently consummated, and that night, Rosamond slept in tranquil serenity, for there was no sweeter slumber to be had than in the arms of her beloved.

For Rosamond, life at Stoneleigh brought more happiness than she could have ever conceived. The days following her arrival were spent in exploration and acclimation, for there seemed to be unending delights to discover both within and without the manor house. She took long walks with her husband in the garden and park, whose terraces and paths held not only fragrant blossoms and picturesque landscapes, but fascinating vestiges of the inhabitants who came before them . . . reminders of the ancient lineage of Earls who had resided there, each generation leaving its mark upon the estate. Sometimes Frederick took her riding across the broad Cumbrian plains and verdant rolling hills of Westmoreland. Other times, they stayed close to home, taking their tea beside the river's bank or their breakfast in the spring arbor.

After a time, of course, the Earl must necessarily give attention to those duties of business which his station required, but Rosamond was no less happy, for she was never neglected and found much to occupy her time within the house itself (whose drawing room contained a fine instrument for her to play upon, and whose vast library held wonders), as well as in acquiring the necessary familiarity with her own role as mistress of the household, in which duties the kindly housekeeper gave her worthy assistance.

After a few weeks deemed appropriate for a newly-married couple to situate themselves, guests began to pay calls. The neighboring gentry were eager to meet the Earl's new bride, being much less inclined toward harboring ill-founded conclusions than their London counterparts, and were thus most welcoming and cordial in their regards. Rosamond's fears of being perceived as lacking in her role as Frederick's wife proved utterly unfounded as their neighbors and guests readily took to her graceful gentility. Indeed, they were quite enamored of the Earl's pretty bride, with her charming appeal and gracious modesty. And she, in turn, found the country gentry to be every bit as engaging as her city coterie and found herself to be missing not at all the London society to which she had been accustomed. This was a gentle, slower-paced world, and she understood Frederick's affection for his family home.

The love that existed between the Earl and his bride was apparent and seemed to touch everyone and everything at Stoneleigh, from the servants, to the guests, to the house itself — filling every corner of the lodge with a lightness and warmth that had not been seen there for many years.

Even when the hunting season commenced, — and Stoneleigh hosted sizable gatherings, for that sport was Frederick's favorite pastime — Rosamond was ever foremost in his thoughts. He went out riding to hunt nearly every day then, whether alone or in a party, but when he returned, he always sought her out, for he knew she was anxious every time he rode out, though she never said so. But often when he went alone, or even sometimes in a group, she would come outside to the terrace to await his return. Once he had handed his horse over to a stable-boy, she would run out to meet him, and no matter the present company, Frederick would put his arm about her, and they would walk back to the house together, his affection ever touched by the joy in her eyes as she beheld his return.

At other times, when the weather was unpleasant or he was in the company of a large number of other men, she would wait for him inside. But he knew where to find her. She would be upstairs, in their apartment, with a ready fire in the hearth and his comfortable armchair positioned before it. Once he had entered and gotten out of his boots and coat, he would settle into the chair, and she would sit upon the stool at his feet, just as she used to do in Lady Abercrombie's library. She would rub soothing balm upon his hands, for gloves gave but little protection during such rough and prolonged riding as hunting entailed. And, just as ever, they would seldom talk, but she would look up at him with shining eyes, and he would look upon her with brooding intensity. And when she had finished tending to his coarsened hands, he would gather her into his arms, and in such a tender embrace would all thoughts of hunts or guests or worldly cares be entirely forgotten.

Truly, the circumstances of their station and environment were merely incidental to their happiness. Frederick Lancaster wanted nothing in the world except to make her happy, and Rosamond desired only to share his love and be with him always. Thus were their wants simple and their contentment great.

There remained only one sorrow in Rosamond's heart and that was her estranged sister, who crossed her mind from time to time and cast a pang of bittersweetness into her otherwise idyllic life.

Rosamond was spared another sorrow, though, due to her husband's vigilant watchfulness over her well-being. Unbeknownst to her, the Earl had forbidden that any London newspapers should be brought onto the estate, including in the servants' hall. Nor were any members of the publication industry to be received at Stoneleigh, including the illustrious Fleet Street entrepreneurs who had been recognizable business associates in London. And so, while Rosamond had certainly been aware that her marriage to Lord Kendal would generate a great deal of gossip in the city, as long as she remained at Stoneleigh, she need never know the extent of such callous intimations.

In their remote haven, the Earl and his bride could easily enough disregard the London gossip, but that did not in any way prevent its commencement, or its subsequent escalation. For theirs was a tale — or at least the appearance of a tale — ripe for the scandal-monger's tongue. And indeed, the insinuations and scrutiny were euphorically set into motion nearly as soon as the Earl's carriage had left Grosvenor Square. Being as the news was never officially announced, the details came out in increments, courtesy of the journalists whose society columns were front-page fixtures. At first, there were just tantalizing hints — "A certain member of the peerage seems to have vacated his seat a bit early this season. And the young lady with whom he fled the city may only be said to have *not* been the wife he so recently divorced." Naturally, that was a prime overture for speculation as to whom the Earl of Kendal "fled" with. The rumors flew indiscriminately, and Lady Abercrombie's hall-tray became flooded with the calling-cards of unsolicited visitors, whom she did not deign to receive.

Then, when it was discovered that the young lady in question was Miss Rosamond Hathaway (and she the offspring of "new money"!), the scandal was taken to new heights, for now the idle and sanctimonious tongues were provided with a target upon which to direct their smug and slanderous innuendos, whispered behind fans and over tea cups in ballrooms and salons across the city. When it was revealed that the Earl and Miss

Hathaway had been married, it hardly deterred the controversial reports, for the self-righteous detractors would readily point out that no matter how lawful the marriage was, it still remained a fact that Lord Kendal had divorced his first wife — and how recently! This was generally followed by a great deal of smug head-shaking and clucking and a comment about how all had been deceived by Miss Hathaway, who had appeared to be a "paragon of virtue". The young lady, of course, must bear the brunt of the blame in such a sordid affair. Though none in society had seemed to possess any knowledge of the situation before its publication, all were now experts in the realm of judgment and hearsay. Sensation was to be preferred over truth, as has been the case in every age, and the marriage of the Earl of Kendal to Rosamond Hathaway provided enough scintillating and speculative material to enliven the social gatherings of the elite for the duration of the season.

Frederick's prediction had been accurate regarding his aunt's advocacy, for Lady Abercrombie's drawing room was one of the few sanctuaries in the city where gossip upon the subject was suppressed. She had immediately and inexorably silenced the first intimations of scandal, and made it very clear that such slanderous implications were not to be repeated within her drawing room or any part of her household.

All of this was bound to be difficult for Mrs. Hathaway, who was so active in society, and whose family had never been the subject of such scrutiny before. Although no one ever put the topic directly to her, of course, she was not oblivious to all of the whispering that commenced whenever she or another family member entered a room or walked by a gathered circle. Aunt Sarah Blakely had a great deal of pity for her "poor sister", and consequently, without any formal invitation or declaration, re-established herself within the household in Grosvenor Square, much to the chagrin of young Tom Hathaway.

Chapter XV

Tom struggled as perhaps no one else in his family did. Ever since he had spoken with Edith and smashed the loathsome flask upon the rocky bank, a change had come over him. He often felt disconcerted and fitful, with an edginess that he could trace to no justifiable cause. He had never loved his work; now he found it burdensome. Although he had always met the requirements expected of him, such achievement had come only as a result of much concerted application, which efforts now seemed overly exerting as he found it increasingly difficult to focus the necessary attention on nearly every undertaking. His father had even summoned him into his office on several occasions to seek explanation for what appeared to be an excess of careless mistakes or unfinished tasks. Tom, unhappily, had no explanation to give, only a promise that he would put forth better effort in the future. Such a general oath did not seem to entirely satisfy his father, which only increased Tom's restive nervousness and added a dimension of dispiritedness.

He no longer went to the club at all; that establishment's convivial pastimes proving too alluring against his self-imposed forbearance. One area that gave him no trouble was sleep. Whatever tenseness or despondency he may have felt during the day in no way brought forth any symptoms of insomnia. On the contrary, he became inclined toward an excess of repose . . . sleeping deeply and heavily, and often requiring awakening by a member of the household, despite the fact that he usually went to bed at a prudent hour.

Tom's world had changed with an unexpected rapidity that made him uncomfortable. He was a naturally cautious and methodical person, and hasty transitions did not suit him. He especially disliked ones as tumultuous as the departure of both his sisters had been. Only a year ago they had been a complacent and harmonious household of five; now he remained the only young person in a household of three. The loss of his younger sister to marriage had caused him substantial consternation, due partly to the astonishing disclosure as to where her affections lay, but more so to the simple loss of her companionship, which he had really only started to lean upon in Lorna's absence. And as for Lorna . . . there indeed was his heart torn. He possessed not the strength of character of either of his sisters, for neither of them seemed to have any ambivalence as to their own feelings or actions, at least in this matter. Rosamond was so guilelessly innocent — it would never occur to her to do anything other than simply wait and hope for her sister's return to virtue. And Lorna . . . Lorna was equally resolved that her life required no reformation.

Yes, Tom knew Lorna's thoughts and inclinations where Rosamond did not. Like his young sister, Tom also had received a letter from Lorna, but unlike Rosamond, he had continued to correspond, for Lorna had found favor with his response to her missive. While he did not think Lorna's choices were right, he could not bring himself to tell her so, for he did not want her to discontinue their relationship (as she certainly would . . . her severance with Rosamond was proof enough of that), and so he had maintained correspondence with her, choosing the comfort of peace over allegiance to his own convictions. He did not tell Rosamond of this in his letters to her, although she sometimes asked in her own correspondence from Stoneleigh if he'd had any word about Lorna.

He did not tell his mother, either, although he suspected she knew. When it came to the subject of Lorna, there was a great deal left unsaid amongst the three Hathaways in Grosvenor Square, but which seemed to be tacitly understood nonetheless. For instance, Tom knew that his father had discovered that Mrs. Hathaway was furtively sending money to Lorna, although if his father knew how regularly, he could not say. Mr. Hathaway had been predictably displeased at such proceedings and had had stern words for his wife regarding the matter. However, Tom knew that whatever avowal his mother may have made, she had not stopped her funding or her correspondence with her eldest child, and he was equally certain that his father was well aware of this and had deliberately chosen to say no more about it, both maintaining a feigned ignorance.

During the months since Rosamond left, Hugh Shadwell did not neglect his old friend, and in his gentle spiritual advocacy as a clergyman and his understanding as an acquaintance of so many years, Tom did find some solace.

There were some changes, though, and some memories which no amount of comradeship or diversion of thoughts could offset. The house itself was changed. Rosamond's piano was silent and untouched. No longer were her pretty baubles and stray trinkets to be found lodged between the sofa cushions or scattered about on the hall-table, under the piano stool, or wherever else she may have carelessly mislaid them. Lorna's vivacious laughter no longer echoed across the parlor, nor was her high-spirited discourse heard at the dinner table. And upon looking into each sister's bedroom, what a contrast was now to be found! Rosamond's apartment, while still bearing its delicate floral accents, was nearly emptied of any small articles or accessories; the drawers and dressing-table devoid of her personal effects, most of which she had taken with her to Cumbria. Lorna's room, on the other hand, might still be thought occupied, for all the customary belongings of a young lady could still be discerned atop the bureau and in the various drawers and cupboards, having left as she did, with only a few possessions which she could carry in her small valise.

Tom did glance into Lorna's room every now and then just to revitalize some sort of connection with the sister he dearly missed. He needed no tangible reminder of Rosamond . . . her letters came so often, and her name was mentioned frequently and openly in the household. But sometimes it seemed to Tom as if Lorna had ceased to exist. There was no talk of her at home or anywhere else, and no certainty of seeing her in the near future. Even her large portrait had been removed from the parlor (though smaller and older ones remained scattered throughout the house). If it weren't for her occasional letters or the intermittent glance into her room, it would be only memories of her that remained. But, while there may have been few tangible reminders of the eldest child, she was very much alive in the minds and hearts of her family in Grosvenor Square. And the silence between those three family members only increased Tom's ambivalence and the ever-increasing dilemma within his conscience.

Lorna awoke to the sound she woke to every day . . . a sound she loved . . . the sound of the sea. It was not a gentle, lulling sound, but rather a coarse, uneven crashing sound as the grey waves collided with the rocks that lined the rugged shore. The sound still thrilled her each morning, even after hearing it for so many months. The little upstairs room in which she awoke was already filled with light, for it was not early, and the functional oblongs of fabric which hung at the windows were hardly adequate substitutes for proper curtains, letting the daylight filter through their sheerness.

She lay there for a few moments, as she always did, letting her eyes adjust to the light and letting her senses make the transition from dreamy sleep to alert wakefulness. She stretched lazily, then turned her head toward Miles, still sleeping, his reddish hair a tangle of unkempt curls all rumpled and disheveled against the pillow. Lorna smiled, rolled over and gave him a kiss upon his ear, then sat up and stepped out of the warm bed onto the cold, hard floor. It always sent a shiver through her which did not abate until she had dressed, which she did next, and hurriedly, to rid herself of the chill all the faster. She sat on the only chair in the room — a wooden slat-backed one borrowed from the kitchen — and pulled on her stockings and shoes then crept down the stairs as quietly as she could, which was only habit, for she knew Miles would not awake, as he routinely slept even later than did she. There was no hall and no doors — the stairs descended directly from the bedroom into the kitchen below. The cottage had but four rooms — two upstairs and two below, but the rusticality was only just beginning to set in for Lorna, and she still found it novel and endearing.

She lit a fire in the stove, for the days were heading into winter and the house was very chilly. She was adept at such a manual task, having done it every morning for the past few months, though she was not particularly fond of it.

One task she had learned to enjoy, though, was cooking, and she put a pot of water to heat on the stovetop as soon as it was ready. Having never had to cook before, it had always been an interesting and appealing activity for her. As a child, she and her siblings were sometimes given by the cook bits of left-over dough to form into little cakes or biscuits of their own, and Lorna more than either her brother or sister had found great enjoyment in handling and kneading the pliable dough, working it into intricate and imaginative shapes that turned out so lovely upon baking that she almost regretted having to eat them. So it was that she was predisposed to think of the preparation of food as being an agreeable and entertaining diversion. This perception gave her a sense of bravery and artistry in her culinary endeavors, and she never seemed to exhaust her cache of ideas in her attempts to create innovative dishes with their meager and repetitious selection of ingredients. Enjoying cooking and excelling at it were two different things, however, and for a young lady who had lived her entire life with a regular cook and with no expectations of ever having to prepare food on her own, it was to be expected that not all of her culinary undertakings should be successful, or even palatable. Fortunately, Miles was not particular about his food. Eating had never been a priority for him. In fact, it was more of an afterthought. More often than not, Lorna had to pry him away from his writing or interrupt his impassioned discourse to remind him to take some sustenance.

Or to remind him of . . . other things. It seemed he had become more and more absorbed in his work as time progressed; preoccupied with important and weighty concerns of humanity's improvement, no doubt.

It had been very strange at first with no regular schedule for eating or sleeping or, indeed, any activity. But without the issues of servants or guests or social obligations, such regularity was unnecessary, and for such a free-spirited pair, was actually impeding. So Lorna had grown accustomed to spontaneity and improvisation. She had given up seemingly every vestige of her former life to be with Miles Anderson in the only way she could — the only way he would have it. And if there was any periodic regret or sadness to be felt, then it was the fault of Society — heartless Society who would never accept them or the life they had chosen; who did not understand the morality of pleasure. Miles had taught her that, and she embraced it.

Lorna reached for her shawl which hung in its familiar place on a hook beside the kitchen door. It was one of her old ones from Grosvenor Square, and while it had been very becoming when first acquired, it had since grown a bit worn from daily use against every element. For Lorna donned it every morning, and indeed every time she left the house, as it was always chilly beside the sea, even in the summer months. Now, being late autumn, the mornings were especially brisk, even as it neared mid-day.

When Lorna stepped outside the kitchen door, she pulled the shawl tighter around her, for a profusion of grey clouds hid the sun and produced (at least the effect of) coldness of temperature. She did not mind, though. The crispness invigorated her, even as did the misty, salty air blown in off the sea, which she inhaled deeply as she set forth along the little footpath which led to the shore.

She followed the path only a short distance while it paralleled the rocky coastline, and she soon came upon a long wooden pier which jutted far out into the cove. She turned off the footpath, stepping up onto the pier's wooden planks and began to walk toward the far end of it, leaving the shore behind. The pier was very old — certainly it was no longer in use — and some of its planks were worn and rotting toward the middle, while many of the boards' edges were splintered and crumbling, but Lorna traversed these spots with ease, for she had made her way thus nearly every morning since she had taken up residence in the little cottage. She bore an affection for the time-worn planks of wood, even in their frailty, which evoked for her a nearness to the depths over which she crossed, until she came to the pier's end. And there she stood for quite a long while; the solitary indication of life above the water's surface, but hardly impassive, for here she felt more alive, more awed, more insignificant and majestic all at once, than anywhere else in the world. And there upon the open water the wind blew uninhibited, whipping through Lorna's long, loose hair, which she made no effort to tie back. She stood gazing across that endless expanse; the churning water bleak and grey under the overcast autumn sky, but to her just as beautiful and mesmerizing as it had been under the clear summer sky only a short time ago. She remembered the way it looked then — its waves calmer and lazy, colored a deep and fathomless blue, like the eyes of her brother and sister.

A shadow as grey as the cloud-reflected waves passed over Lorna's face as the thought of her sister passed through her mind, and despite the vitalizing exhilaration of the fresh breeze and the rolling waves, a scowl creased her brow. No, she must not allow herself to be so severely provoked. She must push all thoughts of Rosamond from her mind. Better to think upon Tom, who was ever loyal to her. But then the scowl would inevitably change to wistfulness, and she must not have that either. Better to focus on just the sea, just the hour, just the cottage and the zealous young man sleeping within.

Lorna began every day with this pilgrimage to piers-end, needing such a communion with the wild seascape and untamed waves. And when she had been sufficiently infused with vigor, she turned her back to the sea and began making her way toward the shore. She walked more briskly back along the footpath than she had in going to the pier, for the damp and chill were truly penetrating, and upon re-entering the cottage's kitchen door, she first removed the pot of hot water before pulling a chair up beside the stove where she sat and enjoyed the warmth for a few minutes.

When she stood, she did not discard her shawl, for the rest of the house was not yet a comfortable temperature, but she had no wish to remain huddled before the stove all morning. She ascended once more the stairs leading into the bedroom, but crossed through that room — still taking care to tread lightly in consideration of the sleeper — and into the other upstairs room, which opened directly off of the bedroom.

This small room was a blunt contrast to the sparsely-furnished bedroom, for it was crammed full of all sorts of assorted miscellany. It was the room they called "the studio", and indeed one corner near the window held an easel upon which sat an unfinished canvas. A half-dozen other canvases leaned against the wall behind it, their subjects completed, but as of yet finding no home of any permanence. The other corner on the window-wall contained the broad wooden desk where Miles sat half the day, and often late into the evening, working on his writing and correspondence. A collection of dried flowers hung from the rear corner of the room, waiting for Lorna to take them down and put them to decorative use, but otherwise serving some purpose in lending a bit of color to an otherwise rather drab and cluttered area. The remainder of the space along the walls was occupied by a wide variety of odds-and-ends salvaged from Miles's London rooms, and which did not seem to belong in any other part of the cottage.

It was to the easel that Lorna crossed and sat upon the stool before it. The canvas was neither large nor cumbersome, and she picked it up, studying it with a critical eye. It was her own work. While Miles was the studied artist, he had passed on to her a love of painting and readily praised her skill. She loved best to paint landscapes, finding she had little talent for the human figure as Miles did, though he preferred sketching his subjects over painting. But she loved the colorful medium, and had even put some of the money sent by her mother toward the purchase of some oil-based paint and the canvasses. She primarily painted the environment around the cottage . . . the rocky coast, the sea in all its moods, and sometimes even the cottages themselves which edged up along the rugged shoreline.

But when she tired of painting reality, she started painting from her memory. Such was the painting she held now, which was nearly finished. It portrayed a scene familiar to both Lorna and Miles . . . the ancient and picturesque well down in the steep ravine where they had gone the day of their first encounter. The image of the romantic old well had always stayed in Lorna's mind, though she had never returned to the actual location since that day. It was the image from her memory which she had painted and she was very fond of the scene, not only for its beauty, but for the memory it represented. Miles had commended her technique, but criticized the accuracy of the physical rendition, having seen the well and ravine many more times than Lorna and quite certain that his own memory should be more precise in this case than hers. It was probably true, but she would never suggest a return to the well's location to verify accuracy . . . not now, though Miles might have been glad enough to make the journey to London.

It was the one concession that Miles had made that, to Lorna, proved his love more than any other. For Miles must carry on his work in reform and philosophy, and London was certainly the preferable location to do such. It was his wish to live there — perhaps the two of them taking a house in Clerkenwell near all the comrades with whom he now carried on his work through diligent correspondence. But in order to be with Lorna in a way she would find acceptable, and in reluctant concession to her family situation, he had agreed to abide with her in the seaside cottage, at least for the present. And so, while he still shunned any notions of sentimentality in speech or ritual, Lorna knew that he loved her nonetheless as he made such a significant sacrifice on her behalf.

She felt restless on this day, though, perhaps due to the desolate austerity of the windswept waves, perhaps due to a remnant of her momentary disagreeable meditation upon the pier; but whatever the reason, she found she could not rally the motivation to take up her brush and work on the painting. She knew better than to work against the tide of creativity —

so she rose again and crossed back into the bedroom.

Atop the bureau was a small box which Lorna had brought with her from Grosvenor Square, and she picked it up. It was a pretty box of alabaster which her father had once given her upon return from one of his travels. It was unpretentious and tasteful; well-chosen to suit a girl of Lorna's penchant for simplicity. Inside, was a collection of small trinkets which she had hastily assembled before her departure from London. None of them had really held any sentimentality for her, and none were valuable . . . she was really not certain what had induced her to bring such a mélange, but every now and then she would lift the box's lid, as she did now, and examine the little collection.

She pulled out a ring — silver, set with a single yellow topaz — that she had once purchased on a whim during a holiday in Canterbury, after which purchase her mother had admonished her for buying such an inferior stone, but Lorna hadn't cared. She liked its warm, golden color, and so she had purchased it and worn it a few times before leaving it to be forgotten; neglected at the bottom of her jewelry-box with her other seldom-worn pieces. Now, though, she took the ring and slipped it onto her finger, admiring its rich hue. She gazed at it there abstractedly for a few moments before, still lost in thought, she removed it from her finger, and after turning it over several times, slid it very carefully onto her left hand. She slipped it off again nearly immediately, for the pang she felt at seeing and feeling it there was not one she liked to contend with.

There were other pangs on other days . . . brought on sometimes when her mind strayed to certain memories or thoughts, but these she also did her best to suppress. She must not let such feelings sway her. The greatest adversary which at times crept into her brain was guilt. But she would repress it again and again. She would not permit herself to feel it. Her best defense was to simply command her thoughts to bend in one direction only: forward. To think on the past would only cause her to weaken her resolve, so she made conscious effort to focus her ruminations only on the present and the future, but mostly on the present. Miles liked to talk about the future of humanity, the future of society, but less so about his own future, or theirs, proclaiming instead the necessity of focusing on the here and now, which "is all we are assured of, so we need to make the most of it", as he liked to say. Lorna found this a useful philosophy to adopt, as it was not only logical but also emancipating, allowing her to be beholden to nothing from her past.

And so Lorna and Miles Anderson lived a very full and exhilarating life together in their little rustic cottage beside the sea, taking care that each moment should be lived to its fullest; each hour should be maximized in its potential to bring pleasure. And whatever thoughts of the past might cross Lorna's mind from time to time, she would never trade her present happiness for a life of mundane convention. Even now, as she placed the ring back in its alabaster box and turned away from the bureau, she found Miles sitting up upon the bed, newly-wakened and looking at her, arousing in her heart the thrilling awareness of her present blissful situation, and chasing away all traces of any desire for ceremonial ring-wearing privileges.

The wintry chill of December is especially felt in England's northern country, but it was not to be found inside the manor of Stoneleigh, for in that grand abode the assiduous domestic staff kept the fires well-tended both day and night for the comfort of all who resided there. Indeed, the house took on an especially warm glow during that convivial month as Rosamond, in collaboration with the excellent housekeeper, had attended to the most agreeable task of adorning the common-rooms with splendid holiday décor, and the guests who visited the estate were welcomed with the sight of beautiful greenery and gold trim bedecking the rooms in a manner that was both festive and elegant. The Master of Stoneleigh was happily amused at the unabashed delight his Lady took in this employment, for nearly every day he was led to some doorway or niche which had been newly-adorned as a result of some enlightened inspiration and which the young Countess was eager to present for his approval.

It was en-route to such an endeavor that Rosamond happened to be passing through one of the main corridors one morning when her husband stepped out of his study and, seeing her there, bid her to come in.

It was an unusual request, for at that time of the morning he usually went over affairs of business with his steward or sometimes rode out to survey tenants' land, and Rosamond always made every attempt to leave him undisturbed during those hours.

But as Frederick stepped aside to allow her to enter the study, she found it quite unoccupied, the steward having apparently already concluded his conference with the Earl. As Frederick closed the door and turned back toward Rosamond, she could see by his countenance that there was something weighing upon his mind. He took her hand and gently led her to the bench before the fire where he settled her with great care, then sat beside her. Rosamond felt instinctively that whatever he was about to tell her was an issue of some sensitivity, and before he even uttered a word, her heartbeat began to accelerate with her trepidation.

"Rosamond," he began, "there is a subject we must address, for I cannot put it off longer." He spoke softly, and as he went on, he looked directly into her eyes, his own dark eyes somewhat troubled, but his voice full of the tenderness he felt toward her. "In only a few weeks I must return to London to take my seat in Parliament. You know how the Session there runs . . . I must stay those months and fulfill my responsibility. But I shall return here as often as I can during that time . . . every chance I have. And I shall take care that you will be looked after while I am gone. You can have your mother here to stay with you if you like, or even Lady Abercrombie could easily be persuaded to give up part of the season in London."

But Rosamond had heard only the first sentence he uttered. She looked at him with eyes wide and gravely somber. "You . . . you would go away to London and leave me behind?"

Her voice sounded so pitifully heartbroken that Frederick frowned with concern and put his arm around her, bringing her close. "If I had only my own wishes to consider, I should not be parted from you for one hour," he murmured to her. "But I must consider your well-being and happiness before all else. I would not for the world subject you to the malicious scrutiny of the London establishment."

Still in her husband's embrace, Rosamond's forlorn words reached his ear as nearly a whisper. "I care nothing about that. I cannot be happy if you are far away from me."

And as Frederick felt a warm and silent tear upon his neck, he could not help but smile affectionately at such a heartfelt affirmation of love.

"My darling," he said reassuringly. "If that is truly how you feel, then you must not be troubled more by this. I assure you, nothing should please me more than to have you with me in London. The thought of leaving you here has weighed heavily upon my heart these recent days. But you must understand why I would not have taken you there without your own consent."

That consent was most readily re-affirmed, to the contentment of both, and as the holidays approached, the household staff was thrust into a flurry of activity as they prepared for not only the Christmas celebrations, but also for the impending departure of both master and mistress to London. And for the Earl and his bride, it was a time of quiet joy and amiable delights, for there would be no forthcoming separation. And if their holidays were touched with a trace of bittersweetness, it was only due to the awareness that they must soon leave their beloved Stoneleigh for a while. Yet how richly gratifying it was to know that such an absence would be but temporary.

Frederick Lancaster was justifiably apprehensive about exposing his wife to the prying eyes and duplicitous tongues of the London gossipmongers, but Rosamond's family there shared none of his trepidation, having joyfully received her letter telling of her imminent return. Her mother, especially, was thrilled at the prospect of having her daughter back in the city for the season. Indeed, Lord and Lady Kendal had hardly arrived in Belgravia (and certainly had not gotten settled or unpacked) when a note was delivered to Rosamond from her mother, asking them to come to tea in Grosvenor Square that very day. Frederick could not take the time for such leisurely diversions, but he urged Rosamond to go and be reunited with her family, as he knew she was anxious to see them.

It seemed strange to Rosamond to arrive at her old house as a visitor, for when she stepped out of the carriage into Grosvenor Square, it was all so familiar and unchanged, it might have been only yesterday that she had last departed the premises. Yet, in reality, it was nearly a year ago since she had taken her leave. As she ascended the front steps, she pondered how the last time she had traversed those steps, she had been Miss Rosamond Hathaway, a member of the household within. She smiled slightly to herself, for while she reveled in such sentimentality, she knew that she much preferred her new role and her new household, however cherished were memories of the old.

The strangeness and novelty of the situation were reinforced as she stood outside the front door and rang the bell. Certainly she had never done so when the house was her own. She glanced back over her shoulder at the waiting carriage, wondering if she ought to have sent the footman to the door instead, as she had been accustomed to do in Cumbria. She couldn't imagine that she should be expected to follow such a formality at her own family's home, but it did feel so odd to be standing at the familiar door, waiting to be admitted.

Agnes opened the door and flashed a welcoming smile of recognition at the sight of her former mistress.

Rosamond smiled back. "Good afternoon, Agnes."

"Good day to you, my lady," Agnes bobbed her curtsey, still smiling genially. "Your mother is expecting you," she added as Rosamond entered the foyer.

What a welcome was in store for her! Her mother did not even wait for her to be shown into the parlor, but came right out to meet her in the hall, and Tom followed directly behind. After a profusion of happy greetings and numerous hugs and kisses, they escorted her into the parlor where Aunt Sarah Blakely and their old friend Hugh Shadwell were waiting beside the tea table. Aunt Sarah greeted her niece affectionately, and Hugh warmly took her hand, then the five of them sat down to tea, and more importantly, to partake of one another's company in the gladsome and lighthearted manner of those who had come together after an extended time apart.

Although regular correspondence had been faithfully exchanged between the youngest daughter and the family in Grosvenor Square, nothing can replace a mother's satisfaction at having her children present before her, and Mrs. Hathaway exclaimed over and over again at how well Rosamond looked — how healthy and rosily glowing was her complexion. It was true. As beautiful as Rosamond had been before she left London, her months of married life had caused her to blossom even further, with a deeper and richer beauty that can only be brought about by such happiness as she had found in her marriage. Tom, also, was well-pleased in his sister's radiant countenance, though he did not voice such sentiments as profusely as his mother.

After several hours of pleasant conviviality, which eventually moved from the tea table to the sitting area, Aunt Sarah took her leave to return to Primrose Hill, and Hugh left for his vicarage, both with Rosamond's sincere wishes that they must soon come to call in Belgravia. Mrs. Hathaway then suggested that Rosamond might like to look into her old room and examine some of the articles she had left there to see if there was anything she should still like to take away with her. Although Rosamond had not missed or required any of the things she left and, indeed, had acquired many finer possessions since her marriage, she did have a curiosity to see her former apartment, so she proceeded up the stairs and down the corridor to her bedroom.

She was rather surprised at her own feelings as she inspected the room and some of the notions inside the bureau and cupboard. She thought she would have been more wistful and nostalgic upon seeing the room, but whether it was because her absence had not yet been long enough to evoke such sentiment, or because she had already taken with her those belongings which had personal significance for her, she could only muster a few fond memories as the room itself was now so bare and devoid of her presence, and her new apartment at Stoneleigh, which was Frederick's also, was so much dearer to her than this room had ever been.

As she sorted through some effects in the drawer of the dressing table, she heard the door being pushed open and, turning, she looked upon a young maid entering with her feather duster. The girl stopped in surprise as she beheld Rosamond at the dressing table.

"Oh, I beg your pardon, Miss Rosamond. I — I mean, Lady Kendal," and the flustered young girl gave a quick curtsey. "I did not know anyone was in here."

Rosamond smiled kindly at the young servant. "It's quite all right, Maggie. I was just about to go back downstairs. You may be about your business here." Rosamond took a closer look at the girl, whom she recognized. "Why, Maggie," she remarked, "this is not your usual domain in the house. Your place was in the kitchen when last I saw you."

"Yes, ma'am." Maggie bobbed again and blushed with some pride. "Mrs. Hathaway gave me a promotion to upstairs maid after Mary was . . . sent away."

Rosamond took note of the maid's hesitation before the last two words, but she did not say anything to the girl except, "Oh, I see. Well, congratulations. I am sure it was a well-deserved promotion." And she smiled again at Maggie before making her way back downstairs.

The girl's words had aroused some curiosity in her mind, though, and when she re-entered the parlor where her mother and Tom were still sitting, she addressed her mother.

"The upstairs maid just informed me that she had been given her position after Mary had been 'sent away'. That is such a curious phrase for her to use. Whatever became of our Mary?"

"Sent away? Is that what she said?" Her mother was duly addled. "Good heavens, I must tell the child to use a different phrase. She has no real knowledge of what did become of Mary, and she makes it sound as if the poor girl had done something to be ashamed of!"

Rosamond looked at Mrs. Hathaway with affectionate consternation — how like her mother to give a roundabout response that was no answer at all.

"Yes, but what did become of Mary?" persisted Rosamond, coming to sit on the sofa beside her mother.

"Oh!" exclaimed Mrs. Hathaway as if she had entirely forgotten the original question. She glanced behind her toward the door to the dining room as if to ascertain that no one was entering, then said to Rosamond in a very low voice, "I've sent her on to Lorna."

Lorna! A name Rosamond had not heard uttered by any member of her family in nearly a year. And to hear it today in such a context was so entirely unexpected that the surprise of it showed plainly upon her countenance. She glanced at Tom who seemed very alert to the discourse, though he said nothing.

Rosamond turned back to her mother, obviously puzzled. 'You sent her to . . . Lorna? For what purpose?"

"To give her a measure of aid in the chores and in the kitchen." Mrs. Hathaway's tone indicated that this circumstance should be evident to Rosamond. "You cannot expect a girl of Lorna's upbringing to be able to keep house with any degree of expertise, even should the house have only four rooms. It was becoming too great a challenge for her."

Rosamond was so amazed at this news that, while she did not pursue the subject further, she could hardly focus her mind on any other topic for the rest of the afternoon.

She returned to Belgravia well before the dinner-hour, her thoughts still attempting to integrate and piece together the implications of such baffling circumstances. She related to her husband that evening the puzzling situation, and though he could give her no insight into her mother's motives, Rosamond found some comfort in the simple act of telling him, and even greater comfort in being once again in his presence and in their own home, however new and unfamiliar the house itself my be. For her, it was a warm and endearing haven. She was glad to have gone back to Grosvenor Square that day, for as much as she loved her family, she had realized that Grosvenor Square could never truly be her home again, for home is not a house, but rather where one's heart lies. And hers lay with her husband. And wherever Frederick Lancaster was, whether at Stoneleigh or in Belgravia, there would be her home.

Rosamond could not get out of her mind the bewildering fact that her mother had sent a domestic servant to assist Lorna, who was leading a life that was categorically antithetical to the very principles that her parents had so avidly believed and instilled in their children, and which principles Rosamond knew were correct. She pondered the issue until it distracted her, and still she could reach no plausible rationale. Other questions had come into her mind as well, so when her brother came to visit her in Belgravia the following week, she broached the issue before him.

"Why ever would our mother do such a thing?" she asked him. "Oughtn't she to be encouraging Lorna to return home rather than helping her to sustain such a dishonorable situation?"

Tom shook his head. "It is difficult to reason out a mother's love for her children."

Rosamond looked to him with some incredulity. "But, Tom, surely you can see that it is not an act of love to perpetuate that which must only hurt Lorna in the end."

Tom sighed, for she had touched upon an issue that he himself struggled with. "What you say is true. Yet it is true as well that a mother likes not to see her children suffer any hardship which she can prevent."

Rosamond leaned forward and spoke earnestly. "Then she should do what she can to persuade Lorna to give up this unrighteousness!"

Tom knew that Rosamond once again spoke truly, and he contemplated her for a moment, noting that some of her vibrance of the previous week had faded. As last he spoke. "It is easier for you to see the truth, for you are so removed from the situation. It is more difficult for one who is very much still a part of Lorna's world to be so objective." His troubled eyes revealed that he might have been speaking as much about his own struggle as that of their mother.

His word triggered a thought in Rosamond's mind — a question she had reflected upon several times since her visit to Grosvenor Square. "Our mother spoke of Lorna's house by the sea. She has been there?"

Tom nodded. "On more than one occasion."

"And Father?"

"To my knowledge, he has never been to see Lorna since he first tried to bring her home . . . when you were still living in Grosvenor Square. But he is well-aware of our mother's actions."

Rosamond could only stare at him in disbelief. Then she slowly turned her eyes away, staring into the abyss. "I have had such . . . faulty assumptions in this matter," she said softly. "I thought that everyone —, well, I had hoped that Lorna —," she broke off, then looked back into her brother's eyes. "You are right. I have been so removed, I do not know anything. I have been in a different world, hoping and praying that Lorna would be guided to return. But now — I can see that she will never be persuaded." She cast her eyes sorrowfully downward. "There is no reason for her to return."

Tom did not like to see his gentle sister so downcast. He rose from his seat and crossed to sit beside her. He took her hand. "You must not feel the situation is hopeless or that Lorna is lost to you forever. Perhaps she can yet be persuaded. She may not be swayed by those who readily accommodate her, but you may be just the persuasion she requires." Rosamond glanced up at him, and he continued. "She has not really changed, Rosamond. I have not seen her, but I correspond with her. She still loves you. I know that she does. I know that she would welcome a chance to see you . . . to talk to you. Won't you go to see her? I will go, too. I do not know if she can be won over, but surely it will do you good to see one another. You said yourself that your distance had given rise to false impressions in your mind. She, too, may be impaired by such assumptions."

Rosamond had brightened visibly upon hearing her brother's suggestion, revealing to him how much she loved and missed Lorna. She gave his hand an eager squeeze. "Oh, Tom — do you think we might persuade her?"

Tom smiled at her. "It cannot hurt to try." He patted her hand. "But first you must ask your husband for permission to go, for I know it is quite a distance."

There was no difficulty in that matter. The Earl knew that the issue had weighed upon his wife's mind throughout the week, and though he did harbor some doubts about the feasibility of persuading Lorna, he gave his consent with hopes that a reunion between the two sisters might put Rosamond's mind at ease. Frederick knew that she would never be able to quiet the dilemma within her heart until she had seen her sister for herself, regardless of the outcome of such a meeting. He agreed to accompany her and her brother and readily offered to provide a carriage for the journey.

The visit did not happen at once. First, Tom must write to Lorna and wait for her response so that a date might be fixed upon. Then, they must go at a time which would not interfere with the Earl's obligations, nor with Tom's work. So, it was not until several weeks after the conception of the idea that Rosamond and Frederick and Tom set out from London upon their excursion to the coast.

The journey took several hours, and most of that time was marked by silence within the carriage's enclosure. It was, of course, always Frederick's nature to be pensively reserved, but Rosamond, too, was quiet upon this day, for inside, her nerves were on edge at the anticipation of a meeting with her sister, and as she watched the scenery pass by, she reflected over and over upon what the encounter might be like — wishing that the driver would urge the horses along faster so that they might arrive at their destination and put an end to her ambiguous conjectures.

Although it was not unusual for Tom to be quiet, his noiselessness on this day hid the fact that there was little tranquility for him within. He must always have a level of discomfort in the presence of his sister's husband, who had been present at such unfortunate events as the opening race and the shareholders' meeting at Smollett's Coffeehouse that must assuredly have presented Tom's character in the worst possible light. While Lord Kendal had never mentioned either incident, his brooding reticence did not inspire in Tom any confidence that the Earl should consider him to be a worthy brother of his fair Rosamond.

And even greater than Tom's discomfort was his agitation. Tom had been uneasy and on edge for many months, and inactivity brought such tenseness to a culmination. To sit idle and silent for so many hours — which at one time would have been a welcome respite — now nearly drove him to distraction. He felt a need to move about, to be free of the confines of the enclosed compartment, and he was uncharacteristically fidgety until Rosamond remarked upon it. Then he made painful effort to contain such external unrest for the duration of the journey. His mind was not at rest, though, and he dealt with not only his own agitation, but also his conflicting feelings regarding the imminent meeting with Lorna. While the visit had been his own idea, as they drew nearer to the coast, he began to worry about the consequences of the interview. His ambivalence upon the matter of his older sister had come into the forefront of his thoughts in recent days. He knew that it was Rosamond who had touched off such ambivalence, however unintentionally. Until she had brought up the subject of Lorna, he had been content to let the matter lie dormant in his mind. He could then unquestioningly carry on his amicable correspondence with their elder sister and fear neither upsetting the peace between them nor pondering too deeply where the futures of all of them might lie. But Rosamond had disrupted that simplistic peace with her guileless insight and impartial candor. The truths she had spoken seemed to nettle those suspended questions in his mind and would not let them return to their state of dormancy. As the carriage rattled along the rudimentary, provincial road that led into tiny Holland Cove, Tom longed for the little glass bottle he had cast upon the riverbank so many months ago.

It had been decided that the best course would be for Frederick to remain with the carriage while Rosamond and Tom went into the cottage to meet with their sister. That way none of the siblings would feel any constraints of formality in their ability to speak openly with one another.

Having no real idea of what to expect, Rosamond was somewhat taken aback at the cottage's rustic exterior, and there was not really even a proper step to stand upon at the front door. Lorna herself opened the door to Tom's knock and very politely asked them to step inside. Rosamond followed her brother a bit timidly into the cottage's interior, which placed her directly into the small, dim sitting-room, for there was no entry-way. There had been no formal greetings exchanged until the door was closed upon the outside world, then everything changed.

Betraying a slightly misty eye, Lorna hugged her brother affectionately and apologized for not having yet responded to his last letter. But when she turned to Rosamond, a surging of emotions suddenly overcame both sisters, and they fell weeping into one another's arms. This went on for quite a few minutes, accompanied by many affirmations of how much they had missed one another and how good it was to see one another again. Lorna finally took a step back to get a better look at her sister.

"You are as beautiful as ever, Rosamond," she said approvingly. "Or ought I to now address you as 'my lady'?" Rosamond laughed through her tears and assured her sister that she would not allow her to adopt any such formality. Lorna went on with her sisterly affection of former days. "To think that you should now be married, and a countess at that!" She took Rosamond's hand. "And see your lovely ring — why the stone is just the color of your eyes! Come look, Miles . . . is it not exquisite?"

And Rosamond's heart skipped a beat as she realized for the first time that there was another person in the room — and such a one as she would not have wished to be present at such a time! But she managed a feeble smile as Miles Anderson came forth and took a cursory glance at the ring, acknowledging both visitors with a somewhat indifferent nod.

Lorna laughed. "Come now! That is no way to greet one another!" She addressed Rosamond: "Despite your rather disastrous first meeting in Grosvenor Square last year, I assure you, you will love Miles as a brother when you know him better."

Miles looked perceptibly uncomfortable at this statement, and Rosamond was shocked to hear Lorna say such a thing. She did not know how to respond, and she looked to Tom, but he was fastidiously avoiding her eye. Clearly, this meeting was not going to play out in the manner Rosamond had imagined. How could she be expected to have open discourse with her sister upon a subject of such delicacy with that man in the room?

Lorna appeared not to notice Rosamond's consternation, for she had gone right on with her blithe chatter . . . telling Tom how well he also looked, all the while setting out plates and cups upon the central circular table. Miles brought in some scones and jam upon a tray, then Lorna sent him back for the teapot and bid the others to sit down.

"You can see how domestic we've become — it is really not difficult to keep house. But you must not think I baked these myself," she laughed as she indicated the tray of scones. "I confess to purchasing them at the bakery this morning."

When Lorna said this, Rosamond wondered where Mary — the servant sent down from their mother — was at present. Certainly she did not seem to be within the cottage, for there were but two rooms on the ground floor, and there was a clear view into the kitchen from the sitting-room. Lorna made no apologies for the size or state of her dwelling and conducted herself as if it was common occurrence for them all to be gathered about such a diminutive table in a sparsely furnished, and yet somehow cramped, sitting room, serving and waiting upon themselves.

Tom had seated himself at Lorna's bidding, but Rosamond hesitated as Miles brought in the teapot. Lorna looked up at her inquiringly as she took her own seat beside Tom. "Come, sit beside me."

Rosamond did so, still tentative in her movements, and Miles sat on her other side. Despite Lorna's attempts at lightheartedness, it was really a rather awkward repast. Rosamond was not at all comfortable in the presence of Mr. Anderson and could not fathom how she or Tom would ever be able to broach the subject which must be discussed. Tom, too, remained fairly quiet, letting Lorna do most of the talking as she related details of the delightful little community into which they had settled and of the beauty and majesty of having the sea practically at their doorstep.

When they finally rose from the table, Miles offered to take Tom outside to observe the view along the coast, to which Rosamond was a bit dismayed to hear him consent, for though it would give her a chance to speak to her sister, she would be deprived of her brother's support. There was nothing she could do to remedy the situation, though, and as the two men left through the kitchen door, the two sisters found themselves facing one another in the little sitting-room.

Lorna seemed determined to keep things between them carefree and impersonal, and she appealed to Rosamond to tell her all about her "dashing Earl" and about life at Stoneleigh. When Rosamond seemed reluctant, Lorna cocked her head inquisitively to one side.

"What? Have you nothing agreeable to tell me of your new life then? I thought surely you'd be bursting with tales of your adventures."

Still Rosamond did not answer immediately. She knew this visit must only be brief, and they must depart soon in order to achieve London before dark. If she did not speak to her purpose now, she might have no opportunity to do so at all.

She turned to her sister and spoke from her heart. "Lorna — this all seems so . . . so unnatural. There are indeed many wonderful things I should like to tell you." She took her sister's hands in her own and spoke very earnestly. "There are many things you and I need to say to one another. Let us say them in a place where we can both be at ease . . . in London . . . in the home of our parents, where you will be welcomed with great joy. Do not hesitate . . . come back with us today — this very hour. You need not even worry about packing any belongings . . . Father will send for them tomorrow or the next day."

Rosamond's fervent appeal was met with a chilly silence. Lorna pulled her hands from her sister's clasp and took several steps back, all the while maintaining her steady gaze. When she spoke, it was with excessive composure and a coolly affected smile.

"Why, Rosamond, my dear, I am afraid you are under some misapprehension. I have no plans to go to London."

But Rosamond pleaded further. "You must have contemplated such a course of action before. You may not be afforded again such an opportunity as this. Tom is here, and my husband is without . . . they will see that you are safely escorted from here and back to London. Please, Lorna, it brings so much grief to those of us who love you . . . to see you thusly wronged!"

Lorna stared at Rosamond with a steely, proud gaze. Her voice held all the coldness of a gusty gale over the sea. "I think you had better not press this issue further. It is bound to lead to unpleasantness for both of us."

And she turned away, busying herself gathering the dishes from the table.

Rosamond was chagrined at such blatant repudiation of her well-intended petition. But she would not easily give up upon her sister.

"You are not yourself, Lorna. You deserve a life better than this. You have been led astray by one who has shown that he has no respect for you, as he so willingly brings dishonor and shame upon you. You cannot long be happy living such a life of ignoble deceit. It is not in your nature."

It was then that Lorna turned upon Rosamond quite suddenly, and looked her straight in the eye. "I do not need to be close to London to imagine what they say about your own — liaison — with the Earl of Kendal. I hardly think you're in a position to criticize me about my love affairs."

Rosamond was truly taken aback by this accusation. Hot tears sprang into her eyes at her sister's injustice. Her voice was tremulous. "You speak of what you know nothing about."

But Lorna ignored this and kept talking. "Or, does ending your 'liaison' with a marriage vindicate such deeds as were done before the marriage vows were taken?"

Rosamond could only stare at her sister in disbelief, stunned and hurt. Tears spilled from her eyes as footsteps were heard in the kitchen. Lorna continued talking as Miles and Tom entered the sitting-room.

"I think you need to understand, Rosamond, that I am quite content in the life I have chosen, and I have no intention of going anywhere without Miles. I think that you had better leave now and not return until you can better show your love as a sister, for indeed, you cannot love me when you do not accept what brings me happiness."

Poor Rosamond was truly overcome at such untruths as her sister had voiced, but Lorna had made her convictions clear, and Rosamond could say nothing, especially not with the two men standing silent in the doorway. Ashamed of her tears before them, and stricken by Lorna's hurtful words, she turned and crossed the room to the door. She tried to hold back any further tears as she left the house, but she could contain them no more once she was outside, and she sobbed quite brokenheartedly as she reached the waiting carriage, where she took refuge in the arms of her husband.

Chapter XVI

Being the subject of scandal and scrutiny does not necessarily ostracize one from society, especially not amongst the London elite. On the contrary, there is nothing they like so much as to have such prominent notoriety in their midst. So it was that Rosamond found herself the recipient of more invitations — and many of them from dignitaries and aristocrats with whom she was hardly acquainted — than she had ever received before. Nearly all of them were declined, of course, but there were a few select venues that were favored with appearances by the Earl and Countess of Kendal. One which they frequented with some regularity was the Kensington residence of Sir Richard and Lady Abercrombie. They did not present themselves more at the lavish dinner-parties — though the Earl assured his wife that by next season they could resume that practice — but they were partial to Lady Abercrombie's formal teas, which were considerably more intimate, though no less illustrious, affairs.

They attended one such occasion shortly after the unfortunate visit to the seaside cottage. Rosamond was not particularly inclined to attend that day — she never had regained the healthy glow she had displayed upon her arrival in London, and she had been feeling poorly of late — but she did not want to unnecessarily worry her husband, who had shown concern for her recent state of listlessness, and so she donned a pretty blue frock and presented herself with her husband in Kensington for tea.

There were more than a dozen in attendance that day, and as it was sunny and pleasant, Lady Abercrombie had set up her tea-table in the conservatory, though there was no formal seating with such a number of guests, but rather people could sit or stand throughout the room, grouped as they wished. As is so often the case, ladies and gentlemen seemed to group themselves according to their sex, and Rosamond stayed close to Lady Abercrombie, while Frederick was drawn into discussion with some gentlemen at the opposite end of the room.

One amongst the guests was an old acquaintance of Rosamond's: Mr. Douglas Trainer, who, despite being recently engaged, several times during the course of the afternoon cast a melancholy glance in the direction of the young Countess. He found himself in conversation with another gentleman who, under no such obligations of engagement, inevitably found his attention drawn to Lady Kendal.

"I say, what an exquisite beauty!" he intoned to Mr. Trainer. "Who is she?"

Douglas Trainer hardly needed to look in the direction of his companion's gaze to know of whom he was so enamored.

"Lady Kendal," he informed the gentleman somewhat glumly. "No doubt you've heard tell of her."

The gentleman nodded, still eyeing the lady appreciatively. "The Earl has a very pretty Lady. I am going to introduce myself to her."

And he would have proceeded in the direction of Lady Kendal, but that Mr. Trainer gave a cautionary shake of his head.

"The Earl is exceedingly fond of his Lady, and he keeps her very well," Mr. Trainer said pointedly. "Although—," and here he peered closer at Rosamond, "she does not look to be so well at present."

It was true. Rosamond, standing near the tea-table with Lady Abercrombie, appeared paler than she had been at her entrance only a short while ago, and her expression was vaguely afflicted and distant, as if she was not at all attuned to the discourse about her.

Frederick, at the other end of the room, was not insensible to this, for though he was in conversation with several other gentlemen, he was ever mindful of Rosamond and periodically cast his eye in her direction. His eyes narrowed in concern, though, and lingered more and more upon her as he perceived her state of progressive unwellness. When he saw her put one hand upon the table as if to steady herself, he did not wait for a break in the conversation or even offer any excuse as he abruptly left his company and made his way toward her. He quickened his step as he saw her other hand go to her temple and her eyes close, the color completely drained from her face. He reached her not a moment too soon, and caught her up just as she collapsed.

Afterward, Rosamond was only able to tell the doctor that her heart had begun to race within her with no apparent warning, and that she was overcome by a feeling of lightheadedness and a trembling that would not abate. She confessed to having experienced similar, though less profound, symptoms for several days beforehand, although she had made no mention of them to anyone, hoping such tendencies would subside on their own.

Doctor Jarrett was unable to provide any conclusive diagnosis for the Earl, who was gravely troubled by his wife's state. The doctor advised him to see that Rosamond received plenty of rest and that nothing should cause her undue worry or anxiety. Frederick would have liked to take her back to Stoneleigh immediately, for he knew that was where she was happiest and could be most at ease, but that he feared such a journey in her present state would be too arduous, and perhaps even detrimental to her recovery. With no physicians in Cumbria of the caliber of the London specialists, such a plan must be delayed until Rosamond's health was established to be substantially improved. Until that time, Frederick took every care that Doctor Jarrett's advice should be followed, so that Rosamond might recover without impediment.

For the first few days, she remained in bed or reclining upon the settee in their apartment. For the next several weeks, her husband insisted that she stay close to home: within the house itself — which was large enough to afford her sufficient diversions — or in the small garden attached. This suited Rosamond tremendously, and she was well-contented to acquiesce, for such disengagement from the tumult and agitation of the city did much to alleviate the trouble which had been in her mind. The household staff was given strict instructions that Lady Kendal would receive no visitors except for family members and a select few close acquaintances such as Edith Byrd and Hugh Shadwell, all of whom were faithfully loyal in providing her with quiet and uplifting companionship, especially during those hours when her husband must be away from the house.

As the days progressed, she did make significant improvement, and while she still did not stray far from home, she would sometimes go for walks with her brother or Hugh about the environs of Belgravia, and at other times Frederick would take her for carriage rides into the parks or along the Embankment.

Eventually, she was able to resume her visits to Grosvenor Square, and on a cheerfully bright day in early spring, she rang the bell at the familiar door and was duly admitted by the ever-pleasant and proper Agnes, who informed her that Mrs. Hathaway was out to Primrose Hill, and Mr. Hathaway and Tom were not yet returned from the office. Rosamond assured her that she did not mind waiting in the parlor, as she knew that her father and brother would be home soon.

After Agnes had made her curtsey and departed, though, Rosamond decided that, instead of sitting idly in the parlor while she waited, she would go up to her old room and take a second look through some of the drawers in the bedside chest, through which she had previously taken only a cursory glance.

As she exited the parlor and began her ascent up the staircase, Rosamond was met with a surprise so unforeseen that it stunned her to the core, and she stopped abruptly with her hand upon the rail. For whom should she encounter descending the same stairs, but Mr. Miles Anderson — the last person she ever expected to see again in Grosvenor Square?

She gasped in astonishment, but Mr. Anderson seemed not at all startled or agitated to see her there. He merely nodded his head with its longish-red hair, bid her a curt "Good day, Lady Kendal", and stepped aside to allow her to pass.

Rosamond did not move, though, and she stood as if rooted to the spot. She finally recovered her senses enough to speak. "What are you doing here?"

Mr. Anderson remained breezily — and even insolently — nonchalant. "I was just on my way out, actually. I have a meeting in Clerkenwell." Seeing that Rosamond did not seem inclined to continue her ascent, he walked down a few more steps, then stopped again. "Oh, if you see your mother, you might mention to her that I will probably not be back in time for dinner, and there is no need to set a place for me. I've already informed the cook. Lorna is meeting me there and will not need any dinner either."

Rosamond stared at him. "Do you mean to say that you're — you're staying here?"

Now it was Mr. Anderson's turn to look surprised, his sandy eyebrows raised disdainfully above his pale eyes. "Why, of course. Did no one tell you? We've been here quite a while now."

Rosamond was bewildered. "But . . . are you and Lorna . . . have you married then?"

Miles wrinkled his brow as if the very suggestion was an affront to his pride. His reply was delivered with more than a hint of supercilious arrogance, "No . . . I am sorry to disappoint you. And now, if you'll excuse me, I mustn't be late." And with a bow that was as condescending as his attitude, he proceeded down the stairs and out the front door, leaving Rosamond stunned and perplexed.

She moved very slowly up the remaining steps and into the upstairs hall. When she reached her bedroom, she did not sort through her bedside chest, but sat upon the bed itself, completely oblivious to her environs, her mind in a whirl of confusion and consternation. She remained thus indifferent to the passage of time, or even to her purpose for visiting Grosvenor Square, until she heard a footstep in the hall, and her mother appeared in the doorway.

"My dear!" Mrs. Hathaway came forward to greet Rosamond. "It is so good to see you out and about once more. How are you feeling?"

Rosamond did not immediately return the greeting and was still in somewhat of a daze as she received her mother's kiss. Her mother bustled on as usual, though.

"I hope you are going to stay for tea? Come downstairs, and we can sit in the parlor and talk. I don't think I've told you about Mrs. Kane's daughters, who just returned from the Continent? They had some very interesting experiences . . . and some adventures, too!"

And her mother waved a hand toward the door, indicating that Rosamond was to follow her downstairs.

Rosamond looked at her mother, then said, "There is a matter of some importance I need to talk to you about. And Father as well."

"Oh." Her mother looked slightly apprehensive, as if she suspected what it was her daughter wanted to discuss and was not anxious to commence the subject. "Well, of course, he's not returned home as of yet."

"It is of no consequence," said Rosamond. "I can wait."

Her mother looked a trifle nonplussed, but led the way downstairs and into the parlor, where she and her daughter spent a half-hour in rather awkward conversation before Mr. Hathaway come home.

He was greatly pleased to see Rosamond and greeted her affectionately. Mrs. Hathaway was wringing her hands, though, and mentioned to her husband that their daughter had requested to speak to them both on a matter of importance. Mr. Hathaway raised his eyebrows and looked inquiringly at Rosamond who was a bit flushed, being unused to confronting her parents on matters of such weight. However, she affirmed with a nod that her mother was correct and asked if they might re-assemble in a place of greater privacy than the parlor afforded. Her father readily consented, seeing that his youngest daughter was in earnest, and suggested that they move into his study.

Rosamond was nervous, but she was also troubled and upset, and such swelling of emotions gave her courage that she might not otherwise have had if she had delayed this discussion until another day. But she did not want a delay . . . she needed answers to her questions, and putting it off would surely only increase her anxiety. So, as soon as her father had closed the study door behind them and without even taking a seat — she was far too agitated — she put the issue to them, her eyes and tone equally troubled.

"Lorna is here, and her . . . companion. They are here together, staying in your home."

For some reason, she addressed this statement to her mother, but as she waited for a response in the silence that ensued, she looked searchingly from one face to the other. Mrs. Hathaway looked hesitantly to her husband who finally spoke up. He, too, looked somewhat flustered, though his tone was calm and even a bit apologetic.

"We were going to tell you, of course. We thought it would be best to wait until you were fully well."

Rosamond felt a pang of indignation which overcame her uncertainty, and the color rose in her cheeks as she leaned forward earnestly. "Because you knew such a situation should upset me . . . because you know that it is wrong!"

Her mother rather bristled at this. "I am surprised at you, Rosamond. You have always spoken of your wish that Lorna should return to us. Now that she is here, you are ill-satisfied."

Rosamond shook her head and spoke with feeling. "It was ever my hope — as I thought it was yours — that she should come home; that she should return to us and leave behind that life which is universally acknowledged to be iniquitous. Yet, you have allowed her to bring that life back with her into your home!"

There was another silence. Both parents were rather taken aback by their usually-demure daughter's courage of conviction.

When Mrs. Hathaway spoke again, it was in a gentler tone. "Rosamond . . . there is something you should know . . . something that may well change your perspective on this matter." She paused before continuing. "Lorna is . . . is going to have a child."

The silence that followed was profound. Rosamond's astonishment and dismay were readily apparent as her eyes widened, and her former earnestness seemed to fade along with the color in her face. She cast her eyes downward as she absorbed this turn of events.

When at last she spoke, her voice was very quiet, but steadfast. "Then that is all the more reason she should be living in a way that is upright. She ought not to be thinking only of herself and of her own pleasures . . . and you will be hurting more than her by your indifference to such transgressions."

Mr. Hathaway spoke firmly. "Lorna is our daughter, and we love her. We will not abandon her when she needs us most."

Rosamond's fervor rose again. "No one is suggesting that you abandon her! Only that you do right by her!"

Her father persevered in his calmly emphatic tone, though his own voice began to intensify. "I know what you are getting at, Rosamond . . . you think that we ought to force a marriage or bar Mr. Anderson from this house and from Lorna's presence. But you underestimate your sister's strong will. She would not come without him. That was her one stipulation."

Rosamond's countenance plainly reflected her disbelief. "Her stipulation? Is it Lorna then who now heads this family? Is it she who makes the decisions?" She shook her head in amazement and even some pity. "I cannot believe what I am hearing. Loving someone means doing what is in that person's best interest, not merely giving them whatever they wish." She paused and looked away reflectively before adding quietly, "I didn't learn that from you." When she looked back up at her parents, she prevailed upon them with gentle intentness. "You are our *parents* . . . is it not up to you to teach the principles of truth, virtue, integrity, and honor — and then uphold such principles yourself, so that your children may profit by your example?"

Her entreaty was met with some coldness by her mother who said, "You are very judgmental for one so young. If you were better acquainted with Mr. Anderson, you would see that he is truly devoted to Lorna . . . in his way. Since entering this house, he has been quite as respectful toward us as any son would be. And," she added with further severity, "I hope that one virtue we have taught to you is compassion. You might be more compassionate toward them. After all, Lorna is your sister."

"My sister has made a mockery of decency!" cried Rosamond. "And you have condoned it — even encouraged it — by your submissive acceptance and accommodation. It is an insult to my brother when you liken Lorna's mongrel-cad to a 'son'!" She had never spoken her convictions so purposefully before her parents, and doing so now made her realize that having been so many months removed from their household did not make her ignorant to the situation, as she had once thought to be the case, but rather such removal had given her a depth of insight. She went on: "I see what the dynamics are here. If you do not meet Lorna's stipulations, she will not allow you to be part of her life anymore. I suppose that I, more than anyone, can ascertain that that is not merely an idle threat on her part." She shook her head sorrowfully, as one who has been gravely disillusioned. "I can see that I was wrong about so many things. I thought your actions where Lorna was concerned came from misguided love. But it is *fear* . . . fear that drives you."

She must have touched upon a precarious point, for after an ominous pause, her father's response was rigidly decisive. "We will not ostracize our own daughter. I think this discussion must be at an end."

But Rosamond sensed that this was merely stubbornness on the part of her father, and she did not relent. "Setting standards of integrity is not ostracizing . . . it is expected! If she chooses not to acquiesce to such standards, then that is her decision. She is then exiling herself."

But her father remained unyielding, and merely said stiffly, "I'm afraid your youth and inexperience discredit you here. You cannot possibly comprehend or evaluate the decisions a parent must make. You would feel differently if it was your daughter."

Rosamond was indignant at being thus patronized, and she lifted her head with spirit. "Do not presume to tell me how I would feel. It is irrelevant, at any rate. If we allowed only our feelings to dictate our actions, we would be no better than animals, who act upon impulse, and the world would be full of Lornas and Mr. Andersons . . . with no regard for virtue."

Mrs. Hathaway, who had not spoken for an interval, now interjected crisply, "You are a fine one to talk about such restraint, considering the circumstances of your own marriage."

A similar accusation by Lorna had reduced Rosamond to tears, yet no tears welled this time. Even as she felt her cheeks flame, she spoke evenly, looking her mother steadily in the eye.

"I will not condescend to defend my virtue or that of my husband. But know this much: Whatever you may choose to think, and whatever my faults may be, I at least have the serenity of knowing that I have lived faithfully according to the principles I have professed. You will not be able to brand me with hypocrisy!"

Mr. Hathaway's words were finally heeded, and the discussion was ended when Rosamond, still carried by the intensity of her fervor, exited the room. It was not until afterwards, when she was enclosed in her carriage and departed from Grosvenor Square that her summoned valor crumbled, and she succumbed to that emotional state which had been fermenting underneath the temporary fortitude.

While her heart was grieved and dismayed by such disaccord between herself and her parents, Rosamond at least had the comfort of having a home and a husband to which she could retreat. Tom had no such recourse. The extent of his self-will was required to resist seeking escape in that which he had foresworn, but which now tempted him so greatly. For while there had been no encounter with his parents on the subject of Lorna — indeed, few words spoken ever between them on the subject — he was not unaffected by her return to London. Tom had always been so quiet and complaisant and obliging. It would never occur to either his parents or his elder sister that he would be any less so now that Lorna and Mr. Anderson had taken up residence in Grosvenor Square. And he had not deviated from his usual disposition. He had returned Lorna's affectionate embraces and good-natured discourse as if there had never been an alteration in their circumstances, for she seemed to desire that her condition and the presence of Mr. Anderson should not be dwelt upon, but rather comfortably accepted. She had, of course, been greatly disappointed by her younger sister's stance, but she had no apprehension as far as her brother was concerned. She knew that Tom could be depended upon to be agreeable, docile, and compliant, and she was not disappointed.

But beneath his outward affability, Tom's mind and heart were in an unceasing state of turmoil. While he believed that the actions of Lorna and his parents were reprobate, he disliked conflict of any kind and would go to great length to avoid causing contention between any parties, particularly if one of the parties was himself. But Lorna's re-establishment in Grosvenor Square had ramifications beyond just the physical presence of herself and Miles Anderson. Other aspects of the household changed as a result of her return. There were not guests at tea or dinner anymore, and his parents attended very few social events — only those that would present no opportunity for intimate discourse with other acquaintances, and Tom wondered if even those appearances would halt in time, for how long would it be before word got out about the "houseguests" of Mr. and Mrs. Hathaway? To what great lengths they went in order to secure their daughter's comfort and love and to assure a hand in the upbringing of her offspring! But as a result of having only one another as constant companions within the house, Tom began to feel the oppressiveness of isolation. And so he took to spending more and more time in Belgravia, where the spaciously comfortable home of Lord and Lady Kendal provided him with respite and diversion. He was always warmly welcomed by Rosamond, and he found there a satisfying feeling of purpose in his usefulness as a companion to her while the Earl attended to his parliamentary duties.

Even with such diversion, though, Tom could not avoid thinking about his own future, which was difficult in the face of so much uncertainty. And how many uncertainties there were! Uncertainty as to the extent of Lorna's intentions to remain established in Mayfair; uncertainty as to the changes that must further occur within the household once her child was born; uncertainty as to his ability and satisfaction in his profession; uncertainty as to his opportunities for someday securing a wife and household of his own. And more than anything, uncertainty as to his ability to continue his life's course without the aid of the little flask which he had so dramatically destroyed, but which could be so easily replaced in a moment of weakness.

As Hugh Shadwell stood before the small congregation gathered within the little church — shadowy and dim as was typical of such rural churches after dusk — leading the services of Evensong, he noted how the attendance at this service had increased since the cold and dismal days of winter had passed. But after those gathered had departed, and as he began extinguishing the candles which lined the walls, a solitary figure emerged from a shadowy recess at the rear of the sanctuary, giving him a momentary start. He almost immediately recognized the figure, though, and his mouth formed into a broad smile as he went forth to greet Lorna Hathaway.

"Lorna! How good it is to see you!" he exclaimed.

Lorna smiled with genuine pleasure at her old friend. "Hugh! How fine you looked up there, leading your 'flock', as it were."

He grinned back at her. "Ah, you ought to come on Sunday and hear me actually preach. You may cringe upon hearing my sermons and change your mind about my abilities as a leader."

Lorna laughed. "Nonsense! I'm sure your natural appeal wins them every time."

He looked a bit rueful as he said, "Well, I hope it is the relevance of my words that wins them, and not my personal charm."

Lorna looked thoughtfully about the darkened sanctuary. "It has been a long time since I have been to Evensong. Yet, listening to you, it was all so familiar." She seemed lost in meditation for a moment before she turned back to him and smiled warmly. "It is so good to see you. I feel I have been away an age. Can it have really been only a year and a half?" She tilted her head and looked at him appraisingly with a sparkle in her eye. "I think that you must have grown older and wiser in that time, for as I watched you up there I saw scarcely any trace of the mischievous little boy who used to run about with us, sailing boats and fishing us out of the water."

Hugh laughed good-naturedly. "Please don't relate any such tales to my congregation. They should never give credence to my sermons again. I have styled myself as a scholarly sage of utmost seriousness."

Lorna did not laugh at his jest, though, and only shook her head. "I never used to believe that you would really and truly take orders, when first you spoke of it. But now that I see you here, in your dominion, it seems so thoroughly to suit you that I can only wonder how I could have ever doubted your success in the profession. I'm sure I don't know why you have not yet taken a wife, though."

She blushed after saying this, for the thought had come to her so naturally that she did not think about the incongruity of such a statement until the words had already been issued.

Hugh did not give any indication that he comprehended such a disparity and only smiled, saying, "You must not give up upon me yet in that regard. I have only just four years of the ministry to my credit and have scarcely had the time to consider such domestic pursuits. I will confide, though, that there are several young ladies who sit here every Sunday who make it a point to smile and blush and look exceedingly demure whenever I greet them or look in their direction."

Lorna laughed at first, but just as quickly lapsed into an attitude of contemplation, staring absently at the wall-sconce where a lone candle flickered, casting exaggerated shadows upon the wall and floor. Her voice was as distant as her gaze as she said dreamily, "Whatever has become of us, Hugh? Nothing has turned out at all the way it should have. When we were children, I had our futures planned with certainty. You were supposed to grow up and marry Rosamond, and Tom was to marry Edith, and I—," she smiled in spite of herself, "I was to go off adventuring upon pirate ships and desert isles." She sighed. "But so much has changed. Nothing has turned out at all the way I had planned." And her hand inadvertently rested upon her abdomen, where her gown fit so snugly that the seams were stretched taut.

Hugh looked at her kindly. "Who is to say what should have been? You know that life is never predictable." His eyes twinkled as he attempted to lift the mood by interjecting some lightheartedness back into it. "I cannot say much for your skill at arranging matches, though. I cannot deny that I also had some notions regarding Tom and Edith, but as for myself . . . if I had ever an idea about growing up to marry one of the Hathaway daughters — as fond as I am of Rosamond, it surely would not have been her, but rather her lively sister who would have had my heart."

Lorna smiled again. "You must not flatter me so, Hugh. Your love as a friend has ever been constant." She frowned, meditating. "I cannot say as much for my sister."

Hugh shook his head. "You must not think that Rosamond does not love you. You would do her grave injustice to think that." His brow creased in thoughtful worriment. "She has not been well of late."

"Yes, I know." Lorna looked down uncomfortably. She did not want to dwell on this subject, but Hugh's previous comments had stirred some resentment within her. "Would you take her part against me, then?"

Hugh gazed at her, comprehending her meaning, and shook his head in gentle warning. "I know what you are getting at, Lorna. I hope that I may ever be your friend, but do not ask me to condone what you know I cannot."

Lorna could not really have been surprised at his answer, but tears sprang to her eyes nonetheless, though she would never allow them to fall. She simply nodded her head in understanding and gave him a half-smile. "No one could ever accuse you of being an unfaithful friend, Hugh . . . not toward any of us. I am truly grateful for your friendship . . . it shall never be severed by me. Do not look for me here of a Sunday, though. This is your realm, and not mine. But for my part, the esteem I have for you is unchanged, and I hope that we may meet again soon. And now, I shall let you get back to your vicarage. Good-night, Hugh."

But Hugh would not let her have the last word. Before she turned to go, he put his hand to her shoulder and said, "Take care of yourself, Lorna, and God keep you."

Chapter XVII

The Earl of Kendal had been detained in a committee meeting since morning, and it was not until he returned to the Upper House Chamber that he was informed by a clerk that a member of his household was waiting to speak to him. Upon entering the Central Hall, he was met by John, the footman, who had hurried forth as soon as he had seen his master exit the House Chamber. The footman was noticeably agitated and gave only the most cursory of bows before speaking, the rapidity of the words exacerbating his tone of urgency.

"My lord, they sent me to summon you back to Belgravia. It is the Countess — she is not well. She was out walking with Mrs. Byrd this morning when she — she collapsed again quite suddenly. It seems she is worse this time, for she still was not revived when I left, though the doctor had been summoned."

Frederick gripped the man's arm, his eyes flashing fire. "This morning? She is still not revived?"

The footman's distress was plain. "I . . . I cannot say, my lord. I came here right away to fetch you and have been waiting since ten o'clock. They said you were in a council meeting and could not be disturbed."

The Earl's scowl would have daunted a stronger man than the robust servant, who looked justifiably unnerved.

"Damned bloody bastards!" Frederick growled under his breath.

He did not tarry to hear any further details, nor did he wait for the footman to have his carriage brought round, but instead hastened directly out through St. Stephen's Gate and stepped into a waiting hansom cab, commanding the driver to urge his horses to the full swiftness of their capability.

Edith Shadwell Byrd was sitting at Lady Kendal's bedside when the Earl entered the apartment. Edith rose, and seeing the Earl's grim visage, set to immediately allay his worst fears.

"She will be all right," Mrs. Byrd assured him, speaking low. "She is only sleeping now, and Dr. Jarrett said she will be tired and weakened for some days, but that she will recover."

Frederick went to Rosamond's bedside, his dark eyes reflecting his concern, and put his hand gently to her cheek as she slept.

"What happened?" he intoned, keeping his voice also subdued. Though the question was addressed to Edith, he did not remove his gaze from his Rosamond's face.

Edith could only worriedly shake her head. "I do not know. We were out walking, just here about the neighborhood, as we have often done before. We had been out about fifteen or twenty minutes and had only just passed the house again when she . . . ," Edith hesitated, frowning as she attempted to remember the exact circumstances. ". . . she gave a sort of moan . . . and when I turned to her, she had gone so dreadfully pale . . . and she — she just fainted away and would not come to. Several passers-by come to our aid, and a servant from one of the houses brought her inside, where your manservant took her and brought her up here. The doctor was fetched right away, and she had begun to revive by the time the doctor arrived. He examined her, then sent us all from the room and spent quite a long while alone with Rosamond — I mean, Lady Kendal," she added, blushing.

Frederick frowned and turned toward Edith. "Did he say nothing to you?"

Edith shook her head. "Only what I've told you . . . that she will recover, though she may be weakened for some time. He could not stay and wait longer for your return, but he emphasized that he must speak with you as soon as possible." She then added rather shyly, "I think he must truly be a good doctor. He spoke to her so very kindly before he left and seemed so genuinely concerned."

Frederick nodded abstractedly. "I will go to see him right away." Then, turning his focus back to Edith — "You have been a good friend to Rosamond, and I know that she is as grateful as I am for your attendance upon her today. You need not stay longer. I will send for her maid to tend to her while I am gone."

But he did not depart immediately. He turned back to the bed where Rosamond had stirred slightly, though she remained deep in slumber, and he softly stroked her forehead with the back of his fingers, reluctant to leave her again.

When the Earl of Kendal emerged from Dr. Jarrett's Harley Street office several hours later, his eyes blazed as dark as thunder. Indeed, every aspect of his being — from his incensed countenance to his purposeful stride — indicated the extent of his embittered fury. He did not climb into his waiting carriage, but walked right past it, his silent ire increasing with each step. Any who chanced to look upon his ominous visage would have readily believed that Frederick Lancaster had once very capably killed a man in a duel, with no regard for the legality of such a contest.

And toward whom should such passionate anger be directed? Not the good doctor who had cared so benevolently for his Rosamond, but rather those to whom the doctor had alluded during his discourse with the

Earl. And how fortunate for those perpetrators that Lord Kendal did not now seek them out . . . though a visit to Grosvenor Square would likely be necessitated at some point. But not now . . . now he must think, and first he must walk, for in such a state of unrest he could not think clearly.

And so he walked. He walked without seeing the people or the shops or the carriages that he passed, and while at first his anger mounted, as he walked on, it gradually diminished to the point where he could deliberate with clarity of mind. And his pace slowed as his rumination intensified, considerably lengthening the duration of his absence, but he took the time required, for he knew that the matters he now contemplated were more crucial than any he had ever been faced with, and that his ultimate decision would significantly impact a life far more precious to him than his own.

By the time he reached again the spot where his carriage awaited, he had concluded his deliberations and determined upon a course of action. He would indeed pay a visit to Grosvenor Square this very day, but first he must return to Belgravia, for he had been too long absent from his wife's bedside.

Rosamond was sitting up in bed, propped up amongst a plethora of pillows, when her husband entered the room. Her eyes immediately lit up upon sight of him, and though she was unable to raise herself, she smiled softly at him.

"How could you have known that I was thinking about you?" she asked as he came to her side. "That you should appear just at that moment?"

Frederick sat on the bed beside her. All traces of his previous moroseness had evaporated at the sight of his fair Lady, and he smiled at her gently as he took her hand.

"I hope your thoughts were nothing but pleasant."

"Of course they were," she said, as if that was the only plausibility. "How else could thoughts of you be, but pleasant? A dream that I had as I was sleeping here brought to mind a memory. The time seems so long ago, yet how dear are such memories to me!" Her voice was not strong, but the warmth of feeling behind it was perceptible. She went on, her eyes distant as she reminisced. "I was remembering the first night I ever went to dinner at your aunt's in Kensington. She let me play upon her harpsichord . . . it is such a lovely instrument, and I was so enchanted by it! But in the midst of my playing, I looked up and saw you looking at me, and I . . . I had this feeling inside of me . . . this sensation that I had felt before when you were near." Even in her state of weakness, a faint blush rose to her cheek. "I feel it even now."

And Frederick had never changed. The passionate fervor in his black eyes revealed clearly enough that he well understood the feeling she professed. He kissed first the back then the palm of her hand, but when he looked back into her face, his countenance was somber. When he spoke, his voice was grave and concerned, but ever gentle.

"Rosamond, my love . . . you have not been well for some time now. I spoke with Dr. Jarrett today." He paused, hesitating, fearing that he would give her any cause to worry. "You must trust me in what I am about to do. I cannot tell you now, for you must rest, but you know that I will always take care of you. You must trust me now."

And Rosamond smiled at him, peaceful and reassuring. "You could never do anything that would make me unhappy . . . unless you would send me away from you," she added with some trepidation.

But Frederick shook his head and reached forward to smooth the top of her black hair. "That I shall never do," he assured her. He stood and pulled the blanket up around her. "And now, you must sleep again. Dr. Jarrett says you must get an abundance of rest in the next few weeks, and I can see that you are already weary again."

It was true. Her eyelids had grown quite suddenly heavy. But before she closed her eyes, Rosamond reached once more for her husband's hand. When he had enclosed it in his own, she smiled at him again, lovingly.

"I think that I have always belonged to you," she murmured. "From the first time I saw you . . . I have always been yours."

After making a brief stop in The City, Frederick spent the remainder of the drive to Grosvenor Square contemplating the purpose of his mission there, with the result being that by the time his carriage came to a halt before the Hathaway residence, his former state of grave displeasure had begun to set in again. So it was with a formidably ominous countenance that the Earl of Kendal was received in the front parlor by Mr. and Mrs. Hathaway.

Mrs. Hathaway was, of course, put into a dither by the unexpected appearance of the Earl, for he had scarcely ever presented himself in Grosvenor Square, and certainly never without Rosamond. After curtseying with as much refinement as could be summoned in her state of agitation, and after the Earl had been seated, she entreated him to take some refreshment. His coldly polite refusal did not deter her, and so determined was she to see to his comfort that she pressed him further until her husband interceded and bid her to respect Lord Kendal's wishes, which had been plainly imparted. Even as Mrs. Hathaway sat beside her husband, though, her flustered state did not subside, and she sat nearly on the edge of the sofa, as if she were prepared to jump up at a moment's notice to attend to the Earl's needs.

Frederick was in no humor for her superficial fuss, though, and he went straight to his purpose, addressing them both with directness, keeping his tone even, despite the dark severity reflected in his eye.

"I'm afraid that I have no pleasant news to convey to you today. Rosamond's state of health has taken a grave turn for the worse quite suddenly. While she was out walking this morning, she collapsed again, and it appears that the fragility of her state, as well as the severity of the circumstances, have left her weakened to a far greater extent than she has previously endured."

Rosamond's parents were duly distraught upon hearing this account of their daughter's precarious state, but Frederick was not swayed by their anxiety, and was, in fact, only irritated by their display. His tone remained steady, however, as he went on.

"We are very fortunate to have the services of an excellent physician who has looked after Rosamond since she first fell ill here in London. He has shown admirable concern for her, and with his intelligence and medical expertise, he has earned her trust and mine. He is very astute and, after speaking with her at length today, was able to gain significant insight into her prolonged frailty of constitution, as well as her recurring symptoms. Although he did not burden her with any explanations, he disclosed to me this afternoon the nature of his discussion with Rosamond, and the conclusions he has thus drawn from it." Frederick scowled. "He also apprised me of the complications which resulted from her loss of consciousness today, and which have so compromised her strength."

Mrs. Hathaway was fretful. "Complications?"

Frederick's black eyes flashed dangerously. "Yes," he said heatedly. "Complications which the doctor recognized immediately, though we should have never identified their meaning. The doctor feels certain, though, that Rosamond was aware of neither her condition nor her loss, for which I am grateful, as she will be spared at least that grief."

Mrs. Hathaway went pale, and there was quite a long, grim silence before Mr. Hathaway spoke up.

"You say the doctor has determined upon a diagnosis as to the cause of . . . everything she has suffered since her return to the city?"

Frederick turned to Mr. Hathaway and there was a certain undertone of intensity to his voice, for here indeed was the heart of the matter. "After speaking with Rosamond and taking into consideration her range of symptoms exhibited over the past months, Dr. Jarrett is convinced that

Rosamond's ailment is due to emotional distress . . . distress so acute that it impacts her physical health."

Mr. Hathaway frowned. "And did she tell him what was causing her such affliction?"

The Earl of Kendal was unwavering in his mercilessly forceful gaze as he looked Rosamond's father in the eye.

"She did not know that he was seeking a diagnosis when he asked if she had any troubles upon her mind, but he informed me that there came a point in their discourse when she became so distraught that she was quite overcome by her emotions. That point occurred when she confided to him some details relating to her family — to *your* family." The underscored emphasis was deliberate and unsparing. Frederick went on, ignoring the stunned looks upon their faces. "I am sure that I need not elaborate upon what aspects of your family situation have caused her such anguish. I myself was aware that the matter weighed upon her thoughts, though I did not realize the extent to which it burdened her." Here Frederick's brow creased, and his eyes betrayed his own affliction. His next words were reflective, as if spoken only to himself. "I am partially to blame, for allowing her to come to London when I could see how happy she was at Stoneleigh. I allowed myself to be swayed by her tears and my own selfish desires." He shook his head with bitter regret. "And now I cannot take her back there." He looked back at Rosamond's parents. "I must take her away from London, away from England. The doctor says she must rest where there is warmth and sunlight, and most of all, where she can have peace in her mind. So I shall take her far away from here."

Mrs. Hathaway's voice was unusually timid and faltering. "Where will you go?"

"The Crown awarded my family a great deal of territory in India. My uncle is a Royal Governor there, and I myself hold several plantations. I will have a new house built upon one of the estates such that she may be afforded every comfort she deserves." He addressed Mr. Hathaway curtly. "I have sold my shares in the Star of India Tea Company. I will not cut off the commodities supplied by my plantations, but I will no longer be involved in any investing or directorial aspects of the company."

While Mr. Hathaway paid heed to this news, his wife was far more interested in her family than in affairs of business, and the Earl's words had given her some alarm, as would any intimation that her involvement in her daughter's life would be severed. She was palpably unnerved as she spoke. "Do you mean to say that Rosamond's sister is the cause of her distress, and that you would take her so far away from us because of what Lorna has done?"

The Earl could not hide his contempt at her refusal to grasp the truth. "No . . . it is because of what *you* have done. I have nothing but pity for Rosamond's sister. She must only be the product of what she has been taught, and I fear that she will one day suffer for the lessons that are even now being impressed upon her brain."

Mr. Hathaway understood well enough Frederick's implications, and spoke coldly. "Then it is us whom you would blame?"

Frederick glowered. "It is because of your deceitfulness and duplicity that my poor Rosamond has suffered such grief. In your cowardly attempts to appease her sister, you have tormented and betrayed Rosamond. You must have been better teachers once, for you taught her too well the lessons of virtue and honesty. Now it is tearing her apart to watch you destroy every edifice of truth you have instilled in her. She cannot reconcile her grief for her sister and her bewilderment at seeing you for the cowards that you have shown yourselves to be!" His heated tone gave way to firm resolve as he added. "But she shall not suffer more. You will find that in striving so to hold fast to one daughter, you have lost the other."

Mr. Hathaway spoke with gruff displeasure. "You are judging us very harshly. After all, you have not sought our account of the situation. We may have justifications that are worthy of consideration. You have heard only Rosamond's impressions and her point of view."

But Frederick had no sympathy for those who had so injured his dearest love. "I assure you, hers is the only viewpoint that concerns me."

Mrs. Hathaway was much subdued when she ventured to speak again. "Even if you do as you say . . . and take her away . . . is there any certainty that she will recover?"

Frederick did seek to allay the mother's fears as he rose and walked restlessly toward the windows. "Rosamond is very young, and the doctor has assured me that she will be able to regain her strength and conceive again. But if it should happen again in her present state, she may lose more than she did today." His black eyes seared with fierce determination as he added, "I will not risk her life!"

This impassioned assertion was met with awed silence as Frederick lapsed into a brooding reverie. When he addressed them again, his tone was brisk and direct. "It will be some time yet before Rosamond is well enough to embark on such a lengthy journey. I am sure you understand that, while we remain in London, I cannot permit her to come to Grosvenor Square again."

"Shall we never see our daughter more, then, in this hemisphere?" fretted Mrs. Hathaway.

Frederick reflected. "That will depend a great deal on Rosamond herself. I am retaining all of my holdings here in England. If, after a time, she has regained her former vitality and laid to rest the troubles in her mind, it is possible that we shall return to England, if that is what she wishes. We would likely settle at Stoneleigh then and not in London. As for your own relationship with her —," He frowned and shook his head. "All I can say with certainty is that I shall never let you hurt her more. But perhaps, in our absence, you will have adequate time to sort out your tangled ideologies, and learn to distinguish between hypocrisy and love."

And it was with this bitter castigation that the Earl of Kendal took his leave from Grosvenor Square.

It was several weeks later when Tom presented himself for tea in Belgravia. It was not his first visit to Rosamond since her tragic relapse, but it was to be a visit of some significance for him. Tom was decidedly downhearted when he arrived, but the sight of his sister did him some good. No longer confined to her bed, Rosamond greeted him from her seat in a cushioned chair in a small sitting-room, wrapped in her shawl. Although she was still not strong, Tom noticed a change in her — a change he had observed gradually taking place over the course of his last few visits. There had begun to be a return of color to her cheek — a soft, rosy bloom that Tom had not seen since she first arrived in London from Stoneleigh. It was faint still, but there nonetheless, and increasingly discernible each time he saw her. And even more gratifying for Tom . . . he noticed that Rosamond was in exceptionally good spirits of late; there was a quiet, cheerful brightness about her, as one whose weightiest cares had been lifted away.

Despite Tom's effort to give his sister no cause to worry, Rosamond detected his despondency and remarked upon it. At first, he attempted to brush off the notion that he should be forlorn, but she pressed him, and her concern was so genuine, and his heart so heavy, that he could not maintain his stoic front longer.

He sighed, resignedly. "My situation is somewhat difficult, I find. Living in the same house with Lorna and her— Well, it is awkward, and I have felt the strain of late. I cannot see how it will improve. And there are other things . . . ." His eyes, the same blue as Rosamond's, were troubled as he contemplated his tribulations. "I . . . I cannot help but feel that our father is disappointed in me . . . I do not show his adeptness in my profession, and, though I would never say as much to him, I am not entirely contented in such a profession. And there are other circumstances as well, which I shall not trouble you with, but which I cannot seem to further ignore. Sometimes I feel quite overwhelmed by it all."

This was quite a speech from her soft-spoken brother, and Rosamond was duly attentive to the gravity of it.

"Poor Tom!" she murmured sympathetically.

"And then, too, there is your approaching departure." He smiled sadly at her. "I shall be sorry to see you go, though I well understand the necessity of your leaving." He inadvertently sighed again. "I almost envy you. If only I could be afforded such an opportunity to leave all of this behind. There is much I should like to leave behind," he added, reflectively.

Rosamond looked at him thoughtfully for only the briefest moment before she leaned forward and grasped his hand. "Tom," she said earnestly, her eyes bright. "Come with us. Come with us to India."

Tom stared at her in disbelief, but Rosamond persisted, the color further heightening in her cheek. "You could, you know. We aren't sailing for several weeks yet. There would be plenty of time for you to prepare."

Tom only shook his head. "Rosamond, you know I cannot do that."

"Why not?"

"Well, I — I—," he faltered, astonished that she should have suggested such a thing. "There are many reasons . . . my position with the company, my responsibilities, our parents . . ."

But Rosamond was quite taken with the idea and would not be put off. "You said yourself that you are unhappy in your position. Who is to say that the opportunities you would wish for are not to be had in India? And I know of no obligations that bind you here. As for our parents . . . you are no longer a child, and surely they know that you will establish yourself elsewhere sometime." She looked at him affectionately and spoke kindly. "'Tom . . . I do not know what all your troubles are." She hesitated. "I . . . I have thought sometimes that there may have been some." She was surely remembering their encounter with Jerry Flynn or his disappointment with Edith, though she made no mention of either situation. She went on, her attempts at persuasion sincerely heartfelt. "This would be the ideal time for you to set out, while you are not bound by anything here. You speak as if you have no hope of ever being released from your tribulations — they must be deeply-rooted, indeed. There is nothing to prevent you from uprooting yourself and starting anew. You can profit by what you have learned here and create a new life for yourself. You may never have such an opportunity as you have now."

Her words were appealing, and Tom almost dared to find hope in new ideas. But still he faltered. There were too many obstacles.

"What would I do to sustain myself in such a distant land where I have no acquaintances?"

But Rosamond was determined to overcome every obstacle he should present. "My husband could help you to establish yourself. He has many connections there, both in business and government. You need only consider what pursuit most interests you." She was beaming, so enamored was she of the plan.

Tom's nature, though, was to doubt. He shook his head, rather shamefacedly. "I would not impose so upon Lord Kendal. I — think that your husband bears no great love for me."

"That is nonsense!" exclaimed Rosamond with feeling. "He has seen what a devoted brother you are to me, and how attentive you have been since I have been unwell. I assure you, your goodness to me has not gone unnoticed by him. He will gladly help you."

A momentary glimmer of hopefulness crossed Tom's face, but it faded as quickly as it had appeared. He knew his sister meant well, but there were some issues that could not be surmounted. He did not know how to tell her what still overshadowed all other justifications, yet he knew she deserved honesty, and so attempted to speak with candor.

"My dear sister, I will not say that your ideas hold no appeal for me, and I have no doubt that in your mind such a plan would be favorable to my well-being, but there are yet reasons why I could never effect such a dramatic transition." He hesitated as he sought the right words to convey his dilemma. "For a man in my position . . . in my circumstances . . . with no wife, no proven accomplishments, no commendations to my name, and with a character that could not be described as bold . . . for such a man to attempt to remove himself so completely from adversity . . . well, it would not . . . it would be —," He broke off, awkwardly disconcerted. But when he glanced rather sheepishly at his sister, he saw in her eyes only compassionate understanding.

She spoke very quietly. "You are afraid that people would see weakness and cowardice behind your actions . . . as if you were running away." She shook her head pityingly. "You think that your character is not bold, not brave. But I think that those who truly know your character would never think you capable of any actions except those that are honorable." She averted her eyes reflectively for a moment, and when she looked up again at her brother, she spoke with thoughtful purpose. "I think that some of your notions of bravery are misplaced. I would think it takes a great deal more courage to depart into the unknown than to stay in the comforts of familiarity."

Tom did not discard Rosamond's ideas as hastily as he thought he would. Though he had said nothing more to her on the subject, after leaving Belgravia he found he could not prevent his thoughts from returning to the conversation held that afternoon. As much as he tried to dismiss such a scheme as unthinkably imprudent, he could not seem to get his sister's words out of his head. *"You can create a new life for yourself. You can start anew."*

If only it was true! He had not even told Rosamond of his gravest troubles, yet she had sensed the extent of his wretchedness and seemed to know that untangling his Gordian knot of hopelessness would require a profound transformation; one that would necessitate complete severance from the life in which his memories, joys, sorrows, and tribulations were inextricably enmeshed.

And yet . . . there were too many fears, too many risks, and, as always . . . too many uncertainties. Such a move would be regarded by his family as a deliberate breach, an affront to Lorna and his parents, a defection. It would radically alter their perception of the character whose image he had so assiduously preserved by his silence and complaisance.

If only he had never picked up a little jewel-flask. If only he had stood up to Jasper Munroe. If only he were more courageous. If only he could have stopped Lorna. If only he had voiced his convictions long ago.

"If only" . . . surely the most mournful phrase in the English language.

And now, the planting of this new thought in his brain had surely doomed him.

"You can start anew."

How many sleepless nights was he to endure if he were to make such a radical decision? How many sleepless nights would he endure if he did not?

Conclusion

It was very early morning when the ship set sail. It was not the first time that the Earl of Kendal and Rosamond had departed before sunrise, but the first time had been in a carriage, and they had left so hastily as not to be noticed, with only her family to see her off. Now there was no need for covertness, and yet there was no family gathered below on the pier to wave them good-bye.

The bulk of their trunks and valuables had been sent on ahead with some servants, and the remainder of their personal effects had been safely stowed inside the main cabin before the Earl had brought his pretty and delicate Countess on board.

They were not alone, though, as they stood upon the ship's deck as the sun came up, casting a soft pink glow over the water. There was another who stood apart, leaning his back against the ship's outer-wall, whose eyes were the same deep blue as the Countess's — the same deep blue of the sea they were about to traverse. He had boarded the ship with the Earl and his Lady, but had kept to himself since then, emerging on the main deck only when he felt the vessel begin to move.

His feelings were profound as he watched the buildings and people on the shore get smaller and smaller. He could not help thinking of another sister whose effervescent brown eyes had turned stormy the last time he saw her. His heart beat with both trepidation and excitement, and he realized that there was now no turning back. What he was leaving behind could not be retrieved. What he was venturing into could not be ascertained. The only certainty was that it would be a change from everything he had ever known. He wondered if change always induced fear.

Tom looked at Rosamond, standing at the rail with her Frederick, watching as the land — England — receded farther and farther into the distance. And he was struck by a thought as he beheld his sister . . . her eyes betrayed no sadness, no uncertainty, no fear, despite the fact that she was leaving behind her homeland, her place of birth. No, all that he saw reflected in her eyes was a calm serenity and even a glimmer of excitement. He pondered this. What was the secret to her tranquility? How was it that she should be so contented and so happy in the midst of such a significant transition? He did not know for certain, but he suspected it had something to do with the soft, luminous glow in her eyes as she looked into her husband's face, and the tender warmth with which his arm enfolded her. Somehow these two had no fear of the journey or of the new life that lay before them, even though it was bound to be different and unfamiliar. Tom was filled with a sudden longing to discover the pathway which would lead him to such peace as they knew, and he could not help but feel that, in spite of his uncertainties, he was at last setting foot upon that course.

Even now, as he contemplated them, he saw Frederick whisper into Rosamond's ear, upon which a soft smile crossed her lips, and she turned toward Tom, her lovely smile widening as she hurried over to him, and clasping his hand, she urged him to join them at the rail, where the view was ever so much better.

In Grosvenor Square, a small boy turned from his bedroom window, where he had been looking out toward the house across the way.

"Mama," he addressed the woman in the room, his head cocked to one

side in puzzlement, "Who is that man with the ginger hair who comes and goes from the Hathaways' house so often? Does he live there? Is he Miss Hathaway's husband?"

The child was bewildered at his mother's reaction, for first her eyes widened, then narrowed, then with a frown, she shooed him away with a stern injunction to pay better heed to his lessons and less to the happenings outside his bedroom window.

She promptly paid a visit to the kitchen, whose staff was always well-apprised of the neighborhood gossip, and then spent a great deal of the evening shut in the library with her husband, which only occurred when there were urgent matters to discuss.